THE
GULF

THE

A NOVEL

GULF

RACHEL COCHRAN

HARPER

An Imprint of HarperCollinsPublishers

THE GULF. Copyright © 2023 by Rachel Cochran. All rights reserved. Printed in
the United States of America. No part of this book may be used or reproduced
in any manner whatsoever without written permission except in the case of
brief quotations embodied in critical articles and reviews. For information,
address HarperCollins Publishers, 195 Broadway, New York, NY 10007.

HarperCollins books may be purchased for educational, business,
or sales promotional use. For information, please email the Special
Markets Department at SPsales@harpercollins.com.

FIRST EDITION

Library of Congress Cataloging-in-Publication Data has been applied for.

ISBN 978-0-06-328412-8

23 24 25 26 27 LBC 5 4 3 2 1

FOR SCOTT

THE
GULF

Part I

1

My mother must have thought I was either blind or stupid, the things she did in front of me. Deaf, too, maybe, considering what she'd say.

Or maybe she just didn't think about me at all. The older I get, the more I think this is the most true.

Usually, if she had to address us kids, she'd talk to my older brother, Robby, instead of me: "Don't come in the room unless I say so—and keep quiet, would you?" When she acknowledged me, though, it came as a remark aimed at someone else, an adult who had her full attention, some guy whose dim motel room would be our home for the weekend, some woman who'd come over late at night and leave first thing in the morning, tottering still high out to the bus stop. "Don't worry about Lulu, she's harmless," my mother would say, or "Who's Lulu gonna tell, her dolls?" as if I had any. In my memories of her— and there are plenty of them, stacked up like dishes overflowing a sink—I remember her talking directly to me only once, the night she left us.

Dead of night. Aunt Cece's front stoop, porch light extinguished. Nothing but my mother's headlights to see by.

"Just a few days, all right?" she'd said, aiming this at Robby, who nodded bravely, and something in that nod told me that he didn't believe her. That I shouldn't believe her, either. I must have started sniffling, because she crouched down in front of me, fixed those red-veined eyes on mine. "None of that, little girl. No one likes a woman who cries for attention." Then, to Robby again, "Now, you just wait until you can't see my car anymore, then you ring that doorbell. Your auntie will see you're out here and bring you right in."

"What if she doesn't?" Robby asked.

"'Course she will," she said, already turned away. "Who'd leave a couple of sweet-faced kids like you on a stoop in the middle of the night?"

I guess I was six or so then, when we came to live in Parson, Texas. Would have been around 1945, right near the end of the war, a world of sugar rations and women being let go from their factory jobs, making way for the boys coming home haggard and rattled from the Eastern Front. After that night, I lived with Aunt Cece for over a decade, then got my own place in Parson after high school; Robby also stayed in the area, settled down young with a wife and a baby, until the draft board came knocking and he shipped out for Vietnam. Parson was home to me, much more than those seedy motel rooms with my mother. When I think of home and family, I think of the frying hog fat smells of Aunt Cece's kitchen, the strains of Spanish music from her ancient radio, the soothing clank of her beaded necklaces when she drew me close in her arms.

But somehow, though nearly a native of Parson, I grew up feeling like an outsider. Maybe it was those first years at Aunt Cece's house, always keeping one eye on the window, half hoping and half dreading that I'd see my mother's car pull up the driveway. Maybe it was all the lying to my classmates—how, to stay at Granbury High, the white school, I had to tell everyone that Aunt Cece was just our housekeeper, that my (real, white) mother was out of town; how this lie kept me from inviting friends over. Maybe it was just those first six years on the road, everywhere in Texas but here: Parson is that kind of town, brutal and inward, the kind to hold a girl's first six years against her.

All of this to explain why I was so drawn to Joanna Kerrigan when she came to school in fifth grade: she was so clearly more the outsider than I was. An aura of oddness, offness, radiated from her. Was it her ghost-pale skin? Her miniature hands? Her eyes as round as coins? She looked more like a porcelain doll sprung to life than a real girl. Even just standing there in the doorway that cloudy morning in 1951, her eyes averted from us, a thumb hooked under her satchel strap, she gave off the impression that she belonged to some other world, as if any second she might turn and disappear through a magical doorway. She made me think of the hidden entrance in *The Secret Garden,* or the wardrobe portal to Narnia in the new book Aunt Cece had bought me. In later days, after everything, I would think of Joanna in terms of the other, darker stories I grew up on, the ones about demon children, foundlings and changelings and babies who are born bad. The ones whose eyes don't catch the sunlight, whose ravenous appetites start to shrink their mothers while they're still inside, then suckle them to dust once they're born.

*The night she came back into my life, I hadn't seen Joanna for fif-*teen years, not since she moved from Parson in our freshman year of high school. I would have assumed her aura of strangeness had dulled over that time, but when I set eyes on her, now a woman in her late twenties, I snapped back to that initial sighting in fifth grade, the unshakable feeling that she didn't belong here. The impression was so strong that, at first, I didn't even feel my anger toward her, all the carefully tended rage of the intervening years. I felt only that original sense of wonder and captivation, of gravity's pull.

I had just stepped out for a smoke in the parking lot at Buck's, the dockside bar I managed and helped tend. Not long ago, Buck's had been the rowdiest place in town, but ever since the storm last summer it had stopped filling up, and most nights we'd just get a few regulars slumped at their pints. It was a gray twilight hour, the night sky already spilling out over the bay, the moon tangled up in the oak branches overhead. I tucked a cigarette between my lips and then realized I wasn't alone: a woman was standing beside a blue Fairlane across the lot. The moon lit her with a pearly light, gleaming along her dark hair like the sheen on a slick of oil.

"Louisa," she said as she walked toward me, her Yankee accent perfectly intact, the rounded vowels that reminded me of Judy Garland. She wore a gray tweed dress, the sort of thing suited to a fancy office, but other than that, she looked much the same, placid and doll-like. "How long it's been," she added when she stopped in front of me.

"Yeah. Long time," I said, too startled to say more. My boots were heavy, rooted against the gravel. I imagined how I looked to her: hardened, aged, boyish with my ear-length hair and sturdy working clothes. Could she see the girl she'd known, the same way I could see this in her? The unlit cigarette tilted from my mouth.

Joanna stepped closer to me. "I just wanted to have a word with you. I know you're aware that my mother died a few months back. Well, I've come to settle her estate. And I know you'd been working with her on the house—the one she was fixing up, up on the promontory?"

At the mention of Miss Kate, I felt my breath catch, my sweat run cold. Aware of her death—that was one way to put it. As far as I knew, Joanna hadn't been in touch with her mother, or with anyone else in Parson, since she'd left town fifteen years ago. Which meant she might not know that I'd been there the morning of her mother's death, had found her sprawled body in the garden. That I'd comforted Joanna's brother in the hours after their mother's death. For the last eight months I'd been mourning Miss Kate, a woman loved and loathed in Parson, who'd stunned the town nearly five years ago by buying the decaying mansion out on the bay.

"We've got a buyer lined up to buy, but they need the place fixed up first," Joanna went on, easy as though we were having a normal conversation. "The storm did a number on it; there's all manner of things washed up in there. But if you're up for the job, it's nothing you couldn't manage—not judging from what I've heard of your skills."

She's been thinking about me, I thought, unable to stop a swell of excitement, the kind I used to get when I felt her attention focus on me. *She's asked around.*

"I'm not trying to save money, hiring you. It's just that most of the professionals are booked until next summer, and I'm hoping to get this wrapped up soon, by the end of the month if possible. And besides, well—" And then she took another step closer, only a single step, but she seemed to grow three sizes larger in my perspective, so that suddenly the memory of the girl was gone, and I was looking at a woman, soft and real and gilded faintly in the light spilling from the open door behind me. "The thing is, I was hoping it would be you, so I could be sure I was working with someone I trust."

The irony of that, I almost laughed out loud. I was probably the only person left in Parson who knew Joanna well enough to hate her. Who had entertained fantasies of killing her.

But she wasn't lying, and she wasn't joking, I could tell. When she said she trusted me, it was because she *did* trust me, and I tried to wrap my head around that but couldn't manage it. Had she gone stupid? She'd always been so bright before, even invasive and uncanny in her quiet little insights. Was it possible that she didn't know, that she simply hadn't realized what she'd done to me?

She'd finally gone quiet, watching me and waiting for an answer. Things were getting louder in the bar behind me, and I heard tonight's serving girl call out for me: "Hey, Lou!" I turned away from Joanna, eager to escape her and close a door between us. But something made me pause, made me look back and say: "I'll think about it."

I hadn't meant to encourage her. But after I locked up the bar that night, I found a slip of paper tucked under the windshield wiper of my truck, and when I tugged it out, I recognized Joanna's handwriting, the same taut, methodical cursive I used to know so well:

If you're interested, meet me at Parson House, first thing tomorrow.

2

For a while I drove around town, past the empty beaches, the abandoned neighborhoods, the heaps of debris that used to be houses, unmade by the water and winds. I'd do this sometimes to relax after work, hoping that Heather would be asleep by the time I came back home. Nothing against Heather, of course: it had been good for us, the last three years, living together since the news of Robby's death. We'd survived that loss together, careful not to cut each other with the edges of our grief. Just that sometimes, after a shift at Buck's, I had no talk left in me, liked to pretend I was the only person on earth. Most nights since the storm, Parson let me have this fantasy, mine the only headlights sweeping along the streets, illuminating one storm-ravaged block after another.

By and large, the town consisted of crabgrassy lawns ringing small, blunt houses, Folk Victorians and Mission Styles put up in the late 1800s, the start of the boom days for Parson's textile factory. Parson had never become a large town—maybe six thousand people at the peak of its industry years in the late '30s—its growth had always been sporadic, in little clusters and enclaves. The town went downhill quickly after the war, when the Parson family closed the factory and moved their money elsewhere, which was one reason I felt such fondness for this tiny Gulf Coast town, an abandoned thing like myself. Over the years I'd come to love Parson for all its idiosyncrasies, and it broke my heart to see it now, to drive past the ruined neighborhoods where Robby and I used to play, my headlights catching warped houses with every window shattered, a grim sequence of cracked-glass stares.

I didn't head out to the promontory, but I did make my way to the turnoff and linger a moment, pushing away the chill I always got driving out that way. This was the same stretch of road where Cass had died, back in high school. It was the road I'd taken out to Parson House, again and again, when Miss Kate had been living there. I hadn't driven down it since the day she died. And now Joanna was waiting down this road. Just my luck that I'd still be hanging around here when she came back. I didn't know whether I wished I'd slipped that net or not.

When I got home, I saw the kitchen light on and Peg's truck parked out front, which meant a grocery delivery. This was a little later than usual, but I didn't think Peg ever slept, always out helping people, delivering things that were needed. And we needed food, all right: Buck's wasn't bringing in much money, and Heather had just quit her job at the one salon left in town. Her pension as a Vietnam widow covered only so much, and most of that money went straight to my niece, Heather and Robby's daughter. When the storm hit in August, Aunt Cece evacuated with Sarah to San Antonio to be safe, and we were supposed to follow as soon as we could. But things hadn't quite worked out that way, and in the meantime we were too proud to ask for help. Luckily, Peg had a good instinct for these things and never treated us like a charity case. She always acted like a friend just stopping by—I couldn't be sure, but I think she did the same for all the women in town she liked to check up on.

In the front hall, some new crates had piled up since this morning, filled with the thrift-store finds that used to hang on our walls, metalwork plaques, watercolor paintings. The walls were mostly bare now. The smell of Heather's cigarettes mixed with Peg's perfume.

They were seated at the kitchen table, and one of the cabinets was partway open, revealing new boxes and cans inside. A Buffy Sainte-Marie record was playing in the next room, filling the tiny house with her crisp, melancholy voice and fingerpicked guitar. It was clear Heather hadn't been expecting company: she was wearing a loose yellow nightdress, and her long Brigitte Bardot hair had been tied back into a fraying braid for the night.

Peg looked up at me with a polite smile and a tip of her Stetson; Heather reached back to me, gave my hand a quick squeeze. "There's beer in the fridge," she said in a tired voice.

"Does Buck always work you this late?" Peg asked, warm and concerned. Peg was older, around Aunt Cece's age, but unlike Cece, she didn't color her hair, which was impressively silver-white. In her dark brown Stetson, comfortably cocked back, she looked like some kind of ice-queen cowgirl. "He ought to let you close up a little earlier."

"I took a drive," I said, and headed for the fridge. To my own ears, I sounded under control, normal, but I heard them both sit up straighter behind me.

"Everything okay?" Heather asked, never one to let it stand.

Heather knew me far too well for me to be able to play dumb. Even Peg, who hadn't known us too well before the storm, probably sensed something off.

So I breathed deep, took my time picking out a Lone Star from all the identical bottles, and then moseyed over to join them at the table. I wanted time to collect my thoughts, choose my words carefully. Finally, slowly, I said, "Looks like Joanna Kerrigan is back in town."

Heather's brow furrowed. She hated Joanna, too, from all the way back.

"Kate's daughter," said Peg. Her voice was casual but careful, as it always was when she brought up Miss Kate, likely aware I was grieving her more than I let on. Peg and Miss Kate had been friends for decades, so it must have been a tough subject for her, too.

I nodded. Took a sip.

"Any idea what she's here about?"

"What else?" Heather said, terse. "It's the house, isn't it? Looking to get every penny."

I shrugged. "I guess she's fixing it up to sell."

"Who the hell is there to buy?"

"Do you know?" Peg asked, gentler and more sincere.

"No," I admitted. "But hey, it's good land. An old house like that, lot of history. If someone was ever going to start up the old factory, Parson House would be the place to live."

Heather shook her head. "Is that factory even standing? There hasn't been anything but fishing here for twenty years."

"There's infrastructure, at least," I said. "The right person—"

"Like Joanna Kerrigan is going to bring the 'right person' to Parson." Heather gave me a weary look: *Please, no more tonight.* I'd been talking a lot lately about the future prospects of Parson, unable to give up on the only home I'd known, but I knew Heather's patience for this talk was running out.

"So who told you?" she asked, leaning on her elbows. "Who'd you hear it from?"

I should have told her the truth. Instead I felt relieved she didn't know I'd talked to Joanna. Without missing a beat, I said, "Danny."

"Figures he'd know," Heather said, curt. "He saw her?"

"Just heard about it, I think."

"I wonder what she looks like now." Heather's voice had an edge to it. "Wonder if she looks more like her mama."

Joanna didn't. She never had. Seth and Cass, Joanna's big siblings, had always resembled their mother. But even within her own family, Joanna gave off that sense of strangeness.

Peg pushed back her chair softly, rose to stand. "Well, I'd best be headed home. But do try to take it easy on Joanna—that family has gone through some real ordeals. I'm sure you well-mannered girls will remember that, won't you? That girl needs our prayers and good wishes, not our judgment."

Heather huffed, but she was smiling. "There you go, always trying to make us into better people. Won't work, you know." She stood to walk Peg to the door. "See you around?"

"I'll come by again," Peg said. "Meantime, you holler if there's anything you need."

After Peg left, Heather got to cleaning up, tossing the beer bottles, washing the crumby dishes. I leaned back in my chair, too tired to talk over the gush of the faucet. Heather must have sensed this, because she waited until she'd shut off the water to turn and speak to me. "I doubt she'll find anyone in town to help fix up that place," she said. "Let alone someone to buy it."

"Hmm," I said, and fell silent. I'd let Heather believe I hadn't seen Joanna, so I could hardly admit I'd heard her mention a buyer, an imminent sale.

Heather sat back down at the table, changed the subject. "You know I packed up some of those boxes and crates today," she said, watching me a little too carefully. "Got everything out of the hall closet. The bathroom's nearly done, too. At this rate, I could be ready by next week.

"Cece called today," she went on. "We talked all about Sarah, how well she's doing. How much she misses me. I'd really love if we could get out of here by next week."

This was something she brought up daily: moving from Parson, joining her daughter and Aunt Cece in San Antonio. We'd packed up two cars just before the storm, and Cece had gone ahead with Sarah, thinking Heather and I would follow in an hour or two, once we'd finished boarding up the house. But Heather and I had gotten stuck in Parson until it was too late to leave, had lived out the hurricane and its aftermath. For a while we thought they'd move back to Parson, once the town got back on its feet, but now, after months of waiting, of watching jobs and people leave, we knew it made no sense to drag Aunt Cece and Sarah back to this dying town. Cece was picking up laundry clients, fixing up a cozy house where we could stay while we found our footing, and all of this made Heather restless, eager to make the move. A few days back she'd given notice at the salon, and over drinks that night, I'd finally admitted what I'd long known was true: there was nothing left for us in Parson, only memories. I hadn't agreed to a time frame for leaving, but now, it seemed, she was push-ing for one. Next week.

"It's too late to talk about it right now," I muttered.

"Tomorrow, before you go to Buck's, you ought to grab a box, start throwing in some of your things. Don't want to leave it all to the last minute."

"Heather," I said, struggling to keep the anger from my voice. "Please? I'm tired."

She didn't push the subject, but her silence was loud as we got ready for bed.

Then we were under the covers with the lights out, and I could feel the tension in the air between us, in her stiff breathing. I rolled over and pressed my hand against her side. Heather had always run hot, her skin giving off warmth like a rock in the sun. With that touch she let out all her air, and I felt her tension bleed away. When she spoke again, her voice was thick, sleepy.

"I just hope Joanna doesn't ask you to help with that house. You never could say no to that girl."

"It's not like that," I said automatically. Then an attempt at misdirection: "Anyway, it'd be good to see the house. I haven't been out there since—"

I'd intended to finish the thought—*since Miss Kate died*—but then stopped myself abruptly. Too late. Suddenly Kate's ghost was there, between us, and I felt that embarrassing prickle at my eyes, the crab claw lodged at the base of my throat, the grief I tried to keep away when anyone else was around, even Heather.

She was used to my long silences whenever Miss Kate came up, always tried to comfort me despite my stubborn quiet.

"You know," she said, "old women fall over sometimes. It's awful that you're the one who found her like that. But there doesn't have to be anything more to it."

"I ever say otherwise?" I asked.

It was a knee-jerk question, one I hadn't thought through. As Heather well knew, I'd often said otherwise: I'd talked for months about the lazy police, the lack of investigation, my lingering questions surrounding Miss Kate's death, until the storm came and distracted me. Since then the topic had settled uneasily into the back of my mind, coiled among all the other loose threads of my past. Heather could have brought this up now, made me answer for my lie, but instead she nuzzled closer to me and let my question pass; I had the yanked-around, grateful feeling a fish must get when you slip it off the hook.

I gathered her up, kissed her sweet and slow, hoping she couldn't tell how riled up these topics had gotten me, hoping that this could be one of those kisses that acts like a bedtime story. It must have worked, because before I was done, I felt her slip, happy and mindless, into sleep. I lay there for a while, relishing the weight of her in my arms, the Coppertone smell of her, the way holding her close helped calm the reeling thoughts I couldn't shake—the ones that had kicked up the second I saw Joanna waiting for me in the moonlight. I hoped she'd forgive me for what I was about to do.

3

The next morning I pulled up to Parson House for the first time since Miss Kate died, and I could barely make out the mansion for all the choking vines. Not quite eight months and already the damn things had grown high as the second-story windows; only the third story and the attic awnings rose out of the green-gray tangle like the head of a gasping swimmer. The front drive gave a partial view of the garden in back, which had also multiplied in wild abundance, fierce and tangled and brimming over the top of the mossy stone wall.

A tidy blue Fairlane was already parked on the front drive. It was early enough that either Joanna was sleeping out here or she'd driven out at dawn. I pulled my C/K up next to the Fairlane, killed the engine, and braced before I could bring myself to leave the truck. Of course what Heather had been hinting the night before, what I'd been so eager to deny, was true. Miss Kate's death still had me in its grips, like a long-ago sunburn that wouldn't stop peeling. And this *was* where it had happened. Right around back, in the tangled garden that once upon a time Miss Kate and I had wrestled into orderly submission—that was where I'd found her. Yet another reason it was a bad idea to be entertaining Joanna's request, and yet another reason I couldn't stop turning the offer over in my mind.

As I sat in my truck and looked up at the house, it came back to me: that morning, after finding the body, the house crawling with a half-dozen cops who seemed more interested in getting a good look than in figuring out how it had happened. For a variety of reasons,

Miss Kate had been even more unpopular among the men of Parson than most independent-minded women, and the police in particular had taken to giving her trouble; buying the old Parson House museum had only painted a bigger target on her, since no one was sure what she was up to out here all alone. That terrible morning, I flinched at every muffled laugh, all the crude rubbernecking, the lack of concern or curiosity. The way they'd handled Seth, too—I'd overheard only slivers of their questioning, but I could see how they smirked and rolled their eyes at his soft voice, his gentle and withdrawn demeanor. Part of me was worried they'd scapegoat him somehow, just because he was different, but they must have dismissed him entirely, figured he didn't have it in him, because their official story was that she'd stepped out into the garden in the morning, and she'd slipped on the slick mud from last night's rain. When I pointed out that her feet were bare and clean, they wrapped me in a blanket and told me I'd had a horrible shock, and wouldn't it be better if I went home and got some rest, they'd drop in to take my statement later on. Only they never did bother to come by. Maybe it was for the best that I was allowed to go on being invisible to them, the way I'd always tried to be.

So the whole thing had a strange, unfinished feeling. I didn't even know what had happened to Seth, hadn't heard from him since that day, though I thought I remembered hearing he'd left town after the funeral. I'd managed to put him—and everything else—well out of my mind until here and now, as I faced Parson House again, which I knew meant returning to all those unresolved emotions. Still, I wasn't planning to stay long. Anyway, the ravages of the storm had done me a favor: the damage had transformed the house, made it difficult to recognize as the one Miss Kate and I had poured ourselves into restoring, the shingles I'd spent weeks of spare hours laying now rippled and torn and missing in patches, the fresh windowpanes punched through, the paint job ripped away as if someone had taken sandpaper to it, so that the place looked like any great house fallen into disrepair, little different from the ramshackle mansions Sarah loved in *Scooby-Doo*.

Eventually I made it out of the car and walked up the stairs to the porch. Even the doorway was covered with vines, the door cracked open a couple inches with one thick vine snaking through it. I knocked; no one answered. I knocked again, really laying into it; still no response. I was about to leave a note, forget this whole business—but I couldn't take my eye from the open door, the faint glimpse of the foyer where I'd spent so many hours with Miss Kate. Hugging tight every time she let me in at my knock. Stepping inside in the middle of a workday for a few seconds out of the streaming sunlight. Playing gin rummy on the marble-topped table while we waited for a deliveryman who was running late.

So I let myself in.

For all that it was open, the door was hard to budge. Vines and other growth snagged in the hinges, dragged stubbornly as I pushed. I tried to imagine Joanna with her tiny frame and slender arms forcing her way through here. She'd probably used the garden door.

I wasn't about to go in the garden, not ever again if I could help it. It was once my favorite place on the property, but the thought of it now made me fight back a quick, unwelcome flash: Miss Kate's head cracked open on the stepping-stones, her limbs splayed out around her like storm-snapped branches, the pale soles of her feet. *Old women fall over sometimes,* Heather had said, like it was natural, but there was nothing natural about the way I'd found her, her head wound gaping like a keyhole, a thick substance seeping out like split yolk.

I struggled harder with the door, distracting myself from the memory, and then managed to squeeze my body through the gap and into the foyer. The odor of sewage and seawater hit me hard: the ripe scent of rot that had soured the streets after the storm, the by-product of sea surge, had not aired out here but lingered, rising from floorboards pickled in brine. That wasn't the only sign of the storm: pellets of broken glass on the floor, catching the light through the vines like a thousand miniature kaleidoscopes; inch-tall ridges of sand brought in by the surge; a large, overturned crab's body, legs clutched in the air, cracked open with the meat picked out by some scavenger. There were scat piles and tracks and, gleaming under the entry staircase, two sets of raccoon eyes, wide and watching. One of them let out a rumbling, chittering cry.

Standing in the storm-wrecked vestibule, I couldn't help but remember the first time I'd been brought here. For a few years in the early '50s—after the Parson family had closed the factory and disappeared somewhere north, washing their hands of the town that had been theirs for a century—the city had decided to keep up the plantation mansion as a museum, with exhibits that celebrated the legacy of Parson, the building of the mansion, the plantation, the textile factory, and the town. Granbury Elementary brought us once when we were young, and a prissy docent with too-firm hair had walked us from room to room, explaining in a Dallas drawl about our heritage. The floorboards had gleamed with fresh polish, the heavy damask curtains barely rustling when my classmates brushed against them. In some rooms a rope cordoned off the original Victorian furnishings, the jade-colored chenille, the lamps with beaded shades, the ceramic curios of hunting dogs and parasoled women. The nursery on the second floor had a shelf of moon-faced porcelain dolls, each with round marble eyes and too-small hands. When I glimpsed Joanna walking past them, shuffling along in the line of students, it occurred to me how well she would have fit there, perched on the shelf right beside them.

Not a foot from where I was standing now, an easel had displayed sketches of the manor's plantation days, the cotton fields dotted with dozens of enslaved workers. The drawings had made me feel dizzy and strange—I remember leaning in close to them, trying to make out the face of a single Black figure, but they were all bent down to their labor, turned away from the artist, away from me.

By the time I entered high school, the town had given the museum up, tried and failed to find a buyer for the property. There was no one in Parson who could afford the price and no one outside Parson who had any interest in such an investment. The empty mansion lost its luster, became the kind of place where teens broke in to drink and smoke and risk unwanted pregnancies. It remained that way for fifteen years, its value falling and falling until finally Miss Kate came along and bought it up out of nowhere, stunned the whole town that this low-class woman had that kind of money. I'd been surprised when Miss Kate asked me to help her fix it up—we hadn't really stayed in touch since Joanna abandoned us both—but it was exciting to be involved in a project like that, and even more exciting to be around Miss Kate again. We'd gotten it halfway back to its former dignity when she died and the storm came.

Which brought me here: standing by the door and watching those raccoon eyes warily, listening for any sign that I wasn't the only person in this house. I walked into the room, the warped floorboards groaning, and then I heard, just louder than the sea breeze, a sound on the floor above me: a desk chair creaking on its casters.

I followed the sound, climbing the stairs carefully. I worried the old wood might buckle under my boot, and with each step I felt a gut-churning sensation of falling, so that when I reached the landing, I stood there gripping the banister for a moment, letting my stomach settle.

Just tell Joanna to go to hell and get out of here, I reminded myself as I walked down the hall. It should be easy. I'd told lots of people to go to hell over the years.

I heard noises from Miss Kate's study, a shuffling of papers like flapping sails in a breeze. The sound paused as I approached, and when I stepped into the doorway, a pale face was already looking up from behind the broad oak desk. I'd hoped for a clearer view of Joanna by daylight, but the windows were so wefted with vines that she sat there as shaded and murky as in the parking lot last night. In this dappled light she looked less like a porcelain doll than an animal cornered in undergrowth: her eyes, glinting seaglass, watched me like the raccoon eyes beneath the stairs.

She's scared of me. That was my first impression. Then, like a predator animal smelling fear on its prey, I thought of what I could do to her. We were a mile at least from the closest neighbor, seven miles and more into town. The exact things Joanna might worry I'd do—strike her, strangle her, push her from the window—I easily could, and there was no one to stop me.

A light passed over her face, and the look of fear was gone. So completely I wondered if it had ever been there.

"Good morning," she said, warm and easy, as if she'd been expecting me at this very moment. "I'm so grateful to you for coming out all this way. I apologize about the state of the house—it does seem hazardous, doesn't it? We have a great deal of work to do, I'm afraid."

I shifted, crossed my arms. "I didn't say I was going to help you."

"No?" Her eyebrows rose as though in genuine surprise. "By all means, we ought to talk about it. Please, feel free to have a seat." She gestured to the nearest chair, which was heaped with papers. "You can put those on the floor, if you like. My mother's papers—I'm trying to put them in order so I can figure out what to do with them."

Something in her words caught my attention, but I couldn't quite identify it.

"I prefer to stand," I said.

Joanna took this in, her hand on what looked like a stack of Miss Kate's letters. "If it's payment you're worried about, all of that will come from the sale, which, as I mentioned, I have already lined up. You can name your price, as far as I'm concerned. Seth and I aren't too bothered about the money."

I should have been concerned about payment—God knew I needed the money—but it was a different question I wanted to ask her. All morning I'd been thinking about the possible buyer of the mansion, what kind of investor might purchase such a white elephant, worth something only if Parson made a miraculous recovery. Heather might roll her eyes at me, but I hoped the buyer had plans beyond the ruined mansion, plans to make use of the old factory building not far off the property, to bring back jobs and prosperity to Parson. I couldn't stomach the idea that my hometown was irredeemable, bad down to its marrow. It would take only one wealthy benefactor to make Parson into a cannery or a meatpacking town, restore its working-class stability, fill the stools at Buck's on Fridays. The thought gave me a kick of queasy, selfish happiness.

But I didn't ask Joanna, too flustered in her presence—angry yet still cowed a little by her delicate, glassy beauty, which beguiled me no less now than as a child.

"So what are you talking about, then?" I asked her. "A percentage of the sale?"

"We'd go as high as five percent." A wobble in her voice: I could push higher if I wanted.

"Thing is, I'm leaving town," I said, surprised at my own words. I hadn't planned to tell her. I hadn't even admitted to myself that it was true.

"Where are you going?"

"San Antonio," I told her. "Heather and me. Aunt Cece went there after the storm, never came back. We'll head out there, help her with the house, with Heather and Robby's kid."

"That sounds nice. Is Robby out there, too?"

I worked hard not to flinch, digging my fingernails hard into my palm. She didn't know about Robby? Where had she spent the last fifteen years, so far from Parson that she'd never learned the consequences of her actions?

Still, the fact that someone thought he was alive stopped me up. In Joanna's mind, at least, Robby was out there walking, talking, breathing. I hesitated, not eager to kill this version of him, maybe the only living version left, by telling her the truth.

"Dead," I finally managed. "Vietnam. Few years ago now."

"Oh, I'm so sorry," she said, but she didn't look it. She still looked like Judy Garland in a movie, choreographed, controlled. She glanced down at the letter in front of her, scanned it with a subtle left-to-right flick of her eyes. That's when I noticed something odd about the papers in the study: as far as I could see, Joanna was putting them all in a single large stack beside the desk, not "organizing" them at all. The papers were either scattered about, waiting for her to review them, or in that one stack.

She's looking for something, I realized. Then my next thought, quick and automatic as a twitch: *Whatever she wants, I can't let her find it*. Part of it was spite over Robby, and part of it was the specter of Miss Kate in the study, this room where we'd talked and laughed hundreds of times at the end of our workday. Joanna had abandoned her mother, and now she felt entitled to root around in her things? All this probably caused Joanna no emotion whatsoever, unless greed was an emotion, the desire to wring every drop of profit from her mother's estate. I wanted to stop her, to shout her away from those letters.

Before I could stop the words, I said, "I could help out for a week or so. Just until Heather and I head off."

If I had been hoping to surprise her, I was disappointed. She only made a pleased noise and remarked, "Wonderful. In that case, we should make the most of today, don't you think? Or do you have other places to be?"

"Buck's," I said. "Tonight. I'm around until then."

I hoped to hell Heather wouldn't have to find out. Sometimes I managed to pick up the odd day job—with any luck, she'd assume that's where I was.

"I could get started with measurements inside," I offered. "Assessing damages, figuring out what we'll need to order."

"I thought it might be better for you to start with the outside," she said, a little too quickly. "There's a machete out in the shed behind the garden. A little rusted, but it should do the job, if you wanted to start in on those vines."

"No need," I said, trying to keep my voice neutral. I didn't want her to know how eager I was to avoid that garden. "I've got my own out in the truck."

"Very well, then."

I turned to leave. The sound of shuffling papers resumed at once behind me. If I was here for the next week, I might have a chance to learn just what she was up to.

Near the doorway, I noticed something familiar on a shelf in the wall, laid on top of some leather-bound books. It was a small weathered notebook, perfectly nondescript to anyone who didn't know better. But I had seen that notebook in Miss Kate's hands a hundred times or more, had watched her hold the phone against her shoulder while she took down notes with the pencil she always kept threaded in the coiled binding. It looked untouched, as if Miss Kate had set it down there and never returned to pick it up.

I grabbed up the notebook as I left the room, held it in front of my body so that Joanna wouldn't see it if she glanced up and watched my retreating back.

I went out to the truck to get my machete, stowed the notebook in my glove box to look over later. Right now the thought of seeing that handwriting was too overwhelming: I could almost picture the deliberate motions of Miss Kate's thick-veined hand with the pencil. She'd been getting frailer those last few months. It had made me nervous for her, all the way out of town like she was.

The one time I'd voiced my concerns about her safety, she'd only laughed and told me she had plenty of protection. "Seth?" I'd asked, dubious, which had gotten her laughing harder: we both knew her son was the dreamy, delicate type, not exactly a guard dog. When she saw I was still troubled, she brought me through the study and into her room and waved me over to her bedside table. There, in the drawer by her bed, was a little snub-nosed revolver. "Always loaded," she explained. "In case anyone wants to give me any trouble."

But this put me even less at ease. To be honest, I didn't care for guns. When people asked me about this—and in Texas, they *did* ask—I told them it was because of how Robby died, but the truth was worse than that. I'd gone out shooting before—I'd even handled guns like Miss Kate's—and it worried me how much I liked it, the feel of a gun's weight in my palm. My whole life, I'd had a temper, had resorted to lashing out whenever I felt backed into a corner. Swinging a punch was one thing; the consequences were minimal, bruises and broken bones. But handling a gun made me deadly powerful, and the thought haunted me: what might happen if I ever got worked up like that with one of those in my hand.

Not that the gun had made Miss Kate any safer in the end. But I couldn't help wondering if Joanna had found the old thing in that drawer—and if so, where she was keeping it these days.

The house loomed above me, full of memories I'd rather not face. Full of Joanna now, too. I'd be smartest to start up my truck and get out of here, regardless of what I'd promised her.

Instead, I climbed out of the truck. I still had questions—about Miss Kate, about what Joanna was looking for up there—and I didn't want to leave Parson without answering them. A week, I'd told Joanna, and I'd meant it. I got my machete from the toolbox in back and strode up to the porch. Those vines were going to be tough work. If I wanted to clear them in the next few days, I'd better get a move on.

4

I spent the rest of the day hacking at vines, the long blade of my machete slicing through their dense, rubbery skin, their lengths heaped around me like a nest of beheaded snakes. Here at Parson House, with Joanna Kerrigan just upstairs, it was hard to keep myself from remembering the past. Usually I could go for months without getting caught up in any memories, could push down those raw feelings when too many beers brought them to the surface. But seeing Joanna again had brought the past back like a sour tide, and as I swung my machete, my arm already sore, a film-reel version of everything started to play out in my mind, and I found myself thinking over how we'd become friends in the first place, when she'd walked into my life and suddenly I could hardly think of anyone else.

And yet for all my obsession, I'd been in no hurry. Though I saw her in class every day, she'd been in town a full month before I got up the nerve to talk to her. I'd watch her from across the room, wondering how someone even *would* talk to a girl like that. I had a few acquaintances at school, other girls from families as poor as mine who dressed in similarly tatty clothes, but these friendships were shallow by necessity: I couldn't risk my white classmates, even the poor ones, getting curious about my home life, asking too many questions about Aunt Cece. So it never much mattered to me how gruffly or rudely I talked to them, as long as I avoided their scrutiny.

Joanna seemed like a different species of girl. Next to her, my acquaintances were dull, blunt objects; even before I spoke to Joanna,

I'd started to distance myself from these other girls. I worried, as kids that age will, that she'd judge me if she saw me with them. Joanna, however, seemed not to see much at all. She was quiet in class, dreamy, her eyes drifting to the window or to a worn book open on her lap, obscured from the teacher's view by her desk. When Mrs. Aster called on Joanna, I'd tense in anticipation, but she always rattled out an answer, demure and correct.

In the end, befriending her was easy enough. It only cost me a punch in the nose.

It happened after school let out one afternoon. Joanna had settled in by then, more or less, had stopped seeming so clumsy with the school rituals, less jarred by every clang of our ancient bell. The other kids had stopped whispering about the "weird" new girl. By that point she was, if not quite one of us, at least a normal part of our world.

Which was probably what made them do it. A trio of boys from our class liked to throw pebbles at girls after school; you'd see them preparing at lunchtime, gathering tiny stones into their pockets. They'd wait beside the path after the final bell of the day, fixing their gaze like buck hunters on the girls streaming out the front door, deciding which ones to terrorize this afternoon. Usually they chose older girls whose breasts were coming in, aiming their pebbles at the new buds under the sweaters. Sometimes the girls were angry, and sometimes they were flattered, and sometimes they ran home crying, which meant they'd get teased the next morning; beyond this, no one ever said much about it. I don't know if it was because they knew I had an older brother in junior high, or simply because I was invisible to boys my age, but I'd never had pebbles thrown at me, except maybe once or twice when they grazed me by accident.

That day the boys picked Joanna as their target. As I walked out into the schoolyard, I saw her cowering in place on the front path, her hands over her face, crying as the pebbles pinged off her. Other girls had the street sense to run, but it was like Joanna not to understand this, to freeze in the midst of danger, to let out a sharp, keening cry at each hit, though I didn't think the boys were hurting her at all. They were laughing like this was the funniest sight in the world, and some onlookers had stopped to laugh, too.

My heart panged with pity, a new emotion for me. I was blushing, upset, and part of me was angry with Joanna as well; I wanted to shake her and tell her to wise up, that boys like this left you alone only when they thought you didn't care. Still, I didn't plan to intervene, had started to walk past her, but then something unexpected happened. Joanna lowered her hands from her face; her big eyes hooked mine like the hypnotic glare of a snake. She didn't say anything—no *please* or *help me*—but all of a sudden my pity had vanished, replaced with a righteous fury, and before I knew it, I was rushing at the boys.

They didn't see me coming: I planted both hands on the biggest boy, Ralph, shoved him down into the dirt. Ralph went boneless, skidding as a cloud of dust whuffed up on impact.

One of the other boys laughed, amazed that a girl could lay out his friend like that. But he didn't laugh for long, not when I punched him right in the stomach and all his pebbles went skittering to the dirt like marbles.

The other kids had stopped walking, transformed from a crowd of children to an eager, bloodthirsty audience—shoulder to shoulder, some of them chanting, egging us on—but when I glanced at them, the only face I saw was Joanna's, her viper's stare pinning me, making me feel invincible.

I was just about to deck the third boy, but that pause had cost me my advantage: before I could lift my arm, his fist slammed hard into my nose. It wasn't the first time I'd been hit, but those had mostly been slaps from my mother, and my head reeled at the impact, my feet a stammering colt's. Through a film of tears, I saw that Ralph was back up off the ground, coming at me fast.

"What in holy hell is going on here?"

It was a teacher's voice, imposing enough to stop the boys in their tracks. I was ashamed to cry in front of Joanna, so I turned on my heels and lit out of there like a jackrabbit, raced down the road and turned the corner and slipped away into the trees.

I thought I'd stay hidden there until the schoolyard cleared out, then make my way home. I knew I must look rough, could feel the blood trickling from my nostrils; Cece would probably faint when she saw me. After a few minutes, I heard the rustles of someone picking through the woods near me. I worried it might be Ralph or the others, but then a delicate Yankee voice called out, "Hello? Louisa, isn't it? Are you there?"

I stepped out of the copse and saw her. Joanna was walking through the brush, her skirt tangled in brambles, a crispy leaf stuck in her hair like a French comb. To my surprise, she looked comfortable, even confident, in the woods, at home in a way she never did in the classroom—as if the forest was where this impossible girl belonged.

It took her a second to see me, but when she did, she didn't wave or smile. She went still, as if she knew I'd come to her.

Of course I did walk up to her. When I reached her, she held out a small, speculative hand and touched my upper lip; her fingers came away red-tipped with blood. It took my breath away, the delicious sight of my stain on her beautiful skin.

She looked so pure, I thought that she would wipe off my blood at once. But she didn't. With a stained finger, she pointed into the deepest part of the woods. "My house isn't far—just a mile or so that way. If you want, we can clean you up before you go home."

That was it. No *thank you*. No mention that I'd defended her.

She took care of me that day. She led me over fallen logs and knotted, messy tree roots, tiptoed over webs of nettles and slick patches of moss. When we made it to her house, she handled me with a gentle touch, washing my face in the icy water that sputtered from a spigot on its side. The house itself was tiny, ramshackle, even—its paint peeling, its rusted gutters draped with spiderwebs—far different from the lavish home I'd pictured for Joanna, three stories at least, her perfect face looking out between lace curtains, the complement to her elegant manner. It was mysterious, the contrast between this girl and her humble home; she was like some princess set here by a curse, waiting for a prince, a fairy godmother. When she ducked inside, she didn't invite me along. She came back out with some slices of bread, which we shared on the walk to my house.

I could have stayed like that forever, just wandering with her, out of the woods and into the streets, grabbing her elbow to pull her clear when a car came rumbling by, her skin porcelain-cool to my hot touch. I was enchanted with Joanna, with the sun-dazzled afternoon, still feeling where her fingers had brushed water over my lips, so enchanted that I was almost home before I remembered Aunt Cece would be there, and I felt such a rush of fear that Joanna would ask about her—would want to know where my real mother was, would wonder if I was actually white or just light enough to pretend, would share this thought with others and get Robby and me kicked out of the school—that I stopped where I stood and, heart thudding, thanked Joanna with such finality that she took the hint and started back toward her own house.

I'd been hoping nobody would notice I'd been fighting, but my nose had puffed up without my realizing it. When I got home, Robby was watching *Man Against Crime* on our fuzzy secondhand television set, but he took one look at me and hollered for Cece. She sat me down and lectured me at length about the dangers of being a girl who makes trouble, and all the while Robby had the television low so he could listen in. Cece was probably right, considering my school, but at the time her words flew past me, wrapped up as I was in Joanna. Eventually she put me to my punishment, scrubbing baked-in stains on her cookware while she bustled around getting dinner ready. I barely noticed the work; in my mind I was in the woods with Joanna Kerrigan, with our gazes and words and fleeting touches, her nimble, nymphlike movements through the trees. I worried that, in school tomorrow, all of this would be gone, like Cinderella's carriage, like a wardrobe that took you only once into a magical realm—that Joanna wouldn't care or even remember what we'd shared, and I'd go back to orbiting her like the moon of some shimmering planet.

But it didn't turn out that way. The next morning she sat at the desk beside mine, and from that day on, we left the school together after the bell; no pebbles ever flew at her again. When some boy did pick on Joanna—for a girl like her, it was bound to happen—I was there at once, scrappy and mouthy, eager to throw a punch. Finally they started to leave her alone, more trouble than it was worth, though sometimes a boy would forget and need to be taught all over again. But by then the boys, the school itself, felt like mere distractions. Our real life started after the final bell each day, when we left the path and slipped into the tree line together, vanishing into an enchanted world that was, for a while, hers and mine alone.

5

M_y favorite bartender!" Adam Stanton shouted as he walked in, as if to a roomful of patrons he could impress. Buck's was almost empty this evening, just a few local shrimpers at the far end of the bar. "I swung by earlier and the place wasn't open yet."

This was true. I'd worked at Parson House today until the last available second, then raced back to town and opened the bar fifteen minutes late.

"My apologies," I said, giving him an obligatory smile.

"This operation getting too much for you, sweetheart?"

I glanced at the empty tables. "Yeah. I can barely keep up."

Adam sat on his usual stool, then unbuttoned and rolled up his shirtsleeves. He was a well-built man of thirty, only now starting to fade from his high school football glory: his sandy blond hair thinned at the temples, a budding paunch that might take on dimension in time. He didn't bother to ask for the Jack and Coke he knew I'd pour him in a moment.

"You've been out in the sun," he said, his eyes moving easily over my body. "You look good with a tan, babe."

Every job I'd had in Parson—and I'd had most of them—came with its drawbacks. For fishing, the smell; for construction, the cuts and bruises; and at Buck's, the creeps. As a matter of fact, our business model depended on them. When I first started here, not long after high school, I'd been serving on the other side of the bar, and Buck had insisted I doll myself up: makeup, low-cut tops, nipped waists.

"Lean low when you set down the tray," he'd said in a businesslike voice, no different than when he'd told me my shift times. "They'll buy more. Tip more. It's good for everyone." The girly, flirtatious role fit me like a scratchy old sweater shrunk in the wash, but I'd needed the job, and it had seemed normal enough for a woman serving beer and shots of whiskey. It took years, but eventually I talked Buck into letting me train behind the bar, and then I slowly ditched my skirts and heels, started dressing in jeans and boots, until in the last couple of years I'd transformed myself into a warm-weather version of Anne Heywood from *The Fox*. By now I was too indispensable for Buck to give me much grief, besides some throwaway comments that I might "catch trouble" dressing like that. *Nothing as bad as dressing the other way*, I didn't tell him.

Still, no clothing in the world could keep a creep like Adam from being a pain. I tolerated him because, back in the day, he'd been friends with my brother. Plus his father was a cop, and Adam himself had recently been appointed county clerk. Buck insisted we keep him happy, that we charge him half price: for business owners in Parson, you could cut a lot of corners if town hall liked you.

So I handed Adam his tumbler and listened gamely to his patter of gossip. The stories around town had gotten thinner since the storm—nowadays we lacked the cast for love affairs and brotherly betrayals. Most of what Adam had on offer these days was suspected insurance fraud and, of course, the running tally of who was leaving town.

He never mentioned the news we never talked about, all the things going on outside Parson: Vietnam, Nixon, the protests. Like most Parson boys, Adam hadn't gone to college, but I'd heard from Buck that he'd pulled some strings to avoid the draft—a major infraction in a patriotic town like Parson, which had sent so many of its own overseas in the last half decade—so the war was an uneasy subject for him. It was uneasy for me, too, led straight back to painful thoughts of my brother. Sadly, the other patrons weren't like Adam: they loved to discuss the war, *our boys* versus the *goddamn commies*, the *blue* versus the *dirty hippies*, like it was all some lethal football game. I couldn't switch them off or turn the dial like I could with the news on the radio. I'd take boring local gossip every time.

Adam was still talking: "And that witch's daughter is back in town, did you hear? Something about the big house. Not that there's anything to do with that hunk of junk, is there? Not exactly a tourist destination. I haven't been out that way in forever."

When I looked at him sharply, he smiled. "Oh, right, you *knew* that Kate woman. You were helping her out there or something when she kicked it."

"Yeah," I said. I grabbed a towel, rubbed hard at a spot on the bar. I tried to keep Buck's words in mind: *Friendly, Lou, always friendly.* "I worked on the house a bit."

He shuddered. "Better you than me. I mean, I know a job's a job and all, but she always gave me the heebie-jeebies. Going around people's houses with those Bibles and whatever else. My ex, she was nicer than me, let her into the house and all that." He snorted into his tumbler. "See how *that* turned out."

Adam's ex was Claudia Reyes, a girl I'd known at the mixed high school after Robby and I were forced to transfer there. They'd been through a sloppy breakup—not a divorce, because they'd never married, though there were two small kids involved who Adam insisted might not be his—and I'd heard the story countless times from Adam's side, in varying degrees of sobriety.

"That old witch, that Darnell woman," he went on, "my dad said the sheriff's office was always keeping an eye on her. He couldn't tell me the details, exactly. But I'm guessing it's something to do with her buying the mansion in the first place. Or maybe her husband disappearing like that. Suspicious stuff, he said."

I didn't respond, and Adam rambled on while I continued to wipe the counter. Truth was, I didn't know how Miss Kate had afforded the house. When I'd asked, she'd only laughed and said that the property had gone unused so long, the county was eager to get it off their hands. *Not that eager,* I'd thought, but I never wanted to push her. She'd seemed delicate those last few months.

But I was familiar enough with Adam's other accusation—the rumor around town that she'd killed her husband, Ed Darnell. On that one, I *had* gotten Miss Kate's side of the story. "Ed ran off," I said during a pause in Adam's monologue. "It's common enough around these parts. And he was a drunk, anyway."

Adam pointed a playful finger at me. "Don't start knocking drunks, Lou. Not when they're the backbone of this fine establishment." His glass was empty; he pushed it toward me for a refill. "You know the women in this town are crazy, right? And Kate Darnell, she was all mixed up with that crew. Those bull-castrating bra-burners or whatever."

I couldn't help but smile. Now he was talking about Peg, who actually *had* done some bull castrating back in the day. Peg had a reputation for helping the women in Parson, which sometimes meant intervening with the men who weren't treating them right. But Peg was hardly a bra-burner, and Miss Kate hadn't been, either. Guys like Adam had only one way of thinking of women who stood up to them.

"No, I mean it," he pressed on, seeing my smile. "You don't know what those women are capable of. This is all hush-hush, of course, ongoing police investigations. But Bruce Dixon, remember him? His wife makes up some story that he raped her or whatever—I mean, come on, she's his *wife*—and then he just goes missing out of the blue, and she takes up with that crowd. And Ed Darnell, too? Too many to be a coincidence. And don't get me *started* on Claudia—"

Here we go, I thought. But just then, thank the Lord, the door swung open, and my best friend, Danny, breezed in.

Adam saw, too, and immediately went quiet, picked up his drink, and slumped off to a table across the room. One of the shrimpers gave Danny a sour look, then went back to his conversation. The Civil Rights Act hadn't reached Parson like other parts of the country, and Danny used to get hassled sometimes in businesses, going all the way back to when we were kids. But ever since the storm had cleared out the town, he said, things had been better. *They don't care so much about the color of my skin now*, he'd told me. *There's not enough people left here to scare one off.*

Danny strode across the room, gave me an ironic salute. "Missed you at the shop today."

Most days, I would go to Danny's auto shop before my shift at Buck's, spend a little time cracking a beer or smoking a spliff.

"Got too busy," I said.

He leaned against the bar, his body angled elegantly. There was no one in Parson, or in all the world as far as I was concerned, quite as beautiful as Danny. That had been true when we were kids, and it kept on getting truer and truer. As time roughened my face, Danny only became more striking, with his narrow cheekbones and his bright honey-brown eyes. The one mar on his face was the long, arcing scar at the top of his forehead, but on Danny, even this didn't look like a flaw. And we didn't talk about that.

With his confidence, his beauty, he could usually pick up men whenever he wanted them, not an easy feat in a town like Parson. In my own single days, the women I went home with were few and far between, maybe four in the span of six years, mostly straight women looking for a thrill, gone by morning. Danny was fastidiously discreet, of course—the town had clear opinions on our kind—but so long as his encounters stayed out of sight, he got by okay. *You'd be surprised who comes over sometimes,* he'd told me once, but he wouldn't give me names, no matter how I pressed him.

"You've been busy?" he asked me now. "Doing what?" He gave me a sly glance, which meant he already knew or had a good idea. Danny knew most everything in this town, one way or another. I'd never quite figured out how he did it.

So I pulled him a glass of Schlitz, told him in a low voice where I'd been today and why. He didn't look surprised at my mention of Joanna, only raised his eyebrows when I told him I'd be working out there for a week. I stuck to the facts, left out the part about the papers in Miss Kate's study, the stack beside the desk that had piqued my curiosity.

"So," he said when I'd finished. "How was it, seeing her again?" He sounded almost excited. We had rarely, if ever, talked about Joanna since she'd moved during high school.

"Do you want to see her?" I asked. "She's not sticking around long."

He shrugged. Like me, Danny had a thing about people leaving him. When Joanna had moved, he'd been in the hospital recovering from the accident. She never wrote or tried to contact him. Didn't try to contact either of us.

"I guess I wouldn't mind," he said finally. "If it happened naturally. People run into people in this town." Then he tilted his glass at me. "But it must be a shock to you, seeing her again."

I looked around, made sure no one was within earshot. "What's to say? She looks just the same."

I could tell he wanted to say more, call me on how I was dodging his real question, but he only shook his head, pressed his lips tight. He disapproved, I could tell that much, but I wasn't sure of what.

I took out my towel, started wiping the bar again. "Money's good. I know the place from back with Miss Kate. Seemed like reason enough."

Danny rolled his eyes. "But aren't you still furious with her? I thought you blamed her for getting you and Robby transferred out of Granbury."

I did blame Joanna, not just for getting us moved to a different school but for all that had happened next. Just before Joanna left Texas, as a final spiteful act, she'd told the administrators at Granbury High School that Robby and I were being raised by our Mexican aunt, that we'd been hiding this for years. While officially, school segregation was coming to an end—*Brown v. Board of Education* had been the year before—Texas was stubbornly slow on the uptake. The governor had threatened to pull funding from schools that integrated; cities like Austin wouldn't try for years yet; and some small towns like Parson resisted—in both official and unofficial ways—well into the '60s.

So this was the powder-keg atmosphere that Joanna's accusation had sparked. The school board was terrified of the possible fallout, the headlines all over the state—that Robby, their star athlete, the once-in-a-generation college-prospects golden boy of Parson, might not be white, might be a half-Mexican boy at Granbury—which, God forbid, could make Parson look like some kind of anti-racist vanguard. Back in those days the school board sent students like this, who didn't meet their standards of racial purity, to Woodman Secondary, the "mixed school" just outside of town: Black and Mexican American students, kids from Central American families, whatever orphans were on the county's dime, the children of poor German immigrants who'd come over after the war. To the school board, this was Parson's concession to integration—not a "segregated school," they argued, but a separate place for students "with different educational needs." If Robby went to Granbury while not being white, if he flourished there despite his "different needs," then their whole argument went up in smoke. And if word got out, if the newspapers called Parson radical, then some school board members probably wouldn't get reelected next year.

The same day our principal received the tip-off, while I, too, was recovering from the accident, the district sent a man to our house right in the middle of dinner, a bulldog official from the school board who sat himself down on our living room sofa and asked bluntly about birth certificates, social security cards, hospital records, and contact information for our real mother and father, which of course we didn't have. "So you don't have a single document to prove your origins?" he said to Robby and me in a cold voice, unsatisfied by the marriage certificate Cece had handed to him, proving she'd married our uncle, Don Ward. Interracial marriages were common enough at the time, but nowhere on the document did it say our uncle was white; nor could we even prove that he was our uncle. If this marriage certificate was our only evidence, then this man's contempt plainly spelled our fate.

"Don't worry," Cece told us, seeing our troubled faces after the intruder had left. "It isn't true. There's nothing they can do to you if it isn't true."

Hell, in a different environment, she might have been right. But the look in Robby's eyes told me he knew what I knew: without Granbury's well-funded football program and the scholarship doors it could open, his dreams of college were over.

It took the school board all of three days to make their decision, during which time they tried to keep it quiet. In Parson this meant that pretty soon everyone was whispering about us, our classmates speculating openly as we walked down the halls at school. We kept our heads down, attended classes like everything was normal, pretended people at school weren't avoiding us like plague victims—everyone except Heather, who stuck by Robby from the beginning.

It had to have been Joanna. She was the only person at Granbury I'd ever told.

So Robby and I were sent to Woodman Secondary. Without his football scholarship, his ticket out, Robby was stuck in Parson, poor, vulnerable, available when the draft board snatched up so many of our best.

Danny knew the broad outlines of this story, and I didn't like to say much about my resentment of Woodman in front of him, since it certainly wasn't the school's fault. And it did give me and Danny those years of high school together to cement our friendship. So instead of answering his question, I flashed him a look. I guess that look told him what he wanted to know, because all the playfulness left his face.

"All right," he said solemnly. "Whatever it is you're up to, that's your business. Just be careful at that house."

I waved this off. "I've done more dangerous jobs."

"Sure. But I've known you a long time: you tend to see only what you want to see. Keep a clear head out there. You might have your reasons to hate Joanna, but she has some reasons to hate you, too."

I couldn't tell whether he was trying to warn me, goad me, or what, but all of a sudden I needed to be alone, away from him, and fast. "I'll see you later, okay? Gotta go get a keg from the shed."

"And I'm guessing you won't stop by the shop tomorrow?"

"If I have time," I said, and left the room without looking back at him. I nursed a cigarette behind the shed—I'd lied about the keg—and when I stepped back into the bar, Danny was gone. Adam Stanton was back on his stool, grinning, ready for another refill.

I'd met Danny in fifth grade, not long after Joanna came to town. It all happened because she invited me over for Christmas.

"What do you mean, for Christmas?" I asked her. We were deep in the woods that afternoon, sitting on a fallen log by a tiny, sun-pimpled pond, one of the places in the forest we'd made our own, a secluded spot to talk and dream and play. There we would lose ourselves in our favorite game, acting out elaborate stories Joanna imagined for us, a skill that always awed me. She'd narrate and stage-direct these stories, and play all the leading-lady parts, the damsels and warrior princesses and fairy queens. Meanwhile I'd become whomever she wanted, sometimes the evil dragon, sometimes the greedy enchantress stepmother, but more often the hero, the defender, the mysterious and debonair savior of Joanna's virtue, fighting off the invisible villains only she could see, her porcelain finger pointing out where these phantoms lurked among the branches.

Our favorite story was Joanna's take on *Snow White*. In her version, the princess had not taken up with dwarves but had hidden herself alone in the forest and begun to learn a magic of her own, a magic of light and music and mysterious potions, which she mixed together out of weeds and ditchwater in an old bright blue Evening in Paris bottle, and which were meant to counteract the vicious magic the evil queen had waiting for her at home. When the queen sent the huntsman after the princess, he became so enchanted by her that he turned against the queen and vowed to serve the princess always. Of all my characters, I liked playing the huntsman best. I never grew tired of the role: hearing the princess's song for the first time, wondering at her beauty when I followed this sound to her clearing, seeing her make her innocent potions out of dirt and pond water, feeling the sweet rush of conversion falling upon me like rain, changing my life forever.

We were right at the conversion scene when Joanna broke out of the story, very rare for her. It took me a second to realize that this wasn't the princess talking to the huntsman—that, out of nowhere, Joanna was asking me, Lou, if I'd like to visit her house for Christmas.

"You know, Christmas Day," she said in a casual voice, under which I sensed some kind of anxiety. "You could come for dinner or something."

"And meet your family?" I asked. We'd been best friends for over a month at this point, but I hadn't gone back to her house since our first day together, and she hadn't come close to mine. Nor did we talk of our homes, our families. I'd often hoped for another glimpse of Joanna's house—I'd been too hurt, too dazzled, that first afternoon to remember my way back—but whenever our play and exploration took us in that direction, Joanna took special care to lead us elsewhere. I was startled that all this evasion would suddenly end with an invitation to her Christmas dinner. "I mean, that could be fun," I added.

She shrugged and rose to her feet, started to clamber delicately up a nearby tree to investigate an abandoned bird's nest, our story evidently forgotten. "My mother wanted me to ask," she said in an indifferent tone. "If you can't come . . . you probably want to be with your own family . . ."

By now my surprise had worn off; I rushed to accept the invitation, told her that I'd be there. As always, I was happy to go wherever Joanna wanted me. Meeting her family could only bring us closer.

"Great. I'll tell my mother," Joanna said as she prodded at the bird's nest. Her lips were pressed tight together, deep lines grooved into her forehead.

Later that night, at the dinner table, I asked Cece if I could go. Only as I was speaking the words—"Can I spend Christmas at my friend's house?"—did I realize that they had an odd sound, that they might carry some harm.

The question clearly startled Cece, but she gave no immediate sign of pain. She tilted her head, her long hair shifting on her shoulder. "You don't want to spend Christmas here?"

I wasn't sure how to answer, because I did love Christmas at home. Cece would start her yearly preparations right after Thanksgiving: the elaborate nativity set, the candy-red poinsettias, the fragrant tree her friend Ruben delivered in his pickup, the swirling colors of our homemade decorations. A few days before, we'd celebrate the feast of Our Lady of Guadalupe, the three of us joined by Cece's Book-of-the-Month friends, an exuberant group of older women from good Mexican families who loved to press quarters into my hand when Cece wasn't looking. Then we'd all sit at the table and enjoy Cece's cooking, the food at its most lavish and showy, conchas and sweet empanadas, hot chocolate sprinkled with cinnamon.

I didn't want to insult Cece: even as a child, I could tell how hard she worked to make the holidays special for us. So I responded with the blunt, selfish logic of childhood: "I love all the stuff you do here. It's really amazing. It's just that I've always wondered what a normal Christmas is like."

Cece didn't answer. Dinner wasn't quite over yet, but she stood from the table and began to pluck away the empty plates, then took them to the sink and busied herself with the washing up. She'd always been small, barely five feet, but she normally thrummed with an energy that made her seem much taller, that filled up the space around her. Now she seemed subdued and still, and I realized she was almost child-sized, barely bigger than I was. Robby shot me a sharp look across the table. I knew I'd said something wrong—though I wasn't exactly sure what—but my intention hadn't wavered. I needed to spend Christmas Day with Joanna.

When Cece came back to the table, there was a wet sheen to her dark eyes, but she managed a brief smile, and she started asking questions about this friend. Where did she live, and what time did she want me, and who was her family, and where did her father work? I was tempted to make up answers, but I owned up to the gaps in my knowledge. It concerned her, I could tell, that checking on these people herself wasn't an option, that our secrets meant she had to remain in the background. I feared that she would say no, that the gulf between her world and Joanna's would keep me home for Christmas. But just when I was about to admit defeat, she relented. "All right," she said, voice clipped. "You take your brother with you."

Robby started to object, but Cece silenced him with a shake of her head. "I don't know these people. You go, too, look out for your sister."

Which was how Robby and I wound up traipsing through the woods on Christmas afternoon. I knew Cece was really sending Robby as a spy—she'd be pumping him for information about my new friend and her family the first chance she got—but I didn't care. He grumbled and griped all the way, but the words slid right off me, my stomach clenched in excitement because I would soon meet Joanna's family, see the spaces where she lived, crawl just that inch further into her life. I was desperate to make a good impression, to get invited back often to her house.

What I remember most about that afternoon is Miss Kate. She was a stocky woman with frizzy brown curls, and that day she met us at the door dressed in a wool Christmas dress patterned with colorful wreaths. She greeted us with exclamations, gave us both familiar hugs, Robby blushing in embarrassment, my head spinning with delight. *She likes us already,* I thought; impressing her would be easy. She led us through the house, which was small, almost crushingly so, the narrow halls and rooms like a network of cluttered rabbit warrens. Still, there was a warmth to it, the warmth of Miss Kate's presence: she made it feel instantly welcoming, loomed large over that space in a way she'd never quite manage, decades later, in the towering rooms and corridors of Parson House.

Miss Kate gathered us all in the kitchen, introduced us to Joanna's siblings: her brother, Seth; her sister, Cassandra. They both looked just like their mother, brown curls, easy smile, ruddy complexion, nothing like their sister. Joanna herself was faced away when we walked into the room, chopping something on the far counter, but even so, the sight of her here shocked me. I'd never seen anyone so out of place in their own home.

The meal was vegetables boiled pale, dry meat, oily pies, nothing compared to Cece's scrumptious fare. But the energy was warm, Bing Crosby and Dean Martin warbling from the radio, and by the time we'd finished eating even Robby had loosened up. Seth brought him outside and showed him around the yard, while Joanna took me to the tiny room she shared with Cass. I could tell at a glance which bed was Joanna's, hers primly made with the blanket tucked tight below the mattress, Cass's wild and unkempt, a stray pillow on the floor.

A neatly kept collection of books ran along the windowsill, fantasy novels alphabetized by author. Joanna was taking me through them, explaining the premise of each, when the front door crashed open across the house. At once Joanna fell silent, tensed and alert, though she didn't turn toward the sound. Her face reminded me of a rabbit hearing a twig snap beneath a coyote's paw.

"Who is it?" I asked in an instinctive whisper. Then, a guess, "Your dad?"

She shook her head, whispered as well. "My father lives in Michigan. That's Ed, my mother's husband. He was supposed to be with his family. I suppose he's come home."

I felt the uptick of tension in the house, an ambient dread flood into the room. Then I heard a male voice, his words indistinct, his tone aggressive.

Calmly though quickly, Joanna had started to clear her books from the sill, stack them on the bed. This completed, she reached down to the frame, pulled the old window open on the winter twilight.

"Well, you and Robby should be getting back home now, don't you think?" she said in a crisp, carefully controlled voice. It was just dawning on me that I'd be leaving through this first-floor window. "This goes right out into the yard," she added, as if it were the most normal thing in the world. "Sometimes I leave for school this way."

The male voice rose again, gruffer and more aggressive than before. So I let Joanna give me a boost out the window; some dry leaves crunched beneath me as I landed in the side yard of the house.

"Will you be all right here?" I asked her. Despite everything, I had half a mind to offer to take her home with me, just to keep her out of harm's way. She shook her head and sighed as if to say: *I'd just have to come back here.*

"Oh, I never got to give you this," she said instead. She leaned out the window and passed me a package wrapped in tatty newspaper. "Open it when you get home."

I found Robby out in the yard, running races with Seth. It made me sad to end their fun—I was thrilled to see them getting along, thrilled that Robby approved of the Kerrigan kids—but it was clear we needed to go. When I told Seth his stepfather was inside, he got the same frightened animal look on his face as Joanna.

Robby and I walked home fast. The adrenaline of sneaking out had me feeling almost jubilant, as well as everything new I'd just learned about Joanna. "Weren't they just great?" I said, grinning.

Robby gave me a look like I was crazy. "You do realize we just had to run out of there. Because their drunk dad came home."

"Stepdad," I said dismissively, as though that made all the difference in the world. Robby could think what he liked. Nothing would touch the treasures I'd gained that night.

We didn't talk much after that. A chill had set into the air, the kind that seldom came to Parson. By the time we made it back to Cece's, we were shivering.

Inside, there was a warm glow, a smell of fresh-baked bread, and, to our surprise, an unfamiliar Black boy seated at the table, sipping a mug of hot cider. Cece greeted us from her seat, not getting up to hug us as we came in through the door, then she said with a smile, "This is Danny. He lives not far away. He's been spending Christmas with me."

I later found out that Cece had discovered Danny, bruised and knocked around, in the woods out behind our house. She took him in and fed him dinner on the spot. At first I almost hated Danny, jealous of him as he sat in my chair drinking the last of the cider, the last pan dulce on his plate. His presence there punched a hole in my perfect night, made me ache for the Christmas I'd missed back here at home.

"What's that?" he asked me. He was pointing at the present Joanna had given me, which I still carried like a talisman, too excited to unwrap it. I'd bought her nothing for Christmas, but she'd cared enough to wrap a present for *me*.

"Nothing," I said, embarrassed.

"That's from your friend?" Danny asked. "The one you just had dinner with?"

I was irritated Cece had told him where I'd been, what I'd been up to. But Cece wasn't paying attention to me; she was picking at a plate of food in front of her, looking comfortable and unbothered in a way that made me feel slighted for reasons I couldn't explain.

"Yeah," I said, trying to hide the present behind my back. "It's nothing."

"You should open it," Danny urged.

I'd planned to open the gift on my own, savoring each second, but I had no way to explain this to the stranger. So I peeled off the flimsy newspaper, which came away like cobwebs, revealing a small book: *The Wind on the Moon*. Joanna had been reading it in class not two weeks ago, her delicate fingers pinching and turning the pages under her desk.

That night I slipped the book under my pillow and slept with one hand on its cover, a place where Joanna's hand had often rested. When I woke, I felt its glossy surface warm against my palm.

Distracted by Joanna, I didn't ask Cece until the next day what had happened to Danny, why he'd been out in the woods behind our house. But Cece didn't tell, claimed not to know, though I suspected she had a theory she was holding back. At the time I figured it must be his family—I knew plenty of parents who knocked their kids around for getting out of line, or for no reason at all. I wouldn't meet his parents for a while yet, didn't know they were gentle and loving, not the type. The most obvious answer never even occurred to me back then: that bad things happened to Black folks in towns like Parson, and this was something Cece could understand in a way I never would.

6

In some ways working for Joanna at Parson House began to feel like two years ago, back when Miss Kate first hired me: I woke before dawn, was already out and working at the house by the time the sun wheeled up above the water, then wore myself down all day and arrived at Buck's so exhausted that I almost nodded off in the lulls between customers. In those days, Miss Kate would bring me a jar of ice water while I worked, chat with me awhile. One time she said, "Part of me wishes you didn't work quite so hard," and then, with a grin and a gesture at the house shaping up around us, "the other part is thrilled that you *do*."

If Joanna noticed how much I was working the first few days, she didn't mention it. It made me miss Miss Kate all the more. By the end of the weekend, I'd hacked most of the vines away from the house, replaced some windowpanes, borrowed Danny's tallest ladder to touch up the paint and trim, all the time half expecting Miss Kate to walk over with a mug of tea for me, shading her eyes and hollering up to ask how I was getting on. Sometimes I'd even forget, for a moment, that Miss Kate was dead, but then I'd see the garden and remember with a violent catch to my breath, like I was finding her there all over again.

I barely saw Heather for a couple days in a row, leaving so early, coming home so late and tired. She didn't know that I was working for Joanna. I knew I ought to tell her, and I tried to do it, too, that very first day. I got home after Buck's and found Heather cleaning out one of our old storage closets, a half-full garbage sack at her side. She gave a little startled jump like she hadn't heard me walk up, then greeted me with a kiss. Even tired as I was, I mustered up all the strength I had and tried to start the conversation, deliberately casual: "Guess what I got up to today?" It must have been too casual, because it set off her own long, eager list of what she'd done—packing, cleaning, all sorts of odd and particular things that had turned up along the way, and did we want to hold on to that old collection of arrowheads or did I think we might toss those out?—and by the time she was done, she must've forgotten how I'd kicked off the conversation. If I'm being honest with myself, I was grateful to have avoided that confrontation, but the next morning when I slipped out, I felt a clench of fear high in my gut, worried she'd catch me. For those first couple of days, she must have assumed I had picked up some of my usual daytime work, or else she must have been too busy, too focused on thoughts of reuniting with her daughter, even to wonder what I was up to. Still, that level of distraction wouldn't last long: I knew I could get caught at any moment.

My main focus had turned to Joanna. While I lashed at the vines, pulled up weeds, slathered on coats of paint, she was always inside the mansion. I imagined her in the study, lost among all those papers. What was she doing, alone in there? What was she searching for in those shadows? And what was she thinking about me, all the while? Was she as aware of me as I was of her? Did my proximity itch her skin, hum like a mosquito in her ears, the same as hers did to me?

I wondered if what she sought might be contained in Miss Kate's notebook, the one I now kept stashed in the glove box of my truck. If so, I hadn't found it. Far as I could tell, the notebook was a sort of journal, little reflections written during the last few months of her life, her observations, anything that struck her interest—*Long walk over the beach this morning; gulls crying, swooping; saw one carry off a mullet that had practically leaped into its talons*—alongside appointments, important dates, addresses of friends. Many notes pertained to Parson House: estimates from local plumbers, contact info for auction houses that might sell the stored furniture, an inventory of antique linens we'd found behind the hidden panel of a closet. I could remember discussing all this with her in those months. "How are we gonna cover this?" I'd asked her, pointing to a column of planned expenditures, prices that seemed far beyond her humble clothes, her run-down station wagon. Miss Kate had pursed her lips, her gaze boring into the numbers like she might change them by force of will. "We'll get it figured out," she'd said. "There's always something to be done."

I found that same column while flipping through the journal at Buck's one night, when everyone had been served and no one needed me for a spell. In stolen moments like these, I read through the journal several times, eager to find anything that might account for Joanna's behavior, but each time the entries seemed less remarkable than before and only made me grieve Miss Kate more deeply.

"I'm determined to make this place work," Miss Kate said to me one evening around a year ago. She'd invited me to stay for dinner and we were sitting at the kitchen table, while Seth stood across the room at the stove, stirring a pot in his bathrobe, whipping up one of his tasty but unambitious meals. As always, he remained almost apologetically quiet, as though he wanted us to ignore his presence.

"Why does it matter so much to you?" I asked her, not for the first time. I knew the official story was that she was fixing the place up for tourism—bringing the place back to its elementary school field-trip glory—but that reason never sat well with me; it seemed like the kind of thing a wealthy local with roots that stretched back to the founding of Parson might do, not a transplant from out of state who, until recently, hadn't seemed particularly well-off in the slightest. But Miss Kate had a slippery way of sidestepping my curiosity, so of course I didn't expect to get anything more than her usual evasive half answers: *Lotta history in a place like this* or *It's a nice place, isn't it?*

This time she narrowed her eyes in thought, seemed to actually consider the question. She cut a wary look at Seth. He stood on the opposite side of the wide kitchen, his back to us, lost in a world of his own. Leaning in, Miss Kate said in a low voice, "You know the history of this place, don't you? The plantation and all that? And then how the Parsons opened the factory and mistreated all those workers?"

"Sure," I said. "Everyone knows that."

45

"Well, doesn't it just make you itch? Thinking about all of that happening in our town?"

I liked that she called it *our town*. Miss Kate and me, both of us transplants from elsewhere—but we could still build a home here if we wanted. All it took was the courage, the willpower.

"But what does history matter?" I said. "Isn't it best to move on?"

I wish Miss Kate had answered this question, but just then came a loud clatter of metal on tile. Seth had been plating up the pasta, and his elbow had knocked a serving spoon to the floor, splattering blood-red sauce everywhere. The nervous man flinched and froze, staring down at the counter, not daring to glance at the mess he'd made.

"It's all right," I said, springing to my feet. Poor Seth: he didn't say a word as I brought the spoon to the sink, as I wiped up the sauce with a rag. Only once the floor was clean did he relax enough to address me.

"Thank you," he said, his voice nearly a whisper as he took the rag from me, not meeting my eyes. He clenched the rag, some sauce spilling over his fingers. "I'm so sorry."

"Nothing to be sorry for. No harm done, right?"

I turned to Miss Kate. She wasn't looking at Seth or me. Her eyes were fixed on the tile by the stove, the red stain I'd swabbed away.

I told Seth to sit, finished plating up the pasta. When I turned around, however, he'd already left the kitchen, slipping out silently in his slippers. "He all right?" I asked Miss Kate.

She looked up from the floor as if startled from her fugue. "Oh, that's just Seth," she said. "Don't you mind about that." Then, in a lighter tone, "It's you who needs to eat, my hardworking girl." That made me glow inside, and I was happy enough to let her oddball son be her problem. I had plenty of my own to worry about.

And now, thanks to Joanna, the house was my responsibility again. I spent my fourth morning at Parson House repainting around the attic windows, those slitlike eyes that peered out of the roof, all the while cursing myself that I'd let three full days pass without getting any closer to figuring out what Joanna was up to. If I wanted to re-solve my curiosity before the week passed, I had to keep an eye out.

Luckily, from that high on the ladder, I could see almost the en-tire property, and so, right before noon, I had a bird's-eye view when Joanna left the house through the garden door. She strode quickly to her Fairlane, which was parked near the back garden gate; when she turned the key, the engine started much quieter than I'd expected, audible to me only because I was straining to hear it. Had I not been up this high, I would have missed her leaving entirely. Joanna pulled away; the Fairlane vanished in the thick of the trees.

Something odd occurred to me now: except for my first day here, Joanna had never parked her car out front where I was working. She kept it back near the garden, out of sight. Was she hiding her move-ments from me? More to the point—did she want me to think she was always here, not let me know when the house was empty? Was there something she was worried I'd find? I thought of the paper she'd been searching for that day in the study.

I set aside my painting things, climbed down to the third-floor windows. These were side-hung, opening out; I swung one wide like a great book. Then I ducked inside and found myself in one of the upstairs bedrooms.

My work with Miss Kate had never reached the third floor. I'd last been in this room twenty years ago, a child on the museum tour. "The servants stayed up here," the docent had told us, "dating all the way back to the house slaves of the plantation days." These narrow bed-rooms had unnerved me, devoid of the lush furnishings on the floors below: bare walls, stark white linens, a metal-bar bedframe. Now the bedframe was bare, its mattress absent, so it looked more like some kind of dismantled cage.

I didn't linger in the room, aware that Joanna could be back any minute. I made my way quickly to the nearest staircase, raced down the second-floor corridor, and entered Miss Kate's study, breathing hard in the half-lit somnolence.

The papers in the room looked different now, as if Joanna had entered another phase of her sorting. There were multiple stacks on the roll-top desk, on the great oak credenza, and I stepped over and started to examine them. It still bothered me, the thought of Joanna sorting and re-sorting these papers—she didn't deserve to feel so close to the mother she'd abandoned, to rummage through her belongings. One stack contained Miss Kate's numerous bills, another her correspondence, a third her family documents. In this third stack I found the birth certificate of Joanna's sister, Cassandra. Cass, who had been my friend, too. Dead fifteen years, in a car wreck not far from this house. I felt an unwelcome chill as I handled it.

As when I read through Miss Kate's diary, my eyes lit on nothing unusual, no secrets Miss Kate had hidden, no hints of the buyer Joanna had lined up. I wondered distantly what I thought I was doing, what Joanna would say if she caught me like this, darting down the huge hallways without permission.

Before she'd moved out to the mansion, Miss Kate had always lived in small one-story houses. She had no clue how to exist in a space this size, and laughed as she told me, "I hate to admit it, but I use three rooms in this whole silly place—the bedroom, the study, the kitchen. Everything else belongs to the dust motes."

The next place to look was Miss Kate's bedroom, spacious, with tall ceilings and a wide, semi-recessed balcony that looked out onto the garden. Sometimes, still dressed in her robe, her hair all big and wild and slept on, Miss Kate would call down to me from the balcony while I worked in the garden, tell me Seth was whipping up some breakfast, and ask did I want to join them. Crossing the doorway, I shivered at her presence in the room.

Of all the rooms I'd seen in the house so far, Miss Kate's bedroom seemed the most alive, the least touched by the wreckage of the storm. Perhaps the balcony had aired it out; perhaps Joanna had tidied a little. All the bureau drawers were pushed in neatly, the curtains around the bed dust-free, drawn closed. I opened the armoire and stared at Miss Kate's clothes, not stiff with salt but soft, like they'd just been washed. Her work clothes, her smocks, her Levi's were folded on a shelf, as though she planned to wake up and put them on tomorrow.

Next to the armoire was the bedside table where Miss Kate had kept her revolver. I slid open the drawer carefully, but the gun was no longer there; I slipped my hand inside and felt around to make sure it hadn't slid into the dark back corners, but all I found was a single book, a Bible, the New World Translation. The sight of it distracted me momentarily from my worry over where that gun had ended up. I picked up the Bible and paged through it, curious. It seemed to be Miss Kate's personal copy: her handwriting was everywhere, underlines, asterisks, annotations in the margins. One bookmarked page showed a verse, circled and underlined as though she'd returned to it many times—Isaiah 1:18.

"Come, now, and let us set matters straight between us," says Jehovah. "Though your sins are like scarlet, they will be made as white as snow; though they are as red as crimson cloth, they will become like wool."

My brain turned to fog, as it always did with Bible verses—the meaning seemed far away, a snippet of an overheard conversation, contextless and senseless. Still, I imagined Miss Kate, alive, reading that verse and feeling moved, moved enough to give it three underlines, and the thought made me miss her with an insistent pain in my chest. What had she been feeling that drew her to this passage again and again? I put the Bible back, slid the drawer shut.

To my left the glass doors of the balcony offered a clear view of the garden. Eight months ago, it was tidy and trimmed; now it frothed and clamored upward with the superabundance of a jungle. Numb, as if in a dream, I opened the doors and stepped to the balcony's edge, looked down into the vicious tangle of overgrowth, hedges and creepers and flower beds that we'd worked so hard to keep separate, now twined together into a single brindled mass. Nothing appeared to have died down there, not from the storm, not from neglect: the garden looked more intensely alive than I'd ever seen it, and it seemed to let out a scraping, breathing sound, the seething of its restless, fecund growth. A moment later, I realized the sound was the ebb of the nearby sea, amplified in this room by some trick of architecture.

I was shaken from my daze by the sound of a car out on the drive. Figuring it must be Joanna's Fairlane, I slipped inside and shut the doors, hurried back through the house the way I'd come. Once I was back out on the ladder, I could see that it wasn't the Fairlane at all but, rather, a giant truck, roaring up toward the house, crooked tailpipe choking out clouds of fume. From my high vantage point I couldn't see it too well, though there was something fluttering from the tail-gate, a piece of cloth that it took me a beat to realize was a flag. The stars and bars of the Confederacy.

The truck pulled up, idled a moment, and I wondered whether I ought to climb down and meet whomever it was or if I should slip back in through the attic window and hide. I wasn't sure if the driver saw me, high up and at an angle as I was, but after a moment they revved their engine twice, angry and aggressive, and then suddenly wheeled around and trundled out of the drive again, spitting gravel as they went.

What had they been doing out here? Out on a joyride? It had felt oddly sinister, the way they'd paused significantly in front of the house. But maybe there was an innocent explanation—they were some local boys who had heard the place was being fixed up and were curious to come take a look? Still, the whole thing unnerved me, and although I knew I was out alone at the house again and could have slipped back in the office for another look around if I wanted, I stayed working out on that ladder until Joanna returned.

She parked by the garden wall again, closed her door softly as if she didn't want to make a noise that would carry. I lost sight of her when she slipped through the garden gate, but soon enough she had come around the front of the house and found me.

Her voice barely reached that far up; she tried only once to be heard, then made me climb partway down to talk. "Got some sand-wiches," she said, lifting up a sack. "Thought you might want to share."

Joanna didn't invite me inside. We sat without chairs on the front porch, away from the sag at its middle planks, my sweat cool-ing under the shade of the awning.

"Where'd you pick these up?" I asked, peeling the waxed paper off my sandwich, which turned out to be tuna fish with chopped celery.

She hesitated. "They're homemade. I'm not sure what's open these days."

"The storm closed a lot of businesses. Restaurants especially."

"Do you think they'll reopen?"

I bristled, knowing what she was really asking: *Will Parson re-cover?* I didn't want to answer that question, not because I didn't know the answer but because I didn't like it, one more reason for Joanna to feel better than the town she'd left behind. Joanna could hear about Parson's death throes from someone else.

So I changed the subject, asked some questions about her life, drifted into the generic catch-up chat she must have had in mind when she made me the sandwich, as if we were just old school friends who'd lost touch for the usual reasons. I told her I'd stuck around Parson, made it sound like I'd worked at Buck's since high school so she wouldn't guess all the job jumping I'd done; to a woman like Joanna, that amount of unsettled might count as a personal failing. Joanna, for her part, had gone in the directions I'd expected: a fancy career path (she was studying anthropology and archaeology, specializing in ancient art), an advanced degree underway (she mentioned a Ph.D. program), a city up north that might as well have been Paris to me (she lived in a place of her own near Chicago). It all sounded so remote and impressive that by the time I'd heard the basics, I was sorry I'd asked at all.

It was tense, and all along I was hoping she'd slip up, say something that gave me a hint as to what she was really doing here, what was going on in that office that she wasn't telling me about. But she dodged all my questions about the house, waving them off or giving cursory, unspecific answers until eventually the conversation fizzled out, and I thought she might make an excuse to leave. Instead she sighed and took a nibble of her sandwich, blinked away from me at the too-bright blue of the sky. I stared at her delicate doll's-face profile, which, despite my anger, despite my obsessive certainty that she was up to no good, still made my body tingle from head to toe. When we were young, no boys had crushes on her—*too weird*, they always said—but it was her otherness that attracted me, that stirred my mind and heart no less than my body. I looked at her chewing mouth, the muscles shifting in her jaw, and felt guilty that Heather didn't know where I was right now.

Joanna had shifted her gaze to the stubbled fields beyond the manor, angled away from me. "You know," she said in a soft voice, "I used to think this place was so inescapable."

"Parson?" I asked.

"It was the whole world back then. Don't you remember?"

I pictured the two of us as girls, running through the woods behind her house, tripping and laughing and pulling each other up roughly by the hand, plucking leaves and ripping them open to release their living scents. The princess and her champion. It was paradise, and she'd wanted to escape? She'd been keeping secrets from me even then? *Wish I'd known how much you hated it*, I nearly said, then stopped myself. "Long time ago," I said. "Can't remember much of anything."

"Really? It's all so vivid to me. Like some book I've read a thousand times."

"Well, I never was much of a reader. Thanks for the sandwich."

She nodded, lost in her thoughts, still staring out over the fields. I didn't know whether she'd ended the conversation or I had, but either way I wished she would look at me again, just so I had a clue what she was thinking, but she didn't. I stood, brushed off my pants, and went back to work.

I wrapped up early that day and stopped by home before heading to Buck's. As I turned the corner onto our road, I caught a glimpse of a yellow car in our driveway. It was all but hidden behind a hedge, but from the color I guessed it was Cece's old Comet wagon. *Great, just great*, I thought. I loved Cece, but she had visited along with Sarah two months back—when she was on the fence about returning to Parson—and her weekend stay had been long enough for her to call the town "a goner" and to set Heather's mind firmly on San Antonio.

"I could leave Sarah with you in the meantime," she'd offered Heather, speaking in a low voice. It was late, and we were sitting in the living room; Sarah had nodded off to sleep in my lap after insisting for half an hour that she wasn't tired. "Just until you can join me in the city."

Heather had looked tempted by the thought, watching Sarah breathe softly against my knee, her long hair half covering her face. I gave Heather an encouraging smile, letting her know I was on board. I liked having Sarah around—the kid reminded me of Robby in about a thousand ways; everything from the set of her pout to her stubborn cowlick felt like having him back. Besides, if Sarah was here, then

Heather might be less eager to get away, might give up the notion of leaving Parson.

In the end she sighed and said, "It's breaking my heart. But there're barely any kids left here. And the school's still not running." She didn't add the other part: money was scarce. Fewer people in town to get their hair done, to tip at the bar. "Besides," she added with a look at me, "we won't be long here, will we?"

Cece was looking at me as well, a look that took me right back to the days when some dumb kid impulse of mine was causing her trouble. I felt a surge of anger at both of them, pressuring me into this decision. Sure, there were times in my life when I'd cursed Parson, hated it—as had just about everyone who'd ever set foot here, at one time or another. But I'd built a life here, a life that may not be available to me anywhere else. I couldn't picture myself somewhere else, far away from the home where people knew me well enough not to get too curious about how I lived and who I lived with, how I cut my hair and the types of jeans I wore.

But that was only part of the reason. The real anger was deeper, more animal, impossible to reach: I didn't want to leave Parson, felt a gripping fear at the notion, and here they were, making me choose between my home and my family. Storms came and went, and Parson had always managed to recover eventually. I felt betrayed by their lack of faith, their unwillingness to believe Parson was coming back for us.

I almost gave them a piece of my mind, but Sarah was sleeping like a cherub against me, so all I did that night was shrug and change the subject. I doubt it would have made a difference: the next day Heather was talking about leaving the salon, asking when I planned to give notice at Buck's. Worst of all, Cece drove back to the city and started her serious nesting, finding new furniture, sewing new curtains, getting her rental house ready for our arrival, which she and Heather seemed to assume was any day now.

Seeing the car in the driveway, I braced myself for a fight. If Cece had indeed come down to Parson, bringing Sarah with her, I doubted I'd have a chance in hell of staying here much longer, of stopping them from whisking me away from the only home I'd ever known. Or else I'd need to stay behind alone while Heather left with Cece, which

I dreaded almost as much. Heather was the only family I had left in Parson, after all, and since we'd moved in together, we hadn't been apart more than a night or two at a time. The thought of living in this house alone, of Heather in San Antonio without me, filled me with a hollow fear, a hot-stove-don't-touch feeling that ran so deep inside me, I didn't want to risk finding out how far it went.

But it wasn't Cece's wagon in the driveway. Just the opposite, in fact: a sleek Corvette painted a similar shade. A new, fancy car, not one I knew. Fay Browne, an old friend of Heather's from school, was sitting in the front seat with her perfectly coiffed hair, just about to pull out as I drove up. I gave her a curt wave; she gave me a fake, painted-on smile. I suspected Fay didn't like me much. She'd been one of the popular girls who'd avoided Robby as soon as he went to Woodman, who'd thought Heather had thrown her future away by marrying and having a child with him. I kept my distance from Fay, talked about the weather if ever forced into a conversation. I was glad to see her drive off.

I found Heather in the living room, dancing to Linda Ronstadt's *Silk Purse.* She grinned when she saw me and held out her hands; I took them and let her lead me into a close sway. Her warm, familiar body melted some of the stress from my shoulders.

"I don't have long," I said, apologetic.

"I know." She pressed her cheek to mine; I could smell the Lux soap she used on her face. "Good news, though. Fay says she can get me a job up in San Antonio. A place to start, at least. Her husband's cousin just bought a salon there."

The last thing I wanted to hear about was San Antonio. "Got herself a new Corvette, huh?"

Heather laughed. "That's the life of a contractor's wife. John's been raking it in lately—folks fixing things up with insurance."

"Hmm," I said, trying to keep the eagerness from my voice. "Sounds like some people aren't leaving."

This was the topic *she* wanted to avoid, and she kissed me gently as the swaying dance continued.

Ever since Heather and I had gotten together, my world had been so solid. No chance encounters with women at bars, no risk of exposure to the town—and, more than that, a kind of settling in my agitated soul, like that scared kid inside me was finally trusting another person with her safety, her happiness, her future. Heather was *home* to me in a way I'd never imagined possible.

But now, for the first time, I felt that stability we'd built here in Parson tugging at the seams. Any minute Heather might decide that I wasn't worth waiting for any longer.

7

The next day, when Joanna left Parson House, I was ready. I hustled down the ladder, started up my C/K, and followed her, trying to keep enough distance that she wouldn't notice. Trucks like mine are common in Parson, and as soon as we hit town, I followed closer.

She wasn't driving aimlessly, every turn she made deliberate, a strange snaking route that took us out to the fringes of Parson, where the houses became smaller and more dilapidated, the kind that looked like a storm had hit them even before the storm. After a while the Fairlane slowed to a stop in front of a squat brown house with its steps caved in. I parked a block away, watching, as for a long minute Joanna lingered in her car.

Is she going to visit someone? I wondered. *Who does she even know in Parson?*

I watched as Joanna climbed out, carrying a small stack of papers. She crossed the unmowed lawn, stepped high to the stairless stoop with the ease of practice, then rapped at the door. It opened almost at once, but she stood so close to the doorway that I couldn't make out who'd answered, tucked inside the shadows of the house. Joanna leaned into the darkness, embraced whomever had greeted her. The door closed behind her.

It would have been smarter to drive back to Parson House, come back later to find out who lived here. Instead I sat there sweating in the hot truck, my gaze moving between that door and the clock in my dash. Ten minutes inched by, then twenty. Finally, at just before thirty, the door opened again and Joanna stepped out. She no longer had the papers, now held a brown paper sack like the one in which she'd brought us sandwiches yesterday.

A man followed her out, walked her across the yard to the Fairlane, taller than Joanna by a considerable height. He kept his back to me so at first I didn't recognize him, but when he stooped to kiss her cheek at the door, I saw the haggard, pallid profile of her brother, Seth Kerrigan.

I took a faster route back to the highway, returned to Parson House before Joanna. When she stepped up to the ladder, asked if I wanted some lunch, I'd calmed some from the initial pain of seeing Seth again. It was little surprise, after all, that Joanna had been visiting her brother, that Seth was still living in Parson. No one I knew had seen him in months, but he wasn't the kind of person who went out much.

What surprised me was how unwell Seth had looked. He had always been something of a retiring, faded boy, but the man I'd just glimpsed looked positively ghostlike. I'd last seen Seth on the morning I found Miss Kate in the garden; I'd kept my distance from him afterward, avoiding those vicious memories. A few weeks later, I'd regretted it, even written a consolation letter to him, but word was he'd moved from the house, and I wasn't sure where else he'd be staying, so the letter never ended up getting sent. More recently, I'd been so distracted by Joanna's return, I hadn't thought to ask where Seth was staying or how he was doing. Now I couldn't help but wonder: how had he been taking care of himself? Why didn't he live in Parson House, like he had when Miss Kate was alive? Why that ramshackle old dump, in the worst neighborhood in town?

And then there were the papers. Joanna knew that soon I'd start working on the inside of the mansion; I'd have access to the study, to things she might not want me to find. But she wasn't transporting all the papers—that would take several boxes—just a stack slim enough to hold in one hand. What, then, was she taking from the mansion, leaving in her brother's care?

I had no specific suspicions; my thoughts were far more primal, superstitious. Watching Joanna with those papers, thinking of her alone in the mansion, I had the same feeling as when I played the huntsman in the woods, leaning around a tree to spy the banished princess muttering incantations, this mysterious girl crouched above her rocks, feathers, and leaves. "What is this girl doing?" I'd think aloud—Joanna pretending not to hear me—and then I'd watch, breathless, for what would happen next, the huntsman and I one and the same in that moment of anticipation, as if she really could set these tokens dancing through the air. All these years later, I was watching Joanna less for signs of vice than for something otherworldly, some unearthly element I knew she contained because I'd witnessed it myself, had even encouraged.

Of course, I didn't actually believe she was performing witchcraft in the mansion, and I certainly didn't ask her about the papers. I stuck to small talk as we ate our sandwiches (tuna fish again), tried not to look too interested as she told me about museums in Chicago—visions of a far-off land, but normal enough to lessen my childhood jealousy and fantasies. I could have asked about Seth without her guessing that I'd followed her, but talking about her brother would start me thinking about Miss Kate, and the last thing I wanted was to get emotional in front of Joanna. I tried to keep at bay the memories of that awful morning with Seth: the two of us sitting on this very porch after I discovered Miss Kate's body, me barely able to catch my breath and Seth patient, stroking my back and humming to me softly, both of us waiting what felt like hours for the police to come. That morning it didn't feel like I'd lost an employer or even a close friend. It felt like I was six again, watching my mother's taillights shrink away into the darkness, never to return.

From the very first, Miss Kate was a mother figure to me. After that Christmas in fifth grade, I could visit her house whenever I liked, show up at the door and always feel welcome, even if Joanna wasn't around. Sometimes, when playing with Joanna in the woods, I'd pretend to get tired or hungry just so we could go back and spend time with her family. I cherished those hours in the house—especially when I learned that Ed, her volatile stepfather, was nearly always away at an oil rig offshore.

I never warmed to Miss Kate's cooking—it had none of the flavor of Cece's—but I loved how the family gathered at the table, the noisy bustle of talk, Seth quoting lines from *The Shadow* from memory, complete with radio sound effects, Joanna chatting with me about her newest book, Cass shooting me sardonic glances whenever someone said something ridiculous, like she and I were wry commentators on this scene. I was always in awe of Cass, the only teenage girl I knew who didn't wear makeup or pin back her hair, her skirts and blouses mussed as if she'd paused for dinner in the middle of some daring adventure. But I was even more drawn to Miss Kate, who always talked to me like an adult, who pulled faces to make me laugh, who greeted me like an old friend when I arrived unannounced at the house, asking me questions, letting me help with her chores. "Welcome, welcome! Louisa's here!" she'd sometimes announce like a circus ringmaster when I arrived, even if there was no one around to hear her.

One such afternoon I found Miss Kate out in the yard with a broken-down table, sweaty and frizzy in a pair of her old overalls. She greeted me with a wave and a motherly pat on the head. "Perfectly good table being thrown out. Someone set it on the roadside out toward town. You know anything about joinery?"

Miss Kate was always like that, looking to save money by fixing things she found. It made me wonder if she'd grown up poor, too.

I shook my head and accepted the screwdriver she set into my hand.

"I don't know much, either," she admitted. "But it can't be too hard. Easier with two sets of hands, I'll bet. Here, I'll hold this leg in place. You see that spot where the screw goes in? Why don't you try . . . hmm, how about that size there? Good, good. Goes in to the right, I think."

These were some of my favorite moments, getting Miss Kate alone so I could capture all her attention. I basked in it like a cat napping in sunlight, the glow of a mother's eyes watching me, the skill of a mother's hands guiding me in a new task. Still, I couldn't let myself entirely off my guard. Miss Kate sometimes asked about my home life, and her attempts to understand me were far more subtle than her daughter's, couched in the language of concern and therefore tougher to dodge.

I was grateful, therefore, that all we talked about that day was the table. After an hour or so, we'd managed to get it sturdy again, so that by the time Joanna heard my voice and came trailing out of the house, we were testing different weights on the tabletop, setting down a vase, a book, a brick, and praying it wouldn't buckle.

Joanna walked up to us, giving Miss Kate a wary, hesitant look. Even as a child, she was often unfriendly to her mother. I was never sure if this was how Joanna always treated her mother, or if she just became unfriendly when I was around. Joanna and I would argue in the woods sometimes, get prickly for no real reason, and when I huffed back to the house alone—Joanna sulking up in some tree— Miss Kate would hear me out, take my side of the argument, shake her head, and say things like: *That Joanna, she's just like her father. She can be a lot sometimes.* Or: *If she ever bothers you, you just tell me, won't you, darling? I'll set her right, okay? She can't go around treating her family and friends like she's head and shoulders high above them, can she?*

As Joanna had approached us that day, Miss Kate had gestured to the table with a flourish. "Just take a look at what Louisa here has made. Aren't you proud of her?"

Joanna's eyes went wide as she took in the table. I bit down on my instinct to correct Miss Kate, to clarify that I'd only helped fix the table; it was too delicious to see Joanna impressed with me. Usually she had the power in our relationship, certain I would follow wherever she led. If Joanna thought I had *made* this table, built it from the ground up, I had no intention of telling her otherwise. For once *she* could be the huntsman stumbling into the clearing. For once she could witness *my* magic.

"I didn't know you could do that," she said, quiet but clearly impressed.

I worried Miss Kate would notice the misunderstanding, correct the record. But she just caught my eye and gave me a tiny wink. "Then I guess you learn something new every day—don't you, Louisa?"

8

The morning after I followed Joanna in my truck, I meant to slip off to work before Heather woke up, but I must have slept in, because I woke to the sound of her on the phone in the kitchen. She was using her sweet voice, so I knew it must be Sarah on the line.

"Is that right?" Heather was saying as I stepped, yawning, from the bedroom. She sat facing the window at the table, her chin propped on her knees; I kissed her bare shoulder as I passed. She gave me a quick, tired smile and went on talking. "And what kind of birdies did you see? Did Aunt Cece help you find them in the book?"

I started a fresh pot of coffee, listening to the call. It sounded like Cece was doing what she did best: taking care of a child, making sure she felt loved while her mother was away. Heather kept her voice happy, chipper, but I could tell she was quickly flagging; by the time I re-filled her mug, her eyes and the tip of her nose were threatening red.

"Give it here," I whispered, holding out my hand.

She nodded, grateful. "Hey, sweetie, Auntie Lou wants to say hi."

"Hey, girl," I said into the handset. "I hear you've been looking at birds."

Sarah's voice had that tinned quality of someone holding the re-ceiver too close. "They have big fat birds here in the city," she ex-plained, eager. "Cece says people feed them in parks."

"That so? Did you get to feed them?"

"We're gonna feed them the day after tomorrow."

"That sure sounds nice," I said. "For the birds, I mean. Getting a home-cooked Cece meal. They'll be big as turkeys by the end of the month."

I expected Sarah to giggle—she'd always had Robby's easy sense of humor—but there was a pause, and when she spoke again, her voice was surprisingly serious, more grown up than I'd heard it before. "You'll be here soon, too, won't you? I want to show you the bird in our yard, but Cece says it might not stay."

"Soon," I agreed.

"Mama says next week."

"Soon," I said again, scared to be too specific, to sound like I was making a promise. "I miss you, sweetheart. Your mom does, too. We both love you so much. And you can call us whenever, you know that."

"Love you," she said, and she must have thought that this was the end of the call, because the line went dead. It stung me a second, the fact that this kid heard *I love you* and thought it meant the same as *goodbye.*

I was still holding the handset when Heather stood and wrapped her arms around me. I was too far from the base to hang it up, so I set it on the table; we listened to the tone, a far-off hum, while we held each other awhile.

"Let's go for a walk," she suggested.

I wanted to say no, make some excuse and get out to Parson House before the heat of the day set in. But Heather seemed fragile right now, and I couldn't bring myself to leave her. Except for a few visits from Peg, she'd been stuck by herself for days on end—my C/K was our only car—and the guilt was getting to me more and more.

"That sounds great," I said, and laced my fingers through hers.

We had started taking walks when we first moved in together, not long after Robby's funeral. I'd agreed to move in because my own place was a shithole, and because Heather needed help with the rent, but living together wasn't easy. Back then we were nothing more than sisters-in-law: all we had in common, more or less, was the pain of losing Robby, which neither of us felt much inclined to speak about, and the love we had for Sarah, who was only a baby back then, and whose smiles and frowns kept reminding us of him, flashing our loss in our faces, so that the way we loved her was mingled with our grief. Not a great environment for a kid to grow up in, particularly not when Heather and I kept bickering with each other, displacing our pain into snide comments about bills and housework.

The walks had started as a peacekeeping measure, something we could do with Sarah—or alone, when Cece could watch her—that didn't require us to talk. Our place was good for walks, too: the house butted up against the woods on one side, and not too far to the other was a stretch of water, so that whichever direction you walked, soon enough you were confronted with nature at rest, the serene lapping of waves or swaying of tree branches reminding you that everything, even death, had a place where it belonged. The walks took us away from the four walls that had become a container for our pain, the roof that cost so much money to keep over our heads. Before long the walks became the place where we opened up to each other, shared stories from our lives—even, eventually, about Robby.

It felt good to talk about him, not just about his life but about his death as well, our anger that our country had killed him with this war. Elsewhere in the country, America was losing its innocence, that rosy glow of confidence in which my generation was raised, the belief that everything we did was right because we were the ones doing it, the heroes of World War II. Young people were standing up against this new war, burning their draft cards and staging sit-ins, but as far as Heather and I were concerned, that could have been happening on a different planet. None of the papers in Parson carried stories about the atrocities being done in Vietnam, and our reasons for being over there were flattened out into diatribes about the Chinese and the Soviets.

In Parson, people liked things to be simple: your country called, you answered. And the death of a soldier was sacrosanct, the most honorable death of them all. You weren't allowed to question the cause, to wish it hadn't happened. Let alone rage against the government that put the soldier there in the first place. After Robby's death, the patriotism here struck me as childish, naive, a lie the town needed to justify the violence being done to its young men.

So we were isolated, Heather and me, not only by our sadness but by our anger. "None of the girls at the salon understand," Heather told me on one of our early walks. "They treat me like it was some sort of accident, like no one could have seen it coming. They're my friends, but I don't understand them, either. Or anyone else in this whole place." When she said this, I understood that *anyone else* meant *anyone else but you*. I remember taking her hand then, grateful she'd said it out loud so that I didn't have to.

During that time our relationship changed. Our routines slotted together, me taking care of Sarah when Heather was at the salon, Heather cooking us dinner in the evening before I headed out to Buck's. Nights I had off, we'd watch television together as a family, *Bewitched* and *Star Trek* and *Petticoat Junction*, until it was time to put Sarah to bed. Every morning I had coffee ready for her, fresh and hot, just as her alarm clock started clanging in her bedroom. Eventually it was my bedroom, too, and I no longer bunked out on the sofa.

It was a first for Heather, being with another woman. I could tell she felt guilty, worried that being with me meant betraying Robby's memory, more than if she'd taken up with another man. I should have focused on helping her work through this, but I had a mountain of my own to climb: sex wasn't strictly new to me, but I'd never lived with a girlfriend before, never even *had* a girlfriend, someone I loved who wanted to build a life with me—someone who made me feel this way, exhilarated but also scared, aware that I had something to lose. Both of us were jumpy, gun-shy, at first—not to mention nervous that the town might notice the change between us, that they'd realize we weren't living together just for Sarah's sake anymore. We'd heard horror stories about men who took up together—an old cowboy couple whose barn had been burned; two high school teachers run out of town overnight—and we feared the punishment that certain factions in Parson might devise for women like us.

Only gradually did we grasp that we were safe here. Men falling in love, living together, sounded an alarm in towns like Parson; it demanded retribution, a forceful defense of the social order. Female affection, however, was nearly invisible. Now that Heather and I were a couple, I started to see echoes of us everywhere: two old biddies who'd run an antique shop on Main Street and had lived together in an old Victorian for forty years; the bait shop woman with the denim shirts whose younger roommate looked like something from a Haight-Ashbury photo, seen together every Friday night at Riley's steak house.

"No," Heather said when I pointed them out to her one Friday, the two women laughing and sipping their wine in a corner of the wood-paneled dining room. "No way."

"Why no way?" I asked. "Just look at them. They'd be playing footsies under the table if they could."

Heather laughed and then quickly brushed my ankle with her own.

Soon we understood that we were better off than these women, even more invisible and protected. When people here looked at us, they saw only family. The memory of Robby was more than enough to explain our living arrangement.

After that we didn't get bold, exactly—even the most obtuse town would know what cuddling at the movies meant, and once Sarah was old enough to babble and walk, we had to be careful about what we got up to in front of her, too, at least until she was big enough to understand the situation—but our walks were solitary, took us far from any roads, so we started to walk hand in hand, stopping at times to kiss in the remote, peaceful inlets along the beach, places where, if I happened to stroke Heather's face, well, there was no one around to see.

Today Heather led the way on our walk. At first I worried she'd head for the woods—I'd been thinking so much of Joanna lately, our whole history together, that the woods had taken on an almost religious significance for me—but to my relief she led us to the beach, a grassy stretch that was more endearing than beautiful in its scraggliness.

We didn't talk until we got there, at which point Heather leaned in close to me, even though there was a road nearby and anyone might have driven past. Since the storm, I sometimes forgot there were people in Parson left to catch us, that maybe now we were less safe than before, since the evacuations had shrunk Parson down to the size of a nosy neighborhood. It felt good to shove this out of my head for a minute and just enjoy the feel of Heather's body against me. Together we looked out at the water, the way the waves seemed to break away from our little beach, splitting like a chevron to the left and right as though trying not to disturb us.

Heather started the conversation as she often did: by letting me in on the one already going in her head. "Cece says she's got the second bedroom made up for us."

"She doesn't mind us sharing?"

Heather smiled. It was a running joke between us: the fact that Cece more than likely understood and supported our relationship—there was only so far small-town denial could get you, and it didn't extend to your own family—but, for the confessional's sake, pretended we were just friends. I never particularly minded that attitude. It was better than the alternatives: lectures on hell, being disowned.

"I'm going to miss Parson, too. I hope you know that," Heather said. "It's always been my home. Just because I want to move doesn't mean I don't love it."

She sounded like she was trying to say something more, something beyond this. I didn't get it, not quite, but I squeezed her hand reassuringly anyway.

"When we have a stable place to live," she went on, "a place we can rely on—I just think, you know, things could be different with us, Lou. Better. And I need that for Sarah: a stable place. It's different when you're a parent, you know. You can't just make decisions for yourself anymore."

I shouldn't have bristled at these words—I was, after all, part of the reason that Heather hadn't lived with her daughter for months—but they rankled me anyway.

"And I'm not a parent to Sarah, am I?" I said before I could stop myself. "I guess half my wages going to her and the other half to you, that isn't enough? I should scare up another half somewhere to split between the two of you?"

Heather tensed under my arm. Neither of us was the placid type, and I could feel the fighting words rise in her, feel her take a breath and try to push them aside. "You've been a huge help," she said, controlling her tone. "You know we wouldn't have made it without you."

I took a breath as well, squeezed her shoulder in apology. This only seemed to make her stiffer. I should have kissed her then, stroked her hair, but my mind was all wrapped up in Parson House, the internal egg timer that had started in me when I first got up and realized I couldn't slip away to my work.

"We can keep making it, you know," I said. "Right here in Parson."

"Oh, come on, Lou . . ."

"No, I mean it," I said, pushing through. "Listen, you're ready to call time of death, but what about Peg? She's staying, isn't she? She's not talking about going anywhere."

Heather hesitated, then relented with a nod. "Sure, she's staying, but—"

"But nothing. Why make Sarah start over someplace entirely new? Why make *us*, for that matter? I'm sure Aunt Cece would come back if everything was how it used to be."

"Aunt Cece *likes* San Antonio. So does Sarah." Heather moved out from under my arm and took both my hands in hers. A real fight was brewing now—I'd already agreed to leave Parson, and here I was rehashing arguments from months ago—but Heather was trying her best to reach me, to stop the fight. "So will we."

"I could find more extra work, not just Buck's," I said. "I'll bet Peg would help connect me with some if I asked."

Heather shook her head. "Just because Peg has plans, property, whatever else is keeping her here . . . we're in a different world than that. You think I want to keep being her charity case? That's what we'd be if we stayed."

"It's no harm to ask for help. That's what community is." I was getting through to her, I could tell. Her eyes were wide and listening. This was my home, and so was she, and I needed her here. If I could just drive it that next step home . . . "And you just said this is your home. Sarah's home. You shouldn't leave your home just because things get rough."

"And if there was a *community* here at all, I'd agree with you," Heather said. "But look around, Lou. It's a ghost town. Pretty soon they'll be selling tickets to tourists to gawp at the empty streets, hear fireside stories about the haunted mansion. Or they'll just knock it all to the ground."

"You don't understand," I cut in, desperate. "Joanna's selling Parson House. She's got the sale lined up, it just needs a little more fixing up, is all. If there's hope for that place—"

Heather's face had gone sharp and still; her hands fell away from mine. "So you have," she said. "You have been going out there."

I didn't respond.

"I knew it," she said.

And with that, Heather turned around and walked off down the beach, toward where the waves were breaking out to the south.

9

I considered following, but I was so worked up, I'd only go on arguing. Now that the cat was out of the bag, I might as well head to Parson House and get some work done.

It was quiet at the mansion when I got there. I'd finished painting the day before and was fixing up the porch, swapping out cracked floor slats, replacing rotted support posts. This was my last task before I started on the interior of the house, which I both dreaded and desired. Working inside felt like a new intimacy, both with Joanna and with my own memories.

I'd managed to lose myself in the work, stop dwelling on the fight, when, in the midafternoon, I heard a car pulling up the front drive. Joanna was at home—we'd had lunch a few hours ago—so I had no clue who might be stopping by. When I came out from under the porch, I found myself face-to-face with Danny.

"What are you doing here?" I asked, happy to see him. I wiped a thick glaze of sweat from my forehead.

"Wanted to see the fruits of your labor," he said. "Also maybe get my ladder back if you're done with it. Got someone else wants to borrow it, and *they're* willing to pay." He smiled.

"Right around here," I told him, leading him toward the side of the house.

He loped after me, hands in his pockets, giving the house a long look as he rounded it. "You're doing a great job," he said. "I drove out here once, after the storm. Looks totally transformed now. Never would have thought one person, in just a few days . . ."

"Well." I waved the compliment off. "The problem was mostly those vines—they were choking the damn thing out. Take 'em down, touch up the paint, it's gonna look a hell of a lot better pretty fast." We reached the ladder and started to break it down together; it was small enough to fit in the back of Danny's truck.

"You almost done, yeah?" he said. "Looks like you must be."

Danny was never good at being subtle; I could tell he had more on his mind. "Maybe. Yeah," I answered. If he glanced through one of the windows, he'd know what a lie that was.

We finished folding the ladder without talking more, walked it back to his truck. I expected Danny to say his goodbyes then, or suggest we chat in the shade, but he just stood there staring up at the house, eyes shaded with one hand.

"Joanna inside?" he asked after a moment.

"Probably. She usually is," I said tersely.

Danny knew me too well: something about my tone was making him uncomfortable. I wondered if he'd talked with Joanna since she'd gotten back. Something told me he hadn't.

"You see much of her?" he asked.

I shrugged. "Now and then, in passing."

This wasn't true, either. Our conversations at lunch weren't exactly friendly, but they were growing longer every day, and today was the longest yet, Joanna telling me about the legal steps for her and Seth to inherit the house through probate. Miss Kate hadn't filed a will, which meant that her assets belonged to her husband, Ed Darnell; but no one had heard from Ed in over five years—not even a private investigator could figure out where he'd gone—so Joanna's lawyer had filed a presumption of death, which would allow Miss Kate's children to inherit Parson House. It was all plenty interesting—and way above my head—but at least Joanna had shared this much with me. It was enough to get me wondering: Was this what she was seeking in the papers? Some clue where Ed had gone?

After lunch, Joanna and I had walked around the house to survey the work I'd done. She didn't know what to look for, so when I'd pointed out the improvements, she'd just hummed and said, "That's wonderful, simply wonderful." I'd never had an easier boss to please: even Miss Kate had often given feedback, pointed out areas that needed touch-ups. When we finished, Joanna put a hand on my back and said, "I can't thank you enough, Louisa." I'd tried to ignore the feeling, but a gentle wave of arousal had passed through my body.

Danny wasn't done asking me questions. "And do you still feel like you did last time we talked?" he said. When I hesitated, he leaned in closer, added in a whisper, "You seemed pretty pissed at her before."

I bit back my knee-jerk response—*Of course, why would I feel any different?*—and stared him down. Danny was no good under pressure, and he hated silence. Over the years I'd gotten more secrets from waiting him out than questions. True to form, he started that hooked-bait wriggle.

"It's just that I'm worried about you," he said. "I know you don't want to leave Parson—what, you think I want you to, either? Thirty years old and I've got to make new friends?" It was an attempt at a joke, but neither of us laughed. He waved a hand. "Hell, part of me thinks the way you do, that people have been too quick to leave this place. It's why I've got no plans to go anywhere. But you and I are in different situations. My business is here, my family is here. And like it or not, *your* family is moving on, and you've got to either move on with them or they'll leave you behind."

"You've been talking to Heather." I crossed my arms high and tight.

"No," he said. Then, more honestly, "This isn't about Heather. She's a grown woman, she can take care of herself. This is about you."

I laughed, bitter and sad. "You my mother now, hmm? You always did have a maternal side to you."

Danny straightened up, annoyed. "You're working yourself down, girl. You looked at yourself lately? You're sunburned and eye-bagged, and you look like you're barely sleeping."

"This is how I worked with Miss Kate," I said. "It's not any different."

"Like hell it isn't. Miss Kate took care of you. Sent you home if you looked too tired. Brought you in for lemonade and tea. You're not a child anymore, but you still need people who care about you. I'm not your mother, no, but you sure could use one right about now."

I was staring down at the driveway. "I've never had a mother."

"Bullshit," he said, and for the first time in a long time, he sounded actually mad at me. "Your aunt Cece—"

"Yeah, sure," I cut in, "and look how *that* turned out. It killed my fucking brother."

I'd never said the words out loud before, that part of me blamed Cece for us going to Woodman, for Robby losing his chance at a scholarship and shipping to Vietnam when his number came up. It gave me a sick rush of pleasure, and then I added, twisting the knife, "No thanks to you, either, come to think of it."

The look of shock and pain on Danny's face gave me another surge of satisfaction. It wasn't until he had turned away and stormed off toward his truck that I realized how harsh I'd been, how sloppy and careless. Danny had been my best friend nearly all my life: it was cruel, monstrous, of me to link him to Robby's death even if Danny had been a link in that chain. I wished I could take the words back but, stunned myself, I just stood there.

Danny pulled open the door of his truck, and I thought he was just being dramatic—he'd had a flair for it, ever since we were kids—but to my surprise, he really did climb in, start up the engine, and take off fast down the drive.

I left work early that day, too upset to focus. I had a couple hours until my shift at Buck's, and I figured now was as good a time as any to have it out with Heather. When I pulled up in the driveway, she was outside taking clothes down from the line.

She didn't greet me when I got out of the truck, just hoisted the basket and turned to head inside. I went after her into the house. "Danny came to see me," I said.

She dropped the basket on the couch, started folding a shirt without looking at me. "So I can't talk to people about you, is that it? I don't have the right?"

"You don't even like Danny," I said, which was true. Ever since high school, not that I knew why.

Heather scowled. "Like I wanted to tell Danny! But it's not like you would listen if Midge or Fay called you. Who else was there?"

Midge Maddox and Fay Browne were Heather's old friends from high school. Back then the three had been top of the heap, the girls watched by all the others for cues. But Heather's star had fallen fast when she kept seeing Robby after he left Granbury. Now she was a war widow, and Fay and Midge were both married to contractors who kept them up in style, whose contracting firms got government grants and actually profited from the storm. The girls were still warm to Heather, but Heather would gripe that she felt like their charity case. One time Midge had offered Heather some nannying work, and Heather hadn't spoken to her for a month.

"Great," I said, throwing up my hands. "So half of Parson knows you've been bitching about me? Bet they can't wait to get rid of me, huh?"

"No one thinks that way. You know that."

"What else are you telling everyone? How I'm keeping you here, keeping you from your daughter? Because that just isn't true. You could go be with her if you wanted. I've never once said you couldn't. Never once."

I hated how calm I sounded. Angry, sure, but under control, which was more than I could say for Heather. She started shouting at me now, which hadn't happened in over a year; it hurt to hear her voice this strained.

"I'm here in Parson for *you*. Don't you get that? You think I don't want to be with Sarah? That I don't miss her every minute? I've had my bags packed for days, Lou—days! But I don't want to leave you to dry up and die here. If I go alone, I'm scared you'll just stay in Parson forever. Even if you're the last one left."

I wanted to tell her this wasn't true, but there was no point. Arguing with Heather was like lying to a mirror: pretty easy to tell true from false.

"My business is my business," I muttered, which was a bridge too far for Heather. She threw down the shirt she'd been folding and refolding, then grabbed up her purse by the door and lit out.

For a while I sat in a kitchen chair, sipping a flat Lone Star I hadn't finished last night. It tasted like punishment. The time for my shift at Buck's approached, and the moon came out like a searchlight looking for me, but I didn't move a muscle. *If I take off now, I could still get there on time*, my mind piped up, even though I wasn't looking at the kitchen clock. *If I take off now, I'll only be five minutes late. Ten minutes late. Fifteen.*

Eventually I picked myself up from the chair. Called Buck to tell him I quit, that I'd be leaving town soon. He started to yell at me for not giving notice, but his heart wasn't in it. I wasn't supposed to know yet, but he told me he'd also been planning to leave, had some family in Galveston he was joining come spring. If I stuck around, I realized, I could buy the bar off him, cheap. Change the name to *Lou's*, stay in Parson forever, pulling pints for shrimpers and dockworkers, wiping up their messes when they left. I ended the call before I felt tempted.

Danny was right. I *was* happy with Heather, happier than I'd ever been. It was easy to forget in this painful in-between space, but being with Heather and Sarah and Cece . . . I might never find a better life for myself. And Heather was right. I had an attachment to Parson that beat out reason, beat out self-protection. If left on my own, I'd stay here until I was no different than those rotted piles of wood that used to be houses. It was as if the six-year-old inside me still held the wheel of my life, didn't want to risk leaving Parson in case my mother finally came back, here to collect me after she'd dropped me off over two decades ago.

10

I drove to a few of Heather's haunts, houses of friends, a park she liked, before I finally went out to Peg's to check if she was there.

Peg had been a major fixture in our lives ever since the storm. Heather and I had tried to leave Parson before Hurricane Celia hit, but Buck had split town as soon as the hurricane entered the gulf, and he'd called me as I was packing the C/K, told me I needed to storm-safe the bar or else I'd lose my job. I assumed he'd done *some* of the work before skipping out, but when I got out to Buck's, I saw he hadn't done a damn thing, hadn't even boarded up the windows. If I'd known how bad the storm would be, I would have gone right back home, driven Heather to San Antonio. But I didn't know. Good jobs were tough to find even back then, and Buck's was busy before the hurricane; with my tips, I was making real money. I wouldn't be hard to replace, and I knew I'd better do as Buck said.

I worked as fast as I could, but it was too late. The storm came while I was still in the bar, and I kept busy to distract myself, packing bottles away into padded crates, tucking them into the storeroom, even as the wind ripped off branches and swung them like battering rams against the window planks, even as roof shingles peeled off with a great sound of tearing paper.

Only when the water came in did I stop working. I weathered the storm on top of the bar while that sewagey water rose toward me, swirling with flotsam and jetsam; while night fell and the wind roared like a steam train overhead. When one of the window planks ripped off, the wind made short work of the pane, and soon there were fractals of glass glinting dangerously in the water, washing along the bar like deadly chips of ice. Snakes and torn electrical cables swam along the ever-rising surface. After a time, a mangy white dog came paddling through the broken window for shelter, but the jagged glass cut the animal and then the air was full of its pained yelps, the foul-smelling water tinted pink with its blood. I called out to the dog, but it wouldn't come near me, and then it went quiet and I couldn't see it anymore in the darkness.

The storm abated just before dawn. Daylight came slowly into the bar, trickling through the broken window. I wished it hadn't. Suddenly, I could see too much: like how the spiders had scurried onto the bar with me, how one had started to spin a web between my shoes.

That was when someone outside wrested the front door open, pushing it against the churning water until it was wide enough for the prow of a rowboat. "If there's anyone stuck in there, you oughta swim on out, fast as you can!" a woman's voice yelled. "I've got you!"

I didn't know it then, but just before the storm, Heather had gone with a band of neighbors to the high school, where a hundred or so people had crouched all night beneath the cafeteria tables. When morning came, a take-charge woman had offered to go out looking for friends and loved ones in her boat. Heather tearfully begged Peg to come find me at Buck's.

Miss Kate was already dead by then, a couple months in the ground, but on first glance, I could've sworn it was her there in the boat to save me. In retrospect this was strange, because the two looked nothing alike: Miss Kate squat and round with frizzy brown hair, Peg tall and slender, hair straight and silver-white. Maybe it was the exhaustion or how shaken up I was; maybe I'd drunk a gulp of seawater. Maybe it was because, before that moment, I'd known Peg only as Miss Kate's friend, thought of them in the same corner of my mind. But on the first glimpse I got of Peg, leaning over the edge of the boat and extending a hand to pull me in, made me think I was reaching toward Miss Kate. Only after I'd settled in the boat, shivering, did I look at her and realize my mistake.

So Peg came into our lives as a hero. I was her first stop of the morning, and when I got my wits back, I spent the day helping her fish people out of other buildings. I threw myself into the work—it took my mind off what had happened—prizing open doors, taking the crowbar to window planks, ferrying people up to the dry part of town.

And she'd been helping us ever since—us and just about every other woman left in Parson. I'd never met someone so insistent about helping people in need, and she'd never asked Heather and me for anything in return. Before then I'd never thought about Peg much, just seen her here and there around Parson House with Miss Kate. Only after the storm did I realize that I'd first met Peg in my childhood, back when she didn't wear men's clothing, when her hair wasn't silver.

Peg didn't bring it up, either. Probably because she was a much different person back then.

She went by Margaret in those days, a friend of Miss Kate's who paid visits to her small, ramshackle house. "Girls, won't you say hello to Miss Margaret?" Miss Kate would call to Joanna and me as we ducked into the kitchen for some potato chips. "Hello, Miss Margaret," I'd say obediently, and sometimes Joanna would say it, too; sometimes she'd only nod.

It wasn't long after my Christmas with Joanna when I first started seeing Margaret there. She didn't stop by much that winter, and I'd barely glance at her, the way children fail to notice adults just passing through their lives. But by next fall she was over at Miss Kate's house a few times a week, and I made more observations about her, noticed her long skirts, her soft-looking hair, the gentle roundness of her face. She kept her stiff cotton blouses buttoned all the way to the neck, far different than the button-down men's shirts she'd wear as Peg years later.

Around this time, the bubbly atmosphere had started to cool at Miss Kate's house: a little less laughter, a little less talk around the dinner table. I thought it just meant that Ed would be home soon—the house always tensed before his visits—but it felt like a cold war was brewing, a war beneath the surface, one I couldn't quite understand. It was subtle, a shift in the air, a new mood of resistance, Joanna and her siblings becoming more petulant, more needlessly defiant of their mother. A few years later, when *Rebel Without a Cause* came out, I was reminded of them at dinner: an angst, a malaise, a sullen challenge in their slumped postures and their tone with Miss Kate, the children eating their meals quickly, as if they couldn't get away fast enough.

Like one night, when Margaret was over for dinner and Cass never came to the table. "Joanna," Miss Kate said, "would you mind fetching your sister?"

"She's not here," Joanna said.

"Have you checked?"

Joanna stared down at her plate. She cut a boiled carrot with the edge of her fork, shrugged.

In a gentle voice, Miss Kate said, "Would you mind going and checking, please?"

It was such a little thing to do—walking down the hall to the bedroom—that I couldn't understand my friend's mulish behavior. Instead of responding, Joanna started to eat her vegetables faster.

"I'm happy to go check, Miss Kate," I offered.

Miss Kate gave me a grateful smile and said that would be lovely. When I reported back that the bedroom was empty, Margaret put down her fork and said, "Perhaps she has an engagement at school? Did she mention anything to you, Seth?"

But Seth, like his younger sister, stayed quiet, hyper-focused on his eating. I couldn't believe my eyes. Cece would have had Robby and me saying Hail Marys if we'd been this churlish with her.

Miss Kate changed the subject, ignoring her the silence of her children. After Joanna and Seth had rapidly cleaned their plates, Miss Kate told them they were dismissed if they liked. They both shot up at once and left, abandoning me with the adults.

That was the last I saw of Joanna that night. After I finished eating, Miss Kate offered to drive me home. "I'm taking Margaret, anyway," she said. I tried to turn down the ride—I didn't want her to know where I lived—but she insisted it was too dark for me to walk alone through the woods, even though I'd done it countless times. So I sat behind the women in the backseat of the station wagon, and Miss Kate started driving us to the outskirts of town. Eventually we reached a small farmhouse and Margaret stepped out into the dusty yard, started walking up the path toward the whitewashed porch, where a much older man sat reading in a rocking chair. Miss Kate told me to climb around front.

"I'm sorry for how my children treated you tonight," she said when she'd started driving. Her tires thudded over the ruts in the old dirt road. "It was so rude of them to ignore you."

I felt a sudden pang of worry. Had Joanna's silence been about *me*? Had I done something to upset her? I thought back through the day, trying to see where I might have made Joanna mad.

"If I could ask you a favor, Louisa," Miss Kate went on. "Please don't tell your parents about that dinner tonight. I'd hate them to think I'd raised uncivilized children. They're not bad, you know—they just need a firmer hand. I'm trying to give them one, but it's hard for a mother alone."

My attention snagged on the word *parents*. Once we got into my general neighborhood, I told her to pull off at a house that looked empty—no cars in front, no light inside. She let me out and I walked up to the door, fiddling with the knob while I listened for Miss Kate to drive away.

Mercifully, she did. Even after her station wagon was gone, I didn't chance the street: I set off running through backyards, keeping to the shadows for the three blocks to my house.

For a while it was a puzzle to me, the reason for all the tension at Miss Kate's house. Then over the school lunch hour one day, not long before winter break, I asked Joanna if Robby and I would be invited for Christmas again. I knew I'd upset Cece last year, and I was tangling with my guilt over letting her down again, but Joanna was everything to me in those days, and my answer would still be yes.

Joanna's mouth flattened, and she shook her head. She stared down at her desk, traced a finger along the wooden grain. "We don't celebrate Christmas anymore," she said.

I couldn't make sense of that, asked her what she meant.

"It's this new church my mother is going to," she said, words careful, like she'd rehearsed them. "They don't allow their members to celebrate Christmas."

"*What?*" I said with a giggle. To me, church *was* Christmas. But

Joanna wasn't laughing, and I realized she might be serious. *No Christmas?* I thought. Other than my mother leaving, it seemed like the saddest thing imaginable.

"But that's crazy," I said. "A church with no Christmas?"

"That's what they believe. That Christmas is bad."

"Well . . ." I began, thinking that over. "At least your birthday isn't far off."

"No birthdays, either. Most holidays, really. Nearly all of them."

"What the hell kind of church *is* this?" I asked. I was indignant, but I kept my voice low.

"I don't know," Joanna murmured. "But Mom's a Jehovah's Witness now. We all are, I guess. So no Christmas."

That year Robby and I celebrated the holiday with Aunt Cece. Whenever I saw Joanna over break, she didn't mention how she'd spent Christmas Day, and I sensed I shouldn't ask.

After that I mostly forgot about Miss Kate's religion, which never came up on my visits to her house. It was not until several months later that I was reminded about it one night while studying for a math test in my bedroom. A knock came at the front door, and I listened as Cece answered and greeted the visitors, who sounded like two women. Then, with sudden clarity, Miss Kate's voice rang out. "Robby? Is that you?"

My ears perked up; I set aside my math book.

"Oh, hello, Miss Kate," Robby said, polite but startled. Then, presumably to Cece, he added, "This is Seth's mother."

This was several months before Joanna would meet Cece, before she learned about our living situation. Back then only Cece's friends and Danny knew.

"Seth's mother," Cece said. "Joanna's as well, then."

"That's right. And this is my friend Margaret. Would you mind letting us inside?"

"Of course, of course. Please do come in. You know, your children have been such friends to Robert and Louisa."

"Thank you," Miss Kate replied. "As have yours."

Cece, I knew, could hear the pointed question in that statement. After a moment's hesitation, she said stiffly, "Oh, these aren't my children. I'm only taking care of them while their mother's away."

I relaxed and focused on my homework again, though the faint buzz of female voices continued from the other room. Before long, Cece saw the women out and wished them a good night; I heard the click as she closed the door behind them.

"What was that about?" I asked, walking out into the kitchen.

Robby had his back to me, washing dishes at the sink. Cece was dropping some papers into the garbage bin. She glanced up at me with a drained, exhausted expression, a look I hadn't seen on her face in years, back when Robby and I were little and would misbehave in public. "It's nothing," she said in a clipped voice. "Nothing at all." She shut the bin lid.

I woke up early the next morning, curious to see what Cece had thrown out. On top of some potato rinds sat two flimsy pamphlets, the top one with the title "Fear of the Sovereign Jehovah." I imagined they must be from Miss Kate's church, because when I fished out the pamphlets, I saw they each had articles that cited Bible verses, line drawings of holy people rising from their graves. Miss Kate and Margaret must have been going door-to-door, inviting people to their church, and just happened across our house. I couldn't help but indulge a fantasy: attending the church every Sunday with Cece and Robby, sitting near Miss Kate and her children, Joanna and me exchanging looks and giggles throughout the entire service, speaking to each other in our silent language. Of course, it wasn't possible; I knew good Catholic Cece would never set foot in a different church, and anyway we couldn't risk being seen as a family, opening ourselves up to a white community that might start asking questions. I lost interest in the pamphlets after a few paragraphs, dropped them back in the trash.

These days I wasn't even sure if Peg still went to that church. Sure, she talked about Jesus and prayer and blessings and that sort of thing, but this was Texas, after all. Miss Kate, as far as I knew, had left the Witnesses years ago, stopped attending long before she died. But when I pulled up at Peg's place tonight and saw a half-dozen cars in her driveway, my first thought was that she was holding some kind of church meeting.

Peg must have been expecting me, because she opened the front door as I walked up the cobblestone path, gestured for us to go and talk in my truck. Every window was glowing in her house, a gabled two-story Tudor, nestled in what once was the rich part of town, now mostly rubble. She'd bought it after the hurricane, the only house in the neighborhood that emerged from the storm unscathed. The property values had fallen, the owners desperate to get out of Parson.

"Heather's here, all right," she told me when we sat down in the truck. "Pretty upset, I'd say."

I didn't know what Peg had deduced about me and Heather, but she'd always treated us like a family unit. Maybe she thought we were just sisters-in-law, held together by the memory of Robby. Maybe, like Cece, she was happy to just look the other way.

"She'll like what I've got to tell her," I said.

Peg studied me a second, then laid a hand on my arm and squeezed gently. "Haven't seen you in a few days. You taking care of yourself, baby?"

"Trying to."

"You should drop by sometime, tell me how you're doing. You're never around when I come over. I want to know my girl's okay."

Peg never had any children. But she had a motherly touch, made you feel safe and calm, like you could fall asleep beside her and she'd watch over you all the while.

"I'll try to find the time," I said. Then added, as warmly as I could, "Sometime soon."

Peg patted my cheek, turned away toward the door. "I'll see if she wants to talk. Can't promise anything."

I watched the house as she disappeared inside. The lace curtain over the bay window blurred my view of the living room, but I could see shapes, dark silhouettes, of people sitting on the other side. I couldn't count exactly how many there were—could have been five, could have been twelve. When Peg stepped in front of the window, the outline of her Stetson was sharp and clear. After a time, several silhouettes stood and moved about the room, and then the front door swung open and Heather was striding across the yard toward me, arms crossed.

She hopped up into the passenger seat and slammed the door shut.

Didn't look my way. Her steady stare through the windshield told me this one was on me; I'd have to start the work of making up.

"I quit Buck's," I said, not wasting time. "Told him I'm going to San Anton."

That got her attention, made her uncross her arms and look at me. Her eyes were tired, puffy in the moonlight; she'd been crying not that long ago. I took one of her hands.

"And Joanna?" she asked after a moment. "You tell her, too?"

This was the tricky part. "I need to finish up the work at Parson House," I said, and gripped her hand so she wouldn't pull it back. "Five, six days, no more than a week. Promise."

I wasn't sure if this was possible, but I knew I needed to say it. Every particle of me hoped I wasn't lying to her.

She let me hold her hand, but she wasn't looking at me anymore. Usually Heather spoke her thoughts right away, but I could tell there were volumes she wasn't saying now.

"You lied to me," she said finally.

"I know. I'm so sorry, hon. I really, really am."

"You don't know how that feels. I never do that to you."

She was right. Heather, Cece, Danny, Sarah—I could count on the honesty of the people in my life, but they couldn't count on mine. The realization hit me with a pang of guilt, guilt I could soothe only by telling myself: *Just a little longer and you can be exactly who they want you to be. Just a little longer and you can make everything right.*

"And why?" she went on. "Why even bother with this house?"

I'd been ready for that one. "For Miss Kate."

Heather shut her eyes. "She's dead, Lou. I'm sorry, but she's gone. You can't bring her back by fixing up some old mansion."

"That house was her dream. Her vision. It meant everything to her."

"But she never even told you why she bought it. It could've been, I don't know, just an investment property or something."

"It was more than that. You know it was."

Heather released a slow sigh. "All right. No more than a week."

I caressed her knuckle. "No more than a week."

She let me drive her home. When we got back, she phoned up Aunt Cece, told her to go ahead and expect us.

"It's about time!" Cece's voice was so excited I could hear it across the kitchen table. "Lou finally give in, did she?"

I was glad to hear Cece so happy, but I flinched at the blame in her words.

"Yeah, just about. She's right here," Heather said, smiling tautly at me, and I couldn't help but wonder what she'd be saying if I weren't in hearing range. It was something I tried not to think about, their long calls on the phone bill, how much time they spent speculating about me.

"You wanna tell Sarah yourself?" Cece asked. "I just put her to bed."

A soft smile lit up Heather's face, so stressed for hours. "Only if she's not asleep already."

While Heather talked to Sarah, I stepped out onto the porch and smoked a cigarette. I thought about how Sarah would feel when her mother walked through Cece's door, back into her life to stay. It was a feeling I'd imagined a thousand times in childhood, the happy ending to the fairy tale that swirled in my head late at night, just before I fell asleep. I was determined that Sarah wouldn't need to imagine the feeling much longer. For her, it would be real. I would make it real.

As I smoked, I noticed some slips of paper on the ground near the front steps. At first they looked like some kind of catalog, but when I stooped to pick it up, I saw it was something else entirely.

The design of the pamphlets had changed since the '50s, when Aunt Cece had thrown away the one Miss Kate and Peg gave her. These days the headline filled most of the cover: "DOES THE BIBLE REALLY TEACH IT?" in big splashy letters. This must have been left for us on the porch, blown to the ground by the wind.

The pages had a dry, porous, paper-bag consistency, and something about their limpness made my skin crawl, like holding a snake. I was walking the pamphlet to the trash barrel, just like Cece had with hers, when I saw that a notecard was marking a middle page. I opened to the page, and a shiver went through me.

The title was "YOUR SINS ARE FORGIVEN: An Article for Parents to Read to Their Children." In chilling singsong text, it told a story of Jesus healing a paralyzed man, proclaiming his sins were forgiven. Then it asked, "What do we learn from this miracle? We learn that Jesus had the power to forgive sins and to make sick persons well. But we also learn something else. We learn that people get sick because of sin."

I couldn't be sure why it had been left here, whether it was innocuous and random or some sort of threat pointed at me. I remembered the Bible next to Miss Kate's bed, the passage she'd circled and underlined. Wasn't it something about scarlet sin becoming white as snow?

Even more chilling than the article, I now saw: the notecard in the pamphlet wasn't blank. In precise handwriting, someone had written an address near the western outskirts of town. And under this: *Sunday mornings, 8:00 a.m. We gather at the Kingdom Hall. Hope to see you there, Louisa.*

Kingdom Hall: I guessed that was what Jehovah's Witnesses called a church. Now that I thought about it, Joanna might have mentioned that term to me when we were kids. Had Peg or one of her friends left this for me? Maybe she was still with the Witnesses after all. I'd have to ask her later. I folded the pamphlet and stuck it in my back pocket.

After the phone call Heather was feeling good. She wrapped her arms around me, kissed me deep. Soon I'd forgotten all about the pamphlet, and I took her to the bedroom and we made love with more energy than we had since before the storm. It wasn't easy to get me shaking, but Heather put her whole self into it, dived down and into me, and soon I felt like I was seeing right through the ceiling, out into the stars beyond. When I finally came down, we held each other for what must have been an hour, sharing the same pillow, our sweat drying under the fan. It was early yet—if I'd been at Buck's, I'd only be halfway through my shift—but soon enough our stillness dragged us gently into sleep.

11

The next morning I finished the porch and started on the inside of the mansion, taking stock of what needed fixing, the materials required. I ought to have felt better now that I wasn't hiding the work from Heather, but something about the house itself felt more menacing once I was inside it. It was one thing to walk through Parson House as I had earlier this week, but to linger here, to absorb its silence, made my body thrum with anxiety, every sense on edge. For the time being, I focused on the foyer and the front room, liking the feel of an exit right behind me. I measured the broken windows, swept out all the dirt and muck, chased away the raccoons and mopped their shit. Then I found where the floorboards had warped the most, rippled up in tiny hillocks, and I weighed them down with blocks of cement in the hope that they would flatten.

All the while I listened hard for Joanna, straining to hear the noises of her daily routine. If today was like the other days, she would leave for Seth's and then drive back, bringing sandwiches for our lunch together on the newly restored porch. I fantasized about the ways she'd praise me, self-indulgent lines like *It's marvelous, Louisa* or *You're a life-saver, I don't know what I'd do without you.* Maybe she wouldn't go that far, sure, but she might touch my knee or shoulder, slightly more intimate than her hand on my back yesterday, and I tried to ignore this thought as I felt an anticipatory warmth. *Don't forget what this woman did to you*, I reminded myself, attempting to quell the fantasy. *Don't forget what she did to Robby.* But still I listened for her all morning.

Every step I took in the foyer gave off a series of echoing creaks, announcing my movements with the clarity of a scream. But I never heard Joanna move upstairs, not once, not even a squeak from the antique chair in the study. Was she keeping completely still, or had she found some silent means of coming and going, some fleet-footed step that allowed her to elude every sound? I envisioned her floating from the house, not bothering with the garden door but drifting out of the balcony in her mother's room, swooping down to the furtively parked car.

Finally, around noon, I heard the soft patter of her footfalls in the upstairs hall. I turned and saw her coming down the stairs in a simple plaid dress, the sandwiches in one hand, her china-doll face smiling at me from the shadows. Back when we were kids, she used to pin me with that smile like a mounted butterfly, used to know my thoughts and feelings before I did, as if my face were a book written in a language she and she alone had grown up reading. She was older now, but that smile was just the same. I glanced away, prayed she couldn't still read my expressions.

Mostly our lunchtime chats had been terse, forced, but there was something different today: I could tell as soon as she sat down and settled her skirt around her that she was feeling easier with me. We sat on the porch and talked long after our sandwiches were finished, even reminisced a little about the old days, those sun-soaked afternoons in the woods behind her house, slipping in and out of identities, genders, stories of capture and rescue, trips to the moon and the depths of the ocean, lost for hours and hours in the hectic joy of our play. I told Joanna how I'd just quit Buck's, how it had turned out he was closing the bar down anyway.

"Will you miss it?" she asked.

"Fuck no," I answered without a beat.

She put a hand over her mouth and laughed, the first time I'd heard that airy sound since she'd returned to Parson, the rare, beautiful, fairy-pure sound that somehow hadn't changed in decades, a second sunlight bursting over the porch. I felt myself blushing, saw that she was blushing, too. Some part of me, far in the back of my mind, wanted to hold on to the sense of danger that had reared up in me as soon as I saw her again, the fury and suspicion that had motivated me to stick around her these last few days; but the impulse to return to the powerful childhood connection was strong, casting over me like a magic spell, making me feel faintly drunk. She was sitting cross-legged on the porch, and I noticed the faint down of hair above her ankles, the hair I'd stroked so innocently as a child, when she was a princess whose tower I'd found, a damsel in distress. Here I was saving her yet again, but not in some fantasy, fixing this mansion the winds and water had ravaged. "I can't believe it's the same porch," she said before I went back to work. "What a miracle worker you are."

      After work that day, I knew I should get back to Heather. I could cook her my famous lasagna, even dig out one of Cece's old recipes. Instead I drove toward the outskirts of town, retracing the roads down which I'd followed Joanna to her brother's house. If I was leaving Parson soon, I wanted the chance to talk to Seth. I hadn't stopped thinking about those papers Joanna had brought over, the best guess I had about what she'd been digging around for in Miss Kate's office. Seth was more open, less circumspect, than his sister. Dreamy, sure, but if I acted casually enough—pretended I was there to say goodbye before moving, maybe—he might just let something slip.

      I found the house without any trouble, parked along the curb. The driveway was empty: either Seth wasn't home or he didn't own a car, had no way to get places himself. This would track with the Seth I knew, who rarely left Parson House during the time he lived there.

      It took a few knocks to rouse him to the door. When he pulled it open, he looked bleary-eyed, as though he'd been sleeping, his face pale and haggard, as when I'd glimpsed him the other day. It took him a moment to recognize me, then he gave me a faint smile. "It's been a long time," he said.

      "Too long," I replied, hoping he wouldn't mention the last time we'd seen each other. The garden, the body, the hours—or minutes?—of waiting for the police. "You been keeping well?"

      "Well enough," he answered.

      Seth sounded sincere, but when he invited me into the house, everything around us disagreed with him. The house was small and ill-kept, its clutter overwhelming, every surface clamoring with empty cans, unwashed plates and glasses, discarded wrappers. Seth, too, looked broken down: he wore a ratty robe over a gray undershirt, and he shuffled around in overlarge slippers, the walk of a much older man. He sat me down in the kitchen, started bustling about to make tea without asking if I wanted any.

I'd known Seth almost as long as Joanna, and even as a child he'd unsettled me a little. Where I came from, boys were tough, flint-eyed, quick with a fist or a cruel laugh. Even Robby, whom I loved more than anyone in the world, had a streak of anger that could burst loose, lash out into violence when provoked, and Danny, though not a fighter, had developed over the years a cagey defensiveness that showed exactly how much tenderness he expected from the world. But Seth seemed like he didn't know what violence was, that his was the same doll's-shelf world as Joanna's, gentle and pure and soft, too soft by far.

If I'm being honest, Seth and Robby's friendship could make me nervous, because the two were so unlike; next to each other, one seemed so fragile, the other so boorish. Whenever they disappeared to build their forts, I always half expected Seth to come home crying, telling us that Robby had hit him, or that Robby had said they weren't friends anymore. It didn't play out quite like that, but when Robby started high school, the day arrived, him waving me off one afternoon when I said let's go to Miss Kate's house. He didn't answer at first when I asked why he wouldn't come, but when I pressed him, he glanced away, mumbled as if it hurt him to say the words: "Because Seth's a loser, all right? He's a fucking loser."

After that, whenever I went to Miss Kate's house, I couldn't look at Seth without feeling ashamed of my brother, without hearing him say *loser* in that contemptuous tone. Even now, in this tiny, filthy house as I waited for my tea, Robby's voice echoed through my mind, and I hated that one of my most indelible memories of my dead brother was that.

Seth sat at the table across from me, set down the mugs of tea, and mixed in some sugar. He gave me two teaspoons, which he'd remembered from our time at Parson House.

"Well," he said, smiling that too-gentle smile, "it's nice to see you, Lou. Didn't expect a visit."

"Just wanted to say goodbye. Heather and I, we're leaving Parson soon. Next week, probably, going up to San Anton. I heard through the grapevine you were out here."

"Yes, it seems like the right time to go, doesn't it? We're leaving, too, soon as we can. Joanna tells me you're working on the mansion. We're very grateful."

I glanced around at the cramped kitchen. "How did you end up in this house, anyway? I thought you might have left town already—you know, after."

He cast a look around as if just realizing where he was. "This house? It's where we lived before Parson House, Mom and Ed and me. After the storm, I moved back here. It seemed safer, and anyway, Joanna said I should. She was a big help. I couldn't have done it alone."

I hesitated. "I owe you an apology, Seth."

He looked surprised at this. "For what?"

"For not coming to see you afterward. For not going to the funeral."

"No need to apologize. It's tough sometimes, isn't it? Like if you'd loved them less, it would be easier to mourn them. I understood."

It was good to hear him say this, but I still burned with guilt. The day of Miss Kate's funeral, I had put on my black clothes but then hadn't left my bedroom; I'd crawled under the covers and stared at the ceiling while Heather stroked my hair. I was shell-shocked at finding Miss Kate's body, at the thought of another casket after Robby's, another preacher saying empty words that wouldn't bring my loved ones back.

I changed the subject. "So where will you be moving?"

"Not sure, exactly." Then, with an apologetic smile, "Maybe Austin? It's where we evacuated to. I liked it a lot. But on the whole I go where Joanna points me."

"You know, I'm not sure I ever asked you why you came back to Parson in the first place. That was, what, six years ago? Seven?"

He shrugged one shoulder of his robe. "Maybe seven, I've lost track. My mother asked me to come, said she needed me. She didn't really, of course, not then. But . . . well, you know what she was like. I felt like I had to."

"What do you mean, *what she was like?*" I asked.

He gave me a curious look. "You were around her as a kid. She could be a very difficult woman."

"Stubborn, you mean? She always had a lot of grit. I respected that."

"Stubborn was part of it," he said, his voice quieter, a little disheartened, like he was disappointed in me for some reason. "But that's not really what I'm saying. Anyway, she's gone now. Maybe it's best if you remember her your own way."

"No, I'd . . . I'd like to hear." A coldness was seeping into my stomach. "You can tell me."

Seth took a sip of tea, looked past me with his foggy eyes. "I loved her, of course. I'm not saying I didn't love her. But we had a tough time of it as kids. Me and Joanna and Cass. Cass probably the worst."

I remembered Cassandra, buoyant, free, filled with the same energy as Miss Kate, only more youthful, more adventurous. Miss Kate poured herself into projects at hand, while Cass seemed bound for something bigger and wilder. I'd always thought Miss Kate adored Cass, and I'd always grieved that her vibrant daughter had died so young, just eighteen the night of the car wreck. If there had been trouble between the two of them, I'd never seen it.

"Are you saying Miss Kate hit you?" I asked. "Hit Cass?"

"No." Then, with a tilt of his head, "Well, not often. What she did—I don't suppose it's something I could describe. But we were miserable there, with our mother. That's why Joanna and I moved, went to live with Dad."

I was feeling more confused by the minute. If all of this was true, if they were really so miserable at Miss Kate's house, wouldn't I have seen something of it? "But you moved right after Cass died. Right after the wreck. I always thought . . ."

Seth stood up and shuffled to the counter, came back with a half-eaten sleeve of saltines. His face wore the same sedate blankness, but I could tell the conversation was affecting him. "Do you remember that summer?" he asked. "The summer she died? Cass, she stayed in Parson to work that job at the diner. But Joanna and I went north to visit our father."

I could only nod. Of course I remembered Joanna's trip north: I'd been devastated at the time, that she would leave me for two whole months.

Seth went on. "It's difficult to describe what it feels like, going from a place like our mother's house to our father's. He's a calm man, kind. He'd finished his education and become a professor since the divorce. Our father listened when we talked, didn't always have some agenda, some threat hanging over our heads. It was like stepping into the pages of some happy, magical book; even the colors seemed to change. Then we came back home to that misery, and a month or so later, Cass died. That was when Joanna asked Dad if we could live with him. We expected our mother to fight it, but she was so shaken up, she let us go."

My mind had snagged on Seth's implications about Miss Kate's mothering—the *agenda* and *threat* he'd mentioned so casually—but I didn't want to risk clamming him up by asking for details, showing my disbelief. Besides, I'd always wondered about Joanna's life after Parson—her life without me. "And how was it up there for you? Better?"

He thought about this. "Joanna, she did well. Graduated near the top of her class, went to Brown. I wasn't like that, though—I struggled. I attended college for a while, but . . . I don't know. After Cass died, after Parson, I always felt like there was an earthquake under my feet. It tired me out, living that way. Some months I barely got out of bed, and then I'd move back in with Dad when I ran out of money. Meanwhile, Joanna, when she called, I marveled at how well she was doing. Going to graduate school. Getting married. She could do all that, but I couldn't."

Married. The word tolled like a bell in my mind. Somehow Joanna hadn't mentioned a husband in our cozy lunchtime chats.

Seth didn't seem to notice my reaction, continued talking. "Sure, she had her problems, too—you couldn't be raised by our mother and not have problems. A hard time making friends, trouble sleeping, a nervous condition . . . . Joanna would tell me about it, it didn't sound easy. But to me it just seemed like she'd made it. *Survived* in a way I hadn't. And maybe it helped that she didn't speak to our mother. That she cut her off entirely. I never quite managed that myself, had phone calls now and then, sent cards on her birthday. Then one day I got another one of those calls from Mom about how she was dying."

"Dying?"

Seth let out a soft, far-off laugh. "What on earth did you two do out there in the woods as kids? You never talked about your lives?"

I bristled at the question, but I couldn't exactly refute it. "Guess not."

"She was always dying, our mother. From this or that, whatever she liked at the time. When she called that day, well—I guess I should have known better than to believe her. I even called Joanna about it, talked it over with her. She told me I'd be crazy to go."

All this was news to me as well: I'd always guessed it was the other way around, Miss Kate helping Seth through his depressions. It wasn't until much later—those last few months, really, out at Parson House—that Miss Kate had seemed to me like she was ill at all. "So you went, just like that?"

He nodded. "I'm not good at saying no. I came down to live in this house, and Joanna and I stopped talking. I never held it against her: anything she told me, she knew my mother would find out in time. Joanna, I think she felt like . . . like if Mom knew anything about her, she could show up at Joanna's place one day, take control of her again, like when we were kids. So for years, I didn't hear about any of Joanna's life—not her divorce, her leaving grad school, none of it."

"She's divorced?" I asked.

"Her husband, he was older, a doctor, a cardiologist. Successful, well-to-do type. Joanna was studying archaeology, and he was helping her pay for the degree. Then she started doing fieldwork and he didn't like that much, her being away so often. Cheated on her, it sounds like, and she left him. But the alimony wasn't much, not enough to stay in her program, and she was working at a museum before she came down here, some low-level job in the archives. Not the kind of job they'd hold for months while she took care of all these things in Texas. So I guess that's gone, too, though she doesn't seem particularly broken up about it."

It struck me how easy it was for Seth to spill Joanna's secrets, the ones she'd concealed from me during our lunches. I was very private myself, and I could see how her brother's openness might have been hard for her over the years. Seth had no secrets from anyone, seemed not to grasp the drama of status, the shame of failure.

With a slow sip of my tea, I tried to take it all in: Miss Kate as an abusive mother, Joanna as a divorcée. I looked at Seth in his ratty robe, in his filthy kitchen, and wondered if he might be exaggerating about Miss Kate, distorting the past. I wanted to ask follow-up questions, press for evidence, but all the questions that rose to my mind seemed too confrontational, even bullying. So I started with a softer question, worded as gently as I could manage: "When I worked for your mother, you two seemed to get along. But it was bad for you then and I just didn't see it?"

He thought this over. "It had gotten better by the time you worked for her. But when I first moved in, Ed was around, drinking more than ever. Mom was miserable in those days. So then we were all miserable together, the three of us crammed in this little house."

"Why didn't you try to leave, then? Go back to your father?"

"He thought she was dying," a voice said over my shoulder. Seth and I both flinched, looked over to see Joanna standing straight-backed in the doorway. "She kept him believing that all the way up until the end." Joanna turned her gaze from Seth to me, and I wondered how long she'd been standing there, whether she'd overheard Seth filling me in on her life. "Outside for a minute?" she said. It didn't sound like a question.

I stood up from the table, the chair legs scraping on the floor. Joanna had already turned away from me, and I followed her tense, abrupt stride out of the house.

As soon as she closed the front door, she turned to me and said, "I am terminating your employment at Parson House, effective immediately. If you have items belonging to you at the house, I expect you to gather them before the end of today. You will be compensated for the work you completed after the sale of the house, as we agreed. And I must ask that you never contact my brother again."

I laughed, even though a chill passed through me at her words. "Joanna, what is this? I'm sorry if—"

"I don't wish to discuss it any further."

"So you're just firing me? Just like that? For what—visiting Seth?"

She didn't respond. Watched me, impassive, flat-eyed.

"You'll never find someone else to do the work," I told her.

"You won't get paid unless the sale goes through, so you might consider sending some business our way. Though I do ask that you refrain from making direct contact with me. Providing them with my number would be sufficient. Good night, Louisa."

She turned toward the house like we were done, but I wouldn't let her slip away that easy. I reached out, gripped her arm tight, pulled her back. Every muscle in my body remembered what it felt like to hit her, that punch to her face the last time I'd seen her in high school. Every muscle ached to do it again.

But before I could form a fist, I froze from the look she gave me. Her face had come alive, her lips curled into a smile, and suddenly I could read exactly how she was feeling, like she'd pulled away the tight-drawn veil she'd been wearing ever since I set eyes on her that night at Rocky's. She was thinking, angry, thrilled: *I knew it.* I had lashed out at her tonight, just like I'd lashed out at her then, and part of her wanted me to hit her now, because it would prove something about me, resolve some question that had troubled her for years.

I let go of Joanna's arm and, with the speed of a wriggling fish, she slipped back behind the door and slammed it closed. The bolt locked with a cold *thunk.* I stood there, breathing hard, and then walked fast to my truck.

At first my driving was aimless, the ruined houses and vacant lots sliding past in the tepid light of sunset. But after a while my heart rate slowed and I realized I was driving out toward the sea, the same shoreline drives I'd loved in that long-ago summer with Cass, the summer that had felt eternal but had turned out to be her last few months of life. When I reached what had been our favorite beach, I parked on the sand and walked out toward the water.

The beachfront was eroded from the storm, and there were shattered planks strewn here and there, fabric and glass and twisted hunks of metal. I tried to remember how it used to be, perfect and smooth in the morning sunlight, so you could lie out starfished after a swim and only worry about a hermit crab maybe pinching you. If I lay out like that now, I'd be cut to ribbons.

Near the shoreline the waves were calm, but the day was clear enough that I could see out to the horizon, where the water rose and frothed and seethed dangerously. Even the seabirds seemed toppled by the wind out there, beating their wings violently against it. I knew I should drive back to Parson House, pick up my tools like Joanna had asked, go home, and tell Heather what she was dying to hear: that there was nothing left to tie me to this place, not anymore. But something was reeling in my mind, a tangled thought, a half-formed question, and I couldn't move from this spot until it took shape.

Joanna had left Parson in high school, had stayed away for fifteen years, had lost touch with her own brother when he moved back here—so Seth said. As far as I knew until today, she hadn't come back to town until last week, when she'd hired me to start the renovations.

But Seth said Joanna had lost her museum job months ago. He said Joanna had helped him move back to his old house after the storm.

How long, exactly, had Joanna been back in Parson?

12

The sun was sinking below the horizon when I reached Parson House to gather my tools. I was eager to pack my truck before the glow left the sky, before full night overtook the mansion. Darkness could come on you suddenly out on the promontory, a complete darkness you never knew, living in town, a desolation that made me long for lighted windows, cars in driveways. The roads had been empty this far from town: I'd passed only one car, a sleek Camaro parked near the turnoff to Parson House, one of its headlights out, the other lonely as a lighthouse beam.

The mansion loomed black above me in the warm purple sunset, like the shape of a house scissored from the air. I left my C/K's headlights on, climbed out and hurried across the lawn, began hauling my tools and supplies from the porch to the truck bed. This took no more than ten minutes, but it was long enough for the edge of the sun to slip below the tree line, for the night to come flooding over me like dark water.

Just as I was carrying the last planks from the porch, the lights on my truck snapped off as if someone had flipped the switch. I dropped the wood in a clatter and then stared out into the night, trying to see who might be there. All I could see was the negative afterimage of the headlights. I suddenly felt dizzy, and I had to crouch low, set my palm on the sandy earth to get my bearings.

Something seemed to be there, stirring in the darkness, the memory of light tucked behind my eyelids. I strained for the sound of other people, footsteps, voices—it seemed for a second like I'd heard some-one shouting—but when I listened carefully, all I heard was myself and the sea.

I considered groping my way to my pickup—it couldn't be far away—but this filled me with a strange fear I couldn't describe. The porch was much closer, a porch I knew well. I could switch on its light, walk easily back to the truck. I made my way up the steps, reached the door, and gripped the knob.

It was locked.

Joanna wouldn't have locked it before she found me at Seth's. She must have driven back here quickly and closed the house against me. She might even be here right now. I should have checked for her Fair-lane while there was still daylight.

I turned and picked my way down the porch steps, deciding to search for my truck instead of knocking, seeking her help. By now my eyes had adjusted to the dark, and after a few paces, I stopped when I saw a soft light swirling deep in the blackness. It was faint as a whis-per, but I couldn't look away. I didn't pause to wonder where the light was coming from; deep inside, I knew.

I started walking toward the glow. I lost all sense of bearings, all idea of where I was; nothing was real except the ground below me, the little light I followed. Even time seemed to lose dimension, stretching out like dripping honey.

What I could use right now was Thomas Wick's lighter, that old scratched Zippo I had seen him slip so casually from his pocket. I could almost hear their footsteps around me, their stifled giggles: Thomas and Danny and Cass. The last night of Cass's life.

The faint light led me to the wrought-iron gate of the garden. Back in high school, when we broke in here, the gate had been locked with a padlock and chain; we'd hoisted ourselves over the garden wall. The chain was gone, and with a gentle push, the iron door creaked open before me. But I hesitated: Could I really set foot in this garden after what I'd seen here? After all this time, did I truly want to face the past?

In the end, the tug was like an undertow, too insistent to fight. I stepped through the gateway.

Inside, the trees and bushes and vines rose up around me in a great wave, like jetting geysers of plants spewing high and cresting downward, all lit by the glimmering clouds of lightning bugs. The greenery braided and tangled together as if trying to form a solid mass, crowd out the air and sky. I could barely see the path of stepping-stones under the grass that brushed my ankles, barely remember the tame garden I'd once managed with Miss Kate. It felt like too much growth, too abundant for just eight months left alone.

The night bugs whirred like pinwheels. Somewhere in the foliage, a black rail chirped in angry blasts, sounding the alarm to my presence. I didn't like to think about all the creatures that must live here, the creatures watching me now, feeling my steps reverberate through this dense, connected world.

Then, suddenly, I was there.

Exactly where I'd hoped never to stand again. The light had led me right to it.

The day Miss Kate died, I had fresh hinges in my pocket. I jingled them like coins as I rounded the house to go inside through the garden. I was rehanging a bedroom door that day, an old battered one there wasn't money to replace. I lingered a moment at the cenizo shrubs near the garden gate, pinching off dead buds among the purple blooms.

When I saw her lying on the path, at first I didn't know what I was seeing. It didn't look like Miss Kate, didn't look like anything human, just an object of cloth and hair sprawled on the stepping-stones. A voice inside me said, *Run*, but I just stood there. Then I recognized Miss Kate's favorite housecoat, its faint floral pattern; then her frizzy locks soaked with a dark substance. The stepping-stone under her head was also stained, and then the whole image resolved and I realized that this was blood on the stone—that this was Miss Kate before me, hurt and bleeding but utterly still.

I called her name and rushed up to her; knelt beside her, looked into her face. This was a mistake: her skull was caved in above her eyebrow, down into her right eye socket. Her eyes were wide and staring, the right eye bulging from the shattered socket, red all the way through.

Then I was moving, skittering away from her, running into the house in search of Seth. He didn't look surprised when I burst into his room, when I shook him awake and told him what had happened, when I rushed out and called for an ambulance on the kitchen phone. Seth seemed only sleepy and disoriented as he trailed me into the kitchen, as he followed me back out into the garden.

He was the one who checked if she was breathing; I couldn't go close again. He rolled her onto her back, stared down at her cratered forehead, her dirt-caked lips. Seth didn't look stunned or frightened, only meditative, thoughtful. Where her body had been, the soil was still drenched with rain.

Later, when I could think clearly, that detail would bother me. After the police had come to the scene, after they'd concluded that Kate had slipped that morning and hit her head on a stone—after the case was considered closed, ruled an accidental death, I couldn't shake the sight of that wet soil beneath her. A few days later I went to the station and discussed my concerns with a sergeant, but the police seemed more than happy with their tidy narrative: the sergeant treated me like some sensitive woman addled by seeing a corpse, scribbled a line in his notebook, and sent me home. But I knew the police had gotten the time of death wrong, that the mud meant she hadn't fallen in the morning—the rest of the garden was dry—but during the rain of the previous night. The soles of her feet had been clean, as if she hadn't taken a step in the garden at all.

Nearly a year later, that stone in the path no longer bore a stain.

Something had drawn Miss Kate out into the garden in the middle of the night, in the middle of the rainstorm. She must have fallen in the water, slipping and going down so fast she didn't have time to reach out and break her fall.

What could have been so important to her, so urgent, that she'd walk out to meet it in her housecoat and her bare feet in that weather? The dark garden around me held no answers, only the chittering hum of insects.

And the light, the one that had drawn me to the garden, pooling down from above. I turned and looked up at the mansion, saw that the light was coming from Miss Kate's bedroom, spilling out over the balcony.

In all the clamor and chaos of that horrible morning, I'd never processed the fact that the spot where Miss Kate fell was just beneath the balcony outside her bedroom.

And then I knew something else—knew it with a certainty that meant I'd suspected it all along.

What was more likely: That Miss Kate would go out in her house-coat in the middle of a storm? Or that she would stand at her balcony's edge?

The balcony railing was high; it came up to my waist, and Miss Kate had been shorter than me, not a tall woman. If she fell from that balcony, most likely she'd been pushed.

A shadow moved across the light, sending shadow-puppet flickers into the garden. I knew from the fluid movements of the shadow that it was Joanna.

When I got back to my pickup, I managed to get the engine going, the headlights on. I threw the planks into the truck bed like I'd been working out front the whole time. I drove quickly back to town, glad to find myself again among the streetlights and paved roads, then pulled into the parking lot of a boarded-up laundromat. I switched on the cab light, dug Miss Kate's datebook from my glove box. I flipped to the middle of the book, the last entries of her life.

The day before her death, she'd had a few meetings. One was with someone marked down as *M*, another with *PCC*. Then, sitting on its own without any commentary, the letter *J.*

Part II

13

I'd already considered Joanna Kerrigan a murderer for years. Ever since Robby died, I had linked his death to her, traced it back to our childhood, as if following the path of a wildfire by the ash it left behind. The trail led back to one event: the day when Joanna met Danny.

For almost two years, throughout fifth and sixth grade, I worked hard to keep these friendships separate. I trusted Joanna deeply—she was my whole world back then—but she still went to Granbury, and I knew what might happen if Granbury found out about Cece, if they knew she was our relative, not our housekeeper. Danny, on the other hand, knew all about our living situation, how we called her *Aunt* Cece. Even then it felt like life and death to me, keeping those two worlds apart.

I thought I'd been so careful, but Joanna must have been spying on Danny and me, or else I'd dropped some clues by accident. Because one summer day, out of nowhere, she walked up while we were playing.

Our play was different from mine with Joanna. Danny and I tended to be rougher, running and shoving and laughing loudly. On hot summer days when the adults weren't paying attention to us, we'd strip to our underwear and swim in the creek near his family's auto shop, hidden from the street by a thicket of trees. Danny's father had impressed upon us the importance of keeping out of view, a lesson Danny took very seriously, and no matter how much fun we were having splashing around in the cool water, we tried to keep an eye out to see if anyone was coming. No one ever did—that is, until the day Joanna found us there.

I had Danny in a headlock and was dunking him playfully while he yowled. The second I saw Joanna, I let him go, stepped guiltily aside in the water.

"Oh, hi," Danny said, startled at this wispy girl in her checkered sundress. He'd heard plenty about Joanna, and I think he recognized her at once. His drenched underwear clung to him, wrinkled like a patchwork of veins; he knelt and hid his pelvis under the water.

But Joanna ignored Danny. She was giving me a curious, confused look, seeming torn between asking to play with us or storming away.

"Joanna, hey!" I said brightly, acting like nothing was wrong. "This is Danny."

I didn't know what to expect. I'd only ever seen her with white people, and things had been tense in Parson lately. Not two weeks ago there'd been an incident downtown when some drunk white men had roughed up Gary Fulton, a Black gas station attendant in his sixties whom Danny's parents knew. Anita from book club had called to give Cece the news, and Cece had prayed at length for Gary when she said grace that night at dinner, tearing up and gripping our hands while the stew sat there getting cold. Even fun, carefree Danny had seemed subdued the next day. "But he wasn't hurt that badly, right?" I said at the time. Danny glanced away, and I regretted my words at once.

Ever since, I'd been trying to be less boorish. But Joanna—I had no idea what she might do or say, seeing me play rough and close with Danny like this. She was from up north, but I knew that people up north could be even more racist than Texans in some ways. My heart pounded hard and tight as I waited for her reaction.

Joanna turned to him and, in her most correct and polite voice, said, "Hello, Danny. Very nice to meet you."

At first Danny didn't seem to respond—his face still wore that cowed, ready-to-bolt expression, and I felt a spike of fear that this was going to be the end of everything—but after a beat Danny pushed a big, bright smile onto his face and replied, "If I'd known you were dropping by, I would've kept my clothes on."

We asked Joanna to swim, but I knew she wouldn't. I couldn't imagine her stripping, leaving her lovely homemade dress on the dirt bank. She took off her flats and sat on a rock and dipped her feet in the water, and the fearful knot in my chest eased as she and Danny kept up an easy chatter, asking each other friendly questions, giving friendly answers. Later, after Danny and I were dressed, she asked me: "Louisa, have you ever shown Danny our special places? In the woods?"

"No way," I said. Of course I hadn't. Those places were sacred, Joanna's territory, and besides, she might have caught us there. I'd play with Danny at home, or in Cece's yard, or at his place; I kept us far from the woods.

Joanna took Danny by the hand. "Here, come with me," she said, her voice all breathless adventure, like she was the heroine of one of her fantasy books. She looked almost like Cass for a moment, daring, fearless. "You'll love it, I know you will."

After this it became the three of us, even after junior high started in the fall. Given my earlier fears, I knew I should have been grateful, especially when our play together remained in the woods, nowhere near Cece's house. Danny joined in our imaginary world, never acted too old for make-believe. At first I was anxious about the role he would play—with a real boy around, would Joanna want me to be her knight anymore? The play sessions had always been so improvisational, me following the script Joanna slowly spun, sometimes contributing lines and plot twists that I thought Joanna would like. What would the addition of a third person, a person with his own tastes and interests, do to our games?

Indeed, the first time we played make-believe together, Danny looked ready to jump into the role of the knight, and it stung me that Joanna didn't correct him. But Danny must have seen something on my face because he stepped back, suggested that he might be a sort of visiting prince from a neighboring kingdom, someone who could fight alongside me against that story's villain. It was enough to give our play a tentative sort of stability, and although I was hurt that Joanna hadn't spoken up for me, I did eventually grow to enjoy the addition of Danny's cast of characters to our stories, someone to fight alongside me against whatever evil foes Joanna dreamed up for us. If someone had to enter our secret enclave, Danny was the best option.

But the truth was, from the first moment I saw Joanna take Danny's hand, something dark had started brewing inside me.

Sometimes I could enjoy myself with them, forget all about my jealousy. But then Danny would make Joanna laugh, and she'd playfully push his shoulder, and I'd feel myself go sullen and quiet, unable to say a word. Alone in my room, I'd think back through our previous day together, fuming at every glance they'd shared, every snippet of conversation that hadn't included me. This was all around the start of my adolescence—my body a painful tangle of desires, my mind a nest of misfiring wires—when I was realizing that my feelings for Joanna were different than just friendship, or at least different than the friendships I saw between other girls. As far as I knew, friends didn't long to kiss each other tenderly, or to hold each other for hours, feel their bodies press together. Friends didn't picture each other naked, didn't struggle with lust that left them blushing and awkward. I didn't know what to make of these feelings other than worrying that there was something wrong with me. But I worried far more that someone—especially a boy—might come between us.

One day I walked to Miss Kate's place and, as I passed the side of the house, saw Danny and Joanna seated in the spreading sycamore tree beyond the yard. Its main branch was just big enough for two people, and Joanna and I often spent time there, one of our special places to make up stories, braid each other's hair. When Danny was with us in the tree, he'd always sit on a separate branch. So it stunned me to see them side by side on the branch I thought was ours, hers and mine, easy as though they were perched on the steps of an ice cream parlor, their words lost in the crackle of wind through the trees. From the light in his eyes, from her gentle smile, I couldn't help but hear a schoolyard rhyme chanting in my head: *Joanna and Danny sittin' in a tree.* Then suddenly, full of chipper happiness, they began to sing together: "Hold Me, Thrill Me, Kiss Me" by Karen Chandler, barely recognizable through their giggles. I watched them for a full minute, neither of them noticing me by the house. Then my stomach clenched and—though they were waiting for me to meet them—I turned and ran all the way back home.

"Is everything all right?" Cece set down her book when I walked in. I told her I felt sick, and she agreed I did look flushed, then she called Robby in from the backyard for a second opinion.

"Sure," he said, feeling my temperature under the guise of ruffling my hair, "you look awful."

Normally I'd have taken a half-hearted swipe at him, but I felt too low even for that.

"You go rest," Cece said. "Robby, help me get some pozole going."

Joanna came before the soup did. I heard her knock, then muffled sounds at the door as Cece invited her inside. The sound of Joanna's voice in my house sent a chill to the base of my spine. The thing I'd worked so hard to avoid had happened: Joanna had met Aunt Cece, was in my home with the smells of pozole cooking all around her, the sounds of Gabriel Ruiz coming from the radio. She would have seen Robby in the kitchen, chopping up chiles for the soup.

"Louisa," she said at my bedside, looking down at me with warm concern. "Are you feeling okay? You're sick?"

It all felt so out of my control. I wanted to yell at her to leave my house right now; she had no right to be here. I wanted to pull her down and kiss her. And I was angry, so angry, at Danny, because he must have given her the directions to get here, even though I'd asked him never to tell her, to pretend he hadn't visited here himself. But some part of me knew better than to blame him, even as confused as I was. This had all come out of my own pettiness: if I hadn't been so jealous, if I hadn't run away from Miss Kate's house, Joanna wouldn't have come looking for me. And she never would have discovered our secret.

By the time the pozole was done, I'd told Joanna everything and felt relieved that she knew the truth after all these years. We both cried a little as I explained about my missing mother, how my aunt Cece had taken us in, how it was so very, very important for Granbury not to know she was our aunt. Joanna held my hands as I talked, and I marveled that I hadn't told her before, this girl whom I loved and trusted more than anyone.

"But I don't understand," she said. "You're white, aren't you? But your aunt is Mexican?"

"She was married to my uncle," I explained. "My mother's brother."

"And where is he?"

I shrugged. "Gone, too."

She gave me a sad, considering look. "It seems your people have a talent for leaving."

The words hit me hard. I'd often thought this myself, but it felt brutal to hear it aloud—too raw and real.

I squeezed Joanna's hands tighter, locked eyes with her. "I'm not going anywhere, ever. I can promise you that."

After Joanna left, Cece came in to check on me. I could tell she suspected I wasn't sick—we'd been through this before on mornings when I didn't feel like school—but today she didn't question my act, just adjusted the pillows behind my head, gazed down at me with a tender, motherly distrust.

"So," she said, "that's the friend you've been seeing so much?"

"Yes. That's Joanna."

"Hmm. For some reason I thought she'd be wealthier."

I looked at Cece, confused about why she had thought this. Was it the way I talked about Joanna? Or maybe something about Miss Kate, a hint of class superiority in her dress or bearing? And what about Joanna's appearance just now had let Cece know otherwise? Joanna was plenty clean, her sundress new and nice. But Cece had a sixth sense about this sort of thing, and Joanna's poverty seemed to soften her toward my friend, bridging the divide between Joanna's world and ours. "She was very polite," Cece added. "She can come over whenever she likes."

This should have thrilled me. Instead, I sensed something Cece was holding back. After a second's silence, she went on: "In fact, I'd much rather if you two play here. And if she can't . . . you keep your wits about you when you visit her house, will you?"

I figured she meant Ed, that she'd heard around town about Joanna's drunk of a stepfather. "Sure," I said. "I'll be careful."

Cece looked at me, considering, as if not certain I'd gotten her point. Then she smiled fondly and placed her hand on my forehead again. "Remember that Christmas when you and Robby caught me putting presents under the tree? For Robby, that was it—I had to come clean about Santa. But you never asked me about it, not even once. And then the next year you wrote to Santa, just the same as before, asking for a dozen things we couldn't afford." I smiled up at her, but it would be years before I began to understand what she was trying to tell me.

At the time, Joanna knowing the truth about Cece didn't seem as dangerous as I'd always feared it would be. Part of me was even relieved. The next time I saw Danny, he apologized for telling Joanna where I lived. "She was so worried about you, I couldn't tell her no," he said, and I didn't bother holding a grudge against him for that. I still prickled with jealousy when I saw them together, but Danny must have guessed I was sore about it, because after a while he started finding little ways to reassure me that he was no threat to our bond— like waving me into the space next to Joanna when we all sat together, or turning to explain their little inside jokes to me so that I could at least pretend to laugh along. It was just like when he'd stepped into the role of the visiting prince: at the time I thought it meant he cared that much about me and my happiness, but looking back, I wonder if he didn't feel like his position was a more precarious one than mine, and he'd switched to people-pleasing as a way of holding on to both Joanna and me.

In the end, I was the one who felt guilty, even foolish, for having kept my worlds apart for so long. Soon enough, Joanna was dropping by the house once a week or more, letting Cece feed and dote on her, sitting on my bed and twisting my hair into braids while I read to her. Then, in freshman year, the trust I'd given her blew up in our faces, and Robby and I were kicked out of Granbury, his scholarship gone and dreams for college dashed. But even then, when he'd started to act sullen and defeated, I'd believed him when he'd said, "We'll handle it, won't we? Don't we have a knack for making the best out of a bad situation?"

It took a while to imagine how that might be possible. Woodman Secondary lacked the funding and resources of Granbury, and the students initially prickled at our presence. At the time I thought they hated us for where we'd come from, but now I think they were only picking up on our resentment of where we were, how disorienting the cold-water splash of displacement was. Part of me was tempted to keep my head down forever, pray my classmates would ignore me all the way to graduation, and the other part of me was scrappy, anxious, jumping to fight anyone who looked at me the wrong way. Luckily, before long Danny had recovered from the crash enough to come back to school. His presence eased everything: when he sat next to me in class or the cafeteria, the tension I felt coming at me seemed to abate, and while the other kids never really became friendly toward me, there was a grudging tolerance that grew gradually into acceptance.

Robby's transformation was more dramatic. He was pretty shaken up in those early days, but he was still Robby: he made new friends after a few months, better and nicer guys who didn't have expensive cars—an old pickup, if anything—but were happy enough to hang out over at Cece's after school. It was one of these friends who set him up with a good construction job after graduation, the company where he worked when he was drafted.

I was stung and bitter at first, but as high school went on, my fury faded. Though Robby and I never fully recovered, though we both spent much more time alone now, we managed to finish our education and get a degree—not always a given in Parson. I couldn't forgive Joanna, but at times I could forget.

But Robby had been alive then. Depressed, maybe, but alive. When the letter came about his death, and then months later, when his coffin arrived at the Corpus Christi airport, all those old memories changed, darkened, ossified. They became part of a different story, the story of his death. Now, when I looked back on those days with Joanna, I saw her not as I'd known her then, my best friend, my enchantress, my secret love. I saw her, instead, as a killer.

And perhaps Robby wasn't the only person she'd killed.

14

Where you going?" Heather asked me.

Soft, sleep-cracked, her voice let me know I wasn't being as quiet as I'd hoped.

"Parson House," I lied.

Heather had no clue that Joanna had fired me yesterday. When I got back from the mansion last night, after seeing that *J* in the date-book, I'd been too shaken up to tell her. I'd downed four beers while she kept up a jaunty monologue about her day: stranded at home with no car, she hadn't done much besides packing and sorting, but she wove this into a pleasant story, a patter I could follow without needing to interject much. She could tell I wasn't up for talking but not in the mood for silence, either.

Though I felt guilty for keeping secrets—Heather deserved better—this morning I was grateful that I'd told her nothing last night. If Heather knew that Joanna had fired me, she would leap on the chance to leave Parson, which I couldn't do now until I knew for sure what had happened to Miss Kate. The police sure as hell weren't interested in solving the questions surrounding her death, and I felt I owed it to her to find some answers.

"You be careful out there," Heather said, half awake. "Had this dream you fell off the ladder."

I shuddered, and the image flashed before me, too frequent and familiar: head cracked open on the pavement.

Heather didn't seem to notice. She gave a sleepy smile. "You could fly, though."

"Well, I'll make sure to wear my wings today."

She yawned, and I could tell she'd decided to sleep a little longer. "I don't trust that damn house. Never have."

A strange feeling rippled through me as I switched on my truck and pulled out of the driveway—a mixture of anger and fear, of self-righteousness and self-doubt, all heightened by a rush of adrenaline that made me grip the wheel tightly, the surge of new awareness awakened in me in the garden last night. Part of me wanted to drive straight to Parson House, confront Joanna, demand answers; part of me, scenting danger, wanted to drop the matter entirely. I kept seeing Miss Kate's bare feet, the swath of mud beneath her—but could it really be true that Joanna had pushed her mother off that balcony? I felt certain that someone had done it—and if not Joanna, then who? Who else would have hated Miss Kate that much, had so much to gain from her death?

I pressed down on the gas and shifted into fourth on an open stretch of road, trees whizzing past on both sides. There was a thrill in hunting Joanna, going after her possible crimes, after so many years of hating the woman, of knowing she deserved a punishment she'd never receive. Because this wasn't just about Miss Kate. This was about the brother Joanna had taken from me, the childhood she'd ruined in retrospect. This was about her firing me yesterday for no reason, just because she felt like it, using me when she needed me, discarding me when I became inconvenient. I couldn't let her get away with this, too: on top of all her many indelible sins, I couldn't stand the thought that she'd taken Miss Kate from me.

Still, I felt how tightly I was gripping the wheel, the rapid thudding of my heartbeat, my temples pulsing as I ground my teeth together. I wasn't doing well, that much was clear. I wondered how long I could live like this, at the outermost edge of myself, staring out into the unknown, nothing in that depth of darkness but a faint wavering light drawing me forward.

I forced these thoughts away, focused on the task at hand. I needed more information about Miss Kate, and luckily there was someone left in Parson who might have answers. I owed her a visit anyway.

It was just after seven a.m., too early to visit most people, but I knew Peg was always up and about with the sun; back when Miss Kate was alive, she used to drop by Parson House first thing in the morning, and sometimes I'd arrive not long after sunrise to find Peg's truck in the circular driveway, the two women chatting in the kitchen over cups of tea. "Morning, Louisa," Miss Kate would say, pulling out a chair for me. "Why don't you join us for a spell?"

I could still see them that way at the kitchen table, one short and squat, the other tall and thin, both looking at me with friendly eyes as their cups steamed before them, birdsong trickling in from the garden, the smell of orange pekoe in the air. One of those tête-à-têtes was the last time I'd seen Peg before the storm, and that morning stood out in my mind because they hadn't invited me to take a seat with them, had just glanced up and gone quiet at my entrance. They looked tense and uneasy at first, a little shaken up, but then Miss Kate flashed me a big smile and I figured everything was fine.

"Say, Lou," she said in a warm voice, "before you get working today, I have a question for you."

"Shoot," I said, grateful the earlier tension was gone.

"This town, you know, it hasn't exactly been kind to you and your family. I remember that horrible trouble with the school back when you and Robby were young."

Peg was watching me intently, so I pushed it down, eager to keep things pleasant. "Sure," I said. "Not that anything like that would happen nowadays. Both the schools are integrated."

Which was only partially true. By the time Parson officially integrated, the next scheme was already enacted: property taxes and racist homeowner policies kept things mostly the same, the rich school white, the poor school diverse.

"Why bring this all up, Kate?" Peg asked kindly, touching Miss Kate's hand with her own. "It must be hard for Louisa to talk about."

"I was just curious if the town ever reached out to you," Miss Kate said to me. "Made any sort of amends."

I thought about Heather tearing up the letter the mayor sent us after Robby's funeral, ripping it into a dozen pieces before she threw it away. "Fuck them," she'd said, the fire in her voice reaching me even through my numbness. "And fuck this whole goddamn town."

The memory pricked my eyes, but I trusted myself not to cry in front of these women. "No, ma'am," I said. "I don't imagine anyone in charge much remembers or cares about that ancient history. You know those guys down at city hall. Probably busier chasing their secretaries."

I'd tried to play it off like a laugh, as if the wound weren't still open and bleeding, as if I wouldn't miss Robby every day for the rest of my life. But Miss Kate must have seen straight through it, because she stood and crossed the room—rickety, old, moving slow—and brought me into a tight hug.

When I drew away from the hug, hoping I hadn't looked too sad or soft in front of this woman who meant so much to me, Peg was sipping her tea, watching us with a thoughtful, concerned expression.

It was this—*Peg's familiarity with Miss Kate, particularly in those* last days—that had me heading out to her place so early in the morning. Before long I was driving down Peg's block, passing the ruined houses and overgrown lots, until I reached her immaculate Tudor, its gables casting long spear-tipped shadows across the lawn.

Two women were crouched in the tidy vegetable garden, pulling weeds. One of them didn't look up when I parked my truck and climbed out; the other peered at me from under her hat brim, then rose and pulled off her dirty gardening gloves.

"Good morning," she said in Spanish, flashing me a big smile. She tilted back her straw hat to see me better. She was in her late twenties, close to my age. I thought I recognized her from high school, someone from Woodman Secondary, or maybe the daughter of one of Aunt Cece's friends.

"Morning," I replied, sticking with English. Not that I couldn't understand Spanish, but it had been a while and I was rusty.

"Are you looking for Margaret?" she asked, switching to English as well.

"If she's around."

"She should be inside," said the woman. "I'm sure she'll be happy to see you, Louisa."

So she did know me. "Thanks," I said, and walked to the door, still trying to place her. As I passed, I felt her turn to watch me, her hat casting a shadow over the doorstep.

A third woman came to the door when I knocked. I almost let out a gasp when I saw her: the poor thing was missing her left eye, the lids stitched together concave over the empty socket. "Margaret's just in the kitchen," she told me in lieu of a greeting; apparently she knew me as well. "We were working on the preserves, but I reckon you two might want some privacy. Tell her to holler if she needs me."

"Sure," I said, and watched her whisk off down the hallway, out of sight.

Peg greeted me with a hug in the spacious, sunny kitchen, the counter covered with rows of empty glass jars. She was dressed in her usual outfit, hard-work boots and jeans and a men's button-down shirt, her silver hair hanging in a narrow braid down her back.

"Things are busy here," I said. "I just got greeted by the Ladies' Home and Garden Brigade."

Peg chuckled. "Always lots of work to do. I'm just grateful for all the help. And speaking of work, sweetie, you look really tired out. I thought you might be getting more sleep now that you quit up at Buck's."

"Heard about that, did you?"

She turned back to the stove, where a large pot was bubbling, emitting a pale orange steam that smelled of persimmons. "Not much to gossip about in this town. Buck was pretty annoyed."

"Yeah, well, fuck him." Then, remembering who I was talking to, I shot her an apologetic smile. "I mean . . . well, you know."

She looked more amused than disapproving. "I *do* know what you mean. I said about a thousand times you were too good for that place."

Indeed she did. Something about Buck leaving me to die in the storm didn't sit right with her.

"Yeah, well, Heather wants to leave town," I told her. "So I had to quit eventually."

Peg was stirring the pot with a large wooden spoon. "And you want to leave, too?"

I shrugged. "Not much to stay for. Even Buck's is closing down soon. Doesn't look like there'll be a Parson much longer."

"It feels that way now," Peg said. "But this isn't the first time Parson was supposed to shut down. Lean years, the factory closing, storms just as bad as this one. Parson always comes back in the end— and always better off than it was before."

I was comforted by these words. Ever since the storm, I'd heard doom and gloom from most everyone in town, dire forecasts of Parson bleeding out and dying. Only Peg ever said anything that made me feel better.

"If you want to stay," she went on, "or if you do leave for a while and then decide to come back, you know I'd be happy to help you. I can't promise much pay, but I can promise good, honest work. A place to live." She gestured as if to take in the women in the garden, her friend helping with the preserves.

"I'm awful grateful," I said truthfully. "And who knows, I might just take you up on it."

She looked happy at that.

Then, because my heart was thudding, because in my mind's eye I couldn't stop staring down that *J* in the datebook, I came right out with it. "I actually was hoping to ask you a few questions, if that's okay. Some things I was curious about. With Miss Kate."

Peg's smile didn't waver, but her expression took on a new gravity, the lines in her forehead more distinct. She nodded at me as if to say *fire away*, then looked down into the bubbling pot.

I hardly knew where to begin with these questions. I was no detective, and as far as the law went, the case was closed, had never been a case at all. If Peg asked me what I was up to, why I was asking questions, I wasn't sure what I'd say.

"You knew Miss Kate pretty well, right?" I began. "And her husband?"

She considered. "Not Ed so much, he was away so often. But Kate and I went to the same church since way back."

"Were you close?"

"Off and on. At one point years ago, we were very good friends.

But the death of her daughter Cassandra, that rattled her considerably. She came to worship, but she didn't socialize as much. Only recently, in the last few years, did we get familiar again."

"How long ago?"

"Not long before she bought Parson House," Peg said. She paused to think, the spoon stopping in the pot. "Maybe five years back it was, around the time that Ed lit out. Kate had started to feel isolated, and buying that house—that was a huge project. She needed to make connections in town if it was ever going to work. That's around when she reached out to you, too, wasn't it?"

"Yeah, it was," I said. Then, slowly, "You know, I never actually knew why she bought that house. I know the official line was that it was about tourism and whatnot, but I never got the story from her. I mean, that mansion—it can't have been cheap. The house she was living in before, it's a total dump. Then suddenly she buys Parson House? She ever talk about any of this with you?"

"Kate was . . . how can I put it?" Peg waved a hand as she searched for the word, slicing the persimmon steam, dispersing the tart sweet smell throughout the kitchen. "Mysterious. Always a bit mysterious, she was. Ever since her kids left, she'd bring in these little projects all the time. Taking in bad dogs, disobedient horses, and trying to break them. I don't know that anything left her care better than she found it. But she never did stop trying, bless her."

"So that's what the house was for her? A doomed improvement project?"

"Of course I can't know for sure," Peg said with a sigh. "I wish she was here for us to ask, I surely do." She left the stove, walked over to where I'd seated myself at the table. Put a hand on my shoulder, rubbed it gently. "I know it's been tough for you since she passed. She was like a mother to you in the end, wasn't she?"

Something in me balked at the word *mother*—not because it was wrong but because it felt dangerous to admit, to make myself that vulnerable. But this was Peg, a woman who'd saved my life, who'd worked hard to keep Heather and me fed since the storm. Whose hand on my shoulder felt like safety, like home.

"Yeah," I said. It took more effort than I expected to let out that one word.

Peg didn't rush me. Didn't take her hand from my shoulder.

Finally I said, "The last few days of her life—was there anything different going on with Miss Kate? Was she acting strange at all?"

Peg gave my shoulder a final squeeze and went back to the stove, turned down the heat on the preserves. "That was, what, eight or nine months ago? Let me think here for a minute." Then, with a smile, "Don't get old, Lou. I can barely remember last week sometimes. Was there something particular you had in mind?"

"Just curious," I said, glancing away from her, ashamed to be lying so much. "I guess I'd like to know if she died happy."

Peg sighed. "I hope she did. She loved that garden. Loved fixing up the house with you. But the month or so before she died, I guess I do remember her being upset."

"About what?"

"The usual sort of things. You know, her husband's parents live in town. And they'd been giving Kate some trouble. It seems he hadn't been in contact with them, either. A man who runs away from his wife, it only figures he'd run away from the rest of his family. There was talk of illegal gambling debts, too—little wonder if he'd want to be scarce for a while. But his parents, they wouldn't believe that, they thought something bad had happened to him, and they blamed Kate. And when she suddenly had enough money to buy the mansion . . . well, it got them fired up against her. I think they even sent some threatening notes."

"Ed's parents have got to be ancient," I said. "How threatening could they be?"

Peg laughed. "They'll be eighty or so, sure. But you'd be surprised. They're rough old Texas stock, tough as leather."

Tough as leather, maybe, but I couldn't picture them shoving Miss Kate off her balcony. Still, it would be worth checking up on them, maybe looking more into Ed.

"And then," Peg continued, "there's the Witnesses."

I remembered the pamphlet I'd found near my porch the other night, inviting us to a service at the Kingdom Hall. It made me itchy to think about. "She wasn't going to that place anymore, was she?"

"That was the problem. See, Kate and I used to be members—avid members—but we'd parted ways with them. We believed and prayed—I do to this very day, in my own way—but we didn't attend their services."

"I bet they were thrilled about that."

She waved a dismissive hand. "They left us alone, mostly. But when Kate bought Parson House, they came sniffing around like everyone else. Wanting to know how she'd bought it and why. They didn't believe the tourism line, either. "

"They were giving her hassle?" I tried to remember anything odd I'd seen, but I'd been so lost in my own world out there, I was sure I'd missed plenty.

Peg smirked. "Kate and I, we were what they called *disfellowshipped*. They were supposed to avoid us—bad influence and all that. Kate pointed that out when they stopped by, and what could they do? They had to leave. We had a good laugh about it the next morning. But we knew that church, knew it must have made the elders angry. Kate laughed, but I'm sure it caused her some grief."

So Peg had left the church—or been forced out, it seemed—which meant she hadn't left the pamphlet for me.

"Sounds like buying the mansion made her some enemies," I said.

"More like it helped her see who her enemies were already. Not that she needed the reminder—neither of us needed that. But the real trouble wasn't outside that house. It was in there with her."

"Wait. You mean Seth?" I'd worried for a second she meant me.

Peg nodded grimly. "He wasn't an easy person to live with. Moody, you know. Taken to long sullen spells. Kate would tell me she was worried about him, and at first I thought she meant worried *for* him, for his well-being. But then I realized it was different. Worried *by* him, more like."

I took this in. Seth was quiet, sure. Sometimes when I worked for Miss Kate, I wouldn't see him for days on end, would feel his presence like a ghost's: objects moved from where I'd last seen them, a chair pulled out from a table, some dirty dishes left on the counter. He seldom spoke around his mother, just smiled morosely at me and let her do all the talking.

And then there were the stories he'd told me—about how difficult Miss Kate used to be, how hard it had been growing up with her. I couldn't bring myself to take what he'd said at face value, but the emotion behind it was true enough. There was resentment there, old but alive. I of all people knew how powerful a long-stoked grudge could be.

"I just saw him last night," I told Peg. "He said he came back to Parson to help Miss Kate. Said she needed him."

"Yes, that's true enough. She wasn't well."

I wondered how long she'd been sick. I hadn't noticed anything until those last few months. Even when I did notice it, I never brought it up with Miss Kate, not wanting to hear more than I could handle, like that she was dying of cancer or had some chronic wasting illness that would slowly kill her over the next decade. After Robby's death, I had a limited capacity for that sort of news. Miss Kate had kept up the house well enough, at least the rooms she used; I thought she might not be that bad off.

"What was she sick with?" I asked. "Did she tell you?"

"I don't think she ever got it diagnosed. Distrusted doctors—ever since Cassandra's death, as a matter of fact. But she always had theories. She did some reading on her own, checked out books from the library. One week I'd see her and she'd think she knew the problem. Then she'd read about some new disease, and that was the one."

Seth had told me as much. "Did you believe she was sick?"

"Near the end, yes," she said without hesitation. "You could see it some days. In her face, in her eyes. Like when a steer's eyes get cloudy and you know there's lung trouble. But I'm not sure she ever did land on the cause of it."

"And Seth . . . did he actually take care of her? I never saw much of that."

Peg hoisted the pot to the sink, poured out its steaming contents in a marigold-colored stream through a mesh sieve. Eventually she answered, "I suppose he did the best he could. But he didn't do much. Not really."

"Then what did she want him for?"

"A mother wants to be with her children," Peg said simply.

"Some mothers," I murmured.

"Kate did," she said. "Better or worse, she wanted them there. Both of them."

I thought once more of the large, lone *J* written in the datebook. Maybe Miss Kate had gotten her wish, after all.

15

I drove back home with two jars of marmalade that Peg insisted I take, as well as the promise of another grocery delivery soon. My mind was lost down a thousand different tracks, drifting back over the final weeks of Miss Kate's life. Distracted, I'd nearly reached the house before I noticed the blue Fairlane in the driveway.

Heather came out the front door as I walked up, barefoot and bra-less, her hair hanging down in a sleepy tangle. Her arms were crossed over her tank top, and I could tell from her expression that I was in trouble.

"Morning," I told her, showing her the marmalade jars. I wasn't sure what was brewing in the house, why Joanna was here, how to play this. "I've been at Peg's."

She ignored the jars. "You got a visitor," she said flatly.

"Yes. I see that."

Heather kept her voice quiet when I reached her on the path, but she might have been shouting for the anger in her tone. "So you've been fired off the Parson House job, huh? Fired yesterday?"

I gestured to the Fairlane. "Is now really the time to talk about it?"

She reached out and gripped the hem of my T-shirt, a gesture both angry and intimate. I felt the neck of the shirt pulling down, the cotton stretching, and I tucked the marmalade jars into my pocket.

"We could have your truck loaded in half an hour," she said. "In *half an hour*, Lou. We could be in San Anton by lunchtime."

When I didn't respond, she kept on. "We just need to get out of this town. Get back to Sarah. To Cece. Don't you see what this god-awful place is doing to you? You're lying to me left and right, making promises and breaking them. All because you're so shit-scared of losing Parson. Trust me—we need to go. Before this place sucks us down any further."

I closed my hands over hers. "Honey," I whispered. I was scared Joanna could hear me somehow, through the doors, the wall. I glanced past Heather, checked the windows were shut.

She clocked the motion, pulled her hands from mine.

"It sounds nice, what you're saying," I said, going for gentle. "San Anton will be great for us. But can we please talk about it later?"

I was surprised to see tears in her eyes. She wasn't a crier, Heather, not really since Robby. "Joanna just fired you, Lou—*fired* you. We should be getting on with our lives, and all you can do is worry she might hear what you're saying. If she wants you back, hell, of course you'll go back. You wouldn't *think* of saying no. But doesn't what I want matter? Answer me that. Don't I matter at all?"

"Of course you matter."

"You haven't acted like it. Not in months. You lie to me like it's nothing."

I wanted to say that she didn't understand anything, that I had more going on than I could tell her. But as soon as I opened my mouth to say it, I had a queasy feeling that made me shut it. I was thinking of those men, the ones who always managed to capture my mother's attention. The ones who had kept her away from Robby and me, made us invisible to her. I knew I was acting just like them, and I hated myself for it.

I closed my eyes, tried to tamp down my racing pulse. The day felt twisted out of shape. "All right," I said.

"All right?" Heather echoed back at me, quick but dubious.

"You're all packed, aren't you?" I said. "We can load your things up tonight, drive out first thing tomorrow."

Heather's face was bright, almost unbelieving, when I opened my eyes. "Do you mean it? Really?"

"I'll need to come back down. There's a little more to do with the house before we quit it for good. Just a day or two." I felt like I was fighting with a rusty hinge somewhere inside myself. Would I really be able to leave Parson and all my questions behind? But here was Heather standing in front of me, smiling like I hadn't seen her smile in weeks, and even as tough as it was, I had to believe this was the right thing to do.

Heather gripped both my hands in hers; I could tell her eyes were welling up. "Thank you," she said. "I mean it. Thank you." She looked like she was going to hug me, but then darted her glance to the window and back to me with a sheepish smile. "Think you can shake her fast?"

"I can try," I said. I braced myself, letting Heather's hands fall away from mine, then we both went inside.

Heather passed right through the kitchen without saying a word, leaving me alone with Joanna. Joanna, who was seated in a burgundy dress at the kitchen table, her slim shoulders pale beneath the straps. I hated to see her here, perched on a chair with wobbly back legs, her elbow rested next to a kidney-shaped stain on the tabletop. It made me notice how small and dingy the house was, made me want to apologize for it. I bit down on the impulse, angry with myself that even now, with all my anger and suspicions toward Joanna, I couldn't stop caring what she thought of me.

I walked up to the table but didn't sit down, leaned back against the fridge. The last time I'd been this close to Joanna, I'd grabbed her, wanting to punch her in the face; I could still feel that buzz of rage pulsing through me. Joanna's gaze met mine, and I knew she was thinking about it, too, my hand on her arm, the violence she'd read in my eyes.

"Morning," she said softly.

I nodded, not sure I could speak. I set the jars of marmalade on the counter.

"I wanted to drop by and apologize," she said, glancing at the jars in that quiet, curious way of hers. "What I said to you last night, how I responded to your presence at my brother's house . . . that was an overreaction."

I nodded again.

"You have your own relationship with Seth. I'm aware of that. It's possible you know him better than I do these days. Which I suppose makes me feel jealous, and guilty, too. He told me what you two spoke of, so I guess you know that he and I lost touch when he moved back here to Parson. When he came to live with our mother."

"He mentioned it," I admitted.

Heather had shut herself in the bedroom, but you could hear everything in the kitchen through the thin plywood door. I worried I'd be asked later on about the visit to Seth that I'd failed to mention.

"I shouldn't have done it," Joanna went on, staring down at the table. "I shouldn't have cut him off like that. He's a sensitive man, Seth, feels rejected easily, and feels it hard. He knew why I took that distance, but that didn't make it easier for him—after I moved, he didn't even have my phone number. I could have been a lifeline for him during all that he was going through down here. Instead I chose to protect myself. And I suppose . . . I suppose I should thank you for being there for him when I wasn't."

"I wouldn't exactly say I was there for him. We just had tea now and then."

"On the contrary," Joanna said, "Seth tells me you were always kind to him. And you helped him manage our mother. She could be a very intense woman, as I'm sure you know. You took some of the burden off him."

Had Seth really told her all this? Perhaps he felt bad about Joanna firing me, wanted to talk her around to liking me again.

Joanna exhaled, then continued, "I hope you can understand my being protective of Seth. But that doesn't excuse my behavior, I know that. And I shouldn't have fired you. If you're willing, I'd like you to return to work at Parson House."

Just as Heather had predicted, I felt a sudden rush of emotion: relief, gratitude, an urge to tell Joanna *yes*, of course I'd come back to the mansion, I could get started again on the front rooms this afternoon. But I was wary of these emotions, aware that I might be feeling them for a killer—was it a smart idea, a *sane* idea, to be out at the mansion, alone on that desolate promontory, away from civilization, with this woman? A woman who was probably armed, carrying the gun from Miss Kate's bedroom, the revolver I hadn't found the other day?

Still, I balked at the prospect of turning her down outright. If I wanted the truth about Joanna, I'd find no place with more access than the house where she spent her days. And I could press for advantages now, be strategic about my approach; I didn't have to be her toy, her puppet. I watched Joanna a minute longer, letting her question hang in the air, saying nothing. Seth had said she had a nervous condition. I wanted to make her nervous.

She sat there placid enough, seemed undisturbed by the silence. But after a moment she spoke again. "We can renegotiate our deal, if you'd like. Allot you a higher percentage."

"I don't need more money," I said, then caught myself. More money would make the move to San Antonio a hell of a lot easier. "How much more?"

Joanna took in a breath, eyes on me as if calculating, though I knew she never would have walked into my house unless she'd already figured out exactly how high she could offer. "If you're able to finish the job, we could go as high as ten percent."

I could feel myself waver. Ten percent on a sale like that was a different universe than five. Slowly, I said, "I'd need some answers."

Something passed across her face—it looked like fear—but she controlled it quickly, gripping the tip of her pointer finger to settle herself. "All right," she said in a hesitant tone, "answers."

"Well, if I'm getting paid in percentages, then I think I deserve to know about the buyers."

Joanna nodded. "I'm arranging all of that. But I can promise complete transparency as soon as I have something solid."

"I thought you had someone lined up."

"It's complicated," she said. "But I can promise you I'm working on it. I assume that isn't your only question?"

I gave my head a subtle shake, inclined it toward the bedroom, where I knew Heather was listening. "Some other time. We'll have a chat, and you'll be honest with me."

"I like to think I've always been honest with you, Louisa."

She said it easy and direct, like a doll with a pull string. The words made me want to laugh, or cry, or flip the table over. Made me want to punch her, most of all. But I just smiled.

"I'll need to talk to Heather about it first," I said. "You know we're leaving town."

She nodded, pushed back the wobbly chair and rose from the stained table, then saw herself out. I sat down at the table, stared at the empty chair that had just held her body. Why had she looked so afraid, so terribly afraid, when I mentioned wanting answers? Would that rattle an innocent person, someone with nothing to hide? She'd squeezed her fingertip red just to keep her composure. And she'd doubled her offer for my work on the house: Was she trying to buy me off, get me to forget my questions? Or was it actual gratitude?

I heard the bedroom door creak open and Heather walking to the bathroom, followed by a weak trickle of water from the faucet. That's where I found her when I got up: brushing her teeth despondently, staring at her under-eye shadows in the mirror.

She spat into the sink when I walked up behind her. "Ten percent of what, I wonder?"

"A lot, I'd guess," I said. "Even if the sale is lower than Joanna wants it to be . . . that great big place?"

Heather hesitated; I could practically hear her brain rattling with the calculations. I hugged her from behind, pressed my face into her hair, shrugged against her back. "It's up to you."

"How much longer, do you think?" she asked.

I didn't know for sure; I hadn't taken in the full extent of the damage inside the house. But I found myself saying, "A couple more days, I think."

She puffed up and deflated again slowly, a long low breath. "It would be nice to show up to Cece's with a little money, wouldn't it? To help pay her back for all she's done?" Begrudgingly, she added, "You know, Fay mentioned a little job I could take on for her the next couple days. I turned it down at first, but if it really *is* just a couple days . . . it wouldn't be so bad. I could pick up some money, too. Help us get settled in San Antonio when we get there."

I knew she'd have been more specific if she wanted me to know what the job was. Nannying, probably—the kind of job that rankled Heather's prideful side and made her resent her old friends. But I knew she was feeling better about me now that I'd made the offer to leave, to quit Parson House. And she wanted to offer me these few days as a gesture of good faith.

And because the money was too tempting to pass up.

I should have been thinking about the money, too. Instead I thought of Miss Kate pushed from that balcony. Her cracked-open skull, the image I could never scrape from my mind. The police who didn't give a damn who'd killed her.

I thought of Joanna in Miss Kate's rooms, raking her hands into every crevice.

Then I sighed and kissed Heather's neck, right at the honey-colored hairline. "Just a little longer," I promised her. I had a chance now, permission to stick around long enough to find out what I had to know. After that, with Heather's help, maybe I really could put Parson behind me forever.

16

I first met Heather when she was in high school. She was in Robby's year and widely considered the most beautiful girl at the school.

I scoffed when I first heard this. "That girl?" I remember saying to Robby. "What's so special about her?" Back then no one measured up to Joanna.

But my brother thought Heather was special, was smitten with her from the first, and when she came up in conversation, he'd get bashful, flustered. Good thing for him, then, that he was starting to make a name for himself at the school. The start of his freshman year, he'd made quarterback on the junior varsity team, and by season's end he was bumped up to varsity with a word from the coach that, if he worked hard, he might get good enough for a college scholarship. When Cece heard this, she teared up with joy, and she began to pray for it at every dinner: "Please, dear God, let Robby's football take him to college."

"Don't get your hopes up," Robby would say, but he'd beam as he said it, then go outside after dinner to throw a football through the tire hung in the yard.

Given what happened later, I wish his coach had never mentioned college, never said *scholarship*. Before he said those words, the future for Robby meant roofing or plumbing, maybe a job with Danny at the auto shop. After those words entered our lives, Robby stopped talking about the future at all, his face too lit up with dreaming, the electric calculations of possibility.

I wanted this future for Robby more than anything else in the world. The only college graduates we'd met were bankers or teachers, and we knew that college could open up many options, jobs that paid good money, houses you didn't rent. He'd talked about starting a business, maybe roofing or something like that, but I harbored bigger ideas—that he'd become a lawyer, a doctor, a politician. My own position had felt so precarious ever since I'd been dropped here all those years ago. But the more influence Robby had when he came back to Parson, the more secure Cece and I would be forever; maybe Cece wouldn't have to work, and I could do whatever I wanted, be whoever I wanted, if my brother was a local big shot. That was the way Parson worked, after all. So whenever he shuffled off to practice, even just with some friends, I knew better than to distract him or tag along, would even take on his chores so that he could go.

"What do you know about college?" I asked Joanna and Danny one day.

Danny shrugged. "There's one in Austin, right? Pretty sure my mother's cousin works maintenance there."

But Joanna's eyes lit up. "My father works at a college," she said. With a glance at Danny, she added, "Teaches, I mean. Philosophy."

I couldn't believe I'd never heard this before. "So you've been to a college?"

This was years before *Dobie Gillis*; I'd seen only a few colleges on the evening news.

Joanna nodded. "When we were little, we'd go to campus with him all the time. He was a student then, but now he teaches there."

"Robby might go to college," I said. "Everyone's talking about it."

This was true. The whole town was looking at him differently, a good crowd coming to see him play at home games—and although I was only in junior high, news of his talent and prospects trickled down to the eighth-grade level. Some of the popular boys in my class started to treat me with more respect; one asked me out. I shut him down harshly, scooped up a handful of dirt, and told him to get lost unless he wanted it in the face.

This was around the time when Heather and I first spoke. I'd seen her around town and out at football games, but one day I was at the grocery store picking up food for Cece, and Heather, who worked as a bagger there, gave me a smile while I stood in the checkout line. Her hair was done up in a horsetail like Bettie Page's, tied with a blue patterned scarf that brought out the color in her eyes. As the cashier rang up my items, Heather looked at me thoughtfully and said, "Is it true about Robby heading to college?"

She knew who I was only because of my brother, but I was flattered that someone like Heather *would* know me. "We're hoping so, sure," I answered awkwardly.

She smiled at me big. "That's amazing. You all must be so proud of him, getting out of Parson like that. Do you live nearby? I could help you carry your groceries."

As always, I was rattled at the thought of visitors to our home. "Not near here," I muttered vaguely, then took the bags and left.

I didn't see Heather again for a while. Not until the summer Joanna left to visit her father.

Before that summer Joanna and I were as close as two people can get: entwined, almost, so that our identities merged for everyone around us. Teachers knew better than to separate us in the classroom; whatever Aunt Cece cooked for me, she made double because Joanna might come over, too; Robby called Joanna our little sister; and Miss Kate had developed a way of running our names together—*JoannaLouisa*—that made me tingle with happiness whenever she said it.

Then, at the start of the summer before high school, Joanna climbed up beside me in the sycamore tree one day, trembling with excitement. She had news: she'd be spending the rest of the summer at her father's house in Michigan.

"Why?" I asked, stunned. I couldn't believe she'd leave Parson. Leave *me*.

She glanced away, realizing her mistake, that I wasn't about to join in her excitement. "No particular reason," she said, and I could tell she was hiding something. "I just wanted to get away from home for a while. So I wrote him and asked, and he sent me the tickets. Seth and I both are going."

Her words baffled me: why would anyone want to get away from

Miss Kate's house? I'd always resented Joanna a little for taking what she had—a real mother—for granted. Now I felt taken for granted as well, Joanna abandoning our beautiful summer together, for which we'd made so many plans. I told her I needed to get home early that day but went to the woods instead, threw rocks at a tree until my heart stopped racing.

When she and Seth left town, I started to spend time with Cass, their older sister. Until then, I hadn't known her all that well: she was four years older than me, untamed in a way that frightened as much as intrigued me. She'd stayed in Parson that summer to waitress at Town Line Diner, and one afternoon I stopped in for a milkshake, saw her in her waist apron, her starched white shirt. When she handed me my check, she told me she was heading to a party that night, told me that I should come, bring Danny along as well.

"Danny? Really?" I asked. Lots of parties in the '50s didn't welcome a Black kid showing up. "You're sure?"

"My friends will be cool," Cass said. Then, with a sly grin, "And if anyone gives him trouble, I'll slug 'em."

At first Danny seemed excited by the prospect of being invited to a high school party. But he said no anyway. "You know what happens to kids like me who go to parties with nice white girls?"

I couldn't argue with that, so I backed off. But Danny kept talking about the party, asking questions about who was going to be there and where the party was going to take place, and eventually he changed his mind, saying he'd go as long as we could set some ground rules: "We stick by the door. We wear shoes that are good to run in. Don't you tell anyone my last name or where my family works."

The party was at a barn on the ranch of Cass's friend—a senior whose parents were out of town for the weekend—and as we walked up the narrow dirt path, I could feel my feet sweating in my gym sneakers. But everyone at the barn was kind to us: no one mentioned our age or the color of Danny's skin. Danny wasn't the only Black kid there, either; a couple of older girls from Woodman were smoking Encores in the corner, plus a guy in a leather jacket who'd driven up from Corpus Christi. Not long after we arrived, the guy stood on a hay bale and read some poetry while everyone sat and listened, snapping their fingers instead of applauding whenever he took a triumphant pause. After this the music and dancing started, and I never thought in a million years I'd be brave enough to join in, but then Cass walked us over to the beer cooler, and no one tried to stop me as I popped a tab and took a precocious chug, and soon enough we'd gotten good and drunk—Danny and me for our very first time—and were dancing with wild abandon to the rockabilly and jazz blasting from the stereo. Suddenly gone was the awkwardness that had plagued our adolescence, Danny's need to linger close to the exit; we felt like new people, untethered and free.

All summer we chased that feeling of freedom, Cass more than happy to help us. By the middle of June she'd bought a car, a beat-up old Clipper, and the salt wind whipped through our hair as we breezed down the oceanside roads with the windows down. We'd find an abandoned stretch of beach and lie there without a blanket, laughing and talking and passing a joint while we stared up into the starlight. We'd drive just to drive, the radio blaring Nat King Cole and Tony Bennett, or we'd end up at some party, smoking and drinking and dancing to Tito Puente. When Danny was busy, she'd take me to the movies—*Land of the Pharaohs, Lady and the Tramp,* whatever was playing.

All that time, the memory of Joanna flickered, wavered, at the edges of my mind. I still felt rejected when I thought of her, and during our one long-distance phone call from her father's house, I was tongue-tied for the whole five minutes, uncertain what to say. How could I explain what this summer meant to me, this joyful, freeing summer that she'd chosen not to share with us? I blamed her for leaving Parson, thought it selfish and silly of her. I never considered, not even once, that something might have driven her away.

The next time I saw Heather, I didn't recognize her at first. Cass had driven us out to a party at the hunting lodge of some rich boy's family, and she disappeared—as she tended to do—not long after we stepped into the swirl of bodies and music. The mounted heads of deer and antelope stared out soberly over the teenagers; pot smoke drifted up in the rafters. Left on my own here with Danny, I felt vulnerable: this place didn't have the casual feel of Cass's beatnik parties, where everyone made a point—sometimes too big a point—of being cool with Danny there. I realized quickly, though not as quickly as Danny, that everyone else here was white.

I took his hand. "You wanna sit down someplace?"

We grabbed a beer apiece and staked out some chairs in a corner. I could sense we were drawing attention, and Danny pointedly dropped my hand when we noticed some gazes lingering on our interlaced fingers. I laughed awkwardly, but Danny wasn't in a laughing mood.

"We can go," I told him. "Cass shouldn't have brought us here."

"No, it's all right," he said. "She drove us all the way out here. We might as well stay for a bit."

We started the serious task of drinking enough to forget ourselves and join in with the dancing—always our favorite part of the night. After a while Danny loosened up, got to talking about the next year at school. We'd both be starting ninth grade, but Danny would stay at Woodman Secondary, which made no distinction between junior high and high school.

"I wish I was moving on to something new," he said. "I'm sick of those ratty old classrooms."

"You're lucky. You don't have to figure out a whole new school, new people to keep happy. Bet your classes are easier, too. Hell, I doubt you even *have* trigonometry there."

I'd meant to make him feel better, but he only seemed tense, even a little pissed. He started looking around the lodge—for Cass, I assumed—and I joined him in gazing out at the dancers. The night felt wrong to me, and I would have been happy to leave this party, spend the rest of the hours out driving.

That was when I spotted her. The lights were low in the lodge and gave the room a murky underwater quality, but she caught my eye as if illuminated in a spotlight, her hair loose and wild and curled elaborately like Rita Hayworth's. She wore a tight green skirt and a tight pearl-colored blouse, and I couldn't look away.

At first she was just a beautiful dancer, effortless, enticing, but after a few glances I realized I knew this girl. This was the Heather whom the boys fawned over, who had talked with me in the grocery store that day. A second later I noticed her dancing partner, a well-built guy a few steps back from Heather, far more constrained as he shook his hips. It was Robby.

He noticed me at almost the same moment, looking over as he sipped from a soda bottle. He laughed and took Heather's hand, led her to where we were sitting.

"Lou," he said, sounding surprised. "That's not *beer* you're drinking, is it?"

My instinct was to put down the bottle, but I'd been imitating Cass lately: I arched an eyebrow in challenge and smiled. "Why, you want some?"

Robby laughed again. "So *this* is what you've been doing all summer? I was wondering. And you, too, Danny? Leading my kid sister down a wicked path?" He clicked his teeth in mock disapproval.

"She's not a kid anymore, Robby," Heather said. She held out a hand to me, pulled me up from my chair. "You're going to be in high school next year, aren't you?"

I nodded, again amazed that this girl knew anything about me.

"See, Robby? Almost in high school. A perfect time to start partying." Then, with a smile at Danny, "Well? Aren't you two going to dance?"

Cass returned to the main room, airy and giggling and twirling, and found us all dancing together to a fast Cajun beat, arms above our heads, feet echoing off the floor planks. Cass shrieked and jumped when she saw us, and we yelled in ecstatic greeting as if we hadn't seen her in years, and then Danny was handing me another drink and the night turned fuzzy and pulsing. One of Robby's football friends, Adam Stanton, strode up to our circle, and at first I thought he might make trouble about Danny—he was looking at Danny sideways with an ugly frown—but then Robby threw an arm around Danny and shouted at Adam, "Hey, why aren't you dancing?" and I guessed that endorsement was enough for Adam, because he stopped looking at Danny and started to move with the music. Everything was fine then, and it seemed the night might just be fun, until Adam started dancing too close to me, brushing up against me every song, and crossing a definite line when he playfully mussed my hair. I was about to stomp his foot with the heel of my boot—an accident; *so sorry!*—when Heather took my arm and drew me outside into the night.

I thought she'd come out to smoke a cigarette—the kind of sexy, grown-up thing I imagined Heather would do—but all she did was walk me in circles out in the yard behind the lodge, her arm linked through mine. My skin hummed where our bare arms touched, soldered together with sweat, the skin drawing apart at times as if from the soft seal of a kiss. After a moment she asked me, "Do you know if Robby's seeing anyone?"

So Heather wanted to date him, make it serious, official. This was wonderful news for Robby—he'd adored her for over a year—but with her slender arm in mine, with her flowery perfume mingling with the white honeysuckle that grew around the lodge, I couldn't help feeling disappointed as I answered, "He doesn't have a girlfriend or anything like that. If that's what you're asking."

"You sure? He seems . . . I don't know. Distracted."

"He's always distracted. Football, scholarships."

"Sure," she said. "Sure." Then, "After college, he wouldn't settle down here, would he? He wouldn't want to *stay* in Parson, right?"

The question startled me. "Why wouldn't he?"

"Oh, lots of reasons. People who go to college, they usually leave here for good. There's a whole wide world out there. Why stay in the same place your entire life?"

For a flash I thought of my mother, the early tumbleweed years that Robby and I had spent with her on the road, cooped up in small motel rooms, eating out of grocery sacks, ignored by the gaunt men who'd take us into their home for a few weeks. That was what leaving, moving around, meant to me: it was a notion incompatible with home, devoid of any stability, and it frightened me to think about.

"Robby's not that way," I said. "His family is here. Why would he want to be away from his family?"

"Well, I'm sure he'd visit," she said easily. "Besides, someday you might want to leave Parson, too."

I almost disagreed with her, insisted that I'd never leave, that *home* was far more important than some "wide world." Instead I let my worries slip into the haze of this tipsy night, the smell of the honeysuckle, the dome of stars curved gloriously above us. I focused on her warm arm, how our hips brushed now and then, the sound of her hair shifting in the summer wind.

I wish that summer could have lasted forever, so full of discovery and promise. But then school started up again, with all its demands and pressures, and the freedom of the summer was consigned to the weekends, and then only if there happened to be a party. Everyone drank harder at these parties, as if determined to cram the fun of a whole week into one night, and there were more fights, more sickness, more car rides home when we knew Cass shouldn't be driving.

Not to mention that things had changed between Joanna and me.

After her trip up north, she had seemed much the same—if maybe a little happier—but I felt like a language barrier had formed between us. She'd speak of her father, so generous, so brilliant, of the museums and concerts and restaurants he'd lavished on her all summer, and her voice would turn to static in my ears. I couldn't see myself in that up-scale world, and it made me jealous, resentful. Nor did she show much interest in my summer of driving and parties.

"My father says drinking like that is a substitute for real culture," she said to me one Saturday after I invited her to a party at a senior's house.

She'd always talked like that—prim, stiff, formal—and I used to find it fancy and impressive. Now it irritated me. "So you don't want to go?"

"I think I'll pass."

Snob, I thought involuntarily, and was stunned to discover I meant it, that I really thought something negative about her. Three months ago, this would have seemed impossible.

In our homeroom, Mrs. Rin didn't know that Joanna and I were supposed to sit together, so we found ourselves on opposite sides of the classroom, too bashful in that new high school setting to make any complaint. For the rest of the day, I saw little of Joanna, all her classes but home economics at a higher level than mine. However much I loved her, however much I felt one with her, high school had revealed a stark difference between us: she was book-smart, meant for bigger things than Parson, and I was something else, headed nowhere. This hurt me, scared me, but I also thought, *Well, isn't this what happens sometimes? Don't friends from childhood sometimes grow apart?* I was committed to our friendship, but maybe there was a future where we wouldn't be entwined, where I'd look back on my time with Joanna with nothing but nostalgia. It seemed possible, even likely.

Or so I thought then. As it turned out, those first few weeks of high school would be the only time when I slipped from Joanna's spell, that cosmic pull, the sense that she defined my entire life. She would leave Parson soon, and we wouldn't talk for over a decade, but I'd still be living in the world she'd created for me.

One Friday night in September we drove out to the promontory and parked in the shadows along the side of the huge abandoned mansion, Parson House. It was me and Danny and Cass and her friend from the school play, Thomas Wick. Joanna opted to stay home and study.

Cass had heard of a way to break into the mansion, which none of us quite believed, but it turned out to work: we just had to climb the garden wall and make our way to the cellar door, which was chained shut but loosely enough to slip through if you tried, all four of us wriggling carefully into that musty, absolute darkness, barely punctured by the wisp of Thomas's Zippo. I was holding on to Danny's arm; I wouldn't have admitted it, wouldn't have blown my cool, but this house spooked the hell out of me, thrilled me, too. I'd come here as a kid on the museum tour, but it had since transformed into something else, a place where your shadow might run away from you, where Bela Lugosi might come rising from a coffin.

Down in the cellar we groped for the stairs, stumbled into heaps of stored furniture, great crates cloaked in cobwebs. Thomas said something about a murder here, and Danny yelped out in fear, and I said, trying not to sound scared, "There wasn't a murder here. They would have told us on the tour," and Cass laughed at all of us and shouted that she'd found the bottom stair.

Fifteen years after that night, I couldn't remember anything else about that trip to Parson House. This was because of my head injury, I figured, and I wondered if it was also something I'd seen, if my mind had decided to wash those memories clear. I knew the facts about that night, but I couldn't recall them happening, nothing beyond me holding Danny's arm down in the cellar, walking with him toward the bottom stair. I could smell his sweat, feel him tremble, and I felt comforted for some reason, as if Danny were absorbing the fear for both of us.

Later that night, as we left the mansion, Cass's car swerved off the road and went crashing into a deep ditch by the roadside. None of us walked away unscathed: Thomas was taken to the nearest hospital, where his five broken bones were reset; Danny was ambulanced all the way to Corpus Christi—because the local hospital took only whites—and needed two weeks of care before he left with a permanent scar on his forehead; I was uninjured except for a harsh, dizzying ringing in my head that came and went for months after; and Cass died in the hospital.

Less than a week after the accident, the official from the school board crashed our dinner with Cece, demanding documents we couldn't provide. We braced for what would come next, so we weren't surprised, a few days later, when the school principal called Robby and me to his office. Mr. James was a big, upbeat man, bald save for a rim of hair, with a gray mustache and baggy dress shirts that never stayed tucked in; his eyes always looked moist, like he'd just stepped out of a windstorm. He told us in an apologetic voice what we'd already guessed: that he'd learned some "information" about us "from a source he couldn't name," information about our family connections, which he'd taken to the school board, and which the board had been investigating. He said he was "heartbroken" about all of this—especially losing a star quarterback like Robby—but there were "protocols to follow here," and "sorry, kids, my hands are tied." If our white parentage couldn't be established, then we'd have to transfer to Woodman Secondary. As I listened to him talk, I saw Robby's football scholarship blinking out of existence around us, his future erased as if by the flip of a switch.

By then I was even more certain Joanna had told Mr. James. She'd been ducking me for days, avoiding my eyes in homeroom, turning the other way when she saw me in the hall, not returning my phone calls. I knew she'd just lost her sister, but I couldn't understand why she was avoiding me—surely she'd be eager for the opportunity to have someone to talk to about how she was feeling? I was so weak with my headaches, so stunned by Cass's death, that I couldn't put in more effort to reach her. I'd been keeping my personal life from Aunt Cece the past few months—she had no clue about my partying; my skill at keeping secrets had paid off here—but I was so upset about Joanna that I broke down and asked her advice. Cece stroked my hair and said, "Honey, the poor girl just lost her sister. Can you imagine losing Robby, how would you feel? She probably just needs a little time."

I could accept Joanna's grief, that she would take some distance from me. But at some point the grief turned angry, turned vengeful, turned into a plan to inflict her pain on me. She must have blamed me for her sister's death, a guilt by association; must have reasoned, in some grief-addled way, that if I hadn't been there, it wouldn't have happened. Maybe she blamed herself for not being there, was lashing out at me instead of facing her guilt. I never knew her reasons, because we never discussed it, why she betrayed me like that after years of friendship, the only person other than Danny whom I'd trusted with the truth about my aunt.

Numbly, still sore all over, my head ringing like an alarm, I walked with Robby through the empty halls to clean out our lockers. Mr. James watched with a sympathetic frown, absently tucking in a shirttail now and then. I could tell he wanted to usher us out before the change of classes, but I kept pausing and losing my focus, and then the bell rang and we were surrounded by an audience witnessing our shame as we picked up the books that wouldn't fit in our backpacks, as we turned and walked down the hall for the last time. I'd never felt more humiliated, more gutted and raw. I couldn't bear to raise my head and see the faces of my classmates, and I remembered the boys in fifth grade who'd fling pebbles at the girls leaving school, how we all had stood and watched them shrink and flee.

Then I did raise my head, and I caught sight of Joanna. She was standing among the others, her eyes wide, her face blank, a thumb curled under the strap of her satchel.

Over the years I'd gotten into dozens of fights for her. It was because of her that I had an instinct for violence: being close to something so soft had made me into something hard. I stared at her, this witch, this betrayer, and then I felt myself running, and I crossed the ground between us so fast she barely had time to respond, her hands not even up when my fingers gripped her hair, pulling her head down and bringing her face with force against my knee. She stumbled back and I flung out my fist and she didn't flinch away, as if she knew she deserved this. My knuckles screamed in pain as they hit the hinge of her jaw.

Then I was being seized, held, pulled away. I was shouting something, I don't remember what. I couldn't hear myself, couldn't hear the other voices, only that terrible ringing inside my skull. Joanna lay on the floor, staring at me in curious silence, until other bodies closed in and enfolded her from my sight. It was the last time I saw her until that night in Buck's parking lot.

And Robby and I, of course, went to Woodman Secondary School. It had fewer teachers, more crowded classes, some carpets that needed replacing, but it was recognizably school, with rigorous lessons and homework that made us ask for Cece's help. In fact, once we'd moved to our new school, Cece became much more involved in our lives outside of the home. Granbury High had been remote to her, a world where she had to remain invisible, but our new classmates were the children of Cece's friends, and she took pride in stepping up like other parents, helping with fundraisers for AV equipment the state refused to buy, or preparing lunches when the school's stoves went out. She kissed our cheeks on the stoop outside before we left for school, clapped the loudest at each graduation. On the whole, we felt more like a family than we had before, and Cece's friends dropped by the house more, joined us for dinners, which livened the place up considerably. It gave me a glimpse of how much she'd sacrificed, taking us in.

So I guess there were ways we had it better at Woodman. Only here, there were no illusions. No one at Woodman dreamed big things about their future, moving to a city or getting a white-collar job. Here, if your family had a trade, then you knew your future, and often you dropped out of school to help them full-time.

I was okay there: I'd never had dreams about a career, not really, and college seemed like something from books, not applicable to my own life. But this new atmosphere hit my brother hard. Woodman

Secondary had no football team, no sports teams at all; Robby exercised, went out running every morning, but I never saw him throw a ball again. As far as I remember, he never complained about this brutal change in his fortune, just seemed sadder, more broken down, more given to quiet spells, one too many beers. It shamed and hurt him to be around anyone who'd known him before, his buddies from Granbury or even good friends like Danny, who came around often enough to spend time with me but from whom Robby kept a careful distance. Heather, to her credit, stayed with Robby through all of this, even though he tried at first to push her away, even though her parents and her Granbury friends like Fay gave her grief about it. Heather must have been disappointed that Robby wasn't her ticket from Parson, but I never heard her complain, and when, a couple years after graduation, she turned up pregnant the first time, they got married. They lost that one before it was born, then two more before Sarah came along.

This was in 1966. Robby was twenty-six years old, about to be a father, when the draft board called him in for his interview. He was right at the upper range of age, and nearly all the draftees so far had been younger, fresh out of high school. None of us expected the board to choose him, especially not with Heather in her condition. But President Johnson had been escalating troop numbers in Vietnam; for this round, they were less choosy. Besides, Robby had always been strong, healthy—he was probably anyone's idea of a good soldier.

After this startling news, Heather and I researched deferments. He could put in for a hardship exception or argue the importance of his civilian duties—before the lottery, plenty of white draftees were granted reprieves if they went looking. But Robby had no interest. "The army'll pay for college," he said. "I'll finally get to go." Anyway, it was what you were supposed to do. Serve your country, fight for freedom: people in Parson never quite soured on that. All the while, I couldn't help tuning in to the news station chatter about student protests, about the dangers of combat, and I sensed a cloud of doom surrounding my brother despite all my attempts to ignore it.

It wasn't logical, but I couldn't avoid the feeling that Joanna had put the doom there, forcing our lives off-track all those years ago. Robby might have been drafted even if she'd never told on us, but getting kicked out of Granbury had taken the fight out of him, made him feel that he didn't deserve a deferment, a life any better than the one he was handed. As I watched Robby kiss Heather goodbye, gently touching the swell of her stomach, I was already thinking back over the past, Joanna's role in all of this. My brother never went to college, never improved his lot in life. He never even met his daughter, all because of Joanna and what she'd done.

17

When I got to Parson House in the morning, Joanna's blue Fairlane was nowhere in sight. I circled the property twice in my truck, even checked for her car in the dense foliage behind the storage shed. I should have guessed she'd start avoiding me now that she knew I wanted answers.

Today I was replacing the broken windowpanes on the ground floor of the mansion. This meant entering rooms I wasn't sure I felt ready to enter, even some rooms I'd never stepped foot in with Miss Kate.

As I got on with my work, my head was full of Cass. All this talk about Miss Kate, the kind of mother she'd been—Cass would have been the one to give me a straight answer. She'd been less sensitive than her siblings, tougher and more exuberant. And in Parson House, where her presence felt strongest, I couldn't help but wish she was here.

A memory floated back to me from the summer we'd gotten so close: parked in a dockside lot, sitting on the trunk of her Clipper, eating sandwiches wrapped in diner napkins while the sun set behind us and the bay scene in front of us lost its colors. Somehow we'd started talking about what had brought her family to Parson in the first place.

I'd heard Joanna's version of the story: after the divorce from their father, Miss Kate had moved the family to stay with her parents in

Louisiana, and it was there that Miss Kate had met Ed one night at a bar. The engagement and marriage had been swift, and afterward Ed had set up his new family in the only place he could imagine putting down roots: his hometown of Parson, where his parents and brothers lived.

Cass's version had the same shape, but she lingered over different details, like what Miss Kate had seen in Ed in the first place. "The way she was brought up, Mom didn't think a woman should be alone, not to mention with three kids to raise. And things were desperate—we were at my grandparents' house, the four of us jammed into a room, Mom and Jo and me in the same bed. Seth slept on the floor." I certainly hadn't heard these details from Joanna; she never implicated herself in the squalor of poverty. "But worst for Mom, I think, was just being at her old house again, her dad barking orders at her like when she was a kid. I think she might have married anyone to escape it. And Ed, he took on all four of us at once, even promised that Mom wouldn't have to work." Cass stared for a moment at the gray, fading horizon. "Or maybe she married him because he was the opposite of Dad."

"Opposite how?" I asked. I was hungry for details of their father, the man Joanna had abandoned me for that summer. Cass gave me a sidewise look, as if she'd picked up on the jealousy but didn't plan to tease me about it.

"Mom, she comes from plain Louisiana stock. Never dreamed much about leaving her town, never thought it'd be an option. Our dad's family was middle class; his father was a lawyer in town—that was a big deal where they came from. Dad planned to leave, educate himself. When Mom managed to snag him, she figured she'd be out of there forever."

"Why did they divorce?"

Cass laughed. "Bet you think I'm pretty upset about that. Truth is, I was so sick of the fighting—screaming late into the night, about bills, about us kids—I was *glad* when they told me they were breaking up. Dad was in school then, which I guess takes a long time—and longer when you've got three kids gumming up the works. There was never much money around, and Mom had expected a higher-class sort of living. For her second marriage, I think she wanted something she understood better. Something that looked more like her own parents. Well, she sure as hell got *that* wish." Cass kicked out her legs, and they thunked back against the Clipper, a soft timpani blast among the ugly chorus of seagull cries.

For a while we sat there, quiet. "I never want to be like that, you know?" Cass said at last. "Choosing something just because it's familiar. I want every mistake I make to be bigger and more beautiful than the last one."

My day at Parson House stretched on as I thought back over this scene, surprised at how vividly Cass's words returned to me. The memory didn't give me the answers I wanted—Cass hadn't brought up the abuse Seth had mentioned—but her words that day gave me an unsettled feeling. I got the sense that Cass was holding something back: there was a bitterness in her conclusion, a boundary line she was drawing between her mother's life and her own, that had made me uncomfortable even at the time. *You ought to be grateful you have a mother at all*, I'd wanted to tell her.

I need a little more, I begged her now. A silent prayer, as if she could hear me.

Before long I'd finished the panes in the kitchen, and my work brought me into the parlor. Miss Kate and I had never worked on the parlor, which she'd said was the room in the worst shape, one we'd tackle after we'd addressed more pressing problems in the house. Years ago, just before they moved out, the museum folks had used the parlor as a garbage room, piling up the furniture not good enough to store or sell, leaving behind their stacks of boxes instead of renting a dumpster.

I hadn't entered this room in decades. My last memory of it was from childhood, back in the museum days, wandering past the wall-length curtains, looking up at the play of sunlight in the facets of the crystal chandelier. Now, as I stood at the door, the thought of the room behind it frightened me for some reason.

I was hoping the knob wouldn't turn in my hand, that Miss Kate had locked it and Joanna never found the key. But the door swung open with a loud, relieved creak.

Until I stepped into the parlor, I thought I hadn't been here since grade school, when the space was all tufted sofas and marble-top tables. But now that I saw it, a graveyard of skeletal chairs and moldy cushions, I realized that, no, I'd been here more recently, I'd seen the parlor much like this before. We'd come here the night we broke in, the night of the car wreck, right at the start of my freshman year. Cass, Danny, Thomas Wick, and me.

But wait, not all of us came to the parlor. It was just Cass and me by that point. We'd lost Thomas and Danny somewhere else in the house.

Cass had a lighter. And we'd sat on that run-down love seat, the one over there across from the window. It was in better shape then, no mold spotting its legs, no water damage. The upholstery was flat enough that I could feel the springs in my seat bones. While we sat there in the dark, Cass had lit up a joint from her Black Cat cigarette tin, its flame end the only light between us.

What did we talk about? I knew we'd talked about something. But all I could remember was what it felt like to sit there, the smoke filling my lungs, the high soothing my fears of the mansion, time slowing down so that it felt like we'd been sitting in the parlor for hours, like maybe we lived here, like this was our home. Like we'd never have to leave if we didn't want to.

It's all right with me, you know. Those words came back to me. Cass said them, right here in this room, and I could remember how good they felt at the time, like all I'd ever hoped for, like drought-breaking rain. I tried to remember more of what she'd said—it hovered right at the edge of my awareness—but I was left with just those seven words, and with Cass's face in the flame of the lighter, superimposed over the room today in the harsh summer sunlight.

I sat down on the floor for a moment, staggered by the memory. It was the first time I'd ever recovered more of that night. It didn't feel like just a memory recovered but a part of Cass, a part of me as well.

Then I got started with the work, putting on my gloves to pick the jagged glass from the frames, heaping the pieces in a pile by the door. Each time I moved from the windows, I passed the love seat, and with each pass, the memory grew stronger. Not all at once but bit by bit, until the entire picture had formed, sepia-tinged like an old film: I could see myself seated on the center cushion and Cass sitting sideways against the scrollwork arm, her bare feet kicked up and rested along on my lap. Their weight like a seat belt holding me secure.

Giggling. The two of us giggling uncontrollably. Cass had been laughing so hard she'd snorted, and this had set us off laughing even harder.

"This room is a gas," she said, and then put on a Cockney accent, her impression of Eliza from *Pygmalion*, one of her best. "I feel like a right proper lady in this gaff."

The weed gave me courage to try the accent myself. "We likes a spot of class, we do!" It came out more Russian than anything, which caused another snort from Cass. I added, "Too bad them boys is missing it."

Which got us both laughing again. But even as I laughed, I was thinking of Danny somewhere else in this house, somewhere alone with Thomas. And it made me nervous, made me suck in a bigger hit when she passed the joint, cough as I let out the smoke.

"He's all right, isn't he?" I said when I got my breath back.

She'd known what I meant. "Thomas is a stand-up guy. He can be kind of an asshole, but, you know. Actors." She made an elaborate gesture. "If you're worried about Danny, don't. He'll be all right."

But I worried about him anyway. Danny had just stopped seeing someone, someone he wouldn't tell me about, and it had ended with bruises. Bruises I knew Cass had seen, too.

And then she'd invited Thomas along tonight like she'd planned for him to have time alone with Danny. Like she knew—even more than I did—what was going on with Danny, what he needed.

"It's all right with me, you know," she said, taking the joint from me. "Danny's different. And so are you. There's nothing wrong with it."

She said this softly, simply, like it was obvious, like any decent person would feel this way. Like I had nothing to hide, nothing to fear from my own desires. Never before then, not for a second, had I thought my desires might be okay, that there might be space in the world for what Danny and I were hiding. The fact that Cass had noticed, that she didn't have a problem with it, was beyond my wildest hopes. It healed a part of me I didn't even know was wounded.

And then, through the bay window before us, the flash of approaching headlights.

Today I stared through that same window, which overlooked the circular front drive. By now I'd picked the glass from the top of the frame and could see the violent blue of the sky, a color that seared me as badly as the heat. A curl of brackish sea air reached me, filled the room with the smell of the sea. The waves hissed and susurrated like conspirators.

I closed my eyes and the sunlight was gone: all I could see was that blazing joint end, and those headlights beaming through the window, and Cass making an exaggerated face of surprise at this unexpected arrival. She stuffed her Black Cat tin into a tear in the love seat's cushion.

I hadn't thought of her Black Cat tin in fifteen years. Surely it was long gone. Any one of the kids who'd sneaked in here over the years would have considered the joints inside a divine windfall. Even as I walked to the love seat, even as I slipped my hand down into the tear in the moldy cushion, I pictured the tin being carried off by some curious animal.

The last thing I expected to feel was the pinprick on my fingertips of its tiny, delicate hinges. I eased the tin from the cushion, tangled in mildewed batting but otherwise the same, as if fifteen years hadn't passed since Cass stood here in this parlor, slid it from her jeans, and asked, *Wanna smoke?*

It's been waiting for me, I thought, then smiled at the idea. I wanted to believe that Cass herself had protected the tin, saved it in the love seat for me to find.

Tenderly, trying not to break the rusted hinges, I prized the lid open.

The joints had degraded over time, and one of them had burst and spilled its ancient, dried-out innards. When I shifted the joints I saw, underneath them, a few slips of paper, the kinds of things Cass would have carried in her smoking tin. A torn-out page of an H.D. poem. An admission ticket to *Harvey*, the school play she and Thomas had acted in that last year. And an unstamped bus ticket from Houston to New York, dated for three days after she died.

18

Over the next few days I cleared the waste and garbage from the mansion, dumping the organic matter out in the bay, the rest in a heap in the yard. The rooms looked picked clean, like a field after the pests had come and gone. With the windows fixed and bare of vines, stripped of their ruined curtains, Parson House felt too full of sunlight, like these old rooms couldn't stand to be so illuminated and exposed. When the windows were open the sound of the sea came in and echoed everywhere, a pulsing swell of cymbals without end.

To clear the house I'd had to enter every room in the mansion, which took the breath out of me at times: either because I remembered the room and the memories made me uneasy, or because I *couldn't* remember, didn't know if I'd passed through there on that night with Cass and Danny. The house was like a labyrinth, like a strange expanding space in one of Joanna's fantasy novels; even after I'd scraped the rooms clean, I kept expecting to stumble into some new stairwell or gallery, or to open a door and discover Cass and me passing a joint as teenagers. *Want to join us?* they'd ask me.

On Sunday I decided to get a later start than usual. I woke up early, though, because I had a different plan for my morning. While Heather slept, I dug around quietly in the kitchen drawer where I'd stashed the Jehovah's Witnesses pamphlet, the notecard that gave the time and address of their service. There was nowhere I wanted to go less, but if someone had a message for me, or information about Miss Kate, I needed to hear it.

The building hardly looked like a church to me, a squat windowless structure at the back of a dusty parking lot, arid fields stretched out on either side. But those strange words from the notecard—*Kingdom Hall*—were carved into the wooden sign out front. It was 8:02 a.m., and the lot was empty except for a dozen cars parked flush against the building, no stragglers walking in, no other cars pulling up late. This was clearly a punctual bunch.

Inside, the small congregation was singing a hymn to an instrumental record; several heads turned in my direction. I sat in the back row, self-conscious about the work clothes I was wearing: boots, overalls, a T-shirt. All the other women wore long skirts and blouses with high collars, like Peg had dressed in when I was a kid. Even the children looked stiff and starched, didn't wiggle in their seats. It was still the '50s here.

After the hymn ended, an elderly man in a gray suit stood up on the dais in front. "If I might direct you to your pamphlets," he said in a shockingly young-sounding voice, "our lesson today is entitled 'Proving Ourselves to Be Men of Goodwill.'"

There was a universal shuffling of pages. I noticed the shelf under my seat, pulled out the pamphlet stowed there, and followed along. The old man read the lesson to us exactly as it was printed, and I found the sentences a little hard to track—all *Christ the Lord* this and *army of heavenly angels* that—but it didn't take a Bible scholar to grasp its grim message: that only a few men had the "goodwill" of Jehovah God, that "according to all the facts and figures" the world was ending soon, and the Witnesses had to be ready.

When the man had finished this delightful lesson, he began to ask us the discussion questions underneath it. Hands flew up all over the room. Instead of giving their own thoughts, however, the congregants just read out the answers printed in the pamphlet, given in footnotes at the bottom of the page. They read them word for word, in an eerily composed monotone. "That was an excellent insight, Sister Carter," the old man would say in response, or "Very interesting connections there, Elder Schafer." Each congregant straightened their spine when the old man called on them, as if reading these footnotes aloud was a real honor.

Something about the robotic performance chilled me, and I almost sneaked out before the seemingly interminable service ended. But someone in this room had invited me, might have a message for me, and they must have noticed me in back: the only person here who'd made it out of the Eisenhower era, who didn't look like a picture from an old Sears catalog.

Sure enough, after the dismissal hymn was over, an older woman walked up to me in the lobby. I recognized her as one of the honored question-readers from the service.

"You're Louisa Ward, aren't you?" she asked.

I told her I was.

"Thank you so much for worshipping with us," she said. "I'm Sister Carter. Sister Ruben and I are the ones who left you the pamphlet. I'm so sorry she couldn't be here today to welcome you, too—she hasn't been feeling well. She'll be delighted to hear you came."

"Is this how things go every week?" I said, too curious not to ask.

"Mostly, yes. Though sometimes there's a visiting speaker down from one of the cities."

I wondered if the visiting speaker drove all that way to read from the pamphlet, too. Sister Carter went on: "There's a reason we invited you here today, Louisa. Sister Ruben and I, we're worried for you."

I tensed. This "worry" might be about Heather, our long-term living arrangement. I readied my denials—*she's my sister-in-law, my brother died, I'm helping take care of their baby*—the words that always stuck like stones high in my throat.

"We know you're friendly with Margaret Muller," she said, "and we just wanted to warn you about her. Calls herself Peg now. Did you know she used to be a sister here? One of the most devout. Then she started stirring up trouble. Her and Kate Darnell together."

My instinct was to defend them, but I needed to hear what this eerie woman had to say. "What sort of trouble?"

Sister Carter pursed her lips as if considering what to reveal. "Those women—they've done irreparable harm to this community. But all of that's in the past. It's not the past I want to warn you about. It's the future."

"What do you mean?"

"Politics, public life, all these earthly things. These are not for us:

our world is the world to come." Her face was stony, serious. "Suffering is to be endured as Jehovah's will. Peg used to believe this, used to await the resurrection. But does she still? I'm not so sure. If you want the true faith, Louisa, you should worship with us here. Not with Peg and those other women she's led astray. She and Kate Darnell."

I was getting the sense that Sister Carter wasn't big on Peg's charity work, helping out the women in Parson. *Suffering is to be endured* didn't sound much like women's rights. I told her she'd given me a lot to consider, but, oh no, I had an appointment in town, I was about to be late.

"Well, do come back," she said. "Next time you can stay for the second hour of service."

Kate and Peg used to go there? I marveled as the Kingdom Hall shrank in my rearview mirror. I tried to picture them twenty years ago—prim, modest women, their blouses buttoned to the neck—so different from the vibrant friends who'd laughed over morning tea at Parson House. They must have gotten something out of the faith, but for the life of me, I couldn't figure out what.

Back home, Heather was up and about, making breakfast. She hadn't expected me, and she greeted me with a kiss, poured the batter for an extra pancake. It was good to spend some time together, even though I felt guilty for all that I was keeping from her these days: I was no stranger to concealing secrets, but this amount of subterfuge was a burden even for me, and lately just looking at Heather made me feel guilty. We chatted easily enough, but I also noticed the tension in her movements, the pointed way she didn't ask where I'd been. Part of me wanted to tell her about my surreal experience at the Kingdom Hall, or to go even further and reveal the head-twisting world of mystery and memory I'd fallen into since Joanna returned. I knew I couldn't leave Parson until I understood. And if I tried to explain to Heather, she'd just tell me to forget the past, to stop this desperate digging for answers, that carrying on like this would only serve to keep us from leaving Parson even longer. I was already putting Heather through so much.

Right around ten-thirty, Heather and I heard a car horn sound in a quick tattoo out front.

"There's Danny," I said, dabbing my mouth with a napkin and standing up. He'd offered to help me haul trash from Parson House out to the dump this morning. He and Heather had never been close, so he usually honked outside instead of knocking at the door.

"You two be safe out there, now," Heather said as she walked me to the door. I could tell she didn't want me to go, and I wished I could stay as well, spend a lazy morning in bed with her, wrapped up in her arms. But if I ever wanted to finish with Parson House, then all the old things needed hauling away.

I met Danny out at his truck, slid into the passenger seat. We were wearing near-identical overalls, and we laughed at this as he pulled out of the driveway. Though I'd fought with him just a few days ago, neither of us mentioned that now, nor had it come up on the phone yesterday when I'd asked if he could help me with some dump runs. We were good at letting things go. One reason I loved being with Danny was that he didn't mind that I preferred to exist in the present, let time and silence swallow up the past. Lately, however, it felt like the past was swallowing me.

The whole ride out to the mansion, Danny was anxious, adjusting his grip on the wheel, shifting in his seat. Finally, in a spirit of mercy, I told him, "Joanna probably won't be there. She doesn't hang around the house much these days."

"Oh, sure," he said, like it didn't matter. But he wasn't shifting anymore.

Just as I expected, Danny's truck was the only vehicle out on the promontory. Joanna's absence the past few days had done nothing but fuel my suspicions of her, and I was biding my time, knowing she'd need to show her face at the mansion sooner or later. Part of me enjoyed this cat-and-mouse game, the sudden shift in our dynamic, the knowledge that my presence here was powerful enough to keep her away from Parson House. When she came back, I'd be ready for her.

Danny wasn't much for silence, and he kept up an easy patter as we loaded the truck bed with rugs and chairs and curtains from the pile, both of us sweating as the sun scaled the sky. It would be a long, exhausting day, and I owed him breakfast and lunch at the very least. Soon the truck bed was full, and we climbed in the cab and set out to the dump across town, glad to cool down in the sea breeze that came flowing through the open windows, the radio playing the steady snare hits of "Suspicious Minds." Everything felt easy and natural for a moment, though I did notice Danny restlessly checking his rearview mirror.

After we emptied the truck, we drove back through town and stopped at Rosette's, a tiny taqueria where we'd eaten since we were kids, closing next month if the rumors were true, though there were a few patrons there when we walked in. I led us to a table in the corner, where, once we'd sat down, I reached in the pocket of my work pants and, after hesitating a moment, took out Cass's Black Cat tin and set it between our place mats.

Danny's face lit up at once. "Wow, where'd you get that? Cass had one just like it."

"I know," I said, giving him a significant look, voice low as if anyone were around to hear us.

His eyebrows twitched toward his hairline. "You've had it all this time?"

"Just found it in the house the other day. Cass left it there that last night. You know, when we broke in."

Normally we never discussed the past, never went further back than the last few months. It felt thrilling to talk about Cass, that girl who, in just one summer, had made us feel whole and accepted in a way we'd never imagined possible. Danny leaned forward, gingerly lifted and opened the tin.

When he saw the ancient joints he smiled, then glanced around to check that no one was watching him, a Black man with drugs in broad daylight. Except for two old women playing bridge in the corner, staring at their cards with a passionate focus, the dining area was empty. He withdrew the little slips of paper, chuckled at the *Harvey* ticket, the lines of poetry. Then he saw the bus ticket. His mouth tightened into a small frown "Oh," he said.

"You knew about that?"

He considered this. "Not exactly. Not that she'd bought a ticket.

But she always talked about it. Getting out." He tapped the ticket fondly. "New York, too. Just her style."

Cass had been planning to move, not even finish high school. All these years later, it had the power to hurt me—that she'd leave Parson, abandon us without so much as a goodbye. Didn't she know how much we needed her, how much she meant to us?

Even as the hurt hit me, I felt a deep sadness for Cass. If she'd wanted to go, if she'd been working so hard to plan for it, the tragedy of her sudden death felt even sharper. She could have bought a bus ticket for a week earlier and might still be alive.

"She tell you why she wanted to leave?" I asked, trying to keep the hurt from my voice. Danny's sympathetic look told me how well that went.

He slipped the papers back into the tin, closed it with a careful click. After a pause he said quietly, "Maybe you'd better talk about this with Joanna."

I stared at him as if to say: *You're holding out on me? Really?*

"Look," he said, "I know you loved Miss Kate. The last thing I want to do is . . . She was important to you, Lou. And she's gone now. So is Cass."

"This is all fifteen years ago. I'm a grown adult. You can tell me. "

"All right, all right. I don't know much. Just what I saw for myself sometimes. Miss Kate . . . she wasn't right. Maybe she'd settled down a bit by the end. But she wasn't a good mother to those kids."

More of what I'd heard from Seth. "She hit them, is that it?" I said, hearing the impatience in my voice.

He shrugged, uneasy. "I'm not sure if she did. Not that I saw. It was more . . . It was different than that. Like it wasn't their bodies she was trying to control. More their thoughts, their feelings, who they were."

"Isn't that just parents?"

He looked out the window beside us to our boarded-up Main Street, stretching in its dusty disuse. "So one time, right? Joanna had brought home a book from school, maybe seventh grade. It wasn't for class or anything; I think her teacher loaned it to her, said she would like it. Anyway, Miss Kate flipped through a few pages, saw the book had some magic in it—witches, fairies, that sort of thing—which went against the teachings of her church. And what did Miss Kate do? She *tore it apart*. Like, right in front of us, page after page, ripping them out. Then told Joanna she wouldn't be eating dinner for the next three days. Joanna was crying, said it was her teacher's book, and Miss Kate called her a liar, said Joanna wouldn't be eating dinner for *five days* now. That was the one time Joanna opened up to me about Kate—when she went running out of the house and I went after her. I asked her had things like this happened before. She said it was pretty common."

I'd never seen Miss Kate act this way; I wanted to minimize the story, even deny it. That sounded impossible. There was no way that could have been happening without my realizing it. Was there?

I did remember that, around seventh grade, Joanna had started giving some of her favorite books to me, insisting I borrow them from her and then never asking for them back. She'd read them over at my house, change the subject if I mentioned her bringing them home.

And there were the dinners at Miss Kate's house—more than a few, now that I thought about it—when Joanna said she had no appetite, wouldn't even bring a plate to the table. I'd just thought she was being difficult.

Then I remembered Cece cooking double for Joanna, heaping more food on her plate than anyone else's, and Joanna, despite her petite size, always eating everything set before her. I remembered she was rounder in the face when she came back from her father's house, her cheeks no longer so hollow. She looked happier than I'd ever seen her.

"And the screaming," Danny said with a wince. "I saw that a few times, too. Miss Kate controlled herself around you and Robby, but me? Joanna's friend from the *mixed school*? No point. That woman would get angry about anything—an unmade bed, something Cass had said, a dirty dish—and she'd gather all three of them in the living room, make them sit there while she told them off for hours. And I do mean *hours*, Lou. One day she got mad at us right after school, and by the time I made it home, the sun was setting."

I could feel my foot jiggling under the table, a dull heat behind my eyes. I wasn't sure if I should hear more, but I couldn't stop myself. "What . . . what would she say to them?"

"What rotten kids they were. Ungrateful, spoiled, sinful. Cass was dangerous, a slut. Seth was a weakling—they were worried he was the wrong way. And Joanna was just like her father: stuck-up, pompous, useless." He shook his head bitterly. "What she'd say about their father, blow by blow, sin by sin, all these old arguments they'd had, like she was reliving all of them in her head. This happened in front of me, I don't know, at least half a dozen times. Who knows how often when I wasn't there. It made sense that all three kids kept out of that house as much as they could."

Danny's words were sinking into me, dropping down fast into the wells of my childhood memory, going off like a depth charge. I'd distrusted Seth when he told me these things, but I knew beyond any doubt that Danny was telling the truth. I didn't want to accept this about Miss Kate, but now I had no choice.

I remembered that night at Parson House, Seth knocking the spoon off the counter, going quiet, skipping dinner because he'd spilled some sauce on the floor. At the time I'd thought him neurotic, but maybe he was afraid of his mother's reaction. I tried to remember Miss Kate's face at that moment: Had she been angry with her son? Upset about the mess? Guilty about his cowed response?

I didn't know how I'd missed all this—the truth about a family I'd known, a home I'd visited, for years. I'd loved Miss Kate, loved Joanna, would have done anything for them. So I guessed I'd seen only what they wanted me to see, what I'd wanted to see myself. I remembered now, too late, Cece's story about Santa, my refusal to see the truth even when the evidence was right in front of me. What an idiot I had been.

Danny was staring at the Black Cat tin. "I'm surprised Cass didn't leave earlier, to be honest. When she talked about it, she said she'd bring me with her if I wanted to go."

That one hurt. "I didn't know you wanted to leave."

"Back then? Sure I did. Or it's more like I wanted the option." He kicked me softly under the table, a friendly thud on my ankle. "No moping, you. I was entitled to feel that way. You got a taste of that dead-end school . . . no money, no hopes, and I had it better than most kids. At least I had Dad's shop waiting for me. But it did depress me sometimes, that my future was already written out for me." He nudged the tin on the table. "Cass was planning to write her own. She probably wanted to leave as soon as she got that Clipper." He smiled. "But that car, hell, that never would've made it to New York. Remember how often we'd pull off the road, need to let the engine cool down?"

"That was a good thing. Gave her time to sober up."

I hadn't meant to evoke this part of the past, but there it was: Cass had died driving the Clipper, maybe because of the weed we'd smoked in the parlor or the wine Cass had brought along. Not that I remembered the crash itself. I remembered only fragments of later that night and the harsh ringing that had started in my head.

The stretch of road where we'd crashed was so empty and abandoned, we were lucky to be found before morning. It was actually Robby and his friends who came across the wreck that night, cruising around in Adam Stanton's Buick. Their headlights caught me as I stood in the middle of the road, blood spattered on my shirt, having stumbled away from the wreck. I had no memory of this; maybe I was delirious, or maybe I was looking for help. To their credit, those football players didn't waste any time: they loaded me up in the Buick, rushed off to call an ambulance for the others. Robby got me back home, sneaked me in without waking Cece, and stayed by my side all night as I vomited into a bucket. He helped clean me up, brought me water, knelt beside me, and prayed, the only time I'd seen him pray outside of church.

"Should I go to the hospital?" I asked him groggily at one point.

He shook his head rapidly. "You want them to find out what you've been smoking? You want to get the police involved? Adam's dad is a cop—he'll get this all hushed up."

"But Robby, my head . . ."

"You'll be all right. You just need some sleep."

I woke up just past dawn, queasy and confused, and saw Robby asleep on the floor beside my bed. I couldn't keep awake for long, drifted off again. The next thing I remember is Aunt Cece's voice from the living room, crying on and off as she talked on the phone.

Danny and I were both lost in our thoughts on the drive back to Parson House, and he switched off the radio when some bouncy

Frankie Valli tune came on. I could tell there were things he was leaving unsaid, glimpses of that summer flashing up inside his mind, maybe for the first time in years. That Black Cat tin had done a number on us: we'd talked more about the past in that taqueria than in the last decade. As for me, I couldn't stop thinking about Miss Kate, what life had really been like for Joanna and her siblings.

I was beginning to see why Joanna might have pushed her mother off the balcony, a motive that ran deeper than any monetary gain. Miss Kate had made life hell for her children, given Seth and Joanna nervous conditions, driven Cass to the wild behavior that killed her. She'd pushed her religion down their throat, made them hide the abuse at home, pretend they were a normal, happy family, that Joanna was so skinny because she skipped dinner sometimes, what was a mother to do? Maybe Joanna hadn't even planned the murder; maybe that quiet, sullen, repressed young woman had lashed out in violence after a lifetime of bottling her anger; maybe, the night of the rainstorm, Joanna, divorced and broke, had come to ask her mother for a loan, the money to continue her doctorate—Miss Kate owned a mansion, so Joanna must have assumed she could afford some tuition; maybe Miss Kate had said the wrong thing to her, some insult from childhood, some barb about Joanna's father, *You're just like him, so hoity-toity, but what about your soul?* and Joanna had surprised herself by rushing at the old woman, shoving her so hard that she'd gone right over the railing, down into the tangled, chittering darkness of the garden below. Maybe the mansion was an afterthought to Joanna, too much money to pass up, especially if you had someone local to help you.

It was easy enough to imagine, this scenario of the murder. I could see myself doing the same, losing control, lashing out at someone who'd ruined my life so completely.

Or maybe someone else had pushed Miss Kate: Ed, her estranged husband, come back to town that night; Seth, her moody son, another victim of her abuse, who'd finally had enough. Maybe other people had wanted her dead as well. The Jehovah's Witnesses, the police. I now understood how little I'd known Miss Kate while she was alive, how I'd seen her as the mother I wanted, not as the woman she was. Maybe this was what she'd loved in me—I still believed she'd loved me—that I was a daughter who knew her as the perfect mother, as the mother she wished she'd been to her own children.

This had made me the only child who'd try to avenge her.

As Danny turned onto the road to the promontory, as the slim brick chimneys of Parson House blurred into sight on the horizon, I knew I'd feel real peace only when I had the answers to my questions, when I understood Miss Kate and Joanna. These were the people who had shaped me, who had formed my love and hate. But could I ever get these answers? Was it reasonable to expect them? Or did most people just live this way, pressed down to the earth by the gravity of their confusion, burdened and buckling under the mysterious weight of the past?

Absorbed in these thoughts, I barely noticed how often Danny was checking his rearview mirror. On the ride to the dump, I'd assumed he was watching so no trash fell out of the truck bed, but the bed was empty now. Finally I said, "What you looking at back there?"

He gestured with his chin. "That Camaro."

I turned around in my seat and saw it: a sleek black Camaro kicking up a cloud of dust, the only other car on this desolate dirt road.

"So what?" I asked.

"It's following us."

"It is? How long?"

"All day. Since we left for the dump." Danny's eyes were narrowed as he looked into the mirror, a wary, sour toughness on his face. "Not the first time someone's followed me in this damn town."

This was a side of Danny I liked, the side that would put up with bullshit only so long. He was a sweetheart most of the time, but he could make a point when he wanted, stand up for himself or others when someone went too far. It was rare, but people remembered, gave him a grudging respect. Not until high school had Danny found this strength, after the car wreck and his injuries, after Cass died and Joanna fled from town.

The Camaro looked like it would follow us right to Parson House. But then it took a right turn down a side road, disappeared amid its dust.

"That was strange," I said.

"Assholes," he muttered.

Then something occurred to me: I'd seen a Camaro at the turnoff the other night, when I'd gone back to the mansion to gather my tools. It was almost certainly the same car. Parson once was full of cars like that—sporty, aspirational cars that spoke of economic optimism—but you didn't see many in town these days.

"You know," I said, "I think I recognize that car."

"Me, too, actually. I think we worked on it at the shop. I got the license."

I smirked. "What will you do? Call the police?"

He chuckled. "That's a good one."

*Neither of us could shake that claustrophobic feeling of being fol-*lowed, so after we finished our work for the day, we headed to Danny's shop to look at his ledgers. Danny's grandfather had opened the shop in his early twenties, a squat tan building with *Joe's Auto* painted on the front, when it opened, the only garage in town that serviced the cars of non-white customers. All the boys of the family were raised to work there, and Danny was the most talented of his generation; he'd been the one to inherit when his father retired, but he had two brothers who helped him out sometimes. Curtis, Danny's younger brother whom I'd known a little at school, was under a candy-red Bug on the car lift when we got there. He gave me a nod in greeting as he turned a bolt with his wrench. "Hey, Lou," he said. "How are things out at the mansion?"

Like most working-class folks in Parson, Curtis was a jack-of-all-trades; I'd worked with him on the odd construction job in the past, called him for advice when Miss Kate needed to find a salvage supplier. He'd since been drafted and done his stint abroad. He'd managed to escape injury, but Danny told me all the clanging in the auto shop stressed Curtis out sometimes. Their third brother, Wallace, had gone overseas several years before, back in Robby's time, and come out of it with a bad arm that made his work here difficult, too.

"The house is getting there," I said. "You should come out and see it someday. I could use your advice."

Curtis shuddered and crossed himself. "Danny's a braver man

than I am. No way I'm setting foot on some old *plantation* property. If the ghosts don't get me, the rednecks will."

Of course, it had occurred to me that Danny might be uncomfortable out at Parson House due to our personal history with the place, but I hadn't thought to wonder if the house's deeper history ever unsettled him. But when I looked at him to gauge his response, he didn't seem to be listening. "Whose is *that*?" Danny asked, looking curiously at the Bug.

"Some Corpus lady passing through," Curtis said, laughing as he worked. "Poor woman looked terrified, breaking down like this in a ghost town. Practically got on her knees, begged me to fix it by nightfall. That's what she said, man. *Nightfall*."

"If you don't, no sweat. The motel could use the business."

"I set her up in the office. Careful, she'll try to order some coffee off you. I thought about giving her motor oil to see if she could taste the difference."

We walked into the office, and the Corpus woman sat up straight in her chair at the sight of us, both filthy from hauling trash all day, giving off fumes fresh from the dump. She was older, dressed in a stiff blouse and an ankle-length skirt, the fingers of her white gloves nervously gripping her purse strap, that breed of Texas church lady I'd hate if I didn't pity them so much. Danny gave her a big customer-service, dealing-with-white-ladies smile.

"There's a little diner just down the road," he said, pointing out the window at the street. "Not half a mile. If you wanted to go get a meal, a coffee, whatever you like."

"Oh," she said. "I was hoping my car would be done by . . ."

"Got at least another couple hours on her," Danny said. "Might as well wait someplace a bit nicer."

Her gaze skittered around the room: the lazily circling fan, the chips in the linoleum floor, Danny in his muck-stained work clothes. She rose with a nod and a grateful mumble and shuffled out into the heat.

Danny lifted a leather-bound book to the counter, started flipping through ledger pages, running a finger slowly down the lines. A framed picture of his grandfather in overalls grinned on the wall behind him.

"Hey," I said as he looked through the book, "you ever talk to Thomas Wick anymore?"

He flicked his eyes at me, suspicious, then went back to the ledger. "Nope. Never."

"You two were close there for a while."

He laughed, dry. "What, for one night? We didn't talk after the car wreck."

"I was just thinking . . . he and Cass were friends, right? Starred in that play together? They probably talked all the time."

Danny didn't respond at once, his head down over a page. Then, in a cagey voice, "What does that matter?"

I wasn't sure how to respond. I didn't want to tell Danny more yet, let him in on my search for answers, which I knew he'd think misguided, maybe dangerous.

"Just curious," I said. "I still think about her a lot, you know."

It wasn't a lie, at least. And I could tell it softened Danny: the next glance he gave me was far more empathetic.

"I do, too," he said softly. "But talking to Thomas Wick? There's no point in that."

He was hiding something from me, I knew it sure as anything. But why would my best friend, a person I trusted even more than Heather, hide something from me about *Thomas Wick*, a boy we knew in high school? I couldn't press Danny on this, not without giving myself away. But I resolved to find Thomas's phone number, to see what I could learn from him.

Just then Danny's finger stopped on a line of the ledger. His brow furrowed and he looked over at me, his lips turned down.

"Adam Stanton," he said. "That's Adam Stanton's car."

167

19

City hall was closed on Sundays, so I had to wait until the next morning to confront Adam. When I stepped into the main office, I saw him behind the counter, hovering over the desk of a harried-looking woman at a typewriter. He smiled big when he saw me.

"Here's a sight for sore eyes! Lou, what a treat! God, I've missed you out at Buck's—it's just not the same. Buck *himself* is working the bar, not much to look at, let me tell you." He pressed his palms together in prayer, gave me an exaggerated pout. "Please tell me you're here just to hang out with me. Want to go for a stroll? I could take my break."

"It's eight-fifteen in the morning," I said. "Y'all just opened."

He checked his watch, grimaced. "Damn. I was thinking I'd been here a couple hours."

I was furious at Adam, but I'd cooled down since last night and had decided to play this friendly. If this creep was stalking me, it was better to put him at ease, not get him all worked up when he found out I knew. Then I could figure out my options.

I leaned against the counter, glanced around at the rows of filing cabinets, the humming fluorescent lights. "That dull here, is it?"

"You have *no* idea," he said. He strode up to the counter and stood across from me; I could smell that morning's cream cheese on his breath. The pocket of his dress shirt had a faint stain, ink that hadn't come out in the wash. "So how you been spending your nights now that you're not the world's best bartender? Getting lots of beauty rest?"

"I've been all right," I said.

"And Heather? She still around town?" He turned back to the woman at the typewriter, a young brunette in thick glasses and a brown cardigan who, from her weary, wilted expression, looked like she spent half her life listening to Adam ramble. "Oh, Lindy, you should have seen her. Heather was just the hottest thing in high school. All the boys went bozo around her. None of us stood a chance around this one's brother, though." He hooked a thumb at me. "Did you know people said he looked like Tony Curtis? The bastard," he added in a fond undertone.

My heart went out to Lindy: she already looked exhausted with Adam, and she was only fifteen minutes into the week. At least at Buck's I could talk to other customers. She gave him a tense, obligatory smile and went back to her Smith Corona.

Adam went on talking. "I've gotten Robert Mitchum, you know, a couple times. Can you see it?" He rested his chin on his fist, posed his face toward Lindy, then toward me.

"Heather's still around," I said, and then decided that this was more than enough small talk. "Hey, I have a question for you."

"Shoot."

"You still driving that big black Camaro? I thought I saw you out around Parson House yesterday."

Something complicated passed across Adam's face—frustration, maybe shame. I got ready for him to deny his stalking, or to cast it in another light, blame it on my "beauty" or something like that; got ready to explain about boundaries, restraining orders if necessary. But then he said in an irritated voice, "You saw it around *Parson House*? What in the world could that bitch be up to?"

Lindy flinched at the typewriter, though her fingers kept tapping at an even pace. *That bitch* could only be Adam's ex-girlfriend Claudia, and it seemed Lindy had heard about his breakup as often I had at the bar. Not hearing him tell that story again had been a major perk of leaving Buck's.

"Claudia has your car?" I asked.

He let out a sigh. "My Camaro. My one true love. They made me give it up, hand her the keys. Now I'm driving my dad's Polara. That rickety old junker's gonna shake apart on me any minute."

I was struggling to catch up: if he was telling the truth, this meant that *Claudia*, my old classmate from Woodman, had been following us yesterday. Why on earth would Claudia be trailing us, or waiting at the turnoff the other night?

"Who's *they*?" I asked him. "Who made you give up the Camaro?"

"Who do you think? That old broad, that bull-castrating freak. Used to live on that ranch outside town."

"Peg?" I asked.

"Peg. That's the one," he said. "And your old boss, too, the witch. Nosy bitches, both of them—no offense to the dead. I heard about them from Dad a few years before Claudia left, how these crones in their sixties were breaking up couples in town, threatening the men, telling them they were 'abusive.'" He made skeptical air quotes with his fingers. "The guys, they'd tell my dad over beers, but they'd never come to the station and press charges. Too embarrassed."

"You mean Claudia left you because of them?"

"Oh, well, it was different with *me*," Adam said defensively. "I mean, they never called me abusive—c'mon, Lou, you know me better than that. I wouldn't hurt a fly, and Claudia's a damn liar if she says I was ever anything but a gentleman. But Kate and that bull castrator, they were knocking on doors, and Claudia was home all the time with her kids—and look, she's never been the brightest, Claudia—so she invites these women in, and they start filling her up with their horse-shit, and then suddenly they're over at the house every day, and I get home from work and all Claudia does is mouth off and fight with me, a whole different person. Then she's telling me she's taking the kids, she's leaving. 'Where you gonna stay?' I want to know, and she says, 'Peg's got a room at her ranch.' I drove out there once, I looked at it, this tiny place in the boonies, a total dump. Now I guess they've all moved to a house in town, but Dad says it's overcrowded, something about fire codes. Says unless they want some legal troubles, they'll need to break up their little utopian lesbian love nest."

Another flinch from Lindy. She sat forward in her chair, closer to the typewriter. Her palm hit the carriage return with suppressed annoyance.

"So, wait, how did Claudia get your car?" I asked.

He forced a laugh, but his ears had blushed a faint red. "That's the saddest part of the whole story. It's a few days after Claudia left, and your boss comes by one night, starts going on about the kids, their school, their doctors, yada yada. Says their mother needs a car. 'Prove they're mine,' I tell her, 'and maybe I'll throw a few bucks her way.'" He laughed again. "Only that's not what they want, they want my damn *Camaro*. Can you believe it? I told her to get off my property, told her I'd take out my shotgun. I put that witch in her place."

"And then you gave her the car? I don't get it."

Adam glanced around, leaned his elbows on the counter. In a softer voice he said, "Well, after I said all that . . . about the shotgun, you know, Kate, she gets all quiet, all intense. Starts asking if I've heard the rumors in town, the ones about men gone missing, getting mutilated. Says her own husband went up in smoke years back, no one's heard from him since. And she's got this evil spark in her eyes the whole time, like she's saying, *I'd love to cut your balls off, friend. Just give me an excuse.* Never thought an old broad could be scary like that."

He rose from the counter, barked out another forced laugh. "I wasn't really scared, of course. But you gotta pick your battles, y'know? Something like that—more trouble than it's worth. Anyway, I got my eye on this gorgeous Firebird now, you've never seen anything so sexy in your life. Couple paychecks and I'll be driving her home."

I'd heard about Adam's breakup before—dozens, maybe hundreds, of times—but he'd left out the part about Peg and Miss Kate, the loss of his precious car. As he talked, I was making connections, thinking over the past week. Claudia, I realized, had been the woman pulling weeds in front of Peg's the other day, the one I couldn't place while she smiled at me from under her straw hat. I'd barely known Claudia at Woodman Secondary, but back then she'd been energetic and boisterous, her voice like a horn call down the halls. At Peg's house she'd been so measured, so quiet and contained.

And in the meantime, evidently she'd spent a lot of time with Miss Kate. What was Miss Kate like with Claudia? A perfect mother, like she'd been with me? Or maybe Claudia saw yet another side of Miss Kate: a religious teacher, a guide to the faith, a devoted reader of scripture. Whereas Adam had met Miss Kate as a fighter, vicious, savvy, relentless. I'd have to track down Claudia and ask her why she was following me around town.

"Did you talk to Kate other times?" I said to Adam.

"Once was enough, believe me. But yes, right, there *was* that time she came here to the office. I let Lindy cover that, took my lunch break. And then she was dead, like, the same week. Ding-dong, I say. No offense."

PCC. Miss Kate had written those letters in her datebook the day before I found her dead. *Parson County Clerk*?

"What did she come here for?" I asked.

Adam's eyebrows went up; his lips tilted in a conspiratorial smirk. "Technically I'm not supposed to give out that information. But just out of curiosity, why would you like to know?"

"It's nothing," I lied, casually tucking some hair behind my ear. "I worked for Kate, but we were never friends or anything. Always got the sense she was up to something fishy."

He clicked his tongue. "Well, we can't leave *that* stone unturned, can we? Lindy, could you pull those records?" he called over his shoulder. "Find out what that witch wanted. Kate Darnell."

Lindy looked pleased to leave the room. After I told her the date of Miss Kate's visit, she walked fast into another part of the office. I heard her sliding open file drawers, flicking through folders.

In her absence Adam leaned on the counter, lowered his voice again. "So do you believe all that? About men getting hurt, going missing? Just over a fight or two with their wives?"

"Nah, I don't think so," I said, deciding to put him at ease, at least until I saw the file.

"I hope you're right. I'd hate to think something bad happened to Ed Darnell."

"You knew him?"

"Just to wave hello," he said. "His job took him out of town a lot, right?"

I nodded. "Oil rig, I think."

"Ed's father is a great old guy, fishing buddies with my dad. Sounds like Ed disappearing hit the poor guy hard. No idea what happened to his son. He thinks Kate and those women did something to him, but Dad couldn't turn up any evidence. Ah, here we are."

Lindy had walked back into the room, slipped a folder onto the counter. She was back at her desk in an instant, inviting as little notice to herself as possible.

"Well, lookee here. A divorce petition," he said after opening the folder.

"Ed and Miss Kate?" I asked, stooping to see.

Sure enough, there it was, filled out in Miss Kate's fluid yet precise handwriting: Katherine Darnell was petitioning to divorce Ed Darnell.

I asked, "Can you divorce someone if he's missing? If you can't find him?"

"Sure, it's legal," he said. "But if she couldn't find him, she would've ticked a different box."

"What do you mean?"

He pointed to a space midway down the page. "This box here. You tick this if you can't find your spouse. Then you need to put an ad in the paper, give them a chance to respond."

I stared down at the form, more confused than ever. Miss Kate had checked the first box, which said that her spouse would sign the papers in person. Had she expected Ed to come into this office? Had she known where he was after all?

Adam let out a long sigh. "Well, that's a relief. If she thought Ed was signing, he's probably not buried in a ditch somewhere. Gotta ring up his old man if I remember."

I'd just realized something else: Miss Kate might have wanted a divorce, but of course, it had never gone through. She'd died the very day she started the paperwork.

Adam wrangled my phone number from me before I left. "I'll have Lindy start digging for anything else Kate Darnell was up to. Bet that's not the only fishy business—I'll let you know. Now that your evenings are free, maybe we can chat about it over some dinner."

Lindy paused in her typing, rolled her neck slowly.

As soon as I got back to my truck, I made my way out to the Darnells' place. I'd gone there as a kid with Joanna and Seth, excited to visit their grandparents' farm, and even had some good memories of playing with the big pack of dogs, chasing chickens in the yard, catching frogs in a stream at the back of the fields. But I'd stopped going out there in sixth grade, after Miss Kate brought Danny along one day and the grandfather wouldn't let him inside the house. Though I'd wanted to throw a rock through the window, I just stalked back to the car.

The trip was less than twenty minutes: soon enough my truck was jouncing up their pitted dirt drive, steering around the yapping dogs that came frothing alongside my tires. I'd been curious about the Darnells for a few days now, ever since Peg mentioned the threatening letters they'd sent to Miss Kate. My ideas were unsteady, half formed, but it seemed like Miss Kate had been in touch with Ed before her death, enough to expect that he'd sign those divorce papers in person. And if Miss Kate had been in touch with Ed, maybe his parents were, too. Ed was key to so many questions, not just about Miss Kate but about Joanna as well. If Ed was alive, if he made himself known, then Parson House was his by direct inheritance. Joanna had no claim to it.

Would Ed kill Miss Kate for the mansion, then lie low until the dust cleared? Maybe even wait for Joanna to finish the renovations, then sweep in, take it over? I had no clue. But one thing I did know for certain: the Parson police wouldn't throw up any barriers. Hell, Ed's *dad* was fishing buddies with the head sergeant.

Mrs. Darnell answered the door in a faded calico dress, stooped and shrunken with age, her hair gone white and wispy. She gave me a scrunched, suspicious look, as if I were out here selling damaged vacuum cleaners. But when I told her my name, she clapped a hand to her mouth, let out a squeal of pleasure.

"Is that little Louisa? Oh my word, it's been *years*, hasn't it? You come right here, look at you all grown."

Her warm maternal hug surprised me, and next thing I knew, I was being hustled inside and led down a hallway lined with photos of her many beefy sons hunting, fishing, holding up beers, occasionally getting married. In the cramped but tidy den sat an older Mr. Darnell, looking like time had been tougher on him than his wife; he'd gone jowly, red-nosed, sun-spotted, and his overalls sagged against him like a slack sail. He squinted at me as I came in the room, but mostly kept his eyes on the television: *Dinah's Place* on mute.

Mrs. Darnell left for a moment and returned with a tray of store-bought cookies arranged in a scallop shell formation. I ate a few to be friendly while we sat down and caught up. "Oh, Chuck, did you hear that?" she said to her husband in a louder voice at one point. "Louisa says she's helping take care of her poor brother's child—isn't that just lovely? You remember Robby, used to visit with Kate's kids? Died over in Vietnam? Chuck was so sorry to hear about that. We both were."

Before I could ask her the questions I wanted to ask, she had started in on her five sons, their jobs, their houses, their wives and children, even their medical problems, like Chuck Jr.'s bum knee. "They might put a metal plate in. Just imagine!" I noticed she never mentioned Ed among her sons, and at last this gave me an opening.

"Do you know where Ed is keeping himself these days?" I asked. "Been a long time since I saw him."

Mr. Darnell let out a sharp snort, his first sign of life. His wife didn't seem to notice. Placid as ever, she said, "It's been a while for us, too. Four, five years? He left town kind of sudden, a ways back. We're not sure where and how he's keeping."

"You haven't heard from him at all?" I asked. "Not a phone call, a letter?"

"That witch woman," Mr. Darnell muttered. His voice was gruff and low, gravel in a shook can. "That goddamn Yankee. Did something to him."

"Now, now," Mrs. Darnell said. She patted his knee softly. "We don't speak ill of the dead in this house."

I turned to the old man. "Y'all didn't like Miss Kate?"

"*Like* her?" he spat, his voice just above a whisper. He was looking at me now. "She murdered my son. Hid his body."

Mrs. Darnell gave me a patient *Don't mind him* smile. "We liked Kate just fine. It was she who stopped coming around here, stopped letting her kids see us. I always thought it might be that church of hers. Lots of strong opinions there."

"Cult," Mr. Darnell said. "Crazy heathen bitches."

"I'm not sure what we did to offend her," she went on. "The beers or cigarettes with the boys, maybe? Or Christmas and birthdays? It came as a surprise, her cutting us off like that. Before then I was sure she liked me—she'd invite me to that church all the time—which, yes, that did become a bit uncomfortable for me. We're God-fearing Presbyterians here. But she didn't pay that any mind. Kept asking."

"Still haven't been able to get rid of all those fucking pamphlets," Mr. Darnell added, his voice growing stronger, a glimpse of the imposing man he'd been once. "She'd fold 'em up, leave 'em around the house. Like a goddamn infestation. And don't get me started on how she treated our boy. He couldn't even watch football, had to come over here to do it. Couldn't crack a beer without hearing about his *drinking problem.* He likes to bet on a race sometimes, and then it's *you're losing all our money to those greyhounds.* She'd cry and scream, that bitch, give him no peace. Ed was too soft with her, that was the problem. Gotta raise a hand if your woman's like that. I'm sorry, but it needs to be done."

There he goes again, Mrs. Darnell's smile told me.

I let a moment pass, let the old man catch his breath. "Before Miss Kate died," I said as carefully as I could, "she received a couple of letters from you. Didn't she?"

"Uppity bitch," Mr. Darnell said. "Putting on airs, buying up that mansion. Meantime, she was living off my son's money."

Mrs. Darnell sighed. "To be honest, we never did know how she afforded that mansion. Where the money came from."

"From *Ed*, that's who," he almost shouted. His face was red, his voice hoarse; he'd need a long nap after this. "Every dime she had, it came from Ed. And answer me this—would Ed have wanted to buy that place, that old useless heap of trash? No, sir, never. He wanted hunting land, that was my boy's dream. So what kind of man lets his money get used like that? A dead one, that's what I say. A dead one."

Mrs. Darnell was patting his knee again. "We did send Kate a few letters," she admitted to me. "I never accused her of *murder*— goodness, no—just said that we missed our boy, that we wished he'd come home. And that if she wasn't around anymore, we were sure he'd come right back. I suppose it wasn't the friendliest letter I've sent, telling her she should leave town and all. But Ed was born here, raised here, a Parson boy through and through. What right did she have to put down roots after she'd run him off?" She shut her eyes, sniffed. Her husband squeezed her hand, brought it to his lips and kissed it.

"The two of us, we haven't got much time left," she said, her voice choked. She reached over to the end table and picked up a framed photograph, black and white, grainy, at least forty years old. It showed Mr. and Mrs. Darnell in their thirties, their five boys standing around them, ranging in age from teen to toddler. "He's our baby, you know. Little Edward. We've done our best by those boys, all of 'em. But Ed, he was always so special."

She pointed at a cherub-faced child. I couldn't see Ed in his features, none of the gruff, grumpy, combative man I'd known.

"Our baby," the old man said, gazing fog-eyed at the photograph. "What did she do to our baby?"

Before I could go, someone thumped twice on the front door and let themselves into the house. Up the corridor lumbered a heavyset guy in a hunting jacket with flannel lining, a matching hunting cap. He favored his left leg as he walked, and I figured this must be Chuck Jr., the one getting a metal plate in his bum knee.

"Dad, Mom," he said bluntly by way of greeting. He glanced over at me. "Who's this?"

His mother answered, "Why, this is little Louisa. Don't you recognize her? She and her brother used to come by here with Ed's kids."

"Those aren't *his kids*, Mom. He just married into that." Chuck Jr. squinted at me, his lips squatting into a scowl. "Ain't you the one got moved from the white school?"

Mrs. Darnell leaned forward and swatted his arm. "It was all a misunderstanding, as I recall. I mean, look at the girl—she's white enough, surely."

I stood. "I was heading out, actually. Got some work to get to."

Mrs. Darnell hugged me again before she let me leave, but Mr. Darnell seemed to have forgotten me. He was staring at *Concentration* on the TV now, a rebus puzzle flipping into view square by square.

Chuck Jr. followed me out to my truck, as though to make sure I didn't dally. In the driveway he stopped in front of me and crossed his burly arms, taut as a seat belt across the barrel of his chest. "You got some business coming by here?" he asked.

His parents were lonely enough to welcome my visit without

question, but Chuck Jr. wasn't the welcoming type. I'd need something better than *for old times' sake.*

"I've been curious what happened to Ed," I said, trying to bait him with part of the truth. "With everything that's happened at Parson House, it just got me wondering."

A quick flicker in his eyes: anger, fear, something else? "You let us worry about Ed."

"Your dad mentioned he'd been gambling. Dog races? Ed ever get into trouble with that?"

Chuck Jr. snickered, but I heard a note of sadness in the noise. "You know who you sound like? Ed's witch of a wife. Ever wonder what happened to *her*?" He walked over to my truck, yanked open the door for me.

The message was clear enough. I didn't push my luck.

20

After the visit to the Darnells, I worked a half day at the mansion, got started on repairs in some upstairs rooms. Things were quiet out on the promontory, and Joanna didn't show up at the house. But at one point I heard the rumble of a truck pulling up the driveway, Stonewall Jackson playing loud on the radio. I peeked out the window, half expecting to see that black Camaro. Instead it was the big pickup I'd seen out there before, the one with a busted tailpipe and a Confederate flag hung across the tailgate.

This time the pickup didn't turn around and leave. Instead it pulled to a stop, and the doors burst open, then two bulky guys in cowboy hats poured out of the cab. I could hear them talking and laughing, but I couldn't make out their words over the twang of Jackson's voice and the growl of the engine. As I watched, one of them meandered over to my truck. The other man crooked his hat against the sun, peered up at the facade of the house.

I gripped my hammer harder, ducked down away from the window. My breath was coming tight and rough, an old fear rising in me. For the most part I could live how I wanted in Parson, dress and talk how I liked and not get much trouble. After all, this was Texas; even the most traditional men liked that the women here could be tough, could spit and ride and cuss up a storm. But men like this were different. Everywhere they went, they acted like they were owed something. If a bar was playing the wrong type of music, they sang drunkenly over it until the bartender gave in. A feminine woman was theirs to harass, and a tomboy was theirs to correct. I'd learned long ago to avoid these types like the devil.

And now I was alone with them in the remotest part of town, where no one would come looking for me for hours.

When I'd seen that truck before, I hadn't guessed who it might be or what in the world they were doing out on the promontory. Truth was, half of Parson drove trucks like that. But now Mr. Darnell's words came back to my mind: Ed had been betting on greyhounds. Dog racing was illegal, which meant that these races were likely run by one of two groups: the Civello family out of Dallas, or the more local Dixie Mafia. The Civellos had operations that stretched far south, while the Dixie Mafia was far less organized, a cluster of good-ol'-boy criminals still moping over the Civil War. Both groups ran puffed-up protection rackets, and Buck needed to pay them off now and then when they bothered to put Parson on their radar.

If the Dixie Mafia had been paying visits to Parson House all this time, did that mean they thought Ed Darnell was out here somewhere?

I stayed crouched under the window, bracing for what would happen next—a holler for me to come out, a hard knock at the door. But before long I heard their truck doors slam shut, their tires rumbling back down the driveway. When I peeked through the window, I caught a glimpse of that big flag flapping in the distance.

Only when I couldn't hear that horrible song did I loosen my grip on the hammer.

When I made it home that evening, I saw that Heather had gone out. Sometimes she went over to her friends' places, Midge Maddox or Fay Browne and their spoiled, fawned-over broods. Hell, maybe Heather was nannying for Fay right now, like she'd planned to do. If that was the case, I felt sorry for her; I knew how much pride she'd have to swallow to make it happen, that she'd never have done it if we hadn't been set to leave town right after.

Alone in the house, I fantasized about finding Joanna and confronting her, forcing her to answer my questions like she'd agreed to do. Even if she resisted, I knew more about Miss Kate now, more about Joanna's life and family, maybe enough to get her blood up, get her talking—especially if I pulled out that Black Cat tin at the right moment. Part of me itched to get back in my truck, drive out to Seth's place, and see if I could track her down.

But I didn't do it. Something told me if I showed up at Seth's house tonight, she'd be on her guard at once, defensive, closed. I needed to wait for the right time, when the two of us were alone, when she was more at ease, not expecting my questions.

I opened a Lone Star and sat down at the phone in the kitchen, started calling information. Before long I'd reached an old landlord of Thomas Wick's parents and, after a few wrong numbers, Thomas's mother in Dallas. I told her I was his friend from high school, just looking to catch up; I didn't say a word about the car wreck or Cass, my real reasons for finding him. He was living in Galveston, she said, working as a teacher. There was tension in her voice as she told me, and I sensed she didn't talk to him much these days. In the end she gave me his number, said she'd better get dinner started. I tapped the switch hook, took a quick sip of beer, and dialed the number I'd written on a napkin.

He answered after a few rings. "Is this Thomas?" I asked him.

"This is he." His voice was still rich and full, and I remembered him in high school, his confident stance on the stage when I saw him in *Harvey*, how his words had carried to the very back of the auditorium. "To whom am I speaking?"

"I'm sorry for calling out of the blue like this," I said. "My name's Louisa Ward. I was in high school with you."

He went quiet for a long moment. When he spoke again, his voice was flinty, brusque. "Hello, Louisa."

"You may not remember me, but I was—"

"I remember you."

It astonished me, the audible hate in his voice. Had he mistaken me for someone else, some horrible tormentor from his school years?

"What can I do for you, Louisa?" he went on. "This isn't exactly a welcome call."

"I was just thinking of you these past few days. I've been doing some work at Parson House—you know, the mansion out on the promontory—and I found a cigarette tin that belonged to a friend of ours, Cass Kerrigan. She'd stashed it in the house that night we all broke in. Do you remember that night—it was Cass and Danny and me?"

"I'm not likely to forget *that* night, am I?"

All right, so maybe he knew who I was; I still couldn't understand his tone. Maybe he hated thinking about what happened, the car wreck, Cass's death. I went on: "Well, in the tin, I found a bus ticket Cass was keeping. Houston to New York, for just three days after the crash."

Another pause. Then, irritated, "Okay?"

"Did she mention that to you?"

"That she'd bought a bus ticket? Fifteen years ago?" he scoffed. "You can't honestly expect me to remember . . . Is this why you're calling me? To have some catch-up chat about Cass?"

"She never told me about it. The bus ticket, leaving town. And we were close that summer. You two, you probably talked a lot, right? You were in that play together, *Harvey*. I found one of the old tickets in the cigarette tin."

"*Harvey*," he repeated, and his voice had softened somewhat. "Yeah, we did that play. Other than that, I'd see her at parties, but I didn't know her well. We'd talk sometimes about skipping town, going to New York, trying to make it. It was just a fantasy for me. But if she bought a bus ticket, who knows, maybe she was going to give it a shot. Never got a chance, of course," he added, and the hate was back in his voice.

I could see it in my mind: Cass as a Broadway star. A spotlight fixed on her in the final scene, the curtains sweeping closed, the waves of oceanic applause in the dark theater. A life she'd never get to live.

If she'd just bought that bus ticket for a few days earlier.

"That night at Parson House," I said, "maybe it was her way of saying goodbye."

"Maybe. Sounds like the sort of thing she'd do."

It did sound like Cass. She'd taken us out there for a reason, and it was clear she'd been trying to set Danny up with Thomas. Maybe Thomas was going through a rough time, too, and she thought they'd be good for each other.

And me also. When she'd said those words—*It's all right with me, you know*—she was saying goodbye to me. She was leaving me with her approval, with words to make me stronger. Words to let me know that *I* wasn't the reason she was leaving, because I'd told her once, drunk and high beneath the summer stars, how I thought everyone would leave me in the end.

"If we're catching up," Thomas said acidly, cutting into my thoughts, "maybe I could ask you a question? Would that be okay with you?"

"Uh, sure. Yeah. Ask away."

"Something I've always wondered. Your brother"—he spat the word into the phone—"and his crew that night, after the crash. Why did they only take *you* with them? They didn't even go over to *look* at the crash, just took you and left. Didn't they have any conscience? That's what I've always wondered, you know. How some people, they just have no conscience."

"I don't remember that night very well," I said, fighting to keeping my voice even. I didn't like his tone about Robby, not at all. "I think my brother said you all were injured, and it wasn't safe to move you. So he called the ambulance."

"Seriously? That's what he said? Danny and I, we were pretty banged up, but Cass? She was bleeding, but she was okay. She was cracking jokes, keeping Danny and me conscious. You know what she seemed most worried about? *You.* Protecting you. She was telling us to lie, to say you'd never been there with us. 'I don't want Lou to get in trouble,' she said. 'If anyone asks, it was only the three of us.' Meanwhile she was putting pressure on Danny's head wound. Then the ambulance finally showed up, and she started screaming at them when they wouldn't take Danny, calling them racists, every name in the book. If your brother had bothered to check on us, he could have taken her right to the hospital. She was just bleeding some, they'd have patched her up. But he left her there to die."

I tried to remember the car crash, the minutes we lay there wounded, Robby driving past in Adam Stanton's Buick, finding me in the middle of the road, dazed, spattered with blood. But I could remember only Cass and me on the love seat earlier that night, the headlights flashing through the parlor window. Then I was back in my bedroom at Cece's house, and Robby was down on his knees beside me, praying hard while I got sick into the bucket.

Thomas went on. "Some stitches—Robby just needed to take her in for some stitches. God, I'll bet you anything she'd be alive. You probably never even thought about that, Louisa. Yet another way you're responsible for her death. My parents, they wanted to go to the police, did you know that? Decided not to, of course. Sergeant Stanton, that bastard, he came out to our house, told my parents there wouldn't be any point to it. Made it clear no one would take the story on *my* word. Danny wasn't talking, either, so nothing ever came of it. We weren't exactly the kind of kids the cops would fight for, anyway."

The police? I couldn't make sense of what he was saying. Did he really blame Robby so much he'd wanted the police involved? Robby had found us, called an ambulance—he wasn't a damn paramedic, he didn't know who you could and couldn't move in a serious accident. What more did Thomas expect of him?

And Thomas was still talking, getting angrier. "You know, my leg, it never did set right. What good is an actor who walks with a limp? That's an actual note I got from one of my professors, by the way. That I'm good at the craft but it doesn't matter, I'm useless for any real roles because I can't *move correctly*. My leg's like that to this day. After four operations. My students snicker at me, do impressions."

A tangle of sorrow had entered his voice; he cut himself off right on the edge of crying.

"Thomas . . . I'm sorry," I said, surprised at the guilt I suddenly felt, the tremor in my tone. "I'm so, so sorry." I wasn't sure why I was apologizing, why he blamed me. But I knew at some deep level I needed to tell him this.

"That doesn't help me much, does it?" he said. "And your brother— I heard he died a few years back. Was he sorry, too? Did he tell you he regretted what he'd done? Or did he die thinking it was all okay— that we were just a couple of pansies who got what we deserved?"

Thomas could have cursed me to hell and I wouldn't have done a thing. But as soon as he spoke of Robby that way, I hung up the phone at once, grateful to cut off that hateful voice.

I paced around the kitchen, took another Lone Star from the fridge. I could understand Thomas getting upset, that my phone call might have brought up tough emotions, especially if the accident had haunted him all his life, like he'd said. I was lucky, it seemed, not to remember much about it. But blaming Robby like that—it was delusional, insane. It sounded like Thomas had brooded for years, had picked Robby as the villain in his life, the handsome football star on whom he could pin his own lost potential as an actor. I understood the impulse, the need to sift back through events, looking for the one right person to blame. It was Cass, of course, who'd crashed the car, but maybe Thomas felt like he couldn't blame her, his beautiful friend cut down so tragically young.

Thomas was wrong about Robby in another way, too. He made it sound like Robby hated Thomas and Danny for what they were. Sure, Robby might have cracked jokes with someone like Adam Stanton, guys on the football team. But I knew him better. By the time I'd finished high school, Robby understood who I was and never treated me with anything but love.

At the auto shop yesterday, Danny had said I shouldn't contact Thomas. Maybe this was why. Danny knew Thomas had an ax to grind, this delusional grudge about the accident.

Just then I heard a car engine outside. I pushed apart the curtains, looked out the window.

A black Camaro was pulling up in the driveway—the same black Camaro that had followed me yesterday morning. The passenger door opened, and out climbed Heather.

21

I hurried out into the yard, expecting the car to screech away at the sight of me. But the Camaro lingered in the driveway, engine idling, black finish glimmering in the dusk.

"What's going on here?" I asked Heather as she came up the path.

She stopped, startled at the jagged edge in my voice. She was wearing one of her nicer blouses and a light coat of makeup, and she gave me a confused smirk, not too friendly. We hadn't been talking much the past few days.

"What, I'm not allowed to go out now? Is that it?" she said.

"No, I . . . That's not what I meant. Is that Claudia Reyes in the car?" The twilight had glazed the driver's-side window; I couldn't see the driver, only a dim reflection of our oak tree.

"She gave me a ride to Peg's. If that's okay with you, Dad. It's four miles. A little far to walk in this heat."

"Were you with her yesterday morning?" I asked.

Heather tilted her head. "God. Jealous much?"

"It's not that. Danny and I, we saw that car around and—"

"I was at home where you left me, you'll be glad to know." She adjusted her purse strap on her shoulder, gestured back toward the car. "Claudia says she wants to talk to you. And if that's the end of my interrogation, Herr Lou, I think I'll go make some dinner."

She walked brusquely to the house, her back arched like she knew I was watching her. She kicked the door closed behind her, just shy of slamming. *Not good*, I thought. I needed to work harder to reach her, to care for her. I was letting my attention get pulled into other things.

Like now: in the driveway I saw the Camaro's window roll down, heard the faint squeak of the window crank. Claudia was watching me from the shadowy interior, her face without expression except for the neutral, unnerving gentleness I'd noticed the other day. She wasn't wearing her gardening hat, and her dark hair fell to her shoulders; like Heather, she wore a nice blouse, as well as a small gemstone pendant on a slim silver chain.

"Good evening, Louisa," she said as I approached, the same reined-in voice that made my stomach clench, I wasn't sure why. "I thought I should say hello. You saw me out on the road yesterday, didn't you?"

I was shaken from my call with Thomas, and that talk with Heather just now hadn't helped. I tried to control my temper as I said, "I'm not sure what that's about, to be honest. Can't say I like it very much. Mind telling me what's going on?"

The look on Claudia's face was innocent, too open, like she'd never tell me anything but the truth. "You are a person who Jehovah God has given many challenges. Now you are surrounded by enemies, by people with unclear motives. I've been asked to keep an eye on you when I can."

The words sounded strange, certainly nothing Claudia would have said when I knew her in school. I didn't know why she wouldn't answer my questions plainly, but it was getting harder to stay calm. "How many times have you followed me, Claudia?"

"Often the past week or so. Back and forth from the mansion. Just to make sure you're safe."

One headlight bouncing on the bumpy road, flashing in my rear-view mirror. No streetlights, too dark to make out the car behind me. Passing the spot where Cass's car went soaring off the road, no clue that the black Camaro trailed me through the shadows.

"Who told you to watch me? Why?" I asked.

For a disorienting second, I thought Miss Kate's ghost might have asked her. A voice whispering beyond the grave, speaking to Claudia as she knelt in prayer, giving her this spiritual mandate.

Claudia said, "I'm sure Peg would explain it to you if you asked. She's never meant to hide her plans from you."

What in the world did Peg have to do with this? "Listen, I'm fine, okay? I don't need your help. Really."

"You don't seem fine, Louisa. Not from what I've observed." The words came out sharp, and she looked like she regretted them at once. She gathered herself, then spoke again more gently. "There aren't many opportunities for women in this town. There never were, even before the storm. We went to school together. Remember how that place felt?"

I knew what she meant. "Like the end of the line," I agreed, confused at this change in subject.

"A lack of options can be a very dangerous thing. It's what got me mixed up with Adam—and worse, before him. There's a woman out at Peg's, her husband popped her eye out when he thought she was cheating. And she and I . . . we're lucky, compared to some."

I didn't need to be told this, either. Growing up a girl in Parson, you heard stories like this all the time. I couldn't understand why Claudia would waste these cautionary tales on me, but I wasn't about to tell her why *I'd* never have those troubles with a man. Then again, maybe it wasn't a man she was warning me off.

"This needs to stop," I told her in a firmer voice. "This needs to stop now."

I'd gone for intimidating, but she wasn't shaken. "I can only do what Jehovah God wills. My will is not my own."

The language she was using kept hitting my ear wrong, buzzing like a flat note. I wished she'd talk like a normal human being. "All right," I said, seeing this was pointless. I wasn't about to start screaming at Claudia in my driveway, not after the day I'd had. "I'll give Peg a call later tonight."

"It would be better if you came to the house," Claudia said.

I bristled at being told what to do, but I nodded. "Okay. I'll come. You can tell her to expect me."

"You're always welcome, wherever we gather," she said.

When I opened the bedroom door, I saw Heather lying on the bed in the half-light, a narrow shape at the far edge of the mattress. She hadn't started dinner like she'd said, just changed into a T-shirt and pajama bottoms—her usual outfit these days—and shut herself in the room. Her back was turned to me, but in the mirror on the closet door, I could see the reflection of her face, pensive, eyes open. I stood in the doorway, hand on the knob, shoulders tense. I wanted to say something sweet and soothing to start our evening on the right note, ease the strain between us, make her face soften and meet my eyes in the mirror.

But what could I say? We'd stopped talking about San Antonio, but it dwelled in the house like a heavy fog, so that we could barely glimpse each other through the haze: she thought I was selfish, I thought she was impatient, and there was no point going over it all again. We passed each other in the empty rooms, spoke to each other with a forced politeness that disturbed me more than fighting. She'd started sleeping in later, going to bed earlier, taking long naps in the afternoon, the most lethargic I'd ever seen her, not at all the bustling, chatty, upbeat woman I knew. But there was nothing for her to do now: the packing was finished except for the toiletries, the boxes stacked in the foyer and living room, and it felt like her spirit had vacated the house already, left me behind with the husk of her body.

That wasn't true, of course. My Heather was here in the room, in that anxious body on the bed, curled quiet, far from me, suffering. I hated that I'd done this to her. I sat on the mattress beside her, the springs creaking under me, began to rub a hand between her shoulder blades. Her back muscles relaxed reflexively, but I knew she wasn't actually relaxed.

"You talk to Sarah today?" I asked, a topic that sometimes brightened her.

A small shrug was all I got.

I tried another inroad. "So you and Claudia are friends now? I didn't realize you knew each other."

She didn't feel like talking, I could tell, but she probably saw no point in being rude to me. "I wouldn't say friends," she answered after a moment. "I met her a few times in high school, back after Robby changed schools. But she's living at Peg's now, and she's not working, so she gives me a ride now and then. Lots of ladies staying in the house there, always someone to help with the kids."

"I talked to Adam Stanton for a bit today. He told me there's so many people in that house, they're exceeding the fire code. Need to find a bigger place."

In the mirror I saw her eyebrows draw together. "Adam was talking about Peg's house?"

This was another source of strain between us: she could tell I was keeping things from her, leaving out details when I talked about my day. I said, "Oh, you know Adam. Always has a good word or two about the ladies in town."

Heather gave a shudder. "Can't believe Claudia was with him. Just the thought of sharing a house with him. Those two boys of hers, they're sweet, but you can tell they have a little Adam in them."

I laughed. "Robby was friends with him. Hard to believe that, too."

"Well, he didn't have much of a choice. On the same team. But in private Robby always called him an asshole."

"Robby didn't like Adam?"

Another shrug, less listless. It felt good to talk about the past, to be back on shared ground: we loved Robby enough to forget our troubles, drift off to an oasis of reminiscence. Right now that was one of the few lifelines we could offer each other.

"All those guys," she said, "it was tough for him. He never said much about it because he was the quarterback, Mr. College Prospects, and he *had* to get along with them. But he didn't like it, all that posturing, all that tough-guy nonsense. It wore him out."

I smiled. "Even when we were kids, he never wanted to be the center of attention. He just wanted, I don't know, a good life for us all. Nothing special, really. And then suddenly, with football, everyone around him was saying, *You're special, you're special, you're number one!* His teammates expected him to act like it. To back it up with all that macho crap."

"He was different around them," Heather said. "He tensed up, talked louder. Then they'd leave and he'd just . . . relax. Let it all loose. I loved seeing that side of him. He'd give me piggyback rides, run me around the yard. He was wacky, you know? Sweet, silly. That's what those guys never saw."

I remembered his broad shoulders, my legs dangling under his arms. "Yeah. He'd give me rides, too."

"He was kind of a weirdo, really. Just a big weirdo."

"I fucking miss him," I said.

She nodded, the pillow shifting under her head. "Every day."

Thomas Wick was so very wrong about Robby. He'd been talking about an entirely different person. But his words had stirred up something in me, a wound that still felt open.

"Do you remember that kid from high school, the one who starred in the school plays? Thomas Wick?"

"Sure," she said. "He was in the accident with Cass, right? Lots of guys called him Thomas Limp after. The pricks."

I felt the same guilt as before, reminded myself his injuries weren't my fault.

Heather asked, "What's got you thinking about him?"

"Just Robby, what a sweetheart he was. I talked to Thomas about the accident," I said. Then, when Heather shot me a surprised look, I added, feeling guilty how easily the lie came, "Years ago, I don't remember when. He acted like Robby was this villain. This evil jock."

"Well, for someone like Thomas . . . I mean, you know what high school can be like. He probably lumped Robby in with that whole group. Football guys."

"But it was more than that. Thomas was mad *about* the accident. Like Robby was cruel or something for what he'd done."

"Huh?" she said. "Robby found you. Called the ambulance."

"That's what I told Thomas. But he was still upset. Said that Robby hated people like him and Danny. It was really weird."

Heather went quiet, thinking. "Yeah, Thomas just didn't know him. It's funny, but that night, the night of the car wreck—that's one of the times I was most proud of Robby."

"Me, too," I said. "He saved us."

"No, I mean before, earlier in the night. God, I haven't thought about this in years. There were a bunch of us out at the football field, drinking, smoking, whatever, just a normal night. And one of the girls, she'd heard that Cass was breaking into Parson House that night. Heard that Thomas and Danny were going with her. The guys, Adam and the others, they were really drunk by then, and they started saying stuff—you know, stuff about Thomas and Danny. Nothing I'd repeat if you paid me: gross, perverted, going into details. They were rolling around on the grass, they were laughing so hard. The girls were just watching them, disgusted, like, *Well, this is just something you have to put up with, I guess.* And they kept looking over at me, jealous, because Robby? He wasn't saying anything at all. He was sitting apart from them, glaring, sipping his first beer, not close to drunk. Hell, it would have been natural enough for him to join in. But the way they were being, he couldn't stand it."

I'd never heard this story before, and I felt a film of tears coat my eyes. If Robby had been that angry, it probably wasn't just for Danny, or for Thomas, whom he didn't know at all. Years after that night, in my senior year of high school, Robby and I would smoke a joint and get to talking on the porch, a quiet, oblique conversation when he'd tell me he knew who I was, that he loved me no matter what. But maybe he'd known about me far earlier, known that night on the football field, and felt an anger, an urge to defend me, to defend people like me, that he knew he couldn't express to his football buddies.

I said to Heather, "Thanks for telling me that. It's a beautiful story. Makes me wonder if he knew about me. You know, way back then."

"Maybe, yeah," she answered, wistful. "I hadn't thought about that. Those guys, though, they were such dicks—after a while they *noticed* he wasn't laughing, that he was angry. Guys like Adam, they love that, love to get under your skin. So they started making it worse, saying even more disgusting stuff, stuff about Cass, too, how Cass would probably jump right in, she wasn't picky. Robby just sat there, fuming. I'd never seen him like that before, like he was losing it or something. Pretty soon us girls, we weren't having fun, we made some excuse and got out of there, piled into Fay's car. But I gave Robby a big kiss before I went, told him he was the best. He barely even kissed me back, he was so mad."

The sun was almost fully set, the slanting beams receded from the curtains. The light in the room was remote, removed, like the glow of a TV in a distant window. I lay down next to Heather and tried to wrap my arms around her, but she pulled away from me, tucked her head down. Then, to my surprise, she shut her eyes and started to cry, quick, gasping sobs from out of nowhere. I took her chin, tried to kiss her, but she turned her face away.

"Is it wrong?" she said, voice barely a whisper. "Please tell me it's not wrong."

"Us talking about Robby? Of course not. It's good we remember him."

She shook her head. "Never mind. Forget it."

"What just happened?" I asked, confused. "I thought . . ."

She was pulling herself together, wiping her eyes. "Yeah, it was good. Good to talk. I maybe could use some time now, though. If that's okay."

I was putting her through so much with the move, the least I could do was give Heather space when she needed it. But she was asking for space more and more, and I felt guilty at my inner sigh of relief, that I wanted this space from her as well.

"You hungry?" I asked. "I could whip up some pasta."

"That's okay. I was hungry before. Not now."

"I might head over to Peg's for a bit. A few things to ask her."

"Sure," she said, her voice faraway, her eyes watching themselves in the mirror. "See you later."

22

It usually cleared my head when Heather and I discussed the past, when we brought to mind all those good memories with Robby. I still missed him, but reminiscing made the pain feel softer and warmer, somehow. But tonight, as I drove out to Peg's house, taking the long route along the ocean, I felt more rattled than ever, my mind a jumble of paranoid thoughts and clues that spilled in all directions. A queasy guilt was growing inside me, souring my stomach, worse than when I'd first talked to Thomas Wick. Just beyond my sight, like the fervid life that swarmed below the dark, churning ocean beside me, there were answers to my questions, something I was missing, giving off a faint glow like jellyfish under the waves, elusive, beyond my grasp. It gave me the same feeling of powerlessness that I'd felt that night sitting on the bar at Buck's while the wind roared above me, while the world around me drowned. Like Robby's letters from Vietnam being three weeks old when we got them, no proof of life at all, his last letter arriving in Cece's mailbox two days after the notice of his death.

I drove down Peg's abandoned block, parked at the curb, walked up her cobblestone path. There was the usual rigamarole at the door, like visiting a minor potentate: a woman I didn't know answered (a fresh shiner under one eye); she went and got another woman, who asked me to wait and closed the door, and then an upstairs window opened and the woman who'd helped Peg with preserves leaned out and called down to me, her hair curled up in rollers, "She'll be right there, Louisa!" and shut the window again. Finally Peg emerged from around the side of the house, smiling easy and natural as she stepped from the shadows, like all of this was normal, like I hadn't just passed through multiple levels of security. The more I learned about this rail-thin, silver-haired woman in her Stetson hat, the more I realized she was a powerful person, not just some friendly local lady who brought over jam and groceries.

That being said, she was brushing flour off the pants of her overalls, giving off the impression that she'd just left some baking project underway. She gave me a big hug, then held me out at arm's length, as always, gave me a once-over. "Not getting more sleep, I see."

"Things have been busy."

She nodded. "Want to go for a drive? Seems like we've got some talking to do."

"Sure."

We climbed into her truck, a brown-and-tan Ranger, which turned over on the second try. We chugged down her empty block, past an abandoned house with half its roof missing, a fallen elm jutting from its shattered porch. A slice of moon peeped out between the branches overhead, keeping tabs on us.

"Heard you talked to Adam Stanton today?" Peg said, breaking the silence.

A shiver of surprise went through me, followed by annoyance. Was nothing I did in this damn town private anymore?

"Who told you that?" I asked.

She chuckled. "I have my ways. But what you were saying, I couldn't quite believe it. That Miss Kate wasn't your friend? Thought she was like a mother to you."

Lindy, I thought. I was annoyed, but I couldn't help smiling—that Peg had a friend in city hall, that whatever Adam said at work went straight to Peg's ears.

"I didn't mean it," I said, flustered. "I just said that so . . . so he'd show me something."

"Miss Kate's divorce papers."

There was no use denying it. "Yeah."

"It's true," Peg said, "she was trying to divorce Ed. Own that house outright. 'Course, she never got the chance, poor woman."

It spun me around inside, Peg knowing all this. But it also felt like a weight lifted off me, that I wasn't the only person in the know. I could talk it through with someone else, someone who cared deeply about the women in this town, who'd built up a network to protect them from the brutal men of Parson.

I said, "Miss Kate, she ticked a box on the form—it said Ed would *sign* those papers. In person. She ever mention that? Tell you where he was?"

Peg shook her head, downshifting as she turned the wheel and left her tattered neighborhood, directing us down the desolate hush of Main Street. A single streetlamp glowed at either end of the lonely stretch. "She kept lots of things to herself, our Kate. Never told me where he was. But she assured me he would sign."

"And what do you make of all that? With the papers, I mean. She filed them one day, dead the next."

"Kate's passing, it's such a sorrow. Of course, I believe that death isn't the end—that if you live your life with love, if you try to make amends where you go wrong, there'll be a better world waiting for you one day, when the judgment comes. Kate believed that, too. So I shouldn't be sad, except that it was so sudden. If I'm honest with myself, I think I looked into it so long, so deeply, because I just couldn't accept that she was gone. But nothing's gonna bring her back. Only the resurrection."

"So you did look into it? It seemed suspicious to you?" I was embarrassed at the fervor in my voice, my need to hear her say *Yes, I do think Kate was killed,* to know I wasn't misguided, brooding on a delusion like Thomas Wick with Robby.

Peg raised a hand, let it fall back on the wheel. "It could've been a murder, no question about that. Could've been an accident—just as likely. And the police don't give two figs either way. Me, I've got my little theories. Sure I do. But in the end, nothing solid."

We were headed out of town, taking an on-ramp of Highway 35, her headlights skimming the long grass that sprouted from the cracks in the shoulder. Peg's face was a dark silhouette against the darker fields in the window. I asked, "Care to share any of those theories?"

She chuckled again. "You've been thinking about this a lot, huh?"

"On and off for months. But then the last week or so, out at Parson House . . ."

"You expect to see her around every corner."

"She's in my head. For sure."

Peg picked up some speed on the highway, her Ranger less rattly on the open road. "So here's the thing: once I started to ponder it, I was stunned how many people might have wanted Kate dead. More people than *me*, even," she added with a laugh. "You have Seth, that son of hers, right at the house when she died—not a big guy, maybe, but bigger than his mother, and moody as anything. You have Joanna, the daughter, who hated Kate, who could've gone out there and done it. You have Ed—and listen, if someone killed her, probably it *was* Ed, because no one had more reason: he loathed Kate, had lots to gain from her death. You have Ed's father, who, okay, that old guy couldn't have done it—but his four other sons, if one got angry, if he thought Kate killed his brother? Who knows; they're local, too, more or less. And you have all those men in town who *despise* Kate and me because we freed their wives or girlfriends from their control. Any one of those guys could have sneaked out to the mansion, waited for the right moment, hit her in the head with a rock. These cops of ours, they don't know a head wound from their rear end, excuse my French. Hell, a few of the wives we freed were *married* to cops. The *cops* could have done it."

I thought of the cops who had shown up the morning I found Miss Kate in the garden—their laughter, their sneering. Had one of them already known she was lying there when he pulled up at Parson House? Had they all already known?

Peg sighed. "What I finally realized was: in a town this size, you've got to live your life. I had, what, thirty, thirty-five people to suspect? All who might've had accomplices, other people in on the murder. I was looking over my shoulder, getting paranoid. And it *still* could have been an accident, because what do I know? I'm not Detective Poirot over here. The main reason I thought it was a murder, it wasn't evidence, really—it's just the men of Parson, I wouldn't put it past them. I look in their eyes, and most of them, I just see killers in waiting. So take that for what it's worth. But I'll tell you one thing, sweetie: Kate Darnell's death—that's a big reason I had Claudia keeping an eye on you."

"What do you mean?" I said.

"This town is *dangerous*, if you haven't noticed. It's rough, it's violent, and justice isn't anyone's top priority. Look what I've had to do just so the women here can live with a little dignity. Right now you're working at a house that my good friend might've gotten killed over. I care about you, Lou. You matter to me. I'm not losing another friend to Parson House."

We drove for a mile in silence, Peg changing lanes now and then, taking a circuitous route around the outskirts of town. I saw why she'd wanted to talk in the truck: she couldn't have talked like this in her house, aired these suspicions with everyone to overhear. I was struggling to take it all in, piece my thoughts together. Was I truly in danger at Parson House? I'd worried that Joanna might have Miss Kate's revolver, but should I be worried about other dangers as well? It felt like every man in town might be watching me out there, waiting to rush from the shadows.

Peg interrupted these thoughts, her voice just louder than the rumble of the tires. "While we're talking, Lou, there's probably some more I should tell you about Kate. I've been holding back, to be honest. You loved her as much as I did. You deserve to know everything. All of it."

As at the taqueria yesterday, I wasn't sure I wanted to know. But I heard myself say, "Please. Tell me."

I thought Peg might tell me about Miss Kate's childhood or some shameful details from her marriage with Ed, details that would make me suspect him even more. Instead she started to tell me about her own parents.

Peg's parents had been born in Germany in the late nineteenth century and had converted to the Jehovah's Witness faith shortly after they married. It was a persecuted religion, frowned on by the government; just after their first child, they sailed to America in search of religious freedom. Peg told me how, despite their hopes of tolerance in America, her family had a tough time for decades in New York, Chicago, Dallas, and had wound up working at the factory in Parson in the 1930s, when they joined the small Jehovah's Witness community. Then the factory became a wartime effort with the start of World War II, began making flags and uniforms, and her father and brother needed to quit, since, as Witnesses, they were pacifists, staunchly anti-war. Her brother was even jailed and beaten as a conscientious objector.

"There was no work for us in Parson," she said. "No one would hire any of us during the war. So I helped my parents put together a little farmstead. Not enough to keep money in our pockets but, after a while, enough to feed us. Those years were rough on all us Witnesses, a time of crisis, directionless. My father was an elder in our church by then, and to him, to the other elders, Parson felt like the last, farthest outpost of the church on earth. They acted like everything could crumble just like that if we didn't hold the faith firm. And we were such a tiny community—nine or ten families during the war—that any broken rule felt like a hole that could sink us all."

This fear had made the elders stricter, their rules more absolute. "I was a full-grown woman," Peg said, "but my father beat me when he thought I'd done something wrong. Either him or one of the elders. My mother, too, she was beaten whenever they liked. All the women and children of the church could be beaten—we were told it was for our own good. It hurts me to think of it now, but that's just how things were. That's how we did things."

I knew lots of people who got beatings at home. Not a lot who liked to talk about it. Peg looked like she was gritting out the words, her eyes fixed on the highway in her headlights.

"We didn't witness much during the war," she said. "Too dangerous. Our boys locked up, the rest of us jobless, people yelling at us in the streets, kids throwing stones. But our elders, they said to get out there, it was still our duty to spread the faith. So, when we knocked on doors, we'd pick certain houses on purpose, lonely people, desperate people, people grateful for any kind word. War widows cooped up with kids; old men in shotgun shacks. Our numbers started to grow, even with the rest of the town hating us. When the war finally ended, that had become our new strategy."

I could see what Peg was getting at. "Miss Kate," I said.

She nodded. "Later on she told me what it was like. She thought bringing the kids to Parson—such a small, traditional place in this new, traditional marriage—would be her best shot at security. For them, for herself as well. But we found her overwhelmed, depressed. Married to Ed Darnell, who was never around, who drank and gambled whenever he was. Three willful children she couldn't control. The first time we knocked on her door? Kate let us right in, made us a pitcher of lemonade. Listened to our message like she was starving for it. It works like that sometimes, you know. People lost, looking for answers, a little structure.

"And once Kate had it, she was off to the races. It gave her a sense of purpose she'd never known before. She was a good Witness. Brought in even more people. There was something shameless about her; she'd witness to anyone. She didn't have those wartime memories, that same fear the rest of us did. The elders took notice of her, made her their special project, started telling her how to handle her children. Hitting her kids wouldn't do much—she was far too small a woman—but she could keep them in their room for days, make them miss their meals, if they disobeyed. The youngest two, Seth and Joanna, they fell in line pretty quick. But the eldest, Cassandra . . . she was wild. Kate forbade her to act in the school play; she sneaked out, got the lead. Kate told her she couldn't have a job—the next thing, she was working in the diner.

"So Kate called in the elders. A few of them, they'd go to the house, they'd bring their paddles. Not sure how often it happened; there was some secrecy around it. But I know my father went. Old as he was, he'd go over there and beat a teenage girl. Just for the crime of acting like a teenage girl."

I'd never known any of this, never suspected it. But I could remember how Cass would have bruises sometimes, dark shadows under her breezy clothes, like dapples on old banana skins. *I keep bumping into tables at work*, she explained once when Danny asked, and then let out a light, airy laugh, tinkling like a bell above a shop door.

The details of her abuse, the full scope of it, scraped me raw. I wanted to ask why Miss Kate had gone along with the elders, had surrendered so much to them. But I was starting to get a different picture of the woman I'd always known. When she was kind to me, it was often at her own children's expense. I'd been so happy to be special, I'd never realized what she was doing, denigrating her children to win my affection.

"How long did this go on?" I asked.

"Years," Peg admitted. "Then, when Cassandra died, I just felt like—"

Peg's voice broke, faltered. I'd never seen her like this, vulnerable, wounded with regret. Beyond her window, a trail of moonlight gleamed along the vista of the bay. She'd taken us off the highway onto the dirt roads outside town, and I realized we'd soon be passing the ditch where Robby had found us that night. Peg was driving us out toward the promontory, the mansion.

She gathered herself, adjusted her grip on the wheel. "Cassandra's death, it shook me up. Changed me. I couldn't think of the church the same way again. I kept my faith—I wouldn't be anything without it. But I started studying the scriptures, finding flaws in some of the rules, thinking how things could be better for the women and kids. I was planning to bring this to the elders—not right away, but when I'd gathered enough arguments to make my case. But I made the mistake of telling Kate about it first."

"She *told* on you?"

Peg gave a grim nod. "Cass's death . . . it had an opposite effect on us. It made me doubt and question, but it drew Kate even deeper into the fold. Looking back, I should have seen it coming. Her kids were gone, she was more alone than ever, more desperate. And her guilt over Cass—the elders made her feel like she'd been a good parent to her children, that their own worldly failings were the problem. So of course she took my 'rebellious' thoughts to the elders—it's what they instructed you to do, after all, to let them know about any dissatisfaction within the ranks. I'm not sure she understood that I'd be disfellowshipped, pushed out of the community. My own parents, they kicked me out of the house I'd *built* for them. Never spoke to me again, rest their souls."

I couldn't help but feel for her: the situation was so much like Robby's and mine, being kicked out like that. I'd had no idea.

"So I set up a life for myself. Got a nice property out in the country, raised a few heads of steer. When women started coming to me from the church, I was ready for them. Battered wives, neglected daughters, mothers scared for their children, all living under the elders, all so grateful to escape them. We didn't leave the faith, just worshipped on our own: we weren't walking away from Jehovah, we were walking away from those *men*. Then, little by little, we started helping other women in town when we could. Only getting tough with the fellas when we needed to." She smiled. "Kate convinced Adam Stanton to give that car of his to Claudia and the kids. Ah, the look on his face! We helped anyone we could. Some of these women joined the faith, but even if not, we helped them. That was our mission."

A picture was forming in my mind: the Miss Kate I'd known in my twenties, the close friend calling me in from the ladder for some tea.

"How did Miss Kate get involved with you all?"

Peg drew in a long, tight breath. "Ed was drinking and gambling more, treating Kate worse and worse. That's why she called Seth to live with her down here—she thought having another man around would keep Ed from hitting her. But Seth didn't seem to notice it.

"Honestly, I would've been happy never to talk to Kate again. But then a pal of mine at the hospital told me that Kate had been there a few nights—Ed had put her in the hospital this time. So I went and visited her room, first time I'd seen her in years, expecting she'd just tell me to get lost. But the abuse, it had changed her. She opened up to me, told me how she'd begged the elders to let her have a divorce. Of course they'd denied her. 'If you want to be treated better, witness to him. Bring Ed into the fold.' And she tried, bless her, but it only made Ed worse. And he was running them into the ground, piling up debt with that hick mob who ran the races. Ed was hinting he might split town, and she was worried the mob might come after her if he left."

"But Ed—was it you who made him leave?"

Peg laughed. "I did give him a talking-to, I won't lie. But Ed would have left all on his own."

A morbid thought occurred to me. "You think his debts caught up with him, wherever he is? He never came back to claim the mansion."

"I'm guessing Ed's just fine," Peg said. "I don't talk about this much, but I ended up arranging a deal with that mob. For Kate's safety, not his. The ladies and me, we started a monthly collection, paying off what Ed owed little by little. It wasn't the first time we'd done something like that—making payments on the husbands' behalf to get them to leave the wives alone—though I will admit Ed's debts ended up being bigger than I'd realized. And those boys aren't renowned for their long-term payment plans. But I guess milking a little from us was better than a big fat nothing from Ed."

"It's the Dixie Mafia, isn't it?"

Peg scoffed. "That's what they'd call themselves, sure. Jumped-up name for a bunch of dropout losers with shotguns."

"I think a couple of them came to Parson House today."

Peg's voice became less easy. "Well, now, I'm sorry to hear that." She took a second, glanced in her rearview mirror. "They probably caught wind of Ed's stake in the place, wanted to make sure he wasn't hiding out there. It won't happen again, I can guarantee you that. I'm making final arrangements now, and soon enough they'll be paid in full. They'll have no cause to go nosing around for Ed's hidey-hole."

"You kept paying them? Even after Kate died?"

"Once boys like that get you on the line, they don't like to cut you loose. I took on the debt when Ed left, which means it's mine now. No matter what we've been through, we've kept up those payments, and we're nearly done. It hasn't been easy."

It was strange to see Peg butt up against the limits of her power, tangling with the type of men she couldn't scare away. "So what happened after Ed left?" I asked.

"The elders found out that I'd helped Kate. So she was disfellowshipped, just like me. I know that hurt her, the rejection of it. But she pulled herself back together in time, realized that my group was just as much of a community. Soon enough she was as devoted to us as she'd ever been to the elders."

We were drawing close to Parson House, Peg slowing her Ranger as it grumbled up the long dirt drive. The mansion was beyond the reach of her headlights at first, so that I could see it mainly by what I couldn't see, the absence of starlight behind its peaks and chimneys. Then the broad bay windows glinted, the columns of the porch resolved, the balcony emerged in its watchful perch above the garden, and the vast house took on a shadowy dimension as it loomed above us, like a dragon winking awake at the back of a cave, lit by the trembling beam of a single flashlight.

Peg parked in the circular drive, looked out at the restored windows, the house front cleared of vines, the roof no longer marred by missing shingles. "You've done a beautiful job," she said, her eyes moving thoughtfully from the porch to the patterned cornice under the attic. "You've got a real gift for this, you know. If you stay in Parson, Lou—I'll tell ya, I could use you."

I was shaken by her stories, but I glowed with pleasure at her praise. To impress a woman like Peg—I could never get enough of such motherly approval.

"You'll have to talk to Heather," I said.

She laughed. "Just sayin'. You have a future doing this kind of work if you want it. Even in San Antonio. You understood this house— what it needed. You showed real care."

I murmured a quiet thanks, too moved to say more.

She hadn't looked away from the manor since we parked. "You know, I remember the first time Kate drove me out here. The first time she said we should buy this place from the town. Things were getting too crowded out at the farm, and the military had started the draft back up, raised the temperature in the entire town. Young men coming home in body bags, lots of fear and anger, lots of women and kids catching the flak. I wanted to help more than anything, but we needed more. We couldn't just cobble together whatever we could day by day—we had to start building a future together. Kate saw that. She had such pluck, such vision. Something like this house, it never would've occurred to me. I took some convincing, to be honest. Told her it was more than we needed. Too much upkeep, too much attention on us."

I was staring at Peg. "I didn't know you were involved with the house."

A tiny smile touched the edges of her lips. "*Involved.* I sank more than half my savings into this place."

"Miss Kate . . . I'd ask her about it, how she could afford a mansion. She'd never tell me."

Peg seemed not to hear me, her eyes faraway, lost either in the past or the sprawling scale of the mansion before us. "She convinced me in the end. Got me to see it, too: what it would mean to move our women out here, to make them shared owners of Parson House. What it would say to the men in town and, more important, what it would say to the women. All the women in Parson. That their time had come. That they were strong now."

A thought was emerging inside me, like the shadowy sprawl of the manor, as we came up the drive. At last I thought I had an answer to one of my questions. Peg was Joanna's buyer.

"So we scraped together all we could," Peg went on. "I wanted to wait and buy the mansion after we'd paid off Ed's debts—because what if those hicks found out, asked why the money hadn't gone to them?—but Kate insisted we act fast. 'If we buy the place straight out,' she said, 'it's not like they can come collect it from under us.' She believed in tangible things. Money could blow away like sand, but property, a house—that was real security. And she wasn't the only one who felt that way; the other ladies fell in love with the idea. We believed in her: this was her dream, her passion. We knew it might take some time, but it was the end of the rainbow for us.

"We gave our money to Kate in cash. The town was dying to sell this place, but those men down at city hall—they'd never sell it to a bunch of 'dangerous women' like us. We needed an individual buyer, a woman with a husband, so those men could think, *Well, Ed owns half of the place*, not guess what we had in mind. Ed hadn't been gone that long yet; people mostly thought he was out at the rig. Our Kate, she went down to city hall, put on the whole dog-and-pony show, told them she'd inherited the money from a 'distant aunt,' wanted to fix up Parson House as a tourist attraction. Those men were thrilled, eager to sell. Probably laughing to themselves at the raw deal she was getting. It worked."

"Until she died," I said.

Peg nodded. "You can see why I was suspicious, why I thought she might've been killed. For years we told no one what we were doing, not even people like you, Lou. We wished we could, believe me, but there was just too much at stake. We were fixing up the house, getting everything ready, and we had it all planned out: on the same day, we'd move the women out here, transfer the deed to common ownership shared among a few of the unmarried women—that way no husbands could come stamping in and muck things up. If we got to that point, then we'd be done, nothing the town could do. But it's possible word got out, that one of our women said something, though they all swear they didn't. Like I said, if the wrong men knew about this, I wouldn't put it past them, coming out here to threaten her—maybe getting carried away."

Everything was making more sense, all the strange sweltering days since Joanna hired me. "So you figured Claudia should watch me. Because these men might try to stop me if they knew you were Joanna's buyer."

Peg shut her eyes, massaged the skin between her eyebrows. She looked less grieved than tired out, exasperated. "Lou, that's the main reason I'm telling you all this. What is there for us to *buy*? We already put in the money. All of us. Some, like me, at a real sacrifice. And not just for the house but to keep Kate safe. I wasn't sitting on some fat bank account: the money, everything I've given, it's come out of my farm, out of the food I could buy for my girls, new shoes for their kids, payoffs to keep their no-good husbands away. The other women, too—you think they can afford to lose what they put up? We've been waiting for years, and we shouldn't have to buy the house *again*. We can't, in fact—not for the price Joanna's asking."

"There's no record of the money?"

"Of course we had a record. Put all our signatures on it. I had a copy, too, that I kept at home, but the storm—let's just say my filing system mostly ended up out in the bay. So Kate's copy, the one in Parson House, is the only one left, but Joanna says she can't find it, that she's been looking, searching the house, all her mother's papers, and it's nowhere. Says our story sounds *far-fetched* to her—unless there's solid proof. I said to her, 'You know your mother didn't have much money. You know Ed was never rich, that grunt job on the rig. You know from her papers that she bought the house outright, not even a mortgage. How do you reckon she did that? I'll tell you how: it wasn't her own money.' Joanna wouldn't listen, just told me again she'd need to see proof. You have to remember how she knows me, Lou. When Joanna left town fifteen years ago, I was a pillar of that church, one of its most active members. The church that turned her mother cruel, that sent elders to beat Cass. She won't just hand Parson House over to a woman she hates. She's saying she's lined up a different buyer, some investor in New York, started negotiations. That's why I was hoping . . . I was hoping you might talk to her, Lou. Because maybe she did find the papers and she just needs some talking around."

I thought about this. "I could try. Doubt she'd listen to me, though. We've got lots of issues from way back in high school."

"Yeah," Peg said on a long sigh. "I was afraid that might be the case. That's another thing about this town. The past dies slow."

I turned from Peg, looked back at the mansion. Suddenly, as if in a dream, I could see Miss Kate's vision of the house: every window lit, the porch lined with wicker rocking chairs, women talking and laughing at their ease in the summer night, a few strolling through the placid garden, children running about in the yard. Miss Kate herself in the kitchen window, humming some old show tune as she bustled between the counters, preparing trays of tea for the others, these women whose lives she'd saved, who could live in freedom now, far from fear. There was no cruelty in this vision, no overbearing presence, no law but love. I even thought I saw Cass and Joanna there, both younger than I'd ever known them, sitting cross-legged in the garden in light cotton dresses, playing pat-a-cake and chanting like little kids.

Part III

Part III

23

After Joanna left Parson in high school, I didn't speak with Miss Kate for over a decade. I knew she was still in town, and I bore her no grudge for Joanna getting us kicked out of Granbury. But what had happened, all that history, felt like a turbulent river coursing between us, too deep and fast-flowing to cross. She was only ever a few miles away, but she might as well have been my birth mother driving off into that eternal night.

The next time I talked to Miss Kate, in my midtwenties, I had just stepped out of Save Mart on an autumn afternoon, my arms heavy with groceries. Miss Kate was walking down Main Street with Seth, and she spotted me and waved before I could duck inside my truck. She gave me a big eager hug, had tears in her eyes when we drew apart, as if she'd been looking for me all these years, as if it were a small miracle we'd found each other at last. Seth offered me a brief hello but then stood back from us, hands in his pockets, watching a few sparrows in the shade of an awning.

"Ah, Louisa. It's been too long," Miss Kate said, gazing up at me. She'd aged a great deal since I last saw her, her skin wrinkled and lax, her hair splotched with gray, looking more like Seth's grandmother than his mother. I thought about books Joanna had given me, stories of fairy worlds where time passes differently than on the human plane.

She asked how I was keeping myself, and I told her that I worked at Buck's, mentioned some odd jobs I'd pick up on the side. I hated catch-up chats like these, when I couldn't hide how little I was making of my life. I could have told her I was helping to raise Sarah, but I didn't want Miss Kate to bring up Robby, not out here in front of Save Mart with my hands full of groceries, though without saying anything about my home and family, I was aware of how empty my life sounded. But Miss Kate said, "You're keeping busy. That's wonderful. I'm so proud of you, Louisa," like I'd told her I was developing a cure for cancer. I didn't ask about her life, afraid she'd talk about Cass or Joanna, make me open those boxes buried deep in myself. Just before we parted, she invited me to dinner, and I gave her a vague yes, wrote my phone number on an envelope from her pocket.

"Kate Darnell?" Heather said that evening in our backyard. "After all these years, she wants to have *dinner* with you?"

I was sitting on a lawn chair, a towel draped over my shoulders, Heather standing behind me as she cut my hair. I'd mostly ignored my hair before I lived with a stylist, would let it grow down to my back and then lop it off at ear length like some hedge I trimmed only when it got unsightly. But I didn't mind these frequent haircuts: I relished the small intimacy of her fingers sectioning my hair, the precise snipping noises of the shears.

I said, "Miss Kate was just being nice, I think. Women like her, they can't say hello and not give an invite. She probably won't follow up."

Lightning bugs glowed in hazy clouds around the yard, and Sarah was nearby, plopped down in the grass, her worn-out Chatty Cathy doll facedown in the dirt next to her. She was plucking up stems and slowly tearing them apart, watching the sinews separate with pious wonder. She was baby-chubby, but I could already see her parents' features in her face: the tiny cleft of Heather's chin, Robby's straight-slashed eyebrows that made her eyes precociously serious.

"Lots of bad memories back when I last knew her," I went on. "You know, Cass and all. Doubt she'd want to think about that, either."

But the next evening the phone rang, and it was Miss Kate. Dinner was warm and friendly, and by later that week, I was out working at Parson House.

From the first I was excited to work for her. Being back in the mansion made me jittery at times, but I didn't mind it so much with

Miss Kate beside me, offering praise every step of the way. She could sense when I got tired out, brought me tea and snacks on a round silver tray, chatted with me about all her plans for the renovation. She never mentioned Ed or Joanna, though she did bring up Seth when he left on his walks, told me she worried that he wasn't doing well, and she wasn't sure how to help a man like him. Other times she'd reminisce about Robby, memories from those long-ago days of our childhood, which felt so distant, like they'd happened in some mythical country sunk into the sea.

One time, only once, she brought up Cass.

It was after dinner, and Miss Kate and I sat in wrought-iron chairs near the entrance to the garden. The ruellia bloomed nearby, its trumpet-shaped flowers open to the fading sun.

"You never knew my daughter Cassandra much, did you?" she said out of nowhere. Her voice was gentle but pained, her gaze turned away. "It's a shame. You would have liked her. She was difficult not to like."

"I knew her a little," I said, not mentioning we'd been friends that last summer. A twinge of guilt passed through me.

"Something about this place, living here . . . it's brought her back to me. I'm not sure why. But sometimes, in the house, it's like she's standing right beside me. Like if I speak to her, she'll hear me. Try to speak back."

I told her this was natural, that I felt this way with Robby, too, sometimes, like I could squeeze a hand that wasn't there, see him smile at Sarah in her crib. But I held back what might have upset Miss Kate, made her think the house was truly haunted: that Cass had been here the night she died, that coming out to Parson House, in many ways, had killed her. I felt like I couldn't tell Miss Kate this. She seemed frail, vulnerable, and I felt responsible for her happiness. Like when Sarah and I were driving and I'd point out a cloud so she wouldn't see the flattened squirrel in the road.

Miss Kate had died here, and her ghost had joined Cass's, both of them whispering in the silence while I put the final touches on my work. For the next few days, wrapped in these thoughts, working long hours, I barely noticed what I was doing, the ways the house was taking shape under my hands. And then one night at sunset, as the long line of the horizon bled below a gibbous moon, I realized I was finished.

The house was far from done. The pipes would need checking, refitting; an electrician should inspect the wiring. None of this was work I could do. But the shell of the house was ready for Joanna's new buyer—or for Peg's group of women if Joanna would accept a lower price.

I took one last walk through the mansion. I supposed I had my answers now, or the most clarity I was going to get. It was time to leave this all behind.

Tonight the sea was strangely quiet, like radio static turned down to a whisper; my footsteps echoed loudly through the rooms. I passed through the servants' cells, thought of this house's unholy birth, a slave plantation that had created the wealth of Parson. I remembered the museum days, trailing with my classmates behind the docent, her polished fingernails pointing out the tidy beds in these quarters. "See how well the slaves were taken care of?" she'd said with a motherly smile. "Why, I'll bet this is bigger'n some of your *own* rooms, isn't it?" I remembered the drawing on the easel, the figures in the fields with their backs turned to the viewer, the backs on which our brutal town was built.

I had an urge to fetch some gasoline, torch the mansion down.

Instead I drifted to Miss Kate's study, moved among her papers as the room darkened toward night, pulled the beaded cord of her banker's lamp. A moth had found its way there, and it flapped around the lightbulb frantically. Standing in this room, amid the detritus of her life—notes, greeting cards, letters, drawings on the backs of past-due bills—I couldn't stop thinking of Miss Kate, what might have happened to her one room over on her balcony. I sat down in the desk chair, the leather cushion creaking, took a deep breath, closed my eyes. The house seemed to gather around me, spacious and silent in the half-light, cleaner now, cleared of clutter, but never at peace or rest, the air in these rooms unsettled by the lives that had passed through here, including my own.

Danny's laugh echoing in the darkness, the thud as he bumped against the wall.

Thomas saying to him: *I'll guide you, just lean into me, I can see all right.* It was a lie—none of us could see, since his Zippo ran out of fluid—but Danny trusted him anyway, a different person then, laughing and happy and full.

You bring your flask? Cass asked Thomas, and I was close enough to her that I felt him hand it over, felt the air shift with their movements, heard the slosh of liquid as she drank.

You boys enjoy yourselves. Cass's hand on my arm, leading me away. *Danny?* I asked. *You all right?*

His small, barely audible laugh told me it was okay, that he felt safe with Thomas. I left them there, followed Cass down to the parlor. We sat on the love seat, smoked, and talked, our last conversation, which only Cass knew was goodbye, her ticket to New York in the tin beside her.

The flash of headlights in the window.

You wait right here, Cass told me, squinting out at the driveway. *I think that's Adam's car. I'll try to get those stupid boys in here, and you can jump out and scare them.* Her voice was sly and playful, giddy with the adventure of this night.

She jumped up, energized, and rushed out of the parlor. She left everything behind: the Black Cat tin tucked in the cushion, her car keys which she'd taken out, using the bitting to fold some loose strands back into the joint. I snatched up the keys, pocketed them before we forgot about them in all this fun.

It's all right with me, you know. Her words echoing in my mind, taking me back to the woods with Joanna, the smooth, tender warmth of her face in my hands. Did Cass know about that, too? Could she tell as easily as looking at me?

I knelt at the bay window, not wanting to give myself away to Adam. I looked out at the headlights, the dark circle of the front drive.

This was where the memory stopped, though I sensed it wasn't finished. I stood up in the study, pulled the chain on the banker's lamp, wandered into the shadows of the hallway like a ghost myself.

Suddenly there were headlights flashing through the window,

coming up the drive, and something struck like a match inside me. I could tell that something dangerous was approaching, rising up inside me and from the hidden depths of the house, as if the two were now the same, my mind as vast and haunted as this mansion. If I wanted, I could try to escape this memory, run from the house, get into my truck, turn up the music, drive. My work here was complete: I never needed to see Parson House again.

But I was tired of running. So I stayed in the shadows, remembered.

*Cass's car keys in my pocket, me watching through the parlor win-*dow. The creak of the front door opening, Cass half skipping down the porch steps, calling out to the car in her joyful, ringing voice. From behind the blinding headlights stepped a man-shaped silhouette, seeming to emerge from the light itself rather than the car. He was walking toward Cass with a quick, tense stride, out of place in the silly revelry of this night. Somehow I recognized the silhouette at once, the familiar outline of that body. It was my brother. Robby.

He was shouting at Cass, words I couldn't make out—only the ugly knife-edge cut of his tone. Cass lost the whimsy in her walk, her body language turning cautious, like she was approaching a bucking animal.

He grabbed her arm, so hard and fast that I gripped the window ledge, stunned, too stoned to make sense of what was happening. Cass yelped in pain, dropped to her knees, but my brother didn't let go. Then a fumble of footsteps on the porch: Danny and Thomas spilling out of the house, down into the driveway and the glare of the headlights.

Robby was still shouting, Danny and Thomas hovering near him. Someone in the car leaned on the horn, let it blare out into the night. I realized with a shiver that no one but us could hear it. That we were all alone out here.

Cass's Clipper was parked nearby. I felt her keys in my pocket. We needed to *go*. Now.

By the time I rushed out onto the porch, Danny was lying on the ground at Robby's feet. Specks of blood on the gravel. Cass still on her knees, a short distance from Robby, holding her arm out to the side as if it caused her immense pain.

I yelled something to my friends, I can't remember what. But suddenly Cass and Thomas and Danny were running, and I was running with them, making for the Clipper like our lives depended on it. Robby was right behind us, a huffing bull about to overtake us, when his teammates got him first, three of them grabbing his arms, pulling him back, barely able to hold him. If I hadn't been so stoned and drunk, I might have turned to Robby then, told him to stop it, demanded an explanation. But I was terrified, blurry, just wanted to escape this desolate place, get back to town. Cass called to me, *You need to drive*, so I rushed into the driver's seat, took out the keys as my friends tumbled into the car around me.

Cass, panting, breathless at my side. Holding her arm out in front of her. *That one*, she said, *the silver key. That one, Lou. Go, go, go.*

The steering wheel rumbling under my inexperienced hands. My first time driving. Cass talking me through the pedal work in a ragged, rapid voice, shifting the gears herself with her good arm. We lurched down the drive, reached a steady speed in second gear, rounded the bend onto the road, and revved into third and then fourth, our speed just over the limit, the house no longer looming in the rearview mirror. Then, when we thought we'd made it, when the adventure seemed over at last, Danny asking Cass about her arm, Thomas muttering about *asshole football players*—just then I saw headlights in the rearview mirror, gaining on us fast. Startled, I pressed down the gas pedal harder.

Fifteen years had passed, but suddenly I could feel that pedal under my foot, the swirl of weed and whiskey and terror inside me. I felt that same terror coming back to me, stammering endlessly. As these memories returned, I had drifted out of the mansion and stood dazed on the front porch, gazing down at the circular drive where Robby, my Robby, had grabbed Cass's arm that night. Why had he done this to her? Who would ever want to hurt *Cass*? And yet so many had hurt her, had treated her like her very presence was an invitation to harm. The sky was huge above me, untouched by any town lights, filled with stars like a stadium of watching eyes.

The headlights' glow growing as they maneuvered down the drive.

The little blue Fairlane was rumbling toward me. Joanna at the wheel.

24

Joanna stepped from the car and shut the door behind her. She wore a thin headband, a green drop-waist dress with a white collar. Wherever she'd been the past week or so—my guess was with her brother—she'd lost her tan from our picnic lunches, her face paler than ever under the starlight. She must have been surprised to see me, standing out on the porch like I expected her, but, true to form, she gave no hint of it, just ran a hand across her bangs, forced a wary smile to her lips.

It was later than I'd realized, all trace of the summer sunset gone. Perhaps she'd been driving out here some nights, checking on my work as it proceeded. I'd startled her, caught her off guard, alone at the mansion with me when she didn't expect it—the moment that the hunter in me had waited for so patiently. But I was scared of any more secrets right now; I could still see my brother shouting on this drive-way, Danny on the ground before him, the spatter of blood. I felt more in the past than the present, a past of bitter truths: I had been driving the car that night, I had crashed into the ditch, I had killed Cass. No wonder Thomas Wick hated me.

But he hated Robby more. Robby, who had been chasing us.

"Hello, Louisa," Joanna said, walking toward the porch. Despite my suspicions, I felt glad to see her. It meant I wasn't alone. She continued, "My apologies for being away the past week. Some business took me out of town, and I suppose I should have called or left a note. But in all the suddenness, I'm afraid I forgot."

In some distant corner of my mind, I was surprised to hear that Joanna had been out of town. Preoccupied as I was, fighting the tremors that raced through my body, I couldn't think of a follow-up question.

"That's okay," I said instead, trying to keep a quaver from my voice. I felt if I glanced back at the parlor window that I'd catch a glimpse of myself: fourteen, gaping at Cass on her knees.

"In any case," she went on, "I trusted you to continue with the work. And I must say, it looks fantastic. You must be close to finished at this point, no?"

"It's done, actually. Finished up tonight."

This halted Joanna in her steps, her low heel clicking on the first stair of the porch. A new brightness shone in her face as she looked up at me, and I remembered all the times that I'd saved her from bullies as a child, how her gratitude was payment beyond measure.

"Well. That is certainly wonderful news," she said. "Just tremendous. And such a relief! Shall you show me around? Or is it too late? I understand if you need to get home. I could look through the house myself."

The thought of driving away in my truck, being alone for even a second, frightened me past reason. "I can show you around. No problem."

She was standing beside me on the porch now, hands on her slender hips, her face harder to see in the shadows. "Louisa, I can't begin to express my gratitude. You'll be paid well, but please know all you've done for me here. It means more than just money."

I killed your sister, I wanted to say. *My brother and I, we killed her. All those years I blamed you for Robby's death, but that was a joke compared to this. These hands right here? They swerved the car off the road. I was drunk, high, fourteen. I had no business driving that car. And Robby, he was chasing us in a rage. Cass died because I was scared of my own brother.*

It hardly seemed true. I wanted to doubt it, to push it away like I'd pushed it away for fifteen years. Now that it was out of whatever tight-lidded box I'd kept it in, I worried I'd never be able to stop watching it, playing on loop in my head.

I said, "Come on, then. I'll show you through the rooms."

The two of us trailed through the house, flicking on lights as we went. Joanna buzzed with happiness behind me, complimenting the windowpanes, the fresh floorboards, the plastered wall holes, the rooms free of mold and mildewy reek. "It's a marvel," she said at one point. "I can't imagine a professional doing a better job. Not that I'm saying you're not professional. Oh my. You know what I mean. Just that this is wonderful."

My thoughts were elsewhere, questioning, reframing the past. Had Joanna known I was driving the car that night, known that Robby was chasing us when we crashed? Someone might have told her: Thomas out of spite, maybe, or even Danny, though he'd never mentioned a thing to me. If she knew, I didn't blame her for informing Granbury about us. I'd have done the same in her place. I would have done even worse.

And Danny—why had he been keeping this secret from me all these years? Maybe he didn't remember, either, concussed himself, traumatized by the violent reversals of that night. But no: the other week at Buck's, he'd said to me, *You might have your reasons to hate Joanna, but she has some reasons to hate you, too,* and a pang of panic had hit me, and I'd hurried outside for a smoke. *That* was what Danny had meant: not my right hook to her jaw back in high school but the crunched-in car in the ditch, the car that my brother and I had put there. Maybe Danny thought *I* remembered, thought this was why I never discussed the past.

Or maybe he had a different reason. *I don't want Lou to get in trouble*—according to Thomas, those had been among Cass's final words. *If anyone asks, it was only the three of us.* By the time Danny left the hospital, the whole incident had died down; Sergeant Stanton, Adam's father, had already intimidated Thomas's parents to keep them quiet. And it wasn't like Robby and I were eager to talk about the crash. So maybe Danny had remembered Cass's request and decided it was better to keep quiet as well.

Joanna and I finished our tour of the house back in the study, where Joanna took an old bottle of whiskey from the shelf, Miss Kate's Glenfiddich. "Would you have a sip?" she asked me.

"Please," I said. "As much as you're willing."

Her smile widened. "Absolutely! You've earned it. You must be exhausted from the work the past few days. Do take a seat. I insist."

She filled a tumbler to the brim, handed it to me, gave herself a generous pour as well. The whiskey was delicious, barrel-aged from Scotland, the good stuff Miss Kate broke out when we finished a major project. Joanna watched how fast I was drinking, my trembling hand on the tumbler. A line appeared across her forehead.

"Are you feeling well, Louisa?" she said.

"Just the heat today. Hot out there. I'm fine."

The liquor burned in my stomach, spread warmly up my chest, settled me somewhat. Usually I had a high tolerance, but I felt almost drunk at once.

Joanna sat on the edge of the desk, her feet dangling above the floor, the most her childhood self I'd seen her since she'd returned. "I have some exciting news to share. And the excellent work you've done here only makes it more exciting."

I drained the last of my drink. Wished I could ask her for a refill.

"We have a new buyer," she continued. "Someone who will pay even *more*. The last buyer was a New York investor, just wanted to turn a profit, made me negotiate at some length. But this new man, Teddy, he's heir to a Houston oil fortune, and he wants a house on the coast for holidays, parties, galas, that sort of thing. He knows how empty Parson is, and he says he doesn't mind. Prefers it that way, in fact. A little peace and quiet, he told me."

I didn't consider what I said next, just knew I needed to say it. The hunter in me had returned, cold, calculating, and I sensed I could throw her off course now, when she was happy with me, sipping her drink, her normal defenses lowered.

"But shouldn't you work something out with Peg?" I asked in an innocent voice. "Her group—they put all that money into this place."

Joanna's smile faded. She looked away from me, out the window. I could see her thinking, wondering how deeply involved I was with Peg.

At last she said, "Whose side are you on here, Louisa? Please be honest with me."

"Can't say that I have a side. Peg told me about this the other night."

"That money you mentioned. The money they 'put into' the house. All I have is their word for it. I haven't found one piece of evidence to suggest it." She gestured to the papers piled around us. "And I've been looking since Peg first told me, searching and searching for evidence of their stake in the property. All I know is this: the deed is made out to my mother, certified by the state. And it's awfully convenient that, as soon as my mother dies, Peg comes knocking."

"Peg and Miss Kate, they were working together. Helping women in Parson."

Joanna gave me a pitying look. "You don't know Peg like I do. She's an awful, wretched woman. Brainwashed."

"Brainwashed?" I asked. "You're talking like this is *The Manchurian Candidate*."

"Closer than you'd think," she said. "Really, Louisa, you didn't see any of it. I don't trust a single word that comes from her mouth. Neither would you if you'd grown up with her."

I nodded, felt a twist in my stomach. "Peg told me about all that. It sounded . . . horrible."

"I'm not a greedy person, Louisa. If Peg's group had truly bought the house, I would do the right thing and sign over the deed to them. But I can't just *give* my inheritance to these religious fanatics because they tell me some story. I have Seth to think of, and that comes first. I need to take care of my brother. Get him away from this terrible place."

To my surprise, I noticed a telltale trembling in her upper lip. This was a trembling I knew well, the trembling that used to precede Joanna's tears. She could have turned her face from me, not let me see it, but she didn't.

I heard a voice speak inside me, cold, alert: *You have her where you want her.* Somehow, despite my confusion, I had angled Joanna into this vulnerable moment.

"Can I ask you a question?" I said, making my voice intimate, soft. "Go ahead."

"You don't have to tell me if you don't want. I'd understand. But . . . how long have you been back in Parson?"

She took a sip of whiskey, her eyes averted. "Longer than I've let on."

"Since before your mother died?"

A few tears glistened in her eyelashes, yet to fall. "Did Seth tell you?"

"I've been putting things together."

Joanna's smile returned, but it was pursed, pained. "Seth. He's too honest for his own good."

"Were you here the day she died?"

She closed her eyes, let out her breath. "I arrived that morning."

I could feel my pulse pick up, as at the start of a chase. "And why did you come here?"

Joanna rested a hand on a pile of papers, looked at the shape of her fingers against the page. Finally she said: "I couldn't stop thinking of Seth. Here. Alone. At my mother's mercy. I'd managed to build a life for myself, but I couldn't forget my brother. I could hardly bear it most days, all the guilt."

"So you came down to see him?"

"Every so often, my mother tried to reach me through my father. She had his address, and she'd send him a letter with a note for me. I always ignored them. But then a message came about Seth: that he wasn't doing well, that he needed me. I knew it might be a trick, but I love my brother too much—I picked up the phone, called her. And she sounded . . . different. Different than I remembered. Weaker, not so forceful and demanding. She told me she was willing to give Seth up. That I could come and take him away, get him the help he needed. So I took some time off work, drove down to Parson. And when I arrived, the situation was nothing like she'd said."

"She'd changed her mind?"

Joanna sat straighter on the desk. Her voice had taken on new animation and was bitter with reminiscence; even her face had changed, looser in anger, less a porcelain doll than a fed-up daughter dealing with a difficult mother.

"Seth greeted me at the door," she continued. "He was stunned, *stunned*, to see me. She hadn't told him I was coming, not one word of what we'd discussed. I'd barely started explaining when my mother heard my voice and interrupted us. She asked to speak with me in private, and . . . and it was all a trick, just like I'd feared. Not that Seth was doing well—I could tell at a glance he wasn't. But she acted like Seth leaving Parson was *my* idea, like she hadn't lured me down here with that carrot. She told me they both were unwell, that Seth couldn't leave because they needed each other. And Parson House—she needed Seth *and me* here to help her. She was dying, she told me, and the house was our inheritance. 'I wasn't the best mother to you,' she said, 'I see that now. And I owe this to you both. To leave you well off.'

"It turned my stomach, Louisa. Oh, it made me sick—those same old lies, that false guilt, her 'death,' our 'inheritance'—all just a way to trap us here, to control us. As if I hadn't been *raised* on her manipulation. But I'd fallen for it, driven down to the Gulf, risked my job for no reason, none at all. I felt her cage closing in around me again. I couldn't stand it."

I took in a slow breath along with these words. I'd wanted answers from Joanna, but *had* she in fact murdered Miss Kate? And what would I do if she confessed? Tie her up in that chair over there, call in our corrupt police force?

Joanna uncapped the bottle, poured herself more whiskey, refreshed my tumbler. There was relief in her voice as well, as if she was glad to unburden herself of this story. She went on: "My mother had something to do in town that day. She said it was important. So after her little speech, she left me alone in the house with Seth. We were sitting in the dining room, and Seth made us some toast, and I told him I wanted to take him away, that I had my car, we could leave right now. He seemed to grasp what I was saying, but he kept talking about Europe, about France, how we'd go visit the Eiffel Tower, ride up to the top. 'Fine, sure,' I said, 'I'll have to save for a while, but that would be lovely. Now pack a bag, we need to get out of here quick.' 'Not now,' he told me, 'tonight. After Mom has gone to sleep. Maybe midnight? That's the right time.' 'No,' I said, 'it has to be this morning, while she's away. Otherwise she might play a trick on us, talk you out of it.' I shouldn't have pushed Seth so hard; I regret that. But at the time, I just . . . I couldn't stop myself. I told him I knew he was unhappy. That he needed help. That I wanted to help him, get him away from her.

"And then—then he stood up from the table. He said, 'Wait right here a minute.' And when he came back, he was holding a gun, this little revolver. 'Our mother's,' he said. He set it down on the table like it was show-and-tell in grade school, like he couldn't see how nervous the weapon made me. 'I used to feel so trapped,' he said, 'like there was no way out. But then I found this in her nightstand. Now I feel so much peace, Joanna, so much peace. I always have a solution now. Things might get bad for me, but I have a solution. I have a plan.'

"I needed to get away from that gun, to get Seth away from it, too. I led him out into the garden, told him he wouldn't need his 'plan.' We could leave at midnight; I'd park around back of the garden and he could meet me. 'Beautiful,' he said, 'and we'll go visit the Eiffel Tower.' Now that I'd seen that gun, I'd agree to anything: yes, I told him, yes, the Eiffel Tower. And then I left before he could change his mind. I went back to my motel. Right before midnight I was back here, behind the garden gate."

I felt a queasy anticipation, sipped more whiskey to settle me. "Did he come out?"

She shook her head. "It was raining like hell that night. I've always hated how hard it rains here on the Gulf—rain like the world is ending. I waited there for three hours, though it felt like more. I couldn't even see out the car windows, it was coming down so hard. It was almost three o'clock, and the rain was driving me mad, and I decided, *To hell with it, I'll go in the house myself.* Maybe the garden door would be unlocked. I'd find Seth's bedroom, lead him outside, suitcase or no. He needed to get out of there.

"I opened the garden gate, started walking toward the door. And then I saw her. My mother, just lying there on the path. I stooped down, looked at her face. She was dead, unmistakably dead. I would have called an ambulance otherwise—I need you to believe that, Louisa. I hated that woman, but I wouldn't have left my own mother there to die. I even took her pulse, in all that rain. And then, well, I panicked. I didn't want to be anywhere near this. I ran back to my car. I drove away.

"I didn't stop until I reached Austin. Dawn had come by then. I stayed in a little nothing hotel for a while, a week, maybe less. Then I came back to Parson, saw Seth through the funeral as best I could. And that's all I know. That's all I know."

Ever since she'd hired me, I'd built up a violent image of Joanna, aiming a gun at her mother, pushing her off the balcony to her death. But I'd also learned in this time that Joanna wasn't the woman I'd thought, and neither was Miss Kate. That violent image of Joanna dissolved before me, and I couldn't see it anymore: only a lonely, frightened woman running back to her car through the garden, the world all black velvet around her, the rain an unrelenting drumbeat echoing from all directions.

Joanna looked at me directly for the first time since she'd started her story. Her eyes had turned puffy and red. "When we were children, sometimes, Seth and I—we'd imagine it together. Her death. Cass never joined in, but Seth and I . . . we'd whisper about it, make up different scenarios. A truck would run her over, back over her again and again. Or she'd be walking down the street and she'd fall in an open manhole. Or her head would just explode. Sometimes, before dinner, we'd shake invisible bottles over her food, murmur the names of poisons. It was a game for us, our favorite game; it gave us a tiny sense of control in that terrible childhood. We never sneaked out at night, like Cass did, so the elders at the church thought she was the problem child. But Cass never wanted her dead."

I took in this story as well, trying to weave the threads of the picture together with the cozy, chatty, festive dinners I remembered at Miss Kate's house as a child. But by now nothing was making sense, and I was starting to feel like my entire past was a fantasy I'd invented, a way to escape the brutal truths around me, like that sunny sketch of Parson House with the workers in the fields, faceless, turned away, their suffering omitted. All this time there'd been so much pain and horror hidden in plain sight. Was it even hidden, or had I just chosen not to see it?

We talked for an hour longer, the night deepening around us, a few birds skittering in the branches outside the window. Joanna told me about the months after her mother's death, how she and Seth had stayed at a hotel in Austin, how he'd seemed to flourish in the larger town, his moods happier, his lows less low, like a wilting plant that finally had sufficient sunlight. The storm came and went, and they didn't even check up on the mansion; Joanna would have been happy to hear it had sunk into the Gulf. But then Peg had found her and called the hotel, had told her about the purpose of the mansion, why Miss Kate had bought it—to help the hurting, endangered women of the town—and said if Joanna came back to Parson, the community of women would buy it from her, continue Miss Kate's plan.

"I was tempted to forget all about the mansion," Joanna said. "But until that call from Peg, I hadn't realized it might be worth real money. Even old and broken down as it was. I had Seth with me, I felt responsible for him, and he hasn't held a job in years—I don't know if he's even capable of it. I'd lost my job while I was down here, and it wasn't like I had other work lined up. Peg calling about the sale—it seemed like my chance to get Seth on his feet, get him out of here. He deserved it after all those years with our mother. I was suspicious about those benevolent plans for the women in town—it didn't sound like the Peg I know, or like my mother, either—but if it got us enough money . . . that was all I wanted."

But Peg hadn't given Joanna the full picture: after Joanna had returned, Peg started talking about all the money her group had already invested, how they couldn't pay that again, how there must be an account of the money somewhere in the house. So Joanna had set up Seth at her mother's old place—it was still in Miss Kate's name—and hired me to restore the mansion. It might not work out with Peg, but by then Joanna had listed the property, spoken with interested parties who were eager to buy up land cheap after the storm. One way or another, she would sell the house and leave Parson forever, pay for Seth to have a better life.

"All this time, Louisa, I've wanted to tell you," she said. "I wanted to explain. But, I don't know, I thought it might scare you off. If you knew I was here the day my mother died. If you knew Peg had made these claims. And I needed your help. There was no one else."

The silence was loud around us. Finally I said: "So you think Seth killed her?"

She took a few seconds to answer. "I've no idea. There's no real evidence, and the case is closed. And my mother, you never really knew her. To make a big enough statement—yes, I believe she might have killed herself. Where I found her that night, it was right below the balcony. If she knew Seth and I were leaving, never coming back . . . that would have been a way to keep a hold on us. To haunt us forever."

The scenario wasn't impossible, but Joanna was making excuses, distracting herself from the truth she couldn't stomach. Everything she'd done since Miss Kate's death—rushing the house sale, keeping Seth at a careful distance from the rest of the world—she'd done because she believed Seth had killed the old woman. Joanna knew her brother better than I did, and it occurred to me with a pang of fear that she might be right. "And the gun?"

"I never found it. Searched everywhere. It's not at my mother's old place, where Seth is living now, I'm confident of that much. And it won't be traveling with us, I'll make sure of it." Joanna paused, seeming to collect her thoughts. "All of this, you must know, I'm only telling you because . . . because I've missed you, Louisa. Painfully at times. Since I went away in high school, I've never had another friend like you. Not even close."

Joanna watched me, waiting to see how I'd respond. She was right; I did want to hurt her. All those years of hating her had hardwired that desire into me. But another thought was gnawing at me: maybe the violence between Joanna and me was over. If she'd stolen my brother from me, then I'd stolen her sister from her. This was how blood feuds started, and if they didn't stop, they bled everyone around them dry.

It could end here. I could let go of my hatred, remember us only as those innocent girls in the forest, the girls joining hands under the cedars and speaking secret words to each other, staring deep into each other's eyes. The girls who knew each other entirely, two becoming one. The way we'd been in that last year, before everything changed.

Heather had asked me once about my relationship with Joanna, whether we'd been "just friends" back when we were young. I'd told her, *Yes, of course, never more than that*—because I didn't want to remember, preferred to lie, forget. Besides, how could I explain it to Heather, the way we'd been as children? We were so joined, so merged, that even kissing felt like a small border to cross, just one more way to entwine ourselves together.

But we had kissed. Many times. The first time late one afternoon, the spring we were thirteen. I had gone to our spot in the woods, not expecting to find Joanna there because we hadn't arranged to meet up. Only there she was, like a figure from a storybook illustration, sitting on a fallen elm and crying. These weren't her usual Hollywood ingenue tears; these tears were ugly and severe, her eyes stained red, her face wet and mottled. I'd playacted this moment so many times— the huntsman stumbling across the princess in the forest—that this time it hardly felt real. When I sat down beside her, asked if she was okay, Joanna threw her slim porcelain arms around me. Our lips pressed together, a dry, clumsy child's kiss that softened, deepened, into something more.

Are we going to talk about it? I asked her the next day, after I'd spent the night thinking of nothing else. *I don't see any need to,* she said, so we hadn't, but the rest of that spring we kept kissing whenever we could, whenever no one could see us but the birds in the budding trees.

This was why it wounded me so badly when she went to her father's that summer. I'd dreamed of a summer in our secret forest, chasing each other through curtains of Spanish moss, her fairy-story laugh tripping like brook water and birdsong, disappearing into my mouth when I pulled her against me. At night I could sneak her into my bedroom, lay her out on my mattress, do more than just kiss her, slip off her sundress, explore the body I loved above all others.

When she left that summer, I felt foolish, rejected. I didn't know she was fleeing her mother, or church elders who beat her sister, or a home life that made her dream of poisons. I just thought she didn't care about me, didn't ache for me like I ached for her. It made me feel like a six-year-old again, standing outside an unknown house, my mother saying coldly, *None of that, little girl. No one likes a woman who cries for attention.* But I'd just misunderstood: Joanna *had* loved me, *had* needed me. Since she'd left Parson, she hadn't been that close to anyone again.

Now, in the lamplit study, I stared at her tentative face, her skin flushed like that spring day in the forest. I wasn't used to feeling this exposed, the pressure of tears behind my eyes.

"Everything that happened back then, in high school," I began. I hoped she knew all I meant: the car wreck, Cass, that cruel punch in the hallway. I couldn't speak of these things, not without crying. "Can you forgive me?"

She smiled sadly. "Oh, Louisa. My sweet Louisa. Can you forgive *me*?"

I rose from my chair, she from the edge of the desk. Her skin was warm when I touched her face, not the porcelain cool I expected. She had a woman's body now, soft against mine, but her lips were the ones I remembered from girlhood, tasted of the same tears. She was gripping my shirt, pulling it over my head. My hands were reaching under her dress, cupping her smooth thighs. And I realized, with a pang of grief, that I'd forgotten to ask her a question all those years ago in the woods, a question that could have changed everything: *Joanna, why are you crying?*

25

Maybe it was cowardly of me, slipping out the next morning without waking Joanna. But when I opened my eyes in Miss Kate's bedroom, when I saw Joanna asleep beside me with the sheet draped over her chest, when I felt the seven-story plunge of guilt inside my stomach, I knew I had to get home fast. Maybe I'd ruined everything with Heather, finally and forever. But every second here could only make it worse.

I picked up my clothes, quiet as I could, and slipped out into the hallway, dressed on the floorboards I knew would creak the least. I thought of sliding down the banister to avoid the creaking stairs, but that seemed too jaunty an exit for this morning of shame. Instead I took the stairs fast, got to my truck in under a minute, drove away before a delicate fairy voice could call me back into that house.

I'd never done this to Heather, never cheated on her, never stayed out all night without calling, never forced her to wonder where I'd gone, if I was injured or betraying her, if I'd come through the door smelling of someone else. Had she waited up all night, called around to friends, asked Danny if he'd heard where I might be? Had she called the kitchen phone at Parson House—the one I'd recently had reconnected—which Joanna and I wouldn't have heard, busy upstairs? Or had Heather gone to bed early, not even all that surprised, my absence just another sign that our lives had grown apart?

I knew only one thing for certain as the mansion shrank in my rearview mirror, as gulls called out, circling above the bay: I didn't want to lose Heather, hated that I'd risked our love last night. Maybe it was forgiving Joanna, putting our past to rest; maybe it was letting myself remember the night of the car wreck, facing at last those strange, disturbing memories of Robby, no longer running from what I knew—but I could see myself more clearly now, see that I'd fenced off my heart like a garden with a padlocked gate, so that anyone who loved me had to scramble over the wall, find me among the tangled vines, the sprawl of untamed growth, an adult woman who'd never stopped being that six-year-old on the stoop, numb with fear and sadness as she watched her mother drive off into the dark. I loved Heather, wanted her more than anything, but these last few months I'd kept her at a distance because it scared me how much I loved her, scared me how completely she could love me in return, scared me how she'd filled my days with kindness and connection, and how hollow my life would become if she ever left me.

Because what was my future without her? Just ghosts, just dust, just Robby's gravestone. Just growing old alone in a dying town. I had no future with Joanna Kerrigan. Even if we had shared a wonderful night, our bodies finding each other's in that transport of forgiveness, those hours in the bedroom like the last lines of a story we'd started writing together in childhood, a book whose covers we both could finally close. This morning I'd seen her asleep on the pillow and understood, for the very first time, that we owed each other nothing: that this was just a woman I had known in another life, and it was time, at last, to move on. I wanted Heather and Sarah and my dear Aunt Cece; I wanted to show the people I loved how much I loved them. I wanted, somehow, to atone for everything I'd done.

And I wanted to be around the people I loved, my family, as I made sense of the memories of Robby that had come to me last night. It took a force of will not to pick the whole scene apart with doubt and disbelief: it was true, I sensed it in my gut, even if I couldn't understand it. Maybe Heather knew something more about that night, about why Robby would have been so furious. Maybe she could help me see the gentle side of him again, the loving side, now that all I could see of him were his swinging fists.

Even as scared as I was of losing Heather, as disoriented as I was about Robby, I felt a new lightness inside me as I drove back home through town. Finally I wasn't fighting the tide pulling me out of Parson; I accepted it, released myself, looked forward to whatever came next, so long as I could share it with the people who mattered. There was dew on the grass, an expectant glow to the angle of the morning sunlight. I drove past the rubble that remained of the town, the streets of my youth that had trapped me here, that were finally letting me leave.

But what would I *say* to Heather? In just a few minutes, when I walked through the door, would I tell her some lie she'd always suspect—one that didn't explain Joanna's perfume on me, my guilty glances? Or would I confess, abase myself, throw myself at her mercy? I didn't know, couldn't predict what I'd say when I saw her face. Either way, I hoped this would soften the blow: I wanted to leave for San Antonio today. Pack the truck, get on the highway, start looking for a job there. Whatever didn't fit in the truck, we could leave it.

Nothing looked out of place as I pulled up to our house: same sagging gutters, same lawn that could use a mow. But I could sense that something was off, feel it like the change in pressure just before a storm, that ominous weight to the air. I took out my keys, unlocked the door, and took a hard swallow, absorbing what I saw, accepting that I deserved it.

The house was clean empty, all the boxes gone. Empty as it had been years ago, back when Robby and Heather moved in here. I felt a flare of anger, of indignation, but I pushed this down, reminded myself, *No, Lou. This is what happens. You brought this on yourself.* I'd kept Heather from her daughter for months, left her alone in the house while I worked that senseless job out at the mansion. Last night I hadn't come home, hadn't even bothered to call.

I said Heather's name as I stepped inside, I'm not sure why. I knew she wasn't in the house, felt silly the second I said it. But part of me hoped I had it wrong, that she'd walk out from the bedroom with her hair in a bandana—pissed off at me, disappointed with me, but here.

No such luck. I walked through the rooms, each one as empty as the last, until I got to the bedroom. There, Heather had stacked my things on the floor in a messy pile, as disordered as the trash outside Parson House last Sunday.

I rang Cece's house, but there was no answer, so I climbed back into my truck, started for San Antonio. Aunt Cece had been offering to drive out here and help us move for months, whenever we felt ready. Heather must have called her last night, asked her to come get her. At least this was what I hoped: I'd checked the whole house twice, but Heather hadn't left me a note.

Soon the last scraps of Parson were winking away in my side mirrors, and not much later I'd crossed the county line. The road took me inland first, the scrubby grass and wind-bent trees of the Gulf giving way to ranchland, fenced-off pastures, and a towering arc of sky. The radio station turned to static and I didn't look for another, just switched it off and listened to the hum of my tires on the road. Now and then I thought of Robby, his silhouette in the headlights, his hand grabbing Cass's arm that night. Had they been involved and she'd hurt him somehow? Did he know she was leaving town? I couldn't begin to explain it, my gentle brother acting that way. I needed to ask Heather if she had any clue as to why.

But I couldn't think of that now, tried to force away the images. Robby was gone, and so was Cass, and obsessing over the past could only ruin my future with Heather. Or maybe that future was ruined already, I wasn't sure.

It was frightening to drive this far from Parson—I'd taken only a few trips over the years, never farther than New Orleans, never longer than a week—but it was thrilling in its own way. Driving, itself, felt new out here, like I knew how to drive only the roads in Parson, like my tires might skid and veer on this unfamiliar terrain, spin out at every bump in the asphalt. What surprised me most was a feeling of hope, a surge of possibility, as I passed the water towers along the highway, each painted with the name of a different small town, towns as full of life and love and loss as my own. I'd never realized before how full the world was of places. Any of these towns could be a home. I could live anywhere, any way, I wanted.

And I'd realized that the only way I wanted to live was with Heather.

I'd known this all along, of course, but I'd never thought too much about it, had treated my love for her like a surface too hot to touch. Plus the way we'd gotten together, not long after Robby's death—it didn't exactly seem like the start of a promising relationship. More like two desperate women using each other to white-knuckle it through their grief. Both of us were brittle, edgy, needy one minute, tired of each other the next.

The first time we kissed was three months or so after moving in together. It was late, and we'd been fighting, probably about house-work or some dishes left in the sink, nothing all that serious, just an excuse to feel anger rather than sadness for a change. We'd put Sarah in her crib an hour before, cooed her off to dreamland, but we'd each had a beer too many, and our raised voices had woken her, started her screaming and crying. Immediately we paused the fight and swooped up to her crib, launched back into our cooing routine, but Sarah kept jerking and punching the air, her face screwed up in purple-red infant rage.

"Shhh, you're okay, honey, you're *okay*," Heather said, grabbing a plush Huckleberry Hound and wagging it in her face. "Everything's all right, sweetheart. Oh yes. You're okay. We're okay. The little dog-gy's okay." The strain of using this singsong voice was wearing on Heather's face, a paper-thin mask over her fragility. She was a per-son who wore her emotions boldly, unashamed of her sadness and anger—a quality in her that awed me; only for Sarah's sake would she cover up her feelings. But tonight the cracks were showing, and the waggling Hound and tense *okay*s were making Sarah wail all the harder.

I took the toy and touched Heather on the shoulder. "You head on into bed," I said.

Technically we were still in a fight—we hadn't resolved anything—but she gave me a grateful, exhausted look and slumped off from the room. Lots of our early fights ended like this, with a small kindness, a sudden joke, a memory of Robby.

"All right, sweet thing," I said to Sarah, wailing away below me. I started talking to her, slow and easy, the way my brother would talk to me when we were little, stranded in some motel room while our mother shot up with a stranger in the bathroom, Robby telling me fairy tales and fables, anything to distract me from the dim, dismal room around us, the closed curtains we were forbidden to ever open. Soon Sarah piped down enough to listen, then started giving me curious looks, and I switched to drawling words she liked, *kitty* and *chime* and *Christmas tree*, and after a while she was finally, blessedly quiet.

When I went to Heather's room she was half asleep, her hair a bird's-nest halo on the pillow behind her. Before I could say a word, she took my hand and tugged me down, kissed me long and full, our tongues pressing together like a thumb wrestle in our mouths. Then we both pulled back and looked at each other and laughed until our stomachs hurt. Maybe because—as we later agreed—lots of our fights had come from how much we'd wanted each other for weeks. It wasn't anything like my first kiss with Joanna, the one that felt as natural as breathing. This kiss was unlikely, unsteady, strange; it made my body heat up like the coils of a radiator. We still fought after that night, but now we had a more engaging way of making up.

Heather had never been with a woman before—but, she admitted, she'd been thinking about it for a while. I could hear the guilt in her voice when she said this, but I could tell it was guilt over Robby—a snarled guilt of grief—more than the thought that we were doing something unnatural. We'd buried my brother only four months ago, but he'd been overseas for nearly a year before then, an absence that Heather could endure when she expected him back home but that reverberated exponentially after his death. Hell, I felt guilty about it, too. But I told myself—perhaps self-servingly—that he'd want us both to be happy anyway, even if he might never have guessed that we'd make each other happy in this way.

Despite her conflicted feelings, despite her Baptist upbringing, Heather was enthusiastic when we were together. Right off she was different from the couple of girls I'd taken home from bars, the *I can't believe I'm doing this!* girls who'd let me show them a good time because they were drunk and curious, though they wouldn't dream of doing the same for me. However I touched Heather, she touched me back, excited and electric. The first time she wrung me out entirely, it took me a while to come to my senses afterward, and when I did, she was looking down at me, her eyes dark-blown like she'd just seen something special, a dolphin breaking the waves or a shooting star.

And she was so fucking beautiful.

When I reached the outskirts of San Antonio, I fueled up and bought a city map. It took some help from the clerk to find the street where Aunt Cece lived; I circled it with a pen, got back in my truck, and entered the maze of the city grid.

I pulled up to Cece's place in the early afternoon, a small, squat bungalow that looked like a gingerbread house with its clay-colored stucco and white trim. There was a patchy yard and a knotted rope hanging from one of the trees. The thought of Sarah swinging there nearly made me cry.

Cece opened the door before I knocked, let out a squeal of happiness. She was dressed in a bright floral blouse, her long black hair pulled back in a bun. "I saw the truck and I thought it couldn't be my little girl! Surely she would have called first!" She wrapped me up in a big tight hug and then herded me through the door. "Come in, come in. See the house, isn't it lovely? I've been doing it up for you ladies. Here, have a seat."

The ceilings were low in the living room, colorful blankets draped across the couch, landscape paintings she'd owned for decades hung on every wall, oils and watercolors of the Gulf Coast I remembered from when I was six, stepping into her home for the very first time. I sank into her old brown sofa—deep, familiar, comforting—and cursed myself that I hadn't moved up here sooner, into this cute little house with my family, that I'd stayed in Parson instead and stirred up all this trouble with Heather. On the coffee table lay this month's book-club selection, *Zelda: A Biography*. Cece went to the kitchen, and I followed her halfway, looking around the house. It was cozy and lovely, with handmade curtains open on the tidy backyard, and I pictured staying with Heather here while we put down roots in the city—a bit claustrophobic for all four of us, maybe, but exciting, too, sneaking kisses where we wouldn't be seen and making love in the dead of night. I could practically see Heather here with me, among the old familiar blankets and paintings, and it made me ache for her.

Cece was talking to me all the while, telling me about a book-club friend who worked at a hotel that was hiring bartenders.

"Or at least they were a week ago," Cece said, glancing out at me through the doorway as she poured some orange juice. "I'll get right on the phone with her about it, soon as you like. But Louisa, dear, you're tired, take off your shoes, those can't be comfortable."

"It's great to see you," I told her. And it was, it truly was. But I had to find out at some point; I steeled myself, asked the question. "Is Heather here?"

Cece brought out the juice to me. "You mean she didn't go back to Parson?"

"What do you mean, 'back'?" I said.

She tilted her head, confused, as she handed me the glass. "Heather was here early this morning. She picked up Sarah and left."

"Wait. She came here on her own? You didn't pick her up?" I was on full alert.

"No . . ."

"Did you see who drove her here?"

"I thought she took your truck. I was working out back, and she was in such a hurry, she barely said hello. I figured we'd have a proper homecoming later."

"Was there anyone else around?"

Cece could hear the alarm in my voice, looked uneasy. "Is everything okay?"

"Yes . . . fine," I lied. "Just crossed wires. It's a busy day, with all the moving."

"I'm sorry I didn't look out front. I just assumed—"

"You did fine. Everything's fine."

While I dissembled to Aunt Cece, I was trying to think, to piece together what had happened. Maybe one of Heather's friends had driven her here to get Sarah, and Heather was staying with them in Parson after all. But there was another, more frightening possibility: that Heather hadn't returned to Parson, that she'd taken Sarah and lit out for somewhere distant, far from me. Maybe she'd gone to her parents in Waco, though she could hardly stand to be near them, they made her so anxious; when they lived in Parson, she'd needed a strong drink after their visits. If Heather had traveled that far from us, if she no longer wanted to live with Cece, no longer felt like we were family—it was my fault, my fault entirely.

"Mind if I make a phone call?" I said in my calmest voice. I wasn't good at faking casual, and Cece looked only partially assured. "Just need to track her down real quick."

Luckily I kept my address book in the truck, in case I needed to make calls from Parson House. While Cece started cooking our lunch, I rang up Heather's parents on the phone in Cece's bedroom. I got her mother, found out Heather hadn't called them in a week. Then I called a few of Heather's friends, but it was the middle of the day and no one answered. I tried Peg's house, and to my surprise, no one answered there, either. Feeling desperate, I tried Danny's shop. Curtis answered and called Danny in from the garage.

"Haven't heard anything," he said. "Are you doing okay, hon? Where are you calling from?"

"I'm at Cece's."

"In San Antonio?" he asked, surprised. "You left without saying goodbye?"

"I haven't moved yet. I just . . . I'm trying to find her."

"Did something happen?"

There were so many things I wanted to discuss with him—Robby and Cass, for one thing, and what he remembered about the night of the accident—but there wasn't time now. I didn't answer his question, just asked, "You got any idea where she'd go?"

He sighed. "What I don't know about Heather could fill a Funk and Wagnalls set. I'll keep an eye out, though."

Finally I called our house, just in case Heather had doubled back there with Sarah. The phone picked up, but it wasn't Heather on the line.

"Hello?" said a hesitant female voice. I recognized it at once.

"Joanna?" I asked.

"Louisa. Oh, thank God," she said on an exhale. "I've been looking for you. Your door was unlocked, and I . . . I'm sorry for loitering here. But I thought you'd be back any minute . . ."

I blushed, kept my voice low, hoping Cece couldn't hear me.

"Look, uh, it wasn't great of me. Sneaking out this morning like that. I owe you an explanation, but right now—"

"That's not why I needed to see you," Joanna said quickly. "We can, yes—we can talk about that later. But there are more pressing matters."

I had no clue where this was going. "Did something happen?"

"It's Parson House. Peg and those women of hers . . . they've come and taken it. They have some kind of paperwork from the county, I can't understand it. They're claiming that *they* own the house, all of them together. And when I tried to ask them questions, they wouldn't answer me at all." Joanna sounded close to tears. "So I called the police, but they told me that the paperwork's official, there's nothing they can do. They kept chuckling while we spoke, like it was all some big joke or something. Then I called my lawyer, but he's out of town, and his secretary says we can set up a 'chat' next week, the insufferable little . . . Anyway, I haven't told Seth yet because I don't want to frighten him. Louisa, that house—it's our *future*."

I didn't respond for a moment, stunned. I knew Peg was a powerful person, but enough to wrangle a mansion from its rightful owners? What was more, how had she gotten the *town* to go along with this? They hated Peg and her group. Finally I said, "I'm in San Antonio right now. Not sure there's much I can do."

Joanna sounded deflated, crushed. "Oh. Well, yes. I understand if you're occupied. I . . . I didn't know where else to turn."

And there it was again, the magnet pull of Joanna, drawing me back to Parson. Right when I'd felt free of her, when I'd embraced a new life. But I had to go back anyway: Parson was the only place to look for Heather now. She was either there with a friend or so far from me that I couldn't reach her.

I sighed. "All right. All right, you just stick there. I'll see if I can talk to Peg."

"You'll help me?" She sounded amazed, as if I hadn't helped her a thousand times before.

"Just get some rest. I'll be back as soon as I can."

"I'll wait. Thank you, Louisa. Thank you."

After we hung up, I dialed the number at Parson House. A woman whose voice I didn't know answered the phone.

"Is Peg around?" I said. "Heard you moved out there today. Thought I'd say hello."

"May I ask who's calling?"

"This is Lou Ward."

"Ah, Louisa," the woman said, her voice serious, focused. "We were given a message for you, should you call."

"You were?"

"Peg says she will speak to you tonight, after sunset. But only if you come out to the manor in person."

"Only in person? Is there—" I began, but I heard a click and the line went dead.

I walked out of the bedroom, told Cece I couldn't stay for lunch, that I had to get back to Parson right away. Cece frowned at me, concerned, and then made me wait while she threw together a jam-and-honey sandwich, my favorite when I was little. She could tell I wasn't doing well, that I was holding things back from her, that I'd only lie to her if she pressed me with more questions. Since the first night I met her, dropped off on her stoop, Cece had astounded and perplexed me, the way she could always read everyone like a book.

"Tell me one thing before you go," she said, wrapping my sandwich in waxed paper for the road. "All this trouble . . . does it have anything to do with that woman Kate Darnell?"

"Miss Kate's dead," I responded, confused. Was there a way Cece didn't remember this? Perhaps, in the chaos of the storm and the move, she'd forgotten.

"Oh, I know. But I wouldn't put it past that woman to kick up trouble from beyond the grave."

There was resentment in her voice, and I felt a keen awareness that I'd put this bitterness there. For years I'd fawned over Miss Kate like the mother I'd lost, all while Cece was doing the hard, thankless work of *being* my mother. I'd never forgiven myself for hurting Cece that Christmas, making her hide her tears when I went to the Darnell house.

"It does have to do with Miss Kate," I admitted. "There's a lot going on in Parson. A lot I hadn't realized before."

"Whatever's going on, you be careful," she said in a worried voice, handing me the sandwich. "You call me later today, okay? Don't forget."

I hugged her and hurried out to my truck, threw the sandwich in the passenger seat.

I used to think this place was so inescapable, Joanna had said a few weeks ago. Maybe she was right. All I wanted to do now was leave Parson, but its tendrils were drawing me back.

26

By the time I made it back home, Joanna wasn't alone anymore. Seth was with her, sitting on the shag carpet of the empty living room, dressed in a rumpled black T-shirt and slacks. He looked the same as when I'd seen him last—soft, pale, unkempt, smiling patiently—and the way he was seated, cross-legged, his big hands on his knees, looked almost like a meditation pose. He reminded me of the hippies who appeared on the news sometimes, blissed out and meditating even at protests of the war.

Joanna seemed like she'd been pacing when I opened the door. She turned and looked at me with the eyes of a fawn in headlights. When she crossed the room and embraced me, I could feel that she was trembling.

"Louisa," she said "It's so good to see you. I worried we'd have to wait longer."

"It's a long drive from San Antonio. Can't just snap my fingers."

"Yes, yes. Of course. Apologies if I sounded . . . We're very grateful."

"San Antonio? Has Heather moved up there already?" Seth asked me from the corner, placid, pleasant. With all the chaos of today, it took me a second to remember why his presence made me uneasy. Last night Joanna had hinted at her suspicions of him killing their mother, described his odd behavior the day of her death.

"We're getting settled," I said to Seth. "Lots of things to sort."

"Do tell her I say hello. She always had the sunniest smile."

Joanna turned to me, said in a low voice, "I'm sorry I brought him here without asking you. I was terribly afraid. Those women, I worried they . . . well, I've no idea what they might do. You should have seen how they came to Parson House today. It was like an invading army."

"They'll probably leave you alone now," I said, trying to assure her. "What they wanted was the house, and it sounds like they got it."

"I can't take any chances, Louisa. They've been following me around—I didn't mention that before because I thought it might just be my imagination. But I saw it out there today, I *saw* it, that black Camaro. They think I killed my mother, that I tried to steal the house—I could see the way they were *looking* at me, disgusted, like I was this *murderer*, oh, I could have screamed. But no, no, I didn't have it in me; I just stayed polite, like this was all under control. 'I'll be speaking with my attorney,' I said, and they *laughed* at me, those hideous religious freaks. And then the police, *they* laughed at me. Has everyone lost their mind? This town—it could drive you mad. And so long as I have a claim to the mansion, I'm a threat to those women, and for all I know they've got a dozen guns over there. And I can't even speak to my lawyer. That bastard's on *vacation*."

She'd started pacing as she talked, running a hand through her hair, the other clenched in a fist at her side. She was wearing the same dress as yesterday, the drop-waist with the white collar, badly wrinkled now. Seeing her like this, I remembered what Seth had said about her nervous condition. It had never occurred to me that Joanna might project such poise, such absolute porcelain calm, because she was frantic inside, riddled with anxiety.

Seth was watching her, bemused, from his meditation pose, as if he couldn't understand all the fuss.

"Why would they think you killed our mother?" he asked her when she finished.

Joanna stopped pacing, shut her eyes, pinched the bridge of her nose. "To get the house. I'm sure they think I killed her to get the house."

"But why would you have to kill her? She was dying."

She let out a slow sigh. "No, Seth, she wasn't. She wasn't dying. She only said that to use you. To control you."

"Actually, this time she was," he murmured.

Joanna opened her eyes, stared at him in disbelief. "Don't you re-member anything? How she'd sit us down when we were little? *It's cancer. I may only have six months. Maybe less.* And we'd cry, dote on her, rush to get her blankets. *Yes, I'm a little chilly. Yes, a little soup would be nice. I'm so sorry that I'll need to leave you. You'll have to care for each other. Your father—you can't ever count on him. But at least we have this time together.* All a lie. Always a lie. Who could do that to their own children?" Joanna was pacing again.

Seth was looking off into the distance. "When I moved back to Parson, I knew she wasn't really dying. I did resent her for that. But that last year or so, Jo, it was real. There was something serious. I mean, you saw her, Lou."

"I just thought she was slowing down a little," I said. "Didn't real-ize it was serious."

Joanna waved a hand, dismissive. "She was the queen of the self-diagnosis."

"She wouldn't go to a hospital, that's true," Seth said. "But when we moved out to Parson House, she started to have . . . I suppose the only word for them is *seizures.* She'd fall suddenly, violently. Nearly cracked her head a dozen times, and I'd turn her on her side to make sure she didn't swallow her tongue. She was falling about once a day near the end. I wanted to tell you about it, Lou, so you'd know what to do if I wasn't there. But she made me promise not to."

I'd never seen Miss Kate fall, but I did remember times when she'd leave abruptly while I worked outside, saying she needed to get out of the sun. Or she'd offer to bring me lemonade, then disappear for over an hour. I'd thought she just needed some rest.

Joanna still looked dubious. She was leaning against the wall, arms crossed. "I never heard about any of this."

Seth said, "After she died, you never wanted to talk about her. And I didn't want to force you. But Mom was different at the end—kind to me, kind to Lou. For years she had never talked about Cass, not once since I came to live with her. But at Parson House, she was bringing her up all the time. Telling fond little stories about Cass as a girl. By then I'd stopped resenting Mom. I was glad to live with her. Glad to help."

Joanna raised her eyebrows. "*Glad?* You wanted to leave her."

"I did?" he asked, perplexed.

"The day I came back to Parson. You agreed to come away with me. To meet me at midnight. Remember? The Eiffel Tower?"

"Jo, if I'd known you were serious . . ."

"Why wouldn't I have been serious?"

Seth smiled, shrugged. "I thought you were playing make-believe, like when we were kids. I hadn't seen you in what, six, seven years? And then you were back, and you were telling this story about saving me, rescuing me, like I'd been captured by pirates or something. It was just like when we were kids, dreaming up fantasies in the woods. It made me so happy to be together again like that."

Joanna stared at him for a long moment, the lines deepening in her forehead. "But your plan. Mom's gun."

A sadness crept into Seth's expression, a new heaviness to his eyes. "You thought . . ."

"I didn't know what to think."

"Oh, Jo. You thought I could hurt someone? With a gun? Our mother?"

"Like you said, it had been so many years. And then you showed me this gun. And said you had a plan. A plan if you felt trapped."

He chuckled to himself. "Oh, Jo. You seemed so worried for me. And I just wanted you to know that . . . that I was okay. To let you see that—I'm sorry if it disturbed you, if it confused you. You've always thought I could be 'fixed,' that I could find some easy answer for my pain. But I've always been unwell, and I'll always be unwell. And if things get too bad, I won't just let myself suffer."

Joanna lowered herself to the floor, rested her back against the wall. She sat like a little girl, hands in her lap, legs stretched out before her. "The gun was to hurt yourself?"

Seth looked down at his sneakers. "*Hurt* is the wrong word. I know it would make . . . a mess. I'd put down sheets, I promise. But it would be a gentle thing for me. A freeing thing."

"Seth," she said, an urgency in her voice. "Where's the gun now?"

He lifted his hands, showed us his empty palms. "No idea. Back at the mansion, I guess? It's not the only way."

The room fell silent while we absorbed that grim statement. Even Seth looked unsettled, as if his "plan" felt different when explained this clearly, not just as a fantasy in his head. Joanna, for her part, stared blankly at a stain on the wall across from her, and I could almost see the painful images playing out in her head, imagining some day in the future, perhaps not far from now, when she'd find her brother like she'd found her mother, all her work to help Seth for nothing. Sheets would be put down beforehand, as if that made any difference.

I looked between these troubled siblings, laid bare in this empty living room, both mysterious to me still. Had one of them killed their mother? It struck me that they were the type of people to do it, people who nursed secret fantasies, who wore masks over their anguish, who were swept up in gusts of emotion, who lost control. I was just the same, in my own way. Perhaps Miss Kate had been, too. *To make a big enough statement,* Joanna had said, she thought her mother might kill herself. But wouldn't Miss Kate have left a note, driven home the guilt, left nothing to chance? Or perhaps it had been a seizure. But the seizures had made her fall down, not pitch forward over a balcony railing.

I turned to Joanna. "I called out to Parson House before I drove back here."

She blinked a few times, taking a moment to refocus. "Yes? Did you speak to Peg?"

"She wasn't around, I don't think. But I'm going out to talk with her later."

"If you could get some clarity from her, Louisa, I'd be *so* appreciative. Maybe she won't bully you like she bullied me. And if you could also see—"

Before Joanna could ask for more favors, the phone started ringing in the kitchen. I walked fast from the living room and snatched up the handset, hoping it was Heather. To my disappointment, a giddy male voice chattered from the earpiece. Adam Stanton.

"Boy oh boy, have I got news for you," he said by way of greeting. "I told you I'd keep an eye out, didn't I?"

I struggled to remember what Adam meant; I tried to forget our interactions as quickly as possible. "An eye out?"

"You'll never guess who just came back from the dead. And got himself *married*," he added, jubilant. Nothing made Adam happier than good gossip. "None other than our friend Ed Darnell."

"Ed's back?" I asked. At these words, I heard Joanna's rapid footfalls from the living room. She looked at me owl-eyed from the doorway.

"In the flesh," he said. "Looks rode hard and put up wet. But he's among the living."

I covered the mouthpiece, whispered to Joanna, "Ed Darnell's back in town. And he just got married."

"Married?" she whispered back, and I nodded gravely. The thought of Ed getting married was like hearing that he'd just been named Miss Texas. I asked Adam, "Who married him?"

He let out a hoot of laughter. "This is the best part of all. It was the bull castrator herself. That vixen Margaret Muller."

I couldn't speak for a moment. Then, in disbelief: "*Peg?*"

Joanna stood next to me and listened in, gnawing a thumbnail as Adam expanded on the news: Ed Darnell had married Peg in a ceremony at city hall today.

"Are you sure about this?" I asked. "There must be some mistake."

"Oh, there's been *plenty* mistake," he said, gleeful. "Happened right here in my office—I was the one who notarized the paperwork. I tell you what, Lou, it was just the strangest sight I ever saw. Peg comes in with two of her women, these divorced broads a little younger than her. The three of them stand at one wall, and then across the room there's Ed, flannel shirt, scruffy sideburns—looks like something from *Planet of the Apes*. Put on some weight, too. Next to him his mom and pops and those four brothers of his, Chuck Jr. and the others, yukking it up, over the moon to have Ed back. But pretty confused about the proceedings underway. Not sure they knew it was a wedding until the justice asked Ed to say *I do*."

I needed to sit down, but there weren't any chairs in the house. I flumped down on the floor and Joanna followed.

"But that's not the half of it," he went on. "The minute poor Ed signs his freedom away to the bull castrator, she turns around and makes him sign a whole other stack of papers right there in my office. A deed of sale, drew it up herself! She makes him give that whole mansion to what she's calling the Sisterhood of Parson County. Her two cronies, they're signatories for the whole group—there's, like, *dozens* of names. Meanwhile, all the Darnells are standing around, no clue what Ed's signing, just champing to get him home and crack some beers. Then the women just march right on out with their papers! Just leave Ed back there. He didn't even get to kiss the bride."

So that was how Peg had done it. She'd tracked down Ed, or maybe she'd known where he was all along. I doubted there'd be a honeymoon.

Adam was still talking. ". . . had Lindy double-check after she left. Not a single married woman on that list of owners. So there's no way Ed can even get it back. Honest to God, I'll never call this town boring again."

Joanna whispered to me, "Where's Ed now?"

"Ed's off to his parents' house," he said when I asked him. "The old man invited me to the party. Might stop by later with my dad."

Predictably, Adam then segued into asking me out—a candlelit dinner at his place—maybe thinking that the gossip had earned him this. I told him I was moving to San Antonio today, and he asked me if I wanted "one for the road." I said a terse *No thanks* and bade him adieu.

Joanna was still gnawing her thumbnail, gazing at the open cabinet doors. "I feel like I'm in that song. The one with the funny farm."

I smiled. "'They're Coming to Take Me Away'?"

"That's the one. But I'm not as crazy as the people in this town. Not even close."

"So . . . I'm guessing that I won't be getting paid."

"Oh, Louisa. What a disaster this all is. I'll take Seth home, and then I need to visit the Darnell place. Talk to Ed."

"What good will that do?"

"I need to find out all I can. Maybe there's some . . . loophole. Some way to proceed."

"Best of luck out there," I said. "Get ready to have some month-old cookies shoved in your face. Mrs. Darnell likes her guests to empty the pantry."

Joanna shifted closer to me on the floor, took one of my hands in hers. I felt the warm, tender, familiar grip of her fingers. "Come with me, won't you?" she asked, her eyes wide, imploring. "It's all been so much today. I don't know if I can handle it alone."

That look had always worked like magic on me, ever since the day in grade school when I saw the boys hucking pebbles at her. I could feel the tidal pull of her, my longing to put a smile on that spectral face. It occurred to me—suddenly, brutally—that Heather had walked out on me, that I could do whatever I liked. If I wanted, I could lift Joanna's palm to my mouth, kiss it slow and sensuous, agree to help her today, sleep with her again tonight, maybe every night this week. I could leave Parson with her, drive off into the sunset like two heroines from our old adventure books.

The fantasy lasted less than two seconds. It was Heather who was my future, and I had to find her.

27

Heather's friends weren't thrilled to see me when I stopped by that afternoon. Both Midge and Fay were at home, all dolled up in their lovely houses; they'd probably spent the whole afternoon primping, preparing a big smoocheroo for their husbands getting back from work. They looked like variations on Carol Brady, if Carol Brady had lived in a ghost town. In high school both had been snotty to me, but now they turned up the fake politeness, said no, they hadn't heard from Heather in a while—was everything okay? She's fine, I told them, though of course I had no idea.

After that I swung by the houses of Heather's lesser friends in town, more acquaintances than buddies, and then a few of her co-workers from the salon. No one had spoken to her lately, and it hurt me to imagine her life these past few weeks, depressed, alone, cutting herself off from everyone.

My next stop was Danny's auto shop. Sweaty and oil-stained, he gave me a hug and then held me by the shoulders and looked at my face, his broad forehead creased with concern. The scar in his hairline, which I'd gotten so used to seeing that it had become almost invisible, stuck out to me, and I wished that I could ask him about Robby and everything else that was on my mind, but there wasn't time. I'd spent so long prioritizing my past, my lingering questions, instead of Heather; now I knew she was all that mattered, even if it meant I never got some of the answers I wanted.

Danny must have known where my head was, that I hadn't

dropped by for chitchat. "No sight of Heather yet," he reported. "But I *did* see that black Camaro again. Headed out south of here."

South of here was Peg's house, a place I needed to check anyway. Sure enough, as I was coming down her street, I saw the black Camaro in her driveway, its trunk popped and crammed with crates and boxes.

I parked at the curb. The once-bustling house looked empty, no women in the garden, no shadows behind the curtains, no one guarding the front door, which was wide open. They must all be out at Parson House, no use for this smaller house. I walked up the cobblestone path and saw Claudia coming through the foyer, carrying a crate stuffed with lamps and bric-a-brac. She was striding fast, her head down, and I wasn't sure if she saw me as she pulled the front door shut behind her and brought the crate to her car.

As I walked up to the Camaro, I noticed something surprising in the trunk: a cardboard box of Heather's old gymnastics trophies. They were stacked willy-nilly among hairbands, pot holders, and Sarah's Huckleberry Hound. I felt a wave of conflicting emotions: relief because Heather was probably in town, hadn't put hundreds of miles between us; worry because Heather had gone to Peg's group, a group who rescued women from undeserving partners. Maybe I fell into that category. Maybe that was why Peg wanted to see me after sundown, after her unpacking was finished: to give me the bad news, to tell me that Heather was moving on.

Claudia shut the trunk as I approached, then turned to me with her benign, unreadable face. I couldn't help but feel irritated at her, this meddling presence in our lives, even if Heather herself had asked Claudia to help.

"Hello, Louisa," she said, her voice eerily calm as ever. "Beautiful weather today."

"Yeah, it's all right. This is moving day, huh?"

"We're relocating, yes."

I scratched the back of my neck. "So listen, uh . . . Heather's out at Parson House? Do I have that right?"

"I'm afraid I'm not at liberty to tell you," Claudia said in a flat voice.

"I mean, I just saw Heather's stuff in your trunk. Peg wants to talk with me tonight. It's pretty obvious what's going on here. If you'd be—"

"I could repeat myself if you like. As I said a moment ago, I'm not at liberty to tell you." There was an edge to her tone, not just polite neutrality.

"Sure, okay, I get it. You have rules. Could you bring Heather a message from me, then? Would that be possible?"

Claudia's lips tilted upward, but not into a smile. It was a sneer, simple in its hostility, its stark judgment of me.

"I don't carry messages for women like you. I don't deal in corruption."

"Excuse me?" I said. My fingers had curled instinctively into a fist; I forced them slack.

"You should have heard Heather last night. So worried something had happened to you. She called Peg, thought you might be injured, working out at Parson House alone. But you weren't alone, were you?" Claudia looked even more disgusted. "We drove out there looking for you, Heather and me. It must have been two in the morning. When we saw your car next to that Kerrigan girl's—we both got the picture."

I couldn't punch Claudia, not if I wanted to win Heather back from them. Nor was she wrong to call me a cheater; I was. But a queasy surge of emotion was roiling my stomach, how I always felt when the wrong people found out about my sex life. I wanted to slap the intolerance off their face, jam their ankle into the claw trap of their bigotry.

Before I could stop myself, I'd already started going off. "I hope you're all real comfortable out at Parson House. I just spent *weeks* there, renovating the place. I was supposed to get paid off the sale, and I suppose you generous women will make that right? You wouldn't make a woman work for nothing, would you? Not the Sisterhood of Parson County."

Claudia was staring past me as if I were no longer there, though her sneer stayed just as firm. Abruptly she strode to her car door, yanked it open with an irritated tug. "You'll have to discuss that with Peg," she said. "She told me about your appointment tonight. Make sure not to miss it."

Claudia slipped inside the Camaro and closed the door. I stood on the lawn and watched her as she backed the car out from the driveway, as she drove away down the wind-ravaged block.

It took everything I had not to drive out to the house straightaway. I was itching for the chance to talk to Heather if Peg would let me. But I knew better than to disobey my marching orders: I was being put in my place, being shown who had the power now, and I had a feeling that if I went storming in before I'd been invited, all the doors would close against me.

So I headed back to my empty house, nervous, angry, impatient for tonight. I found an old Parson Dairy mug among the things in the bedroom, gulped down water until I settled somewhat. There were hours left until sunset, when I could drive out and talk to Peg, and I owed Aunt Cece a phone call—not that I knew what I'd say to her.

"Louisa, you didn't seem well earlier," Cece said just after hello. "Are you doing all right? Please. You can tell me."

How much could I lie to this woman who loved me, this woman who *knew* I was lying? My legs were trembly, my breathing ragged, the phone cord twisted tight around one finger. My voice came out choked when I started talking again. "I messed up, Cece," I said. Feeling the moisture in my eyes, I tried to steady myself. "I don't know if I can fix this. Heather and me, I think it might be over."

For a while the line was quiet; I worried that I'd been too much. *No one likes a woman who cries for attention.* But finally Cece said, "Heather knows you have a good heart. Whatever you've done, I'm sure you can talk it out with her. There's a lot of history with you two. History means something."

"History," I said. "History's the whole reason I'm in this mess."

"People lose themselves sometimes. Make mistakes. When I was young? You'll never be hearing *those* stories—only the priest! But you're a good girl, you always have been. You and your brother both."

I ran a hand down my face. "That's not true. We were awful. We ruined your life."

It was clear to me, the ungrateful brat I'd been as a child. I was a mouth to feed, clothes to buy, the reason Cece couldn't remarry and start over. And how had I repaid her? By watching the window for years, hoping my horrible mother would return. By being ashamed of Cece, hiding our relation, worrying more about staying at Granbury High than about her feelings. I'd been moody, hateful, distant, and in return she'd given me love, far more love than I ever deserved.

Cece's laugh was weary, older than I liked. "It's true, when I saw you on the stoop that night, I sent up a quick prayer. 'SOS, Lord!' Your uncle'd left me because I couldn't have kids; I never thought I'd raise any. And there were times I thought I couldn't do it. Asked God why I had to endure all of it on my own."

Cece had always been careful never to speak of us as a burden—to deny that raising two children alone, with little money or support, had been anything but a joy for her, a gift from God. She must have known this was the story we needed, two small kids whose mother had left them, terrified of being unwanted again. So she stuck to a trussed-up fairy-tale version of her past: *God answered my prayer, sent me two beautiful children.* Even as a kid I wasn't fully convinced; the story brought fleeting comfort. And now, on the phone with her, hearing her say the words *endure* and *on my own*, the truth finally hit me in the heart. It had been the challenge of a lifetime for Cece, raising Robby and me. And here she was, doing the same with Sarah all over again.

"Besides," she went on, and there was a sadness, a deflation, in her voice that pained me, "it was me that ruined things, Louisa. We both know that. Robby getting kicked out of that nice high school. Losing his scholarship. The draft."

"Cece, oh my God," I said, and I started crying, stray tears coursing down my cheeks. "All that bullshit with the school, that wasn't your fault. I should have . . . I should have told you that back then. Not just gone around feeling sorry for myself."

"You were only a child. Of course you were upset."

I sat down at the kitchen table, pinched the bridge of my nose. "I was old enough to know better. To not make you feel blamed."

"Sweetheart, enough of that. You're being too hard on yourself."

But I was thinking of all the people I'd blamed for Robby's death—Joanna, Cece, Principal James, the school board, the government, Lyndon Johnson, even Cass, who'd brought us out to the mansion that night—the sequence of actions and events that I'd clung to like a lifeline, the only sense I'd been able to make out of losing him. Maybe, in the end, losing someone didn't have to make sense. Maybe it was just a fact, the most painful fact of all.

"You aren't to blame for Robby," I told her. "And . . . and Joanna isn't, either, not really." Something old and immobile gave inside me as I said this; I slumped against the table, almost grateful for the punched-out feeling in my stomach. "Cece, you need to understand: you *saved* us. Saved our lives. If you'd tracked down our mother, sent us back to her? We probably would've died out there on the road. You cared for us, you loved us, you gave us a good shot at life. And I wish I'd done more with what you gave me. Because you were the best mother I ever could have had."

Cece was crying as well, less uncommon for her. I heard her sniffing, wiping her eyes with swipes of a tissue. At last she said, "You and Heather, the problem you're having. You make me proud, okay? Talk to her, get through to her. I want my girls here with me."

"I'll do my best," I said. "I swear it."

I couldn't just sit in this empty house, waiting for the sun to go down, brooding about my future, whether Heather would forgive me, whether Peg would let me see her tonight. After Cece and I rang off, I drove out to Seth's place at the edge of town. I might not be saving Joanna anymore, but I could at least check on her.

"She's not back from the Darnells' place yet," Seth said as he led me inside. "But please, make yourself comfortable. It's always so nice to have visitors."

The house was still cramped and cluttered, but overall it looked much cleaner, like Joanna had done some tidying while she'd stayed here last week. Seth was back in his bathrobe, as if his rumpled T-shirt and slacks from earlier had been him getting dressed up.

We went into the kitchen, where he put on the water for tea in an old kettle. He took two mugs I knew from Parson House off the shelf, one with a teddy bear sitting under a rainbow, another a drawing of a young woman seated on a camel. Peg must have let Joanna gather some things before sending her away. I wondered what would happen to the rest of Miss Kate's possessions, now the property of the Sister-hood.

"How are you doing with all this, Seth?" I said.

"With what?" he asked nonchalantly, plucking a tea bag from its box.

"You know, losing Parson House? Your inheritance?"

With the tea bag pinched between two fingers, he paused and stared thoughtfully at the ceiling fan as if he hadn't considered yet that the events of today might affect his life somehow.

"There's something I'd like to show you," he said.

"Okay . . ."

"Watch the water, if you wouldn't mind. I'll be right back."

Seth shuffled down the hall in his slippers, then came back a min-ute later holding a large accordion file. He set it on the table, started rustling through the sleeves stuffed with papers.

"What is all this?" I asked, though I had an idea.

"My mother's papers, mostly," he said as he searched. "Joanna would bring some back from Parson House now and then. Ah, yes, this is the one."

From a center sleeve he slid a crumpled sheet of notebook paper. It had been crunched into a ball and then opened again, smoothed. He held it out to me.

As always, the sight of Miss Kate's handwriting moved me. Her flowing, precise letters filled less than a third of the page. It began: *I, Katherine Mary Darnell, being of sound mind, hereby announce my in-tention to bequeath all my properties to my children—Cassandra, Seth, and Joanna Kerrigan—particularly the mansion at 19 Seaview Road.* She continued for several lines, listing a few items that should go to each of the children, even to Cass, who'd been dead for a decade before Miss Kate bought the mansion. Cass was to receive Miss Kate's Bible, her brooches, her old Chrysler.

"I don't understand," I said.

"Joanna found this in Mom's study months ago," Seth said. "She couldn't make sense of it, either. It was crumpled up in the trash."

I knew nothing about probate law, how inheritance worked. "Can you use this?"

"The lawyer said it has no standing. It's unfinished, unsigned, unwitnessed. But that's not why I thought you should see it." He puttered back to the stove, where the kettle had started to wheeze. "I think that everything in our lives has a purpose, a *reason* we experience it. Don't you?"

"I'm not really sure," I said.

"That's my personal belief. When I have a new experience, I might not grasp the reason at the time: it might seem random, mysterious. But when I look back, I can start to see the pattern, the *purpose*. My mother, she had a plan when she moved out to the mansion. Something to do with Peg—she never discussed it with me much. But the actual reason was how she changed there. She became a different person in that house, a kinder person. My sister Cass came back to her. Not as a ghost, maybe, though it seemed that way sometimes. Like Mom could *sense* Cass at Parson House."

"Sense her?" I asked, feeling a chill of recognition. I could remember the presence of Cass in the house, the beguiling reality of her in the parlor, the study. The slow, persistent rising of memories the longer you stayed in the mansion, memories that felt real enough to touch.

Seth handed me my mug of tea, its steam drifting up between us. He sat across from me, took a tentative first sip. "I'd never bring this up around Joanna," he went on. "It'd only upset her. But sometimes, after Mom had her seizures, she would start to say Cass's name. Talk to her, apologize to her. Mom would say she was sorry over and over, that she 'wouldn't do it again,' like Cass was in the room with us. I could almost feel her there, too, if I'm being honest. I'd bring Mom a glass of orange juice, rub her shoulders until she calmed down."

"*Wouldn't do it again*," I echoed. "Did you have any idea what she meant by that?"

Seth shrugged. "All of it, I'd guess. The things she used to do that made us so miserable."

I thought of the elders beating Cass, the different ways Miss Kate had harmed her daughter. Her living children, too—everything I'd heard these last few days about what a spiteful, controlling, harmful home she'd created for them. "She was feeling guilty at the end."

Seth nodded. "Guilty, yes. And something more. You saw it in the will, didn't you? It was like Cass was alive for her again. She wanted to leave Cass her car. Her brooches."

I pointed to the top lines of the page. "This first part here, about leaving you the mansion. Did Miss Kate ever mention that to you? Was that real?"

"We did discuss it a few times. But she told me I couldn't tell anyone, that it had to be our secret. Anyway . . . it's time for me to forget about Parson House. You can't fight city hall, as they say." He smiled. "I'll just need to see what experience comes next."

I took a slow sip of my tea, thinking. Could it be that Miss Kate had intended to betray the Sisterhood? Abandon her plans with Peg and the women, give the house to her children, "leave them well off"—as Joanna had said in her story last night—because she couldn't bear the guilt, knew how badly she'd failed them as a mother?

"Did you find a later draft of the will?" I asked. "Something more official?"

Seth laughed. "I might be pretty spaced out, but Joanna wouldn't miss something like that. She was digging through the *trash* or I wouldn't even have seen this."

I laughed as well. "Any idea what you two will do after this? Joanna mentioned you wanted to travel."

"Oh, maybe one day. Maybe not. Living in the mansion all those years—it had a purpose for my life, too. For me, I think it was finding Mom's revolver. Ever since I saw the gun, I've felt such peace, such freedom. People are always talking about their 'destiny,' what they dream will happen in their lives. There's all this pressure, all this burden, about their future. But death, you know, that can be a destiny as well. Death can be something you dream of. A thought you come to love."

Seth lifted his mug but didn't sip, just stared out into the dim house, as if death were right there with us, his fond companion.

For a while I didn't know what to say, so I was glad that, before we finished our tea, we heard the front door open and Joanna slink into the foyer. She let out a tired sigh.

"Oh, Louisa, you're here," she said, stepping into the kitchen. She leaned against the counter, the most exhausted I'd ever seen her, her posture stooped, her bangs stuck to the sheen of sweat on her forehead, as if she'd walked back from the Darnell place in the heat. "Nice of you to check in," she added, a weary attempt at politeness.

"How'd it go?" I asked, fairly sure I knew the answer already.

She held up one finger as if to say *Just a moment*, then crouched down to open the lower cabinet, from which she produced a half-drunk bottle of merlot. She put the bottle between her knees and pulled out the difficult cork, then filled up a mug with a gap-toothed clown on the side, stopping only when the wine brimmed at its edge. I watched her slender throat pulse as she drained most of the mug in a single go. She emptied the dregs of the bottle into the mug and sat down heavily beside me, then wiped her mouth with the back of her hand.

"Well," she said, "if there's one silver lining here, it's that I'll never have to see those people again."

Seth rose from his seat and shuffled over to his sister, began to rub her shoulders with a light grip. Joanna let out an even more deflated sigh and rolled her head slowly.

"How is Ed doing?" he asked. "It's been such a long time."

She took another gulp from the mug before she answered him. "Oh, fine. He's still Ed—you know what I mean. Not too easy to be around."

"Seems like you could use more wine," I said.

"Yes. Very true. There's another bottle in the pantry."

After I topped off her mug, Joanna started to tell us the story more coherently. She had driven out to the Darnells' farm, nervous to see her stepfamily after fifteen years with no contact. When she arrived, she found the driveway crammed with pickup trucks, a rowdy gathering of friends and relatives spilling out over the yard. There were kegs of beer, a horseshoe game for the kids, a table of potluck bowls swarming with flies. A guitarist and an accordion player drunkenly dueted on the porch. At the center of the party stood old Mr. Darnell, leaning on a cane, surrounded by a crescent of his wizened drinking buddies. "His oil rig days are done," he was saying loudly, an empty bottle in his other hand. "Moving back to town, our Ed is. He's promised his mother as much."

"Picked the right time," said one of his stooped pals. "Ain't nothing easier than buying in Parson right now!"

Joanna wondered how she'd find Ed in this chaos, but then she heard her name called. It was Mrs. Darnell, swooping over with happy exclamations, giving Joanna a hug and a kiss on the cheek. Her air of happiness had her strutting like a queen around the raucous party. "You heard that Ed was back?" she said, beaming. "It must have been so hard for you, all those years without the man who raised you. He's right inside with his brothers, dear. Oh, he'll be so happy to see you. Father and daughter reunited. He'll be over the moon."

Joanna sincerely doubted this. She found Ed in the crowded living room, slumped down on the sofa with a brother on either side, two more seated on the coffee table in front of him, the burly men laughing and lurching forward to cuff Ed on the back. Ed seemed far less festive: he gulped down a glass of amber liquor and then held it out to a nephew for a refill, a boy no older than ten clutching a liter of Old Grand-Dad. The men were red-faced, extremely drunk, must have started drinking as soon as the wedding ended, if not before. While Ed set into his next glass, the Darnell boys shouted over one another, bringing their prodigal brother up to speed on everything he'd missed: Jim's new Ford F-100, Andy's Winchester Model 70, and—with less enthusiasm—Chuck Jr.'s new baby.

Joanna expected to be ignored, to struggle for Ed's attention in all this ruckus. But as soon as he saw her over his glass, he rose unsteadily and pushed his way through the sea of brothers. He staggered more than walked toward her, looking even drunker in motion than sitting down.

"You wouldn't sell," he growled once he'd led her into a guest room. He dropped down on a chair, spilling some Grand-Dad on his jeans. "Princess Joanna. No compromises for her."

"I beg your pardon?" she asked.

"Hope you're happy, little miss priss. 'Cause neither of us got what we wanted. You didn't get a dime for that house. And I had to *marry* that witch."

"I'm a little confused, Ed. If you could just—"

"Greedy, that's what you are. Just like your mother. Wouldn't take a decent price, oh no, not good enough for Joanna. Needed to hold out for more. Don't you realize what you've done? I have a reputation in this town. *Had*, I should say. *Had*. How'm I ever gonna hold my head up here again?"

By this point, Joanna had realized that Ed was no use to her. This reeking shell of a man couldn't stand up to Peg or scheme to get back the mansion. The best he could do was provide some information. Joanna let him fume for another minute, then said, "But Ed, where have you been the past five years? I looked everywhere."

Drunk as he was, this question stopped his outbursts. He scowled down at the rug like a chastised schoolboy. Finally he said, "Not that it's your business, but . . . I'd built up some gambling debts a few years back. Ain't exactly proud of that, but there it is. Debts I couldn't pay—and not from the nicest people, either. The kind of people that you don't make wait, that you don't skip out on. So I was in a little trouble." He took another sip from his glass. "Well, not *that* little."

Joanna was remembering how much Ed loved to talk when drinking, all those awful nights in her childhood when he was home from the oil rig, rambling at them in the living room while they tried to watch TV. Today, however, it might actually serve her purpose.

"These people—they were going to hurt you?" she asked.

Ed gave a bitter laugh. "For starters. I was thinking I'd maybe run . . . but if they catch you? It'd all be ten times worse. And say they don't catch you—they might go after your damn *family*. Your mother found out about it, sure she did: she was always in my business. And what did she do? She went and told that Peg woman. Last thing I wanted, those crazy ladies knowing all about me, those witches from that church."

Joanna had a feeling that the truth was much different: Ed drunkenly sobbing his troubles to Kate, begging her to find the money for him, to ask anyone she knew—anyone at all—for help. But Joanna wasn't about to contradict him, which might turn him terse and brooding, the other side of his drunkenness. He went on: "And wouldn't you know it, a few days later, Peg shows up with an offer. Says she'll pay these fellas off. But terms! Did that broad ever have *terms*. Tells me she won't pay 'em all at once, no, she'll do it over *years*, and while she's payin', I gotta leave town and not come back, not until the debt is all paid. Not even to see my ma. She says if she finds out I've talked to anyone, she's sending the guys after me, no more payments.

"I have my pride. I kept in touch with my brother Chuck, made sure I heard all the news. I figured it out on my own, why they wanted me away—so me and my family wouldn't interfere with that place your mother decided to buy. Them women and that house, they can all go straight to hell. I'll tell you this much: if Mom and Dad had gotten sick, I'd've been back here in a minute, debts or no debts. You'd better believe that. I'm a lot of things, but I'm not a bad son."

Joanna didn't buy this, either, but she nodded sympathetically. It seemed the death of his wife hadn't tempted him back to town. "But you haven't answered my question. Where *were* you? Not at the oil rig. I tried that."

"You think I trusted Peg? Ha! Not on your life. I disappeared. I got a different job under a different name, looked out for myself. Had a P.O. box in New Orleans, but I was living north of there, didn't want Peg to know, either. Well, a week ago she writes me, says she needs me back in Parson, needs me pronto, not to dawdle. Says she'll pay off all my debts, I'll be done, free and clear. I think great, I can come home again, go fishing, kiss my ma—but then there was always a catch with that one. Oh, nothing big: I just gotta *marry* her. Because *you* wanted more money. You wouldn't sell the damn place, and that witch, that monster, she's my legal wife. You know how long I dreamed of this day, coming back to the house, seeing my brothers? But now . . . I'm a joke. I'll always be a joke."

Peg clearly hadn't told Ed the full story, hadn't mentioned the low price Joanna was offered for the mansion. And why would Peg tell him? She only needed Ed to sign a few papers. Joanna considered enlightening him, filling him in on all the details, but she doubted he'd even remember the next morning. She said it was nice to see him again, then left him drinking and mumbling to himself in the guest room.

Seth had been massaging her shoulders the entire story. "It's good to hear about people celebrating," he said thoughtfully. "It's been such a sad time in this town."

"Seriously?" Joanna said. She brushed his hands away in irritation. "We just lost everything. If you haven't realized, Peg owns *this* house, too. She just hasn't gotten around to taking it from us yet. After all this, we're leaving Parson no better than when we came here as kids. Nowhere to go, nothing in our pockets."

"We'll figure something out," Seth said. "We can live anywhere. Find some work. I don't have much experience, but—"

"'Find some work'? You know what most jobs are like? Dealing with customers, bosses grinding you down. One indignity after another. You won't be able to handle it."

"Maybe I can. You never know. Maybe I can do it this time."

Joanna gave him a sorrowful, disbelieving look. "Maybe you can. But maybe I *can't*. I'm thirty next month," she added miserably. "I was supposed to have my Ph.D. by now. A good job, important work in the field."

"C'mon, Jo. Those are just mental structures. The game they want you to play. Life is more than jobs, money, diplomas. The important thing is—"

"Spare me your Eastern philosophy, Seth. I want to stay pissed off."

I sat at the table with them for another half hour, talking with Joanna about her plans, the sun sinking lower and lower behind the ash trees in the window. I'd almost laughed at the figure of Ed in her story, that bully brought to nothing, but I couldn't help feeling some apprehension: Peg was more powerful than I'd realized, strong enough to keep a grown man in hiding for five years, to outplay the local authorities, to get a mansion for the Sisterhood by sheer force of will. She'd had Ed in her pocket this entire time, the trump card to play if she needed him, if Joanna didn't find the financial papers or sell the house cheaply, spare her the indignity of this marriage. In the meantime, she'd let Joanna renovate the entire mansion for her. Now Heather was out at the mansion, under Peg's care, and I might not get to speak with Heather, to beg for another chance, unless Peg approved. It wasn't like I had leverage on Peg or could demand what I wanted from her. I was tough, sure, but not *that* tough.

When I got up to leave, Joanna walked me outside. We stood in the yard, the last embers of twilight casting shadows down the dilapidated block. A man was working on his truck, his legs sticking out below the undercarriage; a little boy was pedaling in circles on a dinged-up Big Wheel. Joanna's lipstick had smeared on one side, and I resisted an urge to wipe it clean with my fingertip.

"I'm sorry again about all this," she said. "You did marvelous work on that house. I hope they do the right thing and pay you."

"We'll see. Peg's always been very good to me. Though I know you're not her biggest fan right now."

"I imagine she's trying to do good in her own way. I just wish . . . I don't know. I wish my life had turned out differently. That I'd been better to people. That they'd been better to me."

"You and me both," I said.

Joanna was watching me closely in the half-light, like when we were kids and she was about to invent some new fantasy for us, to tell me the roles we'd play in the forest, the monsters we'd need to defeat, the enchanted kingdoms we'd visit.

She said, "You could come with us, you know. Wherever we end up. Out of Texas, certainly. It would be, well—an adventure. We'd be quite broke at first, but things have a way of turning around."

I didn't even feel tempted. "Thanks, but I have a family of my own here. Haven't been acting like it lately, but I do. Hey, get a pen or something, I'll give you my address at Aunt Cece's. Write me a letter when you get a chance. I'd like to hear how things turn out."

"Yes, of course, a letter," she said, nearly hiding the disappointment from her voice. She lifted a hand partway to my face as if to stroke my cheek, then thought better of it and lowered the hand to her side. "And please write me as well, Louisa. You're my oldest friend."

When I drove away, Joanna was standing alone in the scrubby yard, a tiny, pale figure among all that devastation, her wrinkled dress dark in the fading light. How had I ever thought she was my enemy—a villain, an enchantress, a cruel force that had leached all the happiness from my life? She'd always been that little girl standing in the doorway, a thumb hooked under her satchel strap, different from the rest of us. She'd always be shut out from the world we shared, waiting for someone to call her inside, to offer her safety, refuge. As I watched her in the rearview mirror, as I saw her slip into the distance, I knew that person could never be me.

28

In the course of my life I'd seen some unusual days—the hurricane, finding Miss Kate in the garden, the car wreck—but this August day had no competition. I'd woken up in bed with Joanna Kerrigan. Heather had walked out on me. Ed Darnell had come back from the dead; Seth and Joanna had lost everything. Peg had become the most powerful person in Parson. Now, to win Heather back, I'd need to convince Peg. She wasn't a motherly silver-haired woman bringing me groceries anymore. She had me in her power, too, whether I liked it or not.

Peg had been good to me since the hurricane, generous, nurturing, protective. I'd never realized how being protective made you wear two faces: a kind face for the people you protected, a vicious face for the people you protected them against. Maybe all mothers were like this, two-faced at their core, equal parts vicious and kind. And sometimes the lines could blur or the situation could shift, and they'd turn their vicious face on one of their own.

I wasn't sure which face Peg would show me tonight. But I knew that to see Heather again, I'd do anything. Get down on my knees. Plead, bargain, beg.

The mansion came into view on the promontory, no longer dark in the night, its windows glowing, its driveway filled with cars. A new chapter had begun at Parson House, new bodies and lives to mingle with the ghosts of the past. I hoped this chapter would be better than the last one, not ringed with tragedy and haunted by loss. As bad as I felt for Joanna, as much as I could have used the sale money myself, I felt better thinking of these women living out here rather than some Houston oil tycoon.

Best of all would be if I never saw Parson House again. Now, when I looked at it, instead of seeing the memories of my gentle months with Miss Kate, working together to repair the old place, all I could see was the driveway where Robby had grabbed Cass's arm, punched Danny to the ground, lashing out in a rage that seemed impossible to understand. There was the yard where I'd leaped behind the wheel of Cass's car, drunk, high, not even knowing how to work the gearshift, lurching us out on the final ride of her life. There was the house where I'd betrayed Heather, the person I loved more than anyone in the world. I wanted to get Heather out of there, make sure that, together, we put it, and all its history, behind us.

I left my truck a ways down the driveway, behind the scrum of sedans and station wagons parked along the front circle. The black Camaro sat among these cars, gleaming in the moonlight near Peg's old Ranger. My heart was thudding hard, and I tried to steady myself, breathe slowly, as I climbed the porch steps. Empty cardboard boxes covered the porch, probably waiting for a trash haul tomorrow, and I heard voices chattering inside, as well as women singing in harmony, a hymn of some kind. It was hard to believe this was the same house I'd hurried from this morning, trying to reach my truck before I woke Joanna. I could recognize the walls, the windows, the porch planks I'd laid myself, but it was like a body with a new spirit, a new identity.

When I rang the bell, Claudia answered. She had changed into a bleach-white dress with a ruffled fringe. She gazed at me like she had earlier, as if I were some fallen creature, a Judas in their midst.

"You're not welcome inside," she said.

I set my jaw. "Peg said she'd meet me."

"She'll meet you out back," Claudia answered, making a sharp gesture to signal that I should go around the house.

My stomach clenched: that meant the garden.

As I made my way around the side of the house, I had to navigate piles of empty boxes. The women were certainly working quickly to settle in. Just as I got to the garden gate, my foot caught on something I hadn't seen, another pile teetering in the grass, which collapsed, startling me. On instinct I reached down, and my fingers touched metal. I lifted it gently, my hand closing around it as I realized exactly what it was.

A little snub-nosed revolver. The same one Miss Kate used to keep in her bedside table.

I stared at the dark shape in my palm, trying to make sense of it. Joanna had searched this place up and down, looking for the gun without any luck for weeks, or so she'd told me. How on earth had it ended up in this discard pile out on the lawn?

Just then I heard Peg's voice somewhere ahead of me in the garden. Without thinking, I squeezed the gun as safely as I could in my jeans pocket. It was an awkward fit; its hardwood handle jutted like a fin out to the side. I called out a response to Peg, wondering where she was amid all the overgrown grasses, but there was no answer.

I gathered myself, then passed through the garden gate.

It sent a shiver through me, this spectral garden at night. It felt like a seething, living thing. I walked down its tunnel-like path, the very quality of the air changing, sea salt mixed with a brittle, herbal taste at the back of my tongue. I could smell the fresh loam beneath my boots, the mild chocolate scent of the night-blooming daisies, their yellow petals like pennants unfurled to the moon. Amazing, and terrifying, that it had flourished like this with so much neglect.

Farther down the path, near the cobbles where I'd found Miss Kate, stood the lone, rail-thin figure of Peg. She was turned away from me, dressed in trim white pants and a white embroidered blouse, a white Stetson I'd never seen on her. The moonlight glinted along her silver hair, which hung down in a single braid, the palest of the vines in the garden.

Peg turned around to face me. In her white outfit, washed in moonlight, she looked more like Margaret than Peg, a woman of stature, a vision of power. There was something cold and unfriendly in her face. I wasn't sure what game she was playing, but I was determined to win.

"Lou," she said evenly. "Nice of you to meet me here."

"Happy wedding day," I said.

She waved a hand: *Ah, well.* "The good Lord knows that wasn't my first choice. But in the end, the only way. And to think that Ed kept talking about *his* reputation!"

"He says you paid off his debts."

"It was a blessing to check *that* off the list. When you told me those Dixie boys were coming around here, I figured I'd better wrap things up with them. Well, it's Joanna's loss. With the money we'd been collecting to buy her out, we had enough to get those criminals out of our hair." With a nod at my pocket, she added, "I see you found that old thing. That was Kate's, you know."

My hand fluttered to the gun's handle, double-checking that it was there, secure. "Joanna was looking for it all over. Where'd you find it?"

Peg didn't respond to this question. I saw her lips tighten, like she was winching them closed. Like there was something she didn't want to say. I wondered if Claudia had told her about last night, about finding my car and Joanna's out here, guessing what we were up to.

Or maybe it was worse than that. Maybe Heather had told her.

I tried to keep my voice light, friendly, to keep the desperation from leaking in. "I was wondering . . . Heather's here, right? I'd love to talk with her if that's possible."

Peg didn't answer this, either. She plucked at a nearby shrub, tearing a honeysuckle blossom away from the vine, then pinching it and letting it fall to the soil by her boot. "I've done a great deal for you and Heather," she said. "I don't think you'd deny that."

"I wouldn't."

"At one time, Lou, I even saved your life."

"Yes," I said. I was distracted, uncomfortable with how close we were standing to the spot where Miss Kate had died. "I know that. And I'm grateful to you for it, you know I am." The house behind her loomed darkly, so different from the jubilant, glowing facade out front. "Listen," I said, struggling to keep my voice level, "if I can't see Heather right away, I understand. But if you and I have to talk, could we step out of the garden? Maybe go for a walk?"

It was a vulnerable admission, and to my surprise, something in Peg flared when I said it, a shark scenting chum. I could swear she smiled. "That's right," she said. She pointed to the ground at her feet, then waved a hand around like a divining rod. "It would have been around here, isn't that so? Where you found her that morning?"

Panic whip-cracked through me: I felt my pulse quicken, the muscles tighten in my legs. The insects seemed to chitter more loudly in response to her.

"Today," Peg said, looking down at the stones where Miss Kate had died, "signing the papers, moving the women out here? That should have been *our* triumph, Kate and me. Our victory over the awful men of this town. It was Kate's dream first, not mine. But it's funny how things work out."

I wasn't sure why Peg was talking this way. She went on, "Once she moved out of town, started living here, Kate changed, you know. I should have expected as much—it was a pattern for her, after all. Always looking for something to serve, some new zealous devotion. She needed that to give her life structure, I think. Poor thing had been so weak. Here, though, there was firm ground under her feet, property in her name—*her* name, not ours, so no one would get suspicious. She told me she liked the peace and simplicity out here, no husband hanging over her head, time to reconnect with her son. I think she allowed the time for the beast that had chased her all her life to finally catch up with her: guilt. And now that guilt could be reconciled." Her voice changed, became rhythmic and chantlike: "'Come, now, and let us set matters straight between us,' says Jehovah. 'Though your sins are like scarlet, they will be made as white as snow.'"

That verse from Miss Kate's Bible. I wondered if Peg had seen the Bible, too, those same emphatic circles and underlines.

"I didn't understand it all at first," Peg said, rueful and vicious. "But she wanted to talk to me about her children, how she'd wronged them, how she could see that she'd damaged Seth. In ten years I hadn't heard her say Joanna's or Cassandra's name, and suddenly that was all she wanted to talk about. They were real to her out here, her kids, in a way the rest of the world wasn't. 'You wouldn't understand, Peg, you were never a mother,' she started telling me. As if that changed anything. 'You have to leave the world a better place for them. If you haven't done that, you might as well never have existed.' And she talked about *you*, Louisa, how you'd given her a second chance at motherhood. You were quite the inspiration to her. She loved you."

I flinched at these words; there wasn't kindness and pride behind them, not this time. Peg's voice felt like a cattle prod right in my hide, like she was telling me on purpose to upset me. But why? She wanted something out of me, I could sense it—I just couldn't tell what it was. Did she need an apology? Something more?

Peg watched me, waiting to see how those words landed. When I didn't say anything or turn to go, she pressed on. "Looking back, I see it might have been Jehovah's plan for Kate to give Parson House to her children, atone for what she'd done. At the time, though, all I felt was fear. Fear and anger. We'd given her so much money—*I'd* given her so much money, and not just for the house but paying off Ed's debts to keep her safe, to keep him and his family from meddling with our plans for the mansion. If we had to start from zero all over again? It would be a huge financial hit. I'd have to move my women, these poor vulnerable souls, somewhere else. And I owed money to that mob—for *her*? Kate knew that I'd put myself on the line for her in every way there was. And now she wanted to betray us, all of us."

She plucked at the shrub again, only this time she pulled hard enough that the whole thing shuddered as it tore, setting off a rustling that seemed to ripple through the entire garden, above and around and behind us, too. The confusion had begun to disperse: I realized with a flash of frozen shock that I was starting to get a pretty good sense of where this was going. I looked over my shoulder, half hoping and half terrified that someone else had walked into the garden. But no, it was only Peg and me. Still alone.

"The day before she died, I was out here at the mansion. One second we were talking in the kitchen, and the next she was on the floor, having a seizure. Seth came running, said he could handle it, turned her on her side, started rubbing her shoulders. 'Does this happen often?' I asked him. 'Oh yes,' he said, 'almost every day. But Mom didn't want me to tell anyone.' I knew Kate worried about her health—she'd always been like that—but I'd never thought there was anything serious.

"Seth sent me for some aspirin—he said she kept it on the desk in her study. I found the bottle, but then . . . I don't know what made me go looking through her papers. I guess, deep down, I was suspicious of her already. And then there it was, in the bottom drawer of her desk: a typed-up draft of her will with Parson House left to Seth and Joanna. Thankfully not signed, not executed, yet. It looked like she'd typed it herself, like maybe no one else had seen it. But I understood then, like a key turning in a lock, what had changed. As soon as I saw that will, I knew how dangerous she'd become.

"So I took the will and ripped it up. But what difference did that make? Kate could just write another one. At the expense of the poor suffering women of Parson. And after that, do you think my women would have trusted *me*? Stuck around? All the good I'd done, it would be like it never happened. I'd be alone again, flat broke, and with even more enemies than before."

After all the months of confusion, of wondering about Miss Kate's death, it was strange to hear this story, so plain and damning. I felt numb, far from myself, didn't think I could move if I tried, as if I hovered just beside my body. "Why are you telling me this?"

It was as if she hadn't even heard me.

"I didn't plan it, Lou. Not at all. I just knew I needed to scare her straight, take care of it like she and I together had scared off so many deadbeat husbands in recent years. I had to make her understand that her duty was to us, no matter how guilty she felt about her kids. We could talk about helping them, sure we could, but Parson House wasn't the way. Anyway, I let myself in through the garden door. Raining hard that night, torrential. And when I saw the gun on the dining room table—I was here to scare her, wasn't I? I picked it up."

The gun. Left there by Seth. As part of his other, much different plan.

Peg shook her head. "Kate, I'd seen her have a *seizure* yesterday. I was thinking of her as weak, sickly. When I startled her awake in bed, I didn't expect all that fight in her, that toughness. She laughed at me! Reminded me she knew all the things I'd hidden, things I'd done for the elders in the old days. Oh, Lou, those were unforgivable things. And her daughter Cassandra. Kate said she'd tell the women the truth—that it was my fault Cassandra had died."

I could barely feel my body, but my right hand curled into a fist at these last words. As I forced my fingers to uncurl, I felt them brush the grip of the revolver. "That's ridiculous. What do you know about that night? Why would you have had anything to do with Cass's death?"

I thought the move was subtle, but she clocked it, and I saw her eyes flare again. "Cassandra. So rebellious. A burden on her mother, on the church. I was just following doctrine, after all."

"Doctrine . . ." I couldn't finish the sentence.

"I got a call from Kate at the hospital," she went on. "Cassandra had crashed her car, and it was serious, she'd bled out a lot. But the doctors were going to save her." Peg closed her eyes as she remembered. "And I reminded Kate about blood transfusions, the scriptures were clear: they were not allowed. I quoted the passages to her—'You must not eat the blood of any sort of flesh, because the soul of every sort of flesh is its blood.' 'Only flesh with its soul—its blood—you must not eat.'" She spoke these passages in the same rhythmic voice she'd used before. "I told her to intervene before her daughter was defiled. It was her holy duty.

"Kate was terrified, suggestible." Peg opened her eyes, looked at me directly. "I didn't doubt what I was doing, not once that night. That's what my faith was like back then. If it helped the church, I could justify any violence. It was how I'd accepted the violence done to me."

As she spoke, my numbness was wearing off. I was returning to my body, feeling the full depth of my rage. Miss Kate hadn't needed to die. Neither had Cass. But Peg had killed them, ushered them both to their graves.

"You're a murderer," I said, shaken by the rage in my own voice. "They won't punish you for Cass, though they should. But you need to confess that you killed Miss Kate. Accept the consequences."

She shook her head. "The police? Prison? The scandal would break up the Sisterhood, give the men in town their victory. Proof that the women in Parson are crazy, that we need to be kept in line. I'm afraid I can't allow that. But you're right, Lou: I'm a hypocrite, and a sinner, and a killer. Now that my women have the mansion, there needs to be justice. Jehovah won't bless them otherwise. I'm ready for it. I've been cleansed of my sins, asked for His forgiveness. Now all I need is His judgment."

I could feel the sweat on my forehead, a vein pulsing in my neck.

My God, how good it would feel to mete out that justice. The dark garden around me seemed vaster than I remembered, immense as an ocean.

It took the last scrap of willpower I had left, but I gathered my voice, belted out as loud as I could, "Heather! Heather, get out here!"

Peg scowled at me. "There's no need for that, now," she said, sharp and angry. "I'd rather keep this between the two of us, wouldn't you?"

I ought to have run—I could have shoved past her, most likely—but Peg's voice kept me rooted to the spot.

"You know, Lou, I've never met a person in so much denial. Don't you realize what I've done to you? After Cassandra was gone, buried, outside the Kingdom, Joanna still had a chance at being saved. Kate and I just needed to get her heathen friend away from her. We knew about your Mexican aunt. The uncertainty of your birth. How carefully you hid your family. Kate and I reported you."

"You're lying," I said, but knew otherwise. For so long I'd thought Joanna was the only white person who knew about Cece. But those pamphlets in Cece's trash can . . . they'd figured it out after all.

I noticed that my hand rested on the gun, the grip warm against my palm. "Stop," I whispered. I could feel my anger taking over, my self-control slipping.

"And Heather," Peg went on, insistent as a chant. "Did you think I wouldn't try to change your sinful ways? You, well—I don't think I could convert *you*. Heather, she's been studying with us, getting the self-respect to cast you off. Did you even notice? How are you any better than some neglectful husband?"

The truth in that question made me recoil, then clench down again. "At least I'm not a killer. At least I didn't murder my best friend."

"Maybe so." With a ferocity that surprised me, she added, "But as long as I'm alive, you'll never get near Heather or Sarah again."

My fingers had wrapped around the gun's wooden grip; it felt so sturdy, so comforting, nestled in my palm. "You have no right to keep her from me." As I slid it from my pocket, I expected her to fight, to move away. But she raised her hands to her heart and closed her eyes. Something like a smile passed over her face, pained with anticipation.

This was what I'd longed for, what I'd craved, so many years:

the true target of my anger, the skull I could shatter, the heartbeat I could still. The deep scents of the garden twisted tendrils through my mind like a hundred vines swarming up inside me, and the night felt open, potent, wild, transfigured in the moonlight, and Peg was not one woman but all the women I'd known, full of violence and guilt and love and the urge to protect—my mother, Miss Kate, Aunt Cece, Joanna, Cass, Heather—all in one body that awaited the divine mercy of my bullet.

But that smile—her smile jarred me. Her god wouldn't let her end her own life, so she'd decided to *use* me, the most damned person she knew. How was it that I still wanted to do it. To punish her. To please her.

And then a light switched on in an upstairs window, and I glanced away at the mansion. Heather's head emerged from the single brightened window, her long hair drifting in the breeze.

"Lou?" she asked, peering down into the depths of the garden. She must have heard my voice from inside but couldn't see me in the darkness. "What the hell are you doing back there?"

I dropped the gun at once, like a foul thing, my own damnation. I kicked it far off to the side, into the tangled shadows of undergrowth. I kept my eyes locked on Peg while I called up to Heather. Peg was staring at me; her lips were moving fast, but she wasn't making any noise that I could hear.

"Heather. I'm down here . . . I . . . Can I . . . can I come up?" I asked her.

It was out of my control, whether she gave me a *yes* or a *no*, whether I'd get another chance with her, whether I'd drive away from Parson House alone. All those things I'd never trusted—hope, surrender, love—were all I had left.

Then, slowly, I heard her answer.

"Okay," she said guardedly. "Come on up."

"I'll be right there," I called back.

Across from me, in a depth of shadow, Peg sank to her knees, lowered her face into the overgrown grass; I could hear her whispering something, perhaps another prayer. She looked like a grieving mother, like someone who'd just lost the dearest thing in the world. When I spoke to her, she went silent, though she didn't raise her head.

"You love the women here," I said. Considering the rage I'd felt seconds ago, my voice sounded strangely even. "It's your duty to help them, Peg. It isn't 'holy' to leave the people you love. If you want to do the right thing, you'll stay here. You'll suffer from your secrets, and you'll stay here. I won't betray you as long as you leave me and my family alone."

There was something else I needed to say to Peg. It surged up through me like electricity, searing my lungs, burning my throat, setting my tongue on fire.

"I forgive you," I said.

I left her there, hurried for the back door of the house.

The knob was unlocked and I stepped into the hallway, half expecting to find Claudia waiting for me with the rest of the Sisterhood. But for once, the house's mysterious rhythms were on my side. However many women were here, the dark length of the hallway was empty, and the back stairs, too. As quietly as possible, I strode down the corridor to Miss Kate's bedroom.

Sarah was the first to greet me, squealing as I came through the doorway. She wore fuzzy pink pajamas, and Heather stood beside her in running shorts and a tank top, her hair now in a messy ponytail. To my surprise she looked like her normal self, not a pious convert to the Sisterhood.

"Where is everyone?" I asked.

"The front rooms," Heather said. "Peg told us to stay clear of the rooms overlooking the garden for a while. Some of the women thought it must be men from the town, coming by to make trouble."

"Where are your things?" I looked around the empty room. "You aren't staying in here, are you?"

Heather shook her head. "Sarah needed the toilet, and the one downstairs was taken, so we came up here for a minute. And then all of a sudden I hear you shouting my name. Took me forever to figure out where it was coming from—this place is *huge*. What was going on back there?" She took in my breathless, harried face. "You've come to rescue us from the dragon's lair or something?"

I couldn't help myself: I rushed forward and hugged her tightly, felt her sturdy warmth against me. How was it possible that moments ago I'd considered shooting an old woman dead in a moon-dazzled garden?

"I'm sorry," I said softly into her ear. "Heather . . . I'm so sorry. You were right to leave, I deserved it. But if you'll take me back, we can move tonight. We can go right now."

"I need to know something first," she said.

"Anything."

She hesitated. "I saw your truck out here last night, Lou. What the hell was going on?"

I rested my forehead on her shoulder. It might be the last time I ever felt her this close.

"Did you sleep with Joanna?" she asked.

I nodded against her shoulder. I realized I was crying.

"You idiot," she said, too low for Sarah to hear. "You utter, complete bitch."

"You're all I care about, Heather. You and Sarah. We can leave Parson tonight. Never come back here."

"And what about Joanna?"

"She's going north again. And I won't see her, I promise. You're all that matters."

"But Lou . . . you *did* this. How the fuck am I supposed to trust you now? How can I?"

I was trying not to blubber; the words came out fast, desperate. "I fucked up. I fucked up so bad. But nothing like this—nothing like this will happen again. I'll show you. I'll be better."

Heather had stiffened in my arms, but I felt grateful that she hadn't pulled away. I'd never broken down like this with her, and I could tell she was considering my words, weighing her anger, the wounds of betrayal, against the future we might share. Finally she said, "I'm not promising anything."

It was enough. More than I deserved. "You don't need to. Oh, sweetheart, you don't need to." Right then all I cared about was getting her out of there. "Let's go out to the truck. Let's get to Cece's."

I must have sounded serious, or else something about the day she'd spent with these women had thrown her off, because she didn't ask any more questions or put up a fight. Instead—not looking at me, not speaking—she took Sarah by the hand and headed out. The three of us walked together through the blessedly vacant corridor, down the back stairs, and out the garden door. Peg must have pulled herself together, joined the other women inside, because the garden was empty and silent save for the restless thrum of the insects.

The garden didn't look so haunted, so deep and oceanic. Just a lawn that could use a mowing, some plants in need of trimming underneath a mild crescent moon. Sarah reached out toward a lightning bug, but it flittered off into the brush.

29

All of this was over a year ago now. We drove up to Cece's house that same night, a tense and quiet ride through the sprawling Texas dark, Sarah's sleeping a good excuse for our silence. It took a few months to feel like a family again, for the weight of what I'd done with Joanna to ease. By the next morning Heather was talking to me—clipped greetings, terse requests—but she warmed up at a crawling pace, and for weeks I worried that I'd gone too far, given her a wound that would never heal. The fear of that made my chest tight, kept me awake to the early-morning hours. Eventually Heather took pity on me and told me she planned to work things out. "I do mean *work*, though," she said. "It'll be hard."

"I'm not afraid of hard work," I told her.

Even so, I worried it would be like starting over, back in those first months together after Robby's death, both of us edgy and tip-toeing around each other's feelings, breaking into fights in front of Sarah. But so much had changed; we knew each other too well for that. During the days we managed well enough, falling back into our usual rhythms, enjoying the welcome distractions of our new home: the big meals every night, the free concerts in the park, Sarah rushing through the house to show us her crayon drawings and paintings, thrilled to have her family together again. And when Sarah and Cece had gone to bed, Heather and I would go out walking, just like the old days, only here we had the River Walk, vibrant and pulsing with life, and our nice, sleepy little neighborhood full of squat houses and neighbors whose names we were learning, who'd wave to us warmly whenever we walked by.

When we ended up in bed again, it didn't feel like falling back into old habits. It didn't feel like the past at all, or even the present. It felt, for the first time, like we were aiming together at a future worth building.

We've gone back to Parson only one time, about a month after we left, to gather the things we left in our haste: some boxes and crates, my heap in the bedroom, and the furniture we decided to save, like Robby's fanback armchair. The landlord had been griping at us to pick these up, said he was planning to rent the place again, though I doubted he had anyone interested.

The day we visited, I stayed back at our old house while Heather drove out to meet with Claudia at a restaurant by the water. Heather had called ahead to arrange the meeting, an opportunity to pick up some crates she'd stored at the mansion. Like me, she wasn't eager to get all the way out to the house, and I think Claudia was happy enough to keep Heather away, too.

When Heather came back from the meeting, I thought about asking her how the chat with Claudia had gone, digging for whatever information she might have gotten about Peg and the other women out at the house. But Heather seemed tense, so I guessed there had been some harsh words spoken. Only once we'd loaded into the car and I was about to drive us out of town did Heather pull something from her pocket. "Oh, evidently Peg wanted you to have this."

Heather handed me a sealed envelope, and my stomach did a flip. But there was no note inside, just a check for nine hundred dollars. *For improvements, home and otherwise*, read the memo line. My eyes nearly fell out of my head.

"Holy *shit*," Heather said, looking over my shoulder. "Where are we going for dinner?"

We were back in San Anton before sunset, went out for fajitas with Sarah and Cece, watched *The Flip Wilson Show* on the new TV I bought Cece as a surprise.

It wasn't hard to find jobs in the city, Heather at a downtown salon, me at a restoration firm that worked on historic houses. Soon we'd moved into a tiny house of our own, just a few blocks from Aunt Cece, a bungalow with a tile roof and a big front porch. Heather's done it up nice with her thrift-store finds, and I help out how I can, fix things when they break, do my best when she asks for my thoughts on drapes or wallpaper, though she laughs that Sarah's taste is more advanced than mine. It isn't an extravagant life, but sometimes, when Heather's cutting my hair, or when Sarah has a nightmare and comes in to sleep between us, I'm so grateful that it hurts like a punch inside my chest, like my heart might burst open with the feeling.

As for Joanna, I get the occasional letter and make sure to let Heather read them, too. Joanna and Seth live outside Chicago now, Joanna temping to pay her way through grad school, Seth working all-night shifts as a baker's assistant, which suits his schedule fine but keeps him as aloof from the world as ever. When her lawyer got back from vacation, Joanna did have a few calls with him, but he couldn't save a dime of her inheritance. She was angry at first, her letters to me full of bitter complaints, but that's mostly ebbed away. She's started to accept her lot, even sounds excited about her research. I write back to her promptly, warm and friendly letters, giving her our updates, wishing her the best. If there's magic in the world for me now, it's not with Joanna Kerrigan, not even those memories of us as children. It's in the here and now, shopping with Heather, watching Sarah grow, giving in and joining Cece's book club. It's in hearing updates about Parson, how the town is starting to get back on its feet.

Because the town *is* improving—thanks in large part to the women out at the mansion. Each and every one of those women is breathing life into Parson, opening shops and restaurants along the main drag, repairing the buildings out by the bay, rebuilding the rubble into a new, better town. After Peg's women petitioned, the county finally reopened the school, and the children can at last learn in their own town again. There's a sense in the air these days, nothing more than a rumor, but powerful in its quiet: that so long as you're in Parson, Texas, you'd better not raise a hand against a woman or child. If you do, that group of witches up at Parson House might cast a hex on you, might make you disappear forever.

All word of Parson comes to me from Danny, who calls every week and pays us a visit once a month or so. Heather's never thrilled to see him, but he's so gentle and natural with Sarah, I can tell she'll soften up over time. I've never fully understood what they had against each other. On some of his visits Danny spends the night, and then we stay up late and drink on the porch swing after everyone goes to sleep, maybe even smoke a joint for old times' sake. The neighborhood is hushed and still around us, the houses hazy under the streetlamps, charming with their painted shutters and Spanish tile roofs.

"Look at you, acting all grown-up now," he said on his latest visit, after I told him Heather and I had attended a PTA meeting. "Or at least I think that's what adults do. All theoretical for me."

"You're plenty adult," I replied. "You're running the busiest auto shop in Parson."

The town's regrowth meant his shop was getting more customers. I worried that soon he wouldn't have time for these visits.

Danny sipped his beer. "Eh. Runs itself."

We settled into a silence, and I decided that now was as good a time as any. I said, "Do you remember a year or so back, when I found Cass's cigarette tin?"

"Yeah," he replied at once, "that was incredible."

"Well, the day I found it, I started to . . . remember things. About the night she died. About Robby and the car wreck. Before then I couldn't remember much of anything. The concussion or something."

Just like I'd thought, the atmosphere on the porch changed around us. Danny stared out at the sleepy street, didn't speak for a long moment.

Finally he said, "When I got back to school after the hospital, you and Robby were right there in Woodman, in classes with me . . . I could tell how broken up you were, that you didn't want to discuss that night. But I was never sure, you know, how much you remembered. If it was just grief or if the crash had knocked it out of you. Thought that might be a good thing, considering."

"Is it true, then? That I was driving? And what Robby did that night?"

"Couldn't forget that," he said quietly.

"But that wasn't Robby. That wasn't anything like him."

"You talk to Heather about this?"

I shook my head. "I kept meaning to, but I haven't had the guts. Everything has been getting back to normal with us. If I started digging around again . . ."

Danny went silent, thinking. Took a longer sip of his Lone Star.

"Did Heather know about it?" I said.

"No, no. I doubt it. That's not why . . . never mind."

I could feel him holding back, retreating into himself. It was hard for us to discuss the past, and this was the most difficult topic of all. Usually I'd let the subject drop, but tonight I needed to press him. "Danny, if there's something you're not telling me. Please. I have to know."

He took a deep breath. When he spoke, his voice was craggy, uncertain. "At the time, I kind of thought you *did* know. I thought I was so obvious about it, anyone could tell just by looking at me."

"By looking at *you*? I'm not sure when you mean."

"It was that summer," he said, "the summer before high school. And Cass was taking us to parties with her. You remember all that?"

"Yeah. Happiest time of my life."

He smiled. "God, remember how alcohol felt like some magic potion back then? Remember the party we went to, the one at that old hunting lodge? Some rich kid's party."

"Right," I said with a laugh, "all the stuffed heads on the wall."

"Creepy place, kind of. And the kids there weren't that nice to me—it wasn't like most of the parties Cass took us to that summer. I kept getting these looks, hearing these little comments; I thought my head might end up on the wall, too." He shuddered. "Anyway, Cass, she didn't drive us home that night. She'd met some guy, wanted to stay there. So Robby drove us back, and he dropped you off first—you were blotto that night—and then Heather next. And then he was headed to my house, but he said he wasn't tired, asked if we could take a drive. We drove along the beach, just talked for like an hour. He asked me about things: my summer, school, work at the shop. And I asked him about football, scholarships, and he said it was strange to think of leaving Parson, strange but also exciting. I'd known Robby for years, but that was the first time we'd talked like that, just the two of us. I never wanted it to end."

"Did you have feelings for Robby?" I asked, surprised.

"Oh, sure. I wasn't the only one. We all did. He was so strong, and beautiful, and athletic, and funny. You know how he was back then, before he left Granbury. And girls were always trailing after him. I never thought . . . I wasn't expecting that night. I was just happy to get that time with him. That was all."

I waited as he fell silent again, took a few sips of beer.

"Robby, he made the first move," Danny went on. "I still can hardly believe it. When he parked at the beach, it was his idea. When he suggested we go for a swim, that was all him, too. But we didn't go swimming, was the thing. He took his clothes off, and then he saw how I was looking at him, and then he came over and started on mine, too. There was moonlight all along his body. He said he'd never done anything like that before. He was shaking." Danny laughed, soft and fond. "Well, so was I."

"And you . . ." I was stunned at what I was hearing.

"Not that first night. But yeah, eventually, over the summer. We met up every few days, whenever we could. I'd gone stupid with it, daydreams, fantasies about the future, a cabin in the country together, silly stuff. But I wasn't the only one falling in love. Robby made time for me, said he'd never felt this way about anyone. Even when football practice started in August, he'd find times to slip away."

Danny was looking away from me, out at the street; I could tell he was nervous, unsure how I'd react. I reached over, squeezed his fingers. "What happened then?"

He glanced at me, let out a little sigh of relief. "Then the school year started," he said, "and Robby couldn't slip away. Not without being noticed. His friends, his teammates, that gaggle of girls, they were always around. He had to sneak out late at night, but because he didn't get enough sleep for football, he thought he might blow it in front of a scout. The first game of the season, Robby threw that winning pass, remember? And there was that huge party afterward, everyone way more drunk than usual. I looked up at one point, and Robby and Heather were kissing."

I did remember that party. Robby's arm around Heather, everyone giving him elbow bumps, spilling beer from their plastic cups as they shouted toasts to him. Not four weeks later, most would ditch him because they thought he wasn't white. It was one of the last times I'd seen my brother that happy.

"I left," Danny said. "I couldn't handle it. Cass noticed, and she came after me, asked me what was going on. And I started crying and told her everything. I asked her, 'If Robby likes *me* that way, how can he like girls, too?' It was all so new to me then . . . So Cass explained that some people went both ways, liked both girls and boys. It made me feel so jealous, and I told her I wished *I* was like that, could pass as normal. And Cass, she just hugged me, said there wasn't anything wrong with me, I was perfect like I was. Started telling me about guys she knew, people I might like. That there were cities with lots of people like me, clubs and parties just for us. But I didn't want to hear it. I couldn't think about anyone but Robby.

"Then it all happened after the next game, at the party on the beach. At one point Robby gave me this look and I followed him into some trees nearby. And it felt so good, it'd been so long—and we didn't notice Heather walking up, not until the last second. Robby panicked, and he hit me right in the face. Shouted at me, accused me of . . . it's not worth repeating. Heather, I don't blame her for believing him that I'd *attacked* him or whatever. She yelled at me, too, and Robby pulled her away, told her I wasn't worth it. So I left. I ran all the way home. Must have been four miles.

"That's when I understood what Cass had told me. That there were people like me who'd always be vulnerable. And that Robby wasn't one of them. He'd always choose that safety in the end. And Heather, I guess she kept that night to herself all these years. She never said anything to you about it?"

"Never," I said.

He sighed. "Nice of her. Probably thought she was 'protecting' me."

That bonfire on the beach—it was only seven or eight days before we broke into Parson House. Now I understood why Danny had a bruise on his face that week.

I said, "I'm so sorry he hurt you. That's awful."

Danny shrugged. "It wasn't the punch that hurt the most."

I'd had one-night stands turn on me when they regretted what they'd done, tried to blame me for what their bodies had wanted. Those words scarred you; you couldn't look at the person the same way again.

"So after he punched you," I said, "you moved on. Let Cass set you up with Thomas."

He smiled. "Yeah, she was the best. She saw the bruise, and she wanted me to know I had other options. But Robby—he seemed to think we could go back to the way things were. I was what, *fourteen* back then? And he'd hit me hard in the face with all his strength; an inch to the left, he'd have broken my nose. I loved him, but I was done. So I found ways to avoid him. Skipped a couple of parties.

"And Robby, he wasn't used to being rejected. Wasn't used to hearing no. The night we went to Parson House, he'd stopped by the garage a few hours earlier. I hid in the back, told my brother to cover for me. I don't know if he told him we'd be at Parson House with friends that night or what. But I remember feeling good when I saw Robby drive away, looking like he was the one who hurt for once. It was nice to have some power for a change. I was a kid, a stupid kid.

"I couldn't believe it when he showed up at the mansion. Thomas and I were sitting in a bedroom, just talking, when we heard the shouting. We went outside, and we saw Robby, and he was like a different person, so vicious, so violent. He had Cass by the arm, and when I tried to intervene, he laid me out. Then we heard you shout on the porch, and we went running for the car. Once we drove away, I thought we were free and clear. But their car came up behind us, and you pressed down on the gas, and then . . . the rest.

"After that night, everything was different. I came back from the hospital and Robby was at the same school with me, even in some of the same classes. He wasn't the golden boy anymore, no judgy friends, no football pressure. The funny thing is, it might have been possible for us then, if we were discreet. But I'd never felt further from him. Him punching me, the crash . . . I know he felt the distance, too. There was never anything between us again except our connection to you. And you remember how he was then. Low, sad, passive. Not like he'd been. I was glad he had Heather, glad she was so loyal through it all. In the end, me and him, it was just a stupid summer fling.

"But I need to say this, Lou. And you need to believe me. Robby, I don't think he meant to make us crash. He was just blind with anger or fear or whatever that was. When we went into the ditch, he didn't leave us for dead. He pulled over right away. And then you got out of the car, stumbled out into the road—I think it was the shock of his life. Until he saw you on the road, he wouldn't have known that you were there. And he never knew that you'd been driving. Only Thomas and I knew that, and Cass . . . that was what she kept saying while we waited for the ambulance to come. 'Don't mention Lou, don't get Lou in trouble.' So I never said anything, and even Thomas honored her last wish. Listen, I'm not saying it's okay what Robby did. He chased us, and we went off the road. But then he called for help, even if that meant he'd get in trouble. He called the ambulance that saved my life."

After another beer we went back inside, and I spread a sheet and a blanket on the couch for Danny. He started snoring softly as soon as I left the room. I could tell it had been a relief for him, sharing the story after all these years, seeing how much I appreciated his honesty. Everyone, it seemed to me now, lived with a burden of secrets, with dark spaces inside them where the past gnawed away. As I watched him sleep from the doorway, I wished I could wake Danny up and tell him my own secrets, explain about Peg and Miss Kate, the night I'd almost committed murder. But there are some secrets you keep for yourself and some you keep for others. That you carry, like a cross, for the people you love.

I got a Lone Star from the kitchen, walked out to the porch. I drank it slowly on the swing, looking out at my neighborhood. The past seemed clearer to me: Robby's love had curdled into rage, violence, inside him. He'd lost himself for a time, just like Miss Kate and Peg, just like me.

After the car wreck, Robby had turned more inward. He'd had a need to get away from people, take long walks alone. I'd assumed this came from his loss of college, and I'd bitterly blamed Joanna. But now I knew he was also thinking of Cass, the girl whose life he'd ended. Of what he'd seen himself become that night. There was no arrest for the car wreck, no prison, no community service, just a cruel darkness that ate away at him daily. The few times we spoke of the wreck, I always said I couldn't remember much, that I was grateful he'd discovered us in the ditch. But I wonder if he thought I knew more. If he thought, deep down, I might hate him for what he'd done.

I did hate him now, a little. Or at least the violent, controlling man he'd been that fall. But sitting out on my porch, feeling the past rise up around me, what I wanted to say most of all was: *I'm sorry you suffered. I'm sorry you couldn't love who you wanted to love. I'm sorry you never met Sarah—you would have adored her. I'm sorry you died in pain.*

I thought about us as children, something I hadn't allowed myself to do in years. I saw Robby at eight, at nine, at ten, my sweet, lively brother, the boy who loved to play tag, who loved to roll giggling on the lawn. Who jumped up to help with the dishes at night, before Aunt Cece ever had to ask. Who made up stories with me on car trips and always let me pick the ending, whether the hero lived, whether the villain got to fight another day. Who taught me how to climb trees, ride my first bike, stare down a bully.

I could remember a night before our mother left us, when she told us to stay in the car while she visited some friend's apartment. I was four or five years old, and Robby and I sat for hours in the dark parking lot, alone, unprotected, my fear getting worse and worse, every shadow outside more menacing, a demon ready to swallow me. Robby took my hand, told me stories from his favorite comic books. Eventually I started crying, unable to stop myself, and then Robby wrapped his arms around me, let me hide my face against his shoulder.

"Just hold on, Lou," he said. "Just a little longer. We'll make it."

ACKNOWLEDGMENTS

This book exists thanks to the care and support of the following wonderful people:

First, the many workshop leaders and fellow writers at the University of Missouri and the University of Nebraska–Lincoln who gave me so much encouragement, validation, feedback, and advice over the years. I am especially grateful for the rousing enthusiasm of Jonis Agee and the deeply incisive mentorship of Joy Castro. Timothy Schaffert, for years of friendship, wisdom, inspiration, and wit.

All the exceptionally talented and industrious folks at The Clegg Agency who helped shape this book into what it is, particularly the endlessly generous and brilliant Bill Clegg, whose advocacy means the world to me. Simon Toop, for the inspired editorial guidance that helped me see my own work in a new light, and Nik Slackman, Nik Wesson, and MC Connors, for the depth of your insight and for giving so much of your attention and time to this book.

My incomparable team at Harper, including Liz Velez, Katie O'Callaghan, Amanda Livingston, Diana Meunier, Joanne O'Neill, and Karintha Parker. Millicent Bennett, for the tireless attention and unbeatable vision that have brought this book into the world.

The artists, writers, and thinkers in my life who inspire me constantly and whose creativity and kindness have awakened and sustained me in so many ways, especially Meredith, Trevor, Mike, Ryler, Charlene, Nick, Danielle, Anne, Jessica, Jen, Remy, Kate, Adrienne, Alexandra, Mother Amanda, and my wonderful students. David and

ACKNOWLEDGMENTS

Katie—I am constantly motivated by witnessing your brilliance. Ilana, for being the best literary citizen, not to mention one of the most conscientious and compelling artists I could ever be privileged to know.

My amazing family, including Axolotl, Mark, and all the delightful Cochran aunts and uncles. The memories of Bette and Earl, whose loving hearts taught me what family could be. The most dynamic creative collaborators, my siblings Jessica and Viridian, and my immensely supportive, patient parents, David and Angie, for your activism, which has been such a powerful example for me, and for teaching me about the immense joys of art in all its varieties (both the good and the terrible).

Finally, my husband and first reader, Scott, who kindles my creativity every day, and whose measureless love and support are the reason this book was ever written in the first place.

ABOUT THE AUTHOR

RACHEL COCHRAN was raised in Texas and received her Ph.D. in English from the University of Nebraska–Lincoln. She currently teaches literature and creative writing at UNL and is also an assistant editor at Machete, an imprint of Ohio State University Press. Her short stories and essays have appeared or are forthcoming in *The Rumpus* and *The Masters Review* and have won *New Ohio Review*'s Nonfiction Contest.